Praise for Melinda's Choice:

"This has become one of my favorite all-time sci-fi novels. It has a hero and heroine who are older, so we get to see many fascinating dynamics in their relationship. We also get to see how they honor each other's cultures and are willing to learn about them. Melinda's Choice has many reasons for me to love it." 5* Amazon review

"A great alien romance/fated mates... This book will have you feeling all the emotions as you journey with Melinda throughout the story...I definitely recommend this book for my fellow alien romance lovers!" 5* Amazon review

"This is a fabulous book. The way the that author carefully created different cultures and species was masterful." 5* Amazon review

"Great! Melinda has a choice to make. She has two men in love with her. One is a human and the other is an alien. A great plot and the characters are wonderful and carry the book." 5* Amazon review

"Amazing story... This is definitely a little different for me but I loved this book! A love triangle always makes things more interesting, who will she choose?" 5* Amazon review

"O.M.F.G! This was my first sci-fi romance and let me tell you... I'm forever obsessed! ... I never in a million years would ever think I'd be into alien smut... and tail play... but damn... that's all I gotta say." 5* Goodreads review

MELINDA'S CHOICE

M.M. Wakeford

The Venorians and Krovatians

In this series:

Book 1 – Krantor's Mate

One day, on a planet far from Earth, I meet my fated mate. The only problem is, he's in love with someone else...

"Trope busting. Loved it... M. M. Wakeford offers a completely new take on fated mates. With all the expectations that are set with a trope, the author blows it out of the water with her fabulous storytelling." 5* Goodreads review

Book 2 – Melinda's Choice

Two very different men, and yet I want them both. I can't have my cake and eat it though. I have to make a choice...

"This has become one of my favorite all-time sci-fi novels. It has a hero and heroine who are older, so we get to see many fascinating dynamics in their relationship... Melinda's Choice has many reasons for me to love it." 5* Goodreads review

Laijar's Temptation (a prequel novella)

My shuttle crash landed on Earth and now I am stuck here for good, unable to return to my home planet...

Foreword

This is a science-fiction romance novel written for a mature audience. There are sexual scenes that make this story unsuitable for anyone under the age of 18. Please also be aware that there is a non-consensual sex act portrayed in the novel and an unplanned pregnancy. Neither of these are gratuitous but are integral to the plot. If, however, these are triggers for you, then you may wish to skip reading this novel.

Most of the action in this book takes place after the action portrayed in a previous novel, Krantor's Mate. There are references to events that took place in that book, which are briefly explained to the reader. You do not have to have read Krantor's Mate to enjoy Melinda's Choice, which is a standalone.

A note on spellings: I have capitalized the word "human" whenever the alien characters are speaking, to reflect the fact that for them, "Humans" are an alien race. This mirrors the way the humans in the story refer to alien races as Krovatians or Venorians, not krovatians or venorians. I hope that makes sense!

Prologue

Kirimor

"We will be sending a convoy of our ships to the planet Ven in order to retrieve the boral crystals and bring them home safely. We cannot risk them being stolen again."

I nod in agreement, then speak. "There is another matter we must also consider."

The other four people sitting in the circle turn their attention to me. Unlike them, I do not lead any sector of Krovatia, our planet, but as the highest priest in the land, my views are afforded great respect.

"And what is this matter?" asks Denishar, leader of the northern sector.

"Up until now, we have refused to allow foreigners to live on our planet, and we have not shared information about ourselves with our allies. The affairs of Krovatia are a closely guarded secret. As a result, the Venorians were unaware of the power of boral crystals and allowed their planet to be attacked by the Saraxians. We must accept our share of culpability in this matter. Had we been more open with the Venorians, they would have taken greater precautions to protect themselves and to protect the crystals."

"That is true," pipes in Lorifena, leader of the western sector, "but it is a long established Krovatian tradition to keep our culture and practices to ourselves."

I eye her in silence for a long moment. Under the power of my stare, her gray face and breasts darken by several shades. I continue, as if uninterrupted. "In accordance with our long established principles of peace and harmony with our neighbors, we must find ways to develop greater openness with our allies, the Venorians and the Driskians."

"How do you propose we do that?" wonders Nevestor, leader of the eastern sector.

"I think it is time we established closer relations between ourselves and our allies. We could allow a select few of their people to live among us, under close supervision. In return, we would also send some of our people to live on their worlds, in order to encourage a greater exchange of information."

At this, there is a general murmur of voices. Some of the leaders are clearly unhappy at the idea. It is therefore a surprise to hear the remaining person in the room speak in favor of my plan. "We must heed Kirimor's wise words," states Dorishena. At sixty sun rotations old, she is our most experienced leader, in charge of the southern sector. She sits ramrod straight, her legs crossed elegantly beneath her on the floor cushion, her breasts still pert despite her advanced age. "Traditions are not set in stone. We can adapt and make minor changes. I do not see any harm in hosting a small delegation of people from planets that have been our friends for generations."

"I have no objection to this," says Denishar, "as long as it is only a small number of people, and they are properly supervised during their stay."

I turn to the other two leaders, awaiting their decision.

"I do not like it," states Nevestor. "It is too great a departure from the ways of our people."

I level him with a gaze. "Let me ask you this, Nevestor. If the roles had been reversed and our planet was the one about to be attacked by the Saraxians. How would you have felt about the Venorians withholding important information from us about the boral crystals? How would you have felt if your friends and allies had stood by and done nothing to warn you of the threat to your planet? For that is what we effectively did to them—all in the name of protecting our traditions."

He sighs. "I take your point, Kirimor, but the deed is done now. There is nothing we can do to change the past."

"But there is much we can do to ensure the past does not repeat itself. I do not propose that we share state secrets with unfriendly races. I am talking about peoples who we have had harmonious relations with for decades. I believe it would be a positive step, and in accordance with our values, to build greater cooperation between ourselves and our allies."

Nevestor inclines his head. "You make a persuasive argument, Kirimor. If the others are in agreement with this, then I will not oppose the proposal."

I look towards Lorifena. She takes a moment to read the room, then nods in agreement. "I think that we could manage to host a small number of people without too much problem."

"Then we are all in agreement. Let us conclude this meeting as I am eager to get home and take a cooling dip in the pool."

I pick up the tall glass of *nari* on the floor before me and take a long, refreshing drink. Rivulets of sweat run down my chest from the scorching afternoon heat. I take a cloth, dip it into the bowl of ice water and wring it dry. Then I bring it to my heated body, cooling myself down as best I can. Who in their right minds organizes a meeting at such an ungodly time of the day? Personally, I am at my most productive early in the morning, but when I was called to this meeting with the leaders of our planet, I could not refuse.

Now that my objective has been achieved, it is time for me to go. I rise to my feet, swinging my tail in relief. I bow to each of the sector leaders and say, "Go in peace," then take my leave. Quickly, I make my way out to my waiting transport and program my journey back home.

Chapter 1

Melinda

Six months previously

We've pulled out all the stops for this dinner party, no extravagance too much. We've even had real filet mignon, deep frozen, shipped all the way from Earth for the occasion. Tonight, for the first time on our Mars colony, we are hosting five aliens from the planet Ven who will be taking part in our groundbreaking exchange program. They will be trading places with humans in a cultural exchange that will, I hope, grow the cooperation and understanding between our people.

All this is the fruit of many hours of painstaking labor ever since first contact was made with the Venorians last year. I can still remember it like it was yesterday. I'd been fast asleep in bed when I was roused in the early hours of the morning by my head of security.

"Tom," I'd yawned, tapping on my communicator screen sleepily to accept the call. "What is it?"

"Melinda, we're being hailed on our emergency channel by an unknown vessel."

"Could it be the Russians? Have you scanned the vessel?"

"Nothing is showing up on our scans, and it doesn't sound like the Russians. Melinda, whoever it is on the line insists on speaking with the person in charge—that would be you."

Wide awake now, I had sat up in bed. "Ok, patch the call to me but make sure you record everything as you listen in. Have you engaged our security protocols?"

"Yes, of course."

"Ok, let's do this."

A moment later, Tom had murmured, "You're in."

My voice calm, with no hint of the excitement or nerves beneath, I'd said, "Greetings. I am Melinda Garcia, head of the Earth Federation mission on Mars. Who am I speaking to?"

"Greetings to you, Melinda Garcia. I am Pravol from the planet Ven in the second galactic quadrant. We come in peace and would like to make ourselves known to you."

Listening to the strangely disembodied voice speaking through some kind of translating device, I'd become immediately aware that history was being made. But that was only the beginning. Since that initial contact, it has taken time and no little effort to build up a positive working relationship with the Venorians. They are a technologically advanced race, and understandably cautious about who they develop friendly relations with. As a way to help build bridges between our people, we came up with the idea to organize an exchange program. And here we are tonight.

I clink my glass for silence. All eyes turn to me.

"A year ago, I had the honor and privilege to become the first human to make contact with the Venorian people. That fateful day, we took a massive step forward into a greater understanding of the universe around us, perhaps only rivalled by Neil Armstrong's first footsteps on the moon over a century ago. We had no way of knowing if the aliens hailing us were friends or foes, yet we were determined to reach out the hand of friendship. So, it gives me great pleasure to be standing here today, welcoming among us our new friends, the Venorians. Through this exchange program, I believe we will be fostering even greater understanding and cooperation. Welcome, my friends. Let us raise a glass in a toast to our enduring friendship."

I raise my champagne flute, as do others in the room. All too often, the busy nature of my day-to-day life means that I fail to properly observe the moment. This is a rare occasion where I do just the opposite. In the lull as we each take a sip of our champagne, I take time to reflect on just how much we've achieved in one short year and to feel pride for my role in all of this. I, Melinda Garcia, daughter of a humble janitor and a short order cook, have made history. I know mom and dad will be watching the footage of this back on Earth, feeling incredibly proud. Wyatt too. *If only he could have been here with me.* I blink the thought away. No, tonight I will not think of him. With a smile, I turn to the two Venorians standing beside me. "Pravol, Treylor, please help yourselves to some delicious food from the buffet."

It's late and I have an early start tomorrow morning, but sleep won't come. Is it because I indulged in too much rich food from that fabulous buffet? I usually maintain a strict diet and exercise regimen, religiously keeping my forty-one-year old body trimmed and toned. However, it's not every day that real scallops, beef and chicken are on the menu, not to mention the decadent profiteroles and strawberry cream tarts. I couldn't resist helping myself to this deliciousness, even while playing host. The result of this indulgence sits heavy in my stomach.

Perhaps my sleeplessness can be attributed to something else. Among the many visiting dignitaries for last night's momentous gathering was Lucas Rivera, an up-and-coming politician in Washington. I've met him once or twice before in passing. He's about a decade younger than me, with the wits, looks and charm that will get him far in this game. All through the evening, I felt his eyes on my newly ringless left hand as he engaged me in a subtle flirtation. There's definite interest there. Should I encourage it? It's two weeks to the day since I officially became single again. Maybe it's time I dip my toes back into that dating and hooking up world that I inhabited before Wyatt and I became a thing all those years ago. Who better with than a handsome, clever guy like him?

I blow out a frustrated breath. Nah. Men like him always have an agenda. Besides, if I'm being truthful—and the early hours of the morning are always a time for truthfulness—I'm still not ready to move on. Two decades of loving one man won't wash away in a single rinse.

I shift on my pillow, trying to get comfortable, but slumber remains elusive. There's so much to think about and process, not least the momentous hosting of five aliens from the planet Ven. I'd always pictured aliens in my mind as having blue or gray skin, with a tail and maybe some horns and fangs too. But that's not what the Venorians are like at all. In fact, in appearance they are almost like us, just larger and with a bronze tinge to their skin. I'm not sure whether to be relieved or disappointed about that. I've read one or two of Wyatt's beloved science fiction novels in my time, so I've almost come to expect alien life forms to be… very alien.

Having said that, there is one thing very different about these aliens. I'm nearly one hundred per cent sure that they're a telepathic race. The idea was first put in my head by Martha Reynolds, one of the candidates for the Venorian exchange program, when I interviewed her two days ago. She told me she'd glimpsed something in the video footage of my first meeting with Pravol last year that had her believe the Venorians were telepathic. I watched the footage with her several times, but the evidence was inconclusive. Last night though, I decided to put the theory to the test.

The Venorians have a singular form of greeting. They look you directly in the eyes then place a hand on your cheek and join their foreheads to yours for a few moments. When Pravol came to greet me, I deliberately focused my mind on one thought, which I repeated over and over in my head. *You have a bug in your hair. You have a bug in your hair.* Lo and behold, as Pravol stepped away from me, a frown on his serious face, he slipped his fingers into his hair, looking for said bug. It's not proof, but near enough.

It's a shame Martha wasn't one of the final five selected for the exchange program. She deserves to be, with her power of deduction. I did vote in her favor, but the cabal on the selection committee overruled me. Still, I'd be interested in her take on the Venorians now she's had a chance to meet them in the flesh. Perhaps she put them to a similar test as I did last night. I sit up, feeling restless, and say, "Athena, schedule a meeting with Martha Reynolds as soon as possible."

A short time later, Athena, the computer on my communicator and my absolute life saver, responds, "Meeting scheduled with Martha Reynolds at one pm this afternoon."

I lie back again and close my eyes. It's no good. Sleep refuses to come. After a futile minute or two, I sit up again and tuck my arms around my legs in a gesture I've become familiar with in the two lonely years I've spent on Mars. I usually cradle my affection starved body like this just before I cave in and call Wyatt. I really shouldn't. We're divorced now. *Don't do it Melinda. Don't.*

"Athena, call Wyatt."

He answers on the second ring. His handsome face smiles back at me, blue eyes warm with love. "Hey, honey. I've just watched you on the news with the Venorians. I'm so proud of you!"

I smile back. "Thanks."

"How you doing?"

"I'm still buzzing. It's making it hard to settle down to sleep."

"I bet. Well, I hope I'm not adding to the excitement too much by saying everyone back here is talking good things about you. I've had three calls from journalists wanting the scoop on you, plus dozens of calls from friends and family wanting to talk about your meeting with the Venorians. You're quite the celebrity now, honey."

I roll my eyes. "Oh God, please no!"

He laughs. "It's all good. Enjoy the moment!"

I relax my head back against the bed board with a sigh. "Actually, tonight I did just that. It was like I was outside my own body observing myself. I looked at this gathering of the great and good and thought, shit Melinda, you're hosting a dinner party for aliens from a distant planet. What the fuck?"

Wyatt sweeps back a stray lock of dark blond hair, grinning. "That was definitely a pinch me now moment."

"Yeah, it was."

"Tell me all about it."

"Well, for starters, I doubled my usual calorie intake eating from that buffet. The filet mignon was to die for."

"Stop, you're making me hungry. Tell me about the aliens."

"Ok, so here's the thing…"

I tell him all about Martha's theory that Venorians are telepathic and my little test on Pravol tonight. Wyatt listens in wonder. He's always been fascinated by the idea of alien beings. Haven't we all? When I finish my tale, he laughs and suggests, "Next time you greet Pravol, think, *your armpit smells*, and see how he reacts."

"Or maybe, *your dick is hanging out of your pants*," I add cheekily.

"Well, if he's anything like ninety-nine percent of human males, he'll be sure to check himself out."

I get serious all of a sudden and say what's been on my mind. "If you'd been here with me, we could have played this game of catch the telepathic alien together. Wyatt, I missed you tonight."

The smile falls off his face. "I'd have given anything to have been there with you. I'm so sorry, honey."

Really? Then why weren't you here?

Ignoring my errant thought, I reply, "I know. Damn it, I don't even have the right to ask anymore. It's official. We're done."

There's a long silence. Eventually, Wyatt says in a heavy-sounding voice, "I don't know if we'll ever be done."

My face crumples as a sob breaks from me.

"Shit. Mel!" I hear Wyatt call out helplessly millions of miles away.

I wipe the tears and try to get a grip on myself. But I can't. The pain is too raw, and the heightened emotions of the evening have stripped away my control. Another sob breaks from me, then another. I let it all out.

It's a good few minutes before I'm able to stop crying. I clean up my face with tissues and take some long calming breaths.

Finally, I look at Wyatt. He's been silent throughout, his beautiful eyes red-rimmed. "Mel," he says. "That piece of paper can say we're done, but I'll love you forever. I'm sorry I fucked up our marriage. I hate that I've let you down."

We've been over this hundreds of times. Wearily, I rasp, "It takes two, Wyatt. Some of this is on me. But it's done now. We can't take it back."

He doesn't answer, just stares at me, hunger and need evident in his eyes. I drown in his gaze across the millions of miles that separate us. His voice husky, he says, "Baby, I can't let you go feeling like this. Let me make it better."

I know what that entails. We've done plenty of it the last two years I've lived on Mars. Logic dictates we shouldn't anymore, but I put it aside and go with my gut. "Please," I whisper.

His voice takes on an authoritative tone. "Take your top off, Melinda. Show me those gorgeous tits."

My heartbeat picks up as I lift the tank top I'm wearing over my head, baring my naked breasts. As soon as he sees them, Wyatt purrs. "Oh yeah, so damn beautiful. Touch them for me, sweetheart. Squeeze them in your palm, the way I like to do."

I palm my breasts, squeezing the soft flesh. "That's it, baby. Now pinch those nipples hard. Let me see them perk up, nice and firm."

I pinch them between my fingers, feeling a light tremor pass through my body.

"Oh baby, you look fucking gorgeous. My cock's so hard for you."

"Show me," I breathe.

His eyes gleam. "I'll show you mine if you show me yours."

"Deal."

I push down my loose slacks and panties, baring myself fully to him. On screen, I see him stand and slip off the sweat pants he's wearing. His cock is tenting in his boxer briefs, a wet patch forming from the precum. Swiftly, he pulls them down, freeing his lovely, straining erection. My breath catches as I see the glint of gold on the underside. We both got pierced as a ten-year anniversary present to ourselves. While his frenum has a set of gold barbells, I have identical ones piercing my clitoral hood. It's one of the most adventurous things we've ever done as a couple, and for a time, it helped to rejuvenate our marriage.

"Damn, Wyatt. Have I told you lately how beautiful you are?"

He smirks, stroking his length. "It's all yours, baby. Show me that pussy, honey."

I change the angle of my communicator screen so he can see all of me. At the same time, I tap a function on the screen so he's projected in front of me, nearly as real as if he were here. Then, I part my legs and hear his hissed intake of breath as he catches sight of my wet pussy, and the piercing he chose for me.

"Baby, you're the beautiful one," he groans. "Just look at you, swollen and wet, so ready to come for me."

"Make me come," I plead.

"Oh, I will, honey, never fear. First things first, take out the pussy eater in your bedside drawer. I know it's there. Also, get out your fattest butt plug and fill your ass with it."

I reach over and open the drawer, taking out one of my favorite sex toys. It's a simulator of a warm human tongue, programmed to eat pussy in several different ways. I press the button to start heating it up. Then I take out the butt plug and lube it up. Slowly, I ease it into my ass. It takes a couple of gentle pushes in and out before I get it seated fully inside me. Then I grab hold of the pussy eater, now ready to go. Wyatt watches me, a look of hunger on his face. "What I would give to taste your pussy. Put that thing on you, honey, and close your eyes. I want you to imagine it's me eating you."

I set the pussy eater in position over my clit and start it. Immediately, I feel the sensation of a warm, wet tongue licking me up and down in rhythmic motion. Ah, that's good. I lie back on the bed and close my eyes.

"That's it, baby. Let me lick that luscious pussy. Oh fuck, you taste so good."

I moan, feeling the warm wet laps on my clit begin to speed up, fluttering back and forth over my engorged nub and catching ever so slightly on my piercing each time, causing a tingle of pleasure pain.

"Oh baby, I can never get enough of you. If I could, I would sleep with my face buried in your cunt and wake up to the taste of you each and every morning. I'd have the flavor of you infused into my very being. I'm so hungry for you. Feel me eating you. I'm gonna make you come so good."

"Aah," I cry, feeling the sucking motion on my clit and the fullness in my ass. "Oh God. Oh God."

"Just look at you. So fucking beautiful. That's it, baby, come for me."

I let out a loud moan as I feel the orgasm rip through me. Thankfully, the walls of my apartment are fully soundproofed.

The fake tongue on my clit keeps on licking me through each wave of pleasure, unaware that I've reached my climax, but I don't have the will to sit up and switch it off. Instead, I lie back, panting breathlessly, engulfed in the delicious afterglow. I hear Wyatt's voice crooning into my ear.

"That was beautiful, Mel. I love you so much. You can travel light years away from me, but you can never leave my heart."

I open my eyes and look into his meltingly tender gaze. I answer truthfully. "I love you forever too."

My eyes travel down to the cum smeared over his abdomen. "You came."

He laughs. "I did. Do you know what a turn on it is to see you come?" He squeezes his cock, letting out a final drop of his pearly white cum. "How about we take five to clean up, then we both snuggle up in bed and talk awhile?"

"Ok."

I sit up and pull the sex toys out of me, then quickly go to the bathroom to wash up. A few minutes later, I'm back in bed and find Wyatt likewise under the covers in our bedroom back home. I fluff up my pillow and state the obvious truth. "So, we're divorced and still having sex."

"Mel, you've never taken the path well-trodden. Why start now?"

"Oh, I don't know. Because it's the sane and logical thing to do?"

"Perhaps. But we both needed this tonight. Don't second guess what feels right."

I can't argue with that. Already, I feel more calm and centered, ready to face whatever tomorrow morning throws at me. Like it or not, Wyatt is still my lifeline. He's still the person I most want to turn to whenever anything happens. I haven't yet worked out how I'm going to forge a life without him. I guess time will tell. I sigh. "I know. Thanks, honey, I needed that."

We talk late into the night until I give a sleepy yawn, say goodnight and put my head down to sleep.

◆◆◆

Next morning, I'm in my office bright and early as always. I'm pouring myself a second coffee when my assistant, Luis, speaks through the intercom. "Melinda, two of the Venorians, Pravol and Shuban, are here and would like to see you."

"Show them in, Luis, thank you."

I stand and come around my desk to greet the Venorians. "Pravol, Shuban, good morning." As I step towards Pravol, I remember what Wyatt said last night. In my mind, I focus on the thought, *your armpit smells*. I touch my forehead to his. Stepping back, I see him lift his elbow and discreetly try to smell his armpit. Midway through the action, he stops and skewers me with his aqua-colored eyes. "So," he says mildly, "you know."

"Know what?" asks Shuban, looking puzzled.

Pravol inclines his head towards me. "Please, Shuban, greet Melinda as is our custom."

Shuban gravely steps towards me, placing a hand on my cheek and his forehead to mine. This time, I telegraph another thought. *I know you can read my mind.* He steps away, his brow clearing. "Indeed, I can!" he responds to my unspoken thought.

"I'm curious. How does this mind reading thing work?"

"Venorians have neural receptors all over their bodies that can tap into another person's nervous system," explains Shuban. "Through this, we can connect to that person's brain and read thought patterns."

"Can you only do this by touching foreheads?"

"We get the strongest signal that way and it is considered the most polite form of doing so. However, it is possible to get a connection through any physical touch. Give me your hand, Melinda, and think of something. I will demonstrate."

I place my hand in Shuban's much larger one and think of what Wyatt said last night. Shuban's face sets in concentration. Then he lets my hand go with a snort. "Wyatt said you should think their armpit smells next time you greet a Venorian."

"Who is Wyatt?" wonders Pravol.

Shuban takes hold of my hand once more. I let him read me. When he lets go, he tells his fellow Venorian, "Wyatt is Melinda's mate on Earth."

I thought I was telegraphing that Wyatt was my ex-husband. Instead, Shuban seems to have picked up on the fact we are very much unfinished business.

"Ah," says Pravol. "So it was his idea to test me like you did. I would very much like to meet this Wyatt."

I smile, "I'm sure that can be arranged."

"If I may ask," continues Pravol, "how did you become aware of our ability to read minds?"

I gesture towards the couch at the end of my office. "Please, let us sit." We take a moment to settle ourselves down on it, then I answer Pravol's question. "It was Martha Reynolds, one of our shortlisted candidates for the exchange program, who first alerted me to the possibility. I decided to put it to the test last night."

Pravol nods thoughtfully. "The bugs in my hair."

"Precisely."

"Speaking of Martha," Shuban interjects, "she is the reason we have come to see you today."

I raise my brows. "Indeed? How so?"

"It has come to our attention that Martha, uniquely among all other races we have encountered in our space travels, is able to read minds just like us."

"Read minds? How come?"

Shuban shrugs. "As to that, I do not know. However, she was able to correctly read a very personal thought I had about her as we exchanged our greeting. We spoke of it, and she admitted that she had been able to tap into each of our thoughts last night as she greeted us."

I'm floored. Could this mind reading thing also be a latent capability in humans?

"I had no idea this was something we humans could do too. If so, this opens up many intriguing possibilities."

Pravol now assumes the reins of the conversation. "This is what we have come to discuss. We would like to invite Martha on to the exchange program, if she is still willing to come and live on Ven for six moon rotations."

"But who would she trade places with? There are only five of you here."

"There is one person that we do not believe is suitable for this program—Eliza Carmichael. We would like Martha to replace her."

Ah, Eliza Carmichael, the ditzy blonde with a viper tongue who I had the dubious pleasure of meeting two days ago. The other members of the selection committee were adamant about choosing her over Martha, despite my protests. What a gloriously karmic victory it would be if my preferred candidate were to go instead. Cautiously, I say, "I would have to consult with the other members of our selection committee, as this decision is not mine alone to take."

"Very well, but should your committee not approve Martha's appointment on the program, we would also like to make clear that Eliza Carmichael is banned from travel to our planet and will not be allowed to board our ship."

So, the slithery seductress did not make a good impression on them either. "I see. I'm sure we can reach a suitable accommodation. Leave it with me and I will get back to you on this by morning end."

The two stand, our meeting over. Solemnly, they bow and take their leave. As soon as they're out the door, I pick up my communicator and begin making some calls.

Three quarters of an hour later, it's all settled. The selection committee has reluctantly acceded to the Venorians' wishes. Eliza has been informed she is no longer on the program and been escorted back to her quarters to await transport back to Earth. And now, to the best part of all this. I call Martha and ask her to come see me as soon as she can.

It doesn't take her long to get here. I smile at the tall, brown-haired young woman with large gray eyes and freckled skin. "Martha, thank you for coming over so quickly." I lead her over to the small sectional sofa at the far end of my office and invite her to sit, before sharing the good news with her. She stares at me speechlessly.

"Martha? This is what you wanted, isn't it?"

"Yes. I'm just overwhelmed. This is the best news!" Then another thought occurs to her. "Have you spoken to Eliza yet?"

"Yes, I have. Let's just say she didn't take it very well. Said some very unkind things about you. I've arranged for her return to Earth on a transport leaving within the hour, so you don't have to worry about running into her."

She heaves a relieved sigh. "So, what next?"

"You'll be leaving with the Venorians on their ship at 18:00 hours, so make sure you're packed and ready at least an hour before then. Treylor will want to spend some time with you before you go. You can tell her a little more about the specifics of your life on Earth and what she should expect, living in your apartment. She'll reciprocate with more information for you about Ven."

"I look forward to that."

I gaze at her seriously. "Martha, I'm sure I don't need to tell you just how valuable this skill you have could be. More than anyone, you'll be able to get a read on the Venorians and their intentions towards us. I'm nearly one hundred percent sure that they are a benign race that means us no harm, but there is still so much we don't know or understand about them. The intelligence you provide us with from this mission will be critical."

"I understand."

We stand and shake hands. "Good luck, Martha. I've been so impressed with what I've seen from you. I have every confidence in your success on this mission."

"Thank you, Melinda. I really appreciate the vote of confidence."

I smile as I see her out of my office. I have a good feeling about Martha. I do believe she is going to be a great asset for us on Ven.

Chapter 2

Melinda

One month previously

Istretch my arms above my head and flex my neck from side to side, trying to work the kinks out of my body. I've just spent the last two hours writing a report for my superiors back on Earth about the curious happenings on the planet Ven. Out here on Mars, we are first to receive any communications from distant planets such as Ven and the two others we have made contact with through the Venorians—Krovatia and Driskia.

The news that has trickled in recently has made for interesting reading. Who would have thought that the fresh faced young woman I bid goodbye to all those months ago would end up becoming mated to Krantor, the son of Ven's mighty ruler, the Kran? I'm sure not even Martha Reynolds had any inkling of what was to happen to her on that distant planet. In her last dispatch to me, sent a day before her mating ceremony, she sounded happy, excited and very much in love. I'm not surprised. I've seen video footage of Krantor, and he managed to set even my tired old heart aflutter. Lucky, lucky girl.

And then came today's news. I listened wide eyed to dispatches from all five of our humans on Ven. I couldn't quite believe my ears; it all sounded too incredibly far-fetched. I glance again at the executive summary of my report and read what I've written.

> *The Saraxians, inhabitants of a planet in the*
> *far reaches of the second galactic quadrant, have*
> *mounted an attack on the planet Ven. Using*
> *some powerful crystals stolen from Krovatia, they*

*managed to induce a state of mass
unconsciousness in the Venorian population. The
boral crystals are thought to have had this impact
by blocking Venorians' neural receptors and
sending them into shock.*

*In the course of their attack, the Saraxians
stole valuable reserves of the mineral dorenium,
as well as abducted Martha Reynolds, Krantor's
new mate. Krantor and his elite bodyguards—the
somars—were off planet when this attack
occurred, but were able to successfully rescue
Martha, who is thankfully unharmed.*

*Venorians are currently reviewing their
security protocols and discussing punitive
measures to take on the Saraxians. Relations
between Venorians and Krovatians have also
cooled, since the latter failed to properly warn of
the potential dangers of boral crystals to the
Venorian population. All the humans involved in
the Venorian Exchange Program have reported
themselves unharmed.*

Poor Martha, being abducted by these nasty Saraxians. I'm just glad everyone is safe and unharmed. Such drama being played out a few light years away, while here on Mars, life continues to grind at a stiflingly slow pace. God, I can't wait to get off here and return back to Earth for a well-earned break. And to see Wyatt again—my ex-husband who's not quite an ex.

My communicator buzzes with an incoming call. Speak of the devil. With a tired smile, I pick up. "Hey, honey."

He frowns. "You look tired. Is everything alright?"

"Yes, I'm ok. There's been dramatic news from Ven and I've been at my desk for hours drafting my report."

"Dramatic? What's happened?"

Hurriedly, I fill him in. When I come to the end of my tale, he shakes his head in amazement. "Mass unconsciousness! It sounds fantastical."

"I know. I'd barely believe it if it weren't for the testimony of all the humans on our exchange program."

"Will this have an impact on your efforts to build relations with the Krovatians and Driskians?"

"I hope not. It's a delicate situation. If the Venorians decide to cut off their ties with the Krovatians, then we will unfortunately be bound to do so too or risk offending our new allies. But my gut feeling is it won't come to that. The Venorians don't strike me as the type of people to cut off their nose to spite their face. The trade they have with the Krovatians is too valuable to lose. I'll be curious how this plays out though."

"If I were the Venorians, I'd use this as an opportunity to win more concessions from the Krovatians, such as greater access to their planet. Didn't you say they were a closed off, secretive race?"

"Yes. As far as I understand, they don't allow any foreigners on their planet. All their trade with the Venorians is conducted in neutral third-party territory."

"Hmm. Well, if I were a betting man, I'd put money on that changing in the not too distant future."

My eyes sharpen at this. "You think?"

He shrugs. "Just a hunch."

I ponder this. "You might be right. I'll definitely need to keep my ears to the ground."

"No, honey, what you need is to put your feet back on Earth and enjoy a well-earned vacation."

"I can't wait," I say with a sigh. "Have you booked the hotel?"

"It's what I was calling you about. I'm sending the details by message now, but just so you know, hotel is all booked up, including a private hot tub on the terrace. Just think. Fresh air, endless lush green valleys, the two of us hiking by day and relaxing by evening."

"Oh God, that sounds like heaven."

"Just a few more weeks to go."

"I'm counting the days."

"Me too."

"I love you, Wyatt."

"I love you too."

"Bye now."

"Bye, honey."

I end the call, dreaming of that fresh mountain air, and of seeing Wyatt again. Yes, I'm that person who goes on vacation with her ex-husband who's not quite an ex. It's not the most rational thing to do. I'm fully aware of that. When I get back to Earth, me and Wyatt are going to have a talk, that's for sure.

Present day

I'm all packed up and ready to go. My shuttle back to Earth will be arriving soon, loaded with passengers I'm curious to see again. The five Venorians on the exchange program are on their way back home after their six months stint on Earth. They'll be picked up from here by one of their own ships which will be bringing home the humans that have been on Ven, minus Martha. My last job before I begin my vacation will be to invite them all for a debrief.

My communicator buzzes with an incoming call from Tom, my head of security.

"Hey Tom," I answer.

"Melinda, the shuttle is docking in bay six. Could you make your way over to greet the arrivals?"

"On my way."

Opening my office door, I head to the buggy parked in my allocated space outside. I climb aboard and start driving it in manual mode, which is my preference. I could simply program it to take me to bay six, but where would the fun in that be? The drive is short, but a welcome interlude. I pass the main thoroughfare of shops and restaurants before heading east, past the medical bay and further down a long corridor that houses various storage facilities, until I reach the door marked for bay six.

I park and dismount just as the door slides open and passengers begin to stream out. I spot my Venorian friends immediately, their height making them easily recognizable. Pravol and his soon-to-be mate, Treylor, walk hand in hand, followed by the rest of their team. I wave to them and they head towards me, smiling. "Welcome back to Mars," I say, then approach Treylor first for the customary greeting.

She touches her forehead to mine, and steps back with a big grin. "I see you are very excited to return to your home planet and see your mate again."

My mouth quirks into a smile I can't contain. "Yes, I'm looking forward to it."

By now, Pravol is also greeting me, touching his forehead to mine. As he pulls away, he tells me in his usual grave manner, "Wyatt has talked of little else but the vacation the two of you are taking. He cannot wait to be re-united with you."

My heart constricts. Ex-husband or not, I've missed him. Apart from two short weeks last year, we've been separated for nearly three years. We've survived on a diet of regular communicator calls and remote sex. There hasn't been anyone else for me, and I don't believe there has been for him either. I could be wrong. We'll need to have a conversation about our status, and soon.

I greet the rest of the Venorians, inviting them to partake of dinner with me later this evening. With help from my assistant, Luis, I arrange transport for all to the cabins they will be staying in overnight. Then I'm on my way back to my office and to the ten million and one things on my agenda before I take my leave of absence.

Later that evening, I finally sit back at the large dinner table I got Luis to reserve for us at Pico, the premium restaurant on Mars. I take a grateful sip of my wine and ask Treylor, "So, how did you find Earth?"

Her eyes warm with humor, she pronounces, "It was an interesting experience."

"Not a raving endorsement," I say with a chuckle.

She cocks her head to one side. "I greatly enjoyed meeting many different Humans and finding out about their way of life, but my absolute favorite thing was when Wyatt very kindly invited us out to watch a performance of the ballet. That, I adored."

"Yes, Wyatt told me how much you enjoyed Manon."

"It was simply beautiful, and I cried so much at the end. Poor Pravol became much concerned."

He places a hand on top of hers. "My heart, you know that I do not like to see you cry."

"I know, but those were happy tears."

"I see that now."

Watching the absolute care and devotion Pravol lavishes on Treylor has my heart constricting again. Once, I too had my knight in shining armor. I'm still not entirely sure where things went wrong.

I decide to change the subject. "So, I gather you have heard about the Saraxian attack on Ven."

They all nod, looking grave. "My brother Prilor was badly injured in the attack," says Treylor. "If it was not for Krantor's quick action in saving him, he would not be with us anymore."

"I'm so sorry, Treylor," I murmur. "How is Prilor now?"

"He is on his way to a full recovery, thanks be to Lir."

"I'm glad."

"That is why we are anxious to be on our way back to Ven as soon as possible," says Pravol.

"I understand the Venorian ship will be here by morning."

He inclines his head.

"And what of the Saraxians?" I enquire. "How are your people going to deal with them now?"

"The Kran is keen to avoid an all-out war," replies Shuban. "However, we will be drawing up a new exclusion zone, wider than the one in our previous peace treaty with them. They will now not only have to steer clear of the Utar belt, but of an extensive ring around it. We have also imposed a trade embargo on the Saraxians, making it clear we will not do business with any entity that trades with them."

"Will that be enough to deter them?"

"That, I do not know. However, in his address to the people, the Kran made it clear that increasing our planet's security is a top priority. My guess is that we will be expanding our fleet of ships patrolling the area around the exclusion zone."

"And what of the Krovatians?"

At this, Treylor cries out, "They did not tell us about the powerful effects of boral crystals. That was not well done of them! As you may know, we recovered a box of these crystals when Krantor detained a Klixian ship illegally travelling through the Utar belt. Had we known how dangerous they were, we would have engaged far stronger security protocols and avoided this entire attack. But the Krovatians said nothing, even after we informed them of our find."

"Will there be repercussions on them?"

"There will," responds Pravol. "We have increased the price of some of the commodities we export to them and put a temporary stop to our imports of dorenium. However, we have not ceased trading with the Krovatians entirely. Their supplies of medicinal plants are too important for us."

"That is not to say that we have become enemies," adds Shuban. "Far from it. We still see the Krovatians as our allies, but we wish to make our displeasure at their actions clear. We also wish to avoid a repetition of these recent events by improving our communications with them."

"You will know," says Pravol, "that the Krovatians are a very secretive people who keep to themselves. We will be telling them that if they wish to continue being our allies, they must open up a little more."

"Yes," I nod, "that's understandable. Will they agree to open things up, do you think?"

Pravol hesitates, as if not sure whether to share this next piece of information with me. Then, he says, "There is talk of opening up diplomatic relations between our people. I understand our authorities are currently negotiating terms for a mission of Venorians to go live on Krovatia and vice versa."

"Wow, that's a big step forward!"

"It is."

"I suppose there is no hope that they would also accept a mission from Earth on their planet?"

"It is not an impossibility, given that Krantor's mate is a Human. Once we return to Ven and report back on our findings, I am sure we will be more than willing to vouch for your race as peaceful allies of ours. However, one must be prepared for the likelihood that the Krovatian authorities will say no."

I file away this piece of information, undeterred. It may take time, but I see the potential for eventually developing diplomatic relations between ourselves and the Krovatians. It's definitely something I need to discuss on my debrief at the White House when I get back.

We continue our conversation as the meal progresses, but there are no other significant nuggets of information to emerge. Once the meal is over, I bid them goodnight and hurry home to my apartment. I open my front door and toe off my shoes. "Athena, call Wyatt."

A moment later, his handsome face smiles back at me from the confines of his bed. "Hey gorgeous, how was your dinner with our Venorian friends?"

"Informative."

"I thought it might be. I haven't talked politics with Pravol, but I know he's been in touch with his people since that Saraxian attack."

"He has, and what he had to share was very interesting, particularly with regards to the Krovatians."

I give him the gist of the conversation. He listens attentively as I recount what Pravol and Shuban said. Eventually he says, "I can see the wheels turning in your mind, Mel. You're thinking about the possibility of a human mission to Krovatia further down the line."

"It's all to play for, Wyatt. From what I hear, the Krovatians are rich in many valuable minerals and medicinal plants. What a coup for us if we could negotiate our way into trading with them."

"You mean, what a coup for you."

"It's my job to seek out extra-terrestrial opportunities," I say, a little stung.

"I know." He sighs. "We haven't discussed what your plans are once your term on Mars comes to an end."

"I'm not sure yet what I want to do. I'm going to use these four weeks of leave to sound people out and explore possibilities. Hopefully by the end of that, I'll have a clearer picture of my prospects."

"But what is it that you want to do after Mars?"

I shrug my shoulders. "Honestly, I don't know."

"Are you planning to return to Washington?"

Again I say, "I don't know."

Sadness seeps into Wyatt's eyes. "I see," he says flatly.

"Wyatt, let's not argue. I can't wait to get back to Earth and see you. And I'm so looking forward to our vacation. Let's take things a day at a time. I know we need to talk about the future and we will."

"Ok. That's fair."

We talk a little more, then bid each other goodnight.

In the early hours of the morning, the Venorian ship arrives, and with it, the four humans that have been living on Ven. As required by protocol, I'm there to greet them as they arrive. Troy Summers walks out first and grins at me. "Ambassador Garcia," he says, coming towards me.

I shake his hand in welcome. "Call me Melinda. How are you, Troy?"

"I'm good, thanks."

I turn to say hello to the others—Shay Smith, Diego Sanchez and Dimitri Woods. "Welcome back to Mars. I'm sure you'll want to catch up on your sleep and get your land legs back before we have our debrief. How about we meet at eleven for brunch together in my office?"

"That sounds good," smiles Shay.

Eleven o'clock on the dot, they're trooping into my office where a table has been set for our brunch. "Come in. Can I offer you anything to drink?" I ask them politely.

Once drinks are sorted and we're all seated, I begin the debrief. "So firstly, how is Martha?"

Troy is first to speak up. "She's doing great and is very happy in her unconventional menage with all her hunky Venorian males. Last I heard, she had plans to set up a school for Venorians and humans to be educated alongside each other."

"I like that idea. Tell me, what was Ven really like?"

Shay gets a dreamy look on her face. "It was paradise. Perfect weather, beautiful landscapes, gorgeous sexy people, great food. I wish I could go back there already."

"Add to that," says Dimitri, "a highly evolved, sex positive society where there is equality between the sexes like I've never seen before."

"Oh wow, you're really selling it to me."

"And that's not all," adds Troy. "The technology they have is out of this world. I've got hundreds of technical drawings to share with our people back on Earth. I'm pretty sure the information there will make significant improvements to our own technology across the board."

"We're very excited to see what you have, Troy. I can tell you all without a doubt that you have greatly impressed us with the work you've done on Ven. We're so proud of you."

"Thank you," murmurs Diego. "That means a lot."

"Tell me about the day of the Saraxian attack."

"Well, that was one scary bunch of people," says Dimitri. "We were all gathered in the palace with Martha when it happened…"

They all brief me in greater detail about the Saraxian attack on Ven with the boral crystals and how this induced a mass episode of unconsciousness among the Venorian population. As they talk, Luis records the proceedings, which he'll then send me as a written draft. Brunch over, I let them go spend leisure time on the colony before we reconvene. At 18:00 tonight, we will departing on our journey back to Earth.

Chapter 3

Melinda

I pause my hike to admire the panoramic view before me. Grassy alpine meadows and scrubby pine trees cover the land as far as the eye can see. I breathe in the crisp mountain air and drink in the view. I've missed this.

Living on Mars the last three years has been exciting and great for my career, but there were some downsides. I spent my days confined to the artificial space of our indoor city, with no access to the arid landscape outside. It was fine while I was there, but now I'm back on Earth, I realize just how much I've missed being outside, surrounded by the bounty of nature. It makes me wonder how much longer I'm willing to continue with that existence. Over the next four weeks of leave, I need to work out my next move.

Wyatt halts beside me. "It's beautiful, isn't it?"

I take a deep inhale of the fresh mountain air. "It is. I was just thinking how much I miss this when I'm living in an artificially constructed city with no access to the open air."

I walk a little further to find a flat rock to sit on and take off my backpack, pulling out my bottle of water. Wyatt digs into his pack and passes me an energy bar. He sits next to me as we both take satisfying gulps of water and eat our snack.

Finally, Wyatt resumes the thread of our earlier conversation. "It doesn't sound like you want to continue on Mars even if they decide to renew your term there."

"No, I don't think I could do another three years of that life."

"So, what next?"

"I've thought about seeking alternative employment on Earth, perhaps doing some lecturing at universities, but I don't like that idea either. I haven't worked this hard to get to where I am only to give it all up."

I place my chin on Wyatt's shoulder. "The only other possibility that occurs to me is to lead a diplomatic mission elsewhere. There has been talk of establishing an Earth Federation embassy on the planet Ven—which by all accounts is beautiful and lush, a far cry from Mars. Shay Smith described it as paradise. Maybe I should be putting my hat into the ring for that."

"You're sure you want to continue being off planet? There are other avenues you could explore if you wanted out of Mars."

"I've thought about it. I could try to get back into the political game in Washington, but I've been away much too long. Also, my experience on Mars has given me skills and knowledge about inter-planetary relations that few others have. It's one of my strengths, and I have to play to it."

"True, but you'd be living away from humans, among alien species whose way of life is different to ours. Is that what you really want?"

"It's not like humans have endeared themselves to me," I say dryly.

He snorts. "Yeah, I don't know how you did it. The Washington political scene is like a snake pit."

I run a gentle finger along his cheek. "You made it possible. I knew, no matter how vicious things got at work, I could come home to the comfort and normality of you."

He imprisons my hand in his and kisses it. "Oh Mel."

There is a heavy silence between us. Wyatt breaks it with a sigh. "Well then, go for it. They'd be crazy not to pick you."

"We'll see." I lean across and kiss him softly on the lips. "Come on, let's get going."

With that, I pick up my rucksack and put it back on. Wyatt does the same, and we resume our hike.

As we walk, I let my mind wander along with my feet, thinking about my twelve-year marriage to Wyatt. It doesn't take a genius to know he wants me to move back to Washington permanently and give our relationship another chance. I kind of want that too, but I'm on the fence. It wasn't a lack of love that broke us up, nor any infidelity. It's just that our lives were heading in different directions. We were young when we met, still in college. It seemed back then that we both wanted the same things, both of us high achieving and driven.

Things changed a few years ago. Wyatt got off the ambitious, career driven train while I stayed on it. I still sometimes can't believe he ditched his high profile business consulting job and retrained as a goddamn chiropractor. To be fair, he seems much happier now doing a nine to five, away from the high stress environment he was in before. Problem is, it's created a mismatch in our lives. When I was offered the ambassadorship on Mars, we both knew he wouldn't want to leave his budding chiropractic practice and follow me there. So, we separated, eventually deciding to call it quits on our marriage. And now here we are back again. Do I want a repeat?

I study the back of his head as he walks in front me, blond hair darkened by sweat and curling a little at the nape. There's no doubt I love him still. I probably always will. I missed him like crazy on Mars. I don't think I could have survived being there alone without our regular calls and the long chats we had late into the night. He's my best friend as well as my lover. I can't imagine being with anybody else.

When the case is put like this, it seems mad that we ever separated. And yet… If I hadn't left him, I never would have experienced everything I did on Mars. It would have been somebody else, not me, who made first contact with the Venorians, while I watched the news footage jealously from Earth. Now, with the possibility of an ambassadorship on Ven, I'm aching to set foot on that distant planet and experience life there. Getting back together with Wyatt would mean giving up on that dream too.

I blow away a stray strand of hair, feeling frustrated. There are no easy choices. When have there ever? Resolutely, I park these thoughts and decide to enjoy the moment. Quickening my steps, I catch up with Wyatt and grab hold of his hand.

He turns to me, surprised. "Hey."

I kiss his sweaty cheek. "Hey."

"Are you thinking what I'm thinking?"

"I'm thinking, I could murder for a dip in the hot tub right now, how about you?"

He kisses my lips. "I'd happily be an accessory to that murder."

I laugh. "Come on, only another two miles to go."

Some hours later in our room, we both undress and stand, gazing at each other's naked bodies, cataloguing the changes since we were last together. Wyatt keeps himself in shape. There's only a slight thickening at the waist to suggest he's now in his early forties. His golden brown chest hair, very lightly sprinkled with gray, thickens as it trails down towards his groin, where his cock is already rising stiffly, displaying the frenum piercing on its underside.

I see him look hungrily at my pierced clit. Our wedding rings may have come off, but this mutual exchange of body jewelry still exists, reminding us that once, we were together as one.

"Come here," he says gruffly.

I go to him and wrap my arms around his neck. His skin warms mine everywhere we touch. He captures my mouth, and we kiss for a long, long time, reacquainting ourselves with the texture and taste of the other. My tongue reaches into his mouth, playfully tangling with his. Soon, the kiss becomes more heated, our playful licks turning to long, needy strokes and hungry sucks. When finally our lips part, we're breathless.

Wyatt rains kisses along my jaw and to the sensitive flesh of my neck, sending shivers down my spine.

Standing on tiptoes, legs spread wide, I rub my pierced clit against his hard shaft, enjoying the sensation. At the same time, he grinds his cock against me, finding his own stimulation. We discovered this nifty mutual masturbation trick soon after our piercings were healed. We could come just by rubbing against each other, whether standing or lying in bed. It helps that we're about the same height, his five feet eleven only topping me by an inch.

My wetness drips onto his cock, making it easier for him to slide against me. We stand there together in a tight embrace, grinding against each other, moaning and grunting as we seek our release.

"I'm close," I pant.

"Me too," he says huskily, "so we better stop. If I come now, I won't get to fuck you for at least an hour."

"Old man," I tease into his ear.

"Not so old I can't do this," he grunts, as he lifts me over his shoulder, fireman style. He strides over to the balcony door and slides it open, stepping out onto our private terrace. A few further steps has us in the hot tub, where he deposits me gently. We both sigh with pleasure as the warm water engulfs our tired bodies.

"Ah, so good." I stretch my arms and legs, luxuriating in the feel of the warm jets along my aching joints.

Wyatt stretches out beside me with a contented sigh. "That is good," he drawls.

"Better than sex?"

He pretends to consider for a moment, then, putting thumb and index finger an inch apart, he smirks, "Maybe sex is better by this much."

"You'll have to show me. It's been a long time."

"Yeah, I know."

I ask the question that's been on the back of my mind. "Have you—in all this time—you know, been with someone else?"

He takes so long to speak that I brace myself for the answer. "All the time we were married, Mel, I've been faithful. It's been hard, with the long separation. I have needs, like any other human, but I made a vow to you when we got married, and I've kept that vow."

"And what about since the divorce?"

He lets out a long breath. "A week after the divorce, I let Dylan convince me to go out on a date with this girl he set me up with, Callie."

I watch his face intently, my heart sinking.

"So, we went out, had a nice meal—normal, ordinary stuff."

"And?"

"She was nice. Pretty. Intelligent. Kind. We had an enjoyable evening. She seemed to like me, which was good for my ego."

"Wyatt, you're killing me. Just spit it out."

He huffs. "That's what I'm trying to do. It's not easy to talk about this with you." He sighs. "At the end of the evening, I saw her back home and we kissed. I—enjoyed the kiss. She was pretty. She felt good, smelled good, tasted good, and I'm made of flesh and blood. So yes, I kissed a girl and I liked it."

"Don't sugarcoat it," I say sarcastically.

He gives me a pained look. "I'm trying to be honest. So, we kissed and it got a little heated. My cock was definitely on board to take things further, but I stopped. I just wasn't ready to take that big step. For over two decades, Mel, there's only been one woman in my life and my bed. It didn't feel right to be with someone else. So I bid her goodnight, did the gentlemanly thing and left."

"Did you ever see her again?"

He lays his head back against the edge of the tub and closes his eyes. "Next day, I was about to message her and ask for a second date. Then the newscast came on with footage of your first contact with the Venorians and everything got forgotten for a while. I got swamped with calls, remember? And then you called and we ended up naked, having remote sex. I thought all that would end with the divorce, yet here we were at it again. You were so gorgeous as you came, and I realized no other woman, no matter how pretty, holds a candle to you. That piece of paper that says we're divorced can't speak for what's between us. I'll always love you, Mel. You're it for me."

I swallow the lump in my throat as he continues. "I figured, if there's even the smallest chance that we could be together again, then I wouldn't ruin it by sleeping with someone else. So, my hand's been kept busy, trying to ease my long suffering cock. I'm yours, Mel. The question is, after all this time, are you mine?"

"There's been no one else, only you."

"I sense a but."

"But the problems that broke us up are still here."

"You want to go to Ven," he states flatly.

"I want to go to Ven. I want more than the conventional, nine-to-five lifestyle you seem to crave."

"What if you don't get the Ven ambassadorship?"

"Then I'll keep trying for something else, maybe Krovatia or Driskia. In any case, do you really want to predicate our getting back together on my career disappointment?"

"No, of course not! I'm no consolation prize."

"And you shouldn't be."

"Mel, I want you to have your dreams and your success. I never want to be the guy that cuts you down."

I tuck my head against his familiar, comforting chest. "I know."

"All I've ever wanted is to share my life with you."

"But my life took me to Mars, and yours stayed here."

He sighs. "Don't I just know it."

I kiss him just below the collar bone. "There's no point going over this again. What's done is done. One day, you're going to meet some fine woman and fall in love again. I just know it. And yes, it will hurt and sting, but I'll get over it. We've made our choices."

He strokes my hair gently. "Are you sure?"

I don't answer. Instead, I say, "Maybe us sleeping together while I'm here isn't the brightest of ideas. Do you want me to move to another room for the rest of our stay?"

His arm around me tightens. "Hell no!"

I snuggle up to him in relief. "Ok."

After a time, he says, "Perhaps it'll be the other way. One day, you'll meet some fine man and be the one to fall in love again."

"Maybe," I murmur, though in my head I think it unlikely. I look up into his eyes. "Enough talk. Let's enjoy the here and now. Take me to bed, Wyatt, and fuck the living daylights out of me."

His mouth curves into a grin. "At your command, ma'am."

In one swift move, he stands us up in the tub and marches me out, stopping only to reach for a fluffy set of towels. Quickly, he dries us off, then he's leading me to the bed, pushing me down onto my back. Next moment, he's opened my legs wide and buried his face in my pussy. He licks me like a starving man with long laps of his tongue up and down my clit, tugging gently at the piercing with each stroke and making my nerve endings tingle. It feels so incredibly good. I close my eyes on a sigh, losing myself in the pleasure of his touch.

After a while, his finger joins his tongue, stroking along my slit to gather lubrication, before making its way down to the rosebud of my ass and slipping gently inside, as deep as his knuckle. He knows just the way I like it. With his finger, he fucks my ass while still licking my pussy in long, rhythmic strokes. I writhe beneath him. Oh God that's good. I'm so, so close.

Sensing my impending orgasm, Wyatt's tongue and finger pick up speed, the one fluttering up and down my clit, and the other massaging my ass with shallow strokes. I cry out as I start to come, and that's when he catches one of the barbells on my clit with his teeth and tugs it, sending me into heavenly convulsions. "Oh God!" I shriek as I feel myself pulse endlessly. His tongue continues lapping at me through my orgasm, only stopping once I lie still beneath him.

When he lifts his head to look at me, I pant, "You are a fucking genius."

He smirks, wiping my juices from his face with the back of his hand. "First orgasm on my tongue. Second one, on my cock." As he says this, he lifts my legs up high, tucking my ankles on his shoulders. He takes his cock in his hand and positions himself at my entrance. Just as he's about to enter me, he pauses and asks, "Do I need to put on a condom?"

"It's fine. Get in there already."

With a quirk of his lips, he obliges. In one thrust, he buries his length inside me. Wyatt's cock isn't massive. It's not tiny either, just proportional to his body size. However, in that position with my legs raised, and with the stimulation from both our piercings, I feel the penetration to the very core of my being—not to mention that core is still throbbing and engorged from my orgasm. I gasp at the intrusion. "Oh yeah! Feels good."

Eyes burning with desire, Wyatt begins to fuck me mercilessly, making me moan louder and louder with each thrust. My starved body drinks him in. As he senses my orgasm approaching, Wyatt slips a finger to my clit, rubbing gentle circles around the engorged nub. Ever since I had it pierced, sensation there has been enhanced and it's made it easier to achieve multiple orgasms, something I used to struggle to do. His next thrust takes me over the edge. With a shudder, I come, pulsing around his cock, feeling the contractions deep within me. Wyatt drives into me a few more times, then he too comes with a loud groan.

Still joined, he leans down to kiss me. "Thanks, honey, I needed that," he murmurs.

I brush back his tousled hair. "Me too."

We hold each other close until, with a sigh, Wyatt pulls out. Grabbing some tissues from the bedside table, he wipes the excess cum dripping from my body. Then he pulls the covers over us and tucks me to his side. "Come on, let's get some sleep."

I yawn. "Good idea. Goodnight, honey."

"Goodnight, sweetheart."

Much later, I wake, my sleep patterns still not adjusted to being back on Earth. I rest my head on the pillow next to his and trace gentle circles with my fingers on his chest. "Wyatt," I whisper.

"Mmm," he grunts.

"When you were saying your wedding vows, did it ever cross your mind that one day, we would have to break them?"

He traps my hand to his heart. "No, not in a million years."

We're silent as I resume tracing circles on his chest. Then I ask, "Do you ever regret us not having kids?"

He shifts a little, coming fully awake. "I wouldn't have minded having kids, but I don't have regrets. In any case, I see my brother's children a lot and get the best of both worlds — the fun parts without the responsibility." He runs his fingers through my hair on the pillow. "Why do you ask? Do you have regrets?"

"No, not really. Just like you, I get to play auntie with Harper's kids. I get moments though, you know, when I wonder what it would have been like to grow a baby in my belly and to nurture a new life. But then, I realize it just couldn't have worked. Not with my life the way it is."

He strokes my cheek gently. "How about now? Forty-one is still possible if you wanted to try for one."

"Are you saying you'd have a baby with me if I wanted to?"

"In a heartbeat, yes."

I take a shaky breath. "Jesus, Wyatt. You make it so fucking hard."

"Hard to do what?"

"Hard to get on that spaceship and pick up my life on Mars."

"Then don't. Nothing's stopping you from staying here. You said yourself you wanted a change."

"For one thing, Wyatt, we're divorced. Remember? And yes I want a change from living in the artificial world of Mars where I don't get to step outside for some fresh air. But that doesn't mean I want to quit."

He rubs his eye irritably. "And then we're back to square one." After a while he says, "I'm sorry. I didn't mean to rehash all this."

"Don't be. I was the one who started this conversation." I huff out a deep breath. "I'm sorry, I shouldn't have."

He sighs. "Come here."

I let him spoon me to his body and close my eyes. Later, much later, sleep eventually comes.

Chapter 4

Melinda

Decision made about the direction I want to take in my career, I make a plan of action. As soon as we get back to Washington, I start contacting people. My first port of call is my good friend, Elise Dawson, who is probably the only person I trust in the shark infested waters of the Washington political scene. We interned together at the same congressman's office many years ago. Now, she works as a lobbyist, and her eyes and ears are everywhere.

We meet for brunch at our favorite eatery in Penn Quarter. I've already been here a few minutes and ordered my drink, when I see her glide smoothly towards my table, looking well put together as always. I stand and give her a hug.

"Melinda, how good to see you."

"You too, Elise. You're looking well."

She brushes her hair back and smiles wickedly. "It's the latest toy boy in my life. Keeps me young."

I laugh. "That it does!"

We settle down at our table and order our food. Once that's out the way, she leans back in her chair and observes me. "So, tell me your news."

For the next few minutes, I update her on the latest happenings from my Mars posting. I ask her about the new gossip in town and she fills me in. By this time, our food's arrived, and I take a moment simply to enjoy the pan fried fish and fresh crisp salad on my plate. That's another thing I miss on Mars. Apart from a couple of special occasions where we've had real meat sent to us from Earth, the rest of the time our food has consisted of rehydrated protein, pasta and rice, with a few vegetables grown in the hydroponic greenhouses. It's not bad, and the food has gotten better over the past year, but nothing beats the fresh stuff here on Earth.

I'm savoring the last bite of my fish when Elise raises an elegant brow and regards me with her warm brown eyes. "So, Melinda. What next for you? If you're looking to get back in the Washington scene, I have a few suggestions for you."

I put my fork down. "Actually, no. I was thinking more in terms of a diplomatic mission to Ven."

"Ah. Are you sure you want to go on living off planet?"

I smile. "That's the same thing Wyatt asked, and the answer is yes. Don't get me wrong, I've missed Earth. Just being able to walk outside in the fresh air is a gift. But now that I've had a taste of life beyond our planet, I'm hungry to explore and know more."

"How's Wyatt? I haven't seen him in forever."

"He's doing well. The practice is booming. I think he made the right choice, switching careers. He's a people person and a giver. Being a chiropractor suits him a hell of a lot more than the cutthroat world of business."

"You may be right. I'm curious. How is it working out between you two?"

"It's good. We're still friends."

Elise scrutinizes me in silence. I blurt, "Ok, maybe a little more than friends."

"Don't tell me you're sleeping with your ex?"

I flush and study the dessert menu with rapt attention.

"Jesus, Mel. What are you thinking?"

"I know it sounds all kinds of wrong, and we'll stop doing it someday—when he meets someone else and it gets serious. Until then, it just feels natural to be together when we can."

"Sweetie, he's not your husband anymore."

"You don't need to tell me that. I know."

"But you still haven't got him out of your system."

"It's hard to move on from someone who's been an important part of your life for so many years," I say quietly.

She shakes her head disapprovingly. "Well, I guess then it's all the more reason to get well away." She pauses and regards me speculatively. "The Ven ambassadorship has yet to be decided and it could be yours if you play your cards right. I warn you though, there's some stiff competition for the position."

"Who?"

"Lucas Rivera."

"Well color me surprised. I knew there must have been a reason for him coming to Mars to see off our candidates for the exchange program."

"He's hungry for a slice of the intergalactic political pie. Just like you, he sees the potential there. But you have advantages you need to press. Your expertise, your existing relationships with the Venorians, the prestige of having been the person to make first contact with them. It's all to play for."

"So, who do I have to see to make this happen?"

"For starters, get yourself a meeting with Peyton Miller."

Peyton is the President's chief of staff, and as luck would have it, I already have an appointment with her as part of my Mars debrief. "That I can do."

I keep busy the next few weeks, paying a visit to my parents and to my sister Harper. I shop for a new wardrobe—when it comes to fashion, the amenities on Mars are severely lacking. I make calls, do some schmoozing, and start the momentum going for my candidacy. Each night, I sleep in Wyatt's arms, taking comfort and pleasure from him but all the while knowing how fleeting this feeling is. One day soon, as Elise said, I will have to get him out of my system, permanently. That day hasn't come yet.

I'm focused on getting all my ducks in a row, one of which is this meeting I have today with Peyton Miller. I dress with care, wanting to project the right image. Slipping on a newly bought fitted navy pant suit, with a coral pink blouse beneath, I examine myself critically in the full-length mirror. I keep to a strict fitness regimen, so despite my middle age, I'm still trim and toned. I turn sideways to observe my figure. My breasts are small, but that's no bad thing in my line of work. I don't have to worry about lecherous individuals looking down my cleavage when I'm trying to be taken seriously. Despite my Latin heritage, I don't have a big booty either. My butt is ordinary—not flat exactly, but not the type that men, or women, lust after. Again, an advantage workwise. I do everything in my power to appear business-like and professional. Nothing about me screams "sexy lady".

Strong arms slip around my waist and draw me against a hard, muscled chest. I breathe in Wyatt's seductive scent, musky and woodsy, a combination of him and his cologne. Closing my eyes, I bask in the pleasure of being in his arms. It feels so good. He kisses the side of my neck and murmurs in my ear, "Good morning, sexy lady."

I can't help laughing at that. "Wyatt honey, you've got to get your eyes examined. I was just admiring how unsexy and professional I look."

He turns me around so we're both facing the mirror. I take in my wavy dark brown hair that has not even a hint of gray, thanks to regular tinting treatments. It's been cut and styled at the salon just this week in wispy bangs that frame my face. My brows have been lasered to a neat arch above my dark, long-lashed eyes, which are my best feature, I think. I'm no beauty. My mouth is a little too wide, my nose too snub, but I look eminently presentable, so I'll take that.

Wyatt too is perusing me in the mirror. "Look at you, Mel. One gorgeous, sexy lady."

I turn in his arms with a smile and kiss him. "I think you might be just a tad biased, but thanks." I step back and point to myself. "So, what do you think. Will this do for a meeting at the White House?"

He draws me to him and kisses me once more. "You look great."

An hour later, I arrive at my destination and get through the security checks. I'm not kept waiting long. Peyton strides in, her blond hair coiffed to perfection, a warm smile on her face.

"Melinda, it's good to see you!"

I stand and shake hands with her. "Likewise, Peyton. It's been a while."

"Come on through, I'm sure we've got lots to talk about. I know we've had our weekly video chats, but there are things that can only be discussed in person."

I follow her to her office and sit on a dark leather sofa. Peyton settles herself down in an antique armchair to my right. Without further ado, we get into the nitty gritty of my debrief. Peyton's aide, a serious looking young man, sits to one side, taking down the minutes of our meeting. We're interrupted several times with calls, a few from the President herself, but we manage to get through the business at hand. I give her my candid and considered report on our relations with the alien races we've so far made contact with—the Venorians, of course, the Driskians and the Krovatians. There are a few other inhabited planets that we've discovered through our contact with the Venorians, such as Sarax and Klix, but these are considered too risky for us to approach at this time. I set out my views on which direction we should be heading, what potential advantages we could gain from further engagement with these planets and a little on the possible threats.

As the meeting is winding down, I look for an opportunity to discuss my own future plans. She presents me with it in her next question, "So, Melinda, I know you'll soon be coming to the end of your term on Mars. Have you had any thoughts about extending it? We're all aware just how critical you have been to our interplanetary relations, and we would hate to lose you."

I decide to make my pitch rather than answer her question directly. "Peyton, thank you for asking. I'm keen to continue putting that expertise to good use. The past three years have given me valuable insights into interplanetary politics, and one of these is that we have to tread carefully. As we've seen with the Venorians, these alien races are hesitant to share their more advanced technology with us—who they see as a backward planet—but with careful nurturing of the relationship, we've been able to make headways. For example, the improvements we've been able to make to our space technology, enabling our ships to travel more quickly over longer distances, are the direct result of over a year of cautious negotiations between ourselves and the Venorians."

She nods. "And you, Melinda, were at the forefront of these negotiations, as we well know."

"What I would hate to see," I continue, "is those efforts wasted because someone less familiar with the intricacies of these negotiations were put in charge. I see interplanetary relations as something very long-term. First and foremost, we need to develop the relationship between ourselves and these planets, and build the trust. The fruits of careful relationship building will be reaped further down the line, but impatience with the process could set us back decades."

"I couldn't agree more. So, does that mean you would be willing to carry on as our ambassador on Mars?"

Now comes the more difficult part. "I see my role evolving beyond that. Through careful effort these past three years, my team and I have been able to build a solid foundation on Mars, enabling someone else to step in and take over. From my perspective, the next frontier is establishing diplomatic missions on these alien planets, starting of course with the planet Ven. I have already built strong relationships with the Venorians, and I know how to work with them. Not to mention I've also got a good friendship with Martha Reynolds, Krantor's mate, and an important inside track for us with the Venorians."

Peyton frowns. "So, you're looking to lead the Earth Federation mission to Ven. I have to tell you, Melinda, that there are several other parties interested in that position."

"So I hear, but I hope I make a strong case for my candidacy."

Peyton smiles. "That you do. If it were up to me, no question you would be top of the list. However, there are other considerations at play. Some have argued that it's time for a fresh face to lead the diplomatic effort."

"Someone such as Lucas Rivera?"

"You have good sources. There is the argument that continuing to have you lead the negotiations with the Venorians is not in our best interests. Having the same face as the spokesperson of humanity could become a hindrance rather than a help."

My hackles are up, but I try to stay focused. "It's important to remember that it is not just me that's been at the forefront of the negotiations, but a whole team of the brightest and best. Our track record speaks for itself."

"I hear you, Melinda, but there is also another issue. As you know, this is a mission of the Earth Federation, not simply the United States. There have been rumbles that our next ambassador to Ven should not be an American. The Europeans have put forward their own candidate, and the Chinese have thrown in their support behind that person. Since the US has been at the forefront of the technology that has enabled us to build the Mars colony, we have a lot of clout and could insist on our own candidate. My reading of the situation, however, is that the President feels we should cede on this particular appointment, and focus our efforts on future missions."

My heart sinks. "Is it a done deal then?"

"Not quite, but a decision should be made by Friday. I will personally relay the gist of this conversation with the President and make representations on your behalf. Knowing your interest in the position could sway things. No promises though."

I can feel the meeting drawing to an end and try to think quickly on my feet. "You say the focus would be on placing Americans in future missions. Any idea what those could be? The Driskians?"

"Possibly. I'm not at liberty to disclose the information with anyone yet, but Melinda, if the Venorian mission does not come through, I'm confident there will be other avenues of interest for you. That's all I can say for now."

I stand, knowing the meeting is over. "Thanks, Peyton. I appreciate it."

I return home in a pensive mood. I'm not one to wallow in disappointment. Already, my mind is jumping ahead to those other avenues Peyton mentioned. It's been nearly a month since I returned from Mars, and quite possibly, some new information has been relayed to Peyton that I have not had access to. There are only two other alien races with whom we've made contact, the Driskians and the Krovatians. No humans have been to their planets yet, as they are much further away than Ven in our galaxy. Our contact so far with these two races has consisted of video calls mediated by the Venorians.

Without Venorian spaceships, there is no way we could travel to these planets. There has been talk of human missions to these worlds, but as I said in the meeting, these negotiations take a long time. The Venorians are not simply going to invite us to travel on their ships so we can visit other planets. It makes me wonder what possible conversations have been going on at a higher level than I've been privy to. My understanding was that missions to Krovatia and Driskia were years away, yet Peyton made them sound a lot more imminent.

I spend the rest of the afternoon going over all the information I have on these two planets. The Driskians are a reptile-like race whose slightly alarming physical appearance belies a deeply peaceful nature, or so the Venorians assure us. Their planet is hot and dry, though not arid like Mars. There are lakes and oceans, as well as cooler uplands where most of their agriculture takes place. They trade in minerals, such as dorenium, which I understand is an important energy source used to power spaceships and other industrial processes.

My knowledge of the Krovatians is more limited. All I know is what I've heard from Pravol, Treylor and Shuban. I know that the Venorians are in the process of negotiating a diplomatic mission there, but I'm assuming humans have not been invited to the party. Or have they?

Reviewing this information now, I come to the conclusion that it must be Driskia that Peyton has in mind. I try to imagine myself living among a race of lizard-like people and feel a sense of excitement tinged with disappointment—excitement at exploring a new frontier, but disappointment that I won't get to live on Ven, which I've heard so many good things about. And I guess another few years of sexual abstinence lie ahead of me. Perhaps I should invest in a new set of vibrators—or even a sex bot.

I'm in the kitchen, chopping up vegetables, when Wyatt gets back from work. He comes straight to me, wrapping me in his arms. "Hey there beautiful, how did your meeting go?"

"Hmm, some positives and some negatives."

"Oh yeah? Just give me a few minutes to freshen up and I'll come help you. Then we can talk some more." He kisses the top of my head and disappears up the stairs. A few minutes later, he's back, freshly showered and wearing comfortable sweatpants. He comes over to me. "What are you making?"

"Just some tacos. Could you make up a salsa with the chopped onions and tomatoes there?"

"Sure thing." He reaches over to one of the kitchen cupboards and takes out a bowl. "So, talk to me."

I tell him about my meeting with Peyton. He listens to me in attentive silence. When I come to the end of my tale, he frowns. "Mel, are you really prepared to go live in an unknown planet all on your own apart from a handful of other humans in your delegation? What if it isn't safe?"

"I'm not too worried about safety. The Venorians have interacted with the Driskians for decades, and by all accounts, they're an extremely peaceful race."

"I worry about you."

"I know you do, but it will be okay. I'm sure of it."

"So, you're still set on this? There's a plan B, you know. Didn't Elise say she could help you get back into the political scene here?"

"She did, but the more I think about it, the more I'm sure I want to continue working in interplanetary relations. I don't want to get back into politics here. Now that I've had time away from that toxic environment, I'm not too keen to get back into the snake pit."

Wyatt heaves a long breath as he takes the bowl of salsa to the table and starts setting it with plates and cutlery. "No, I guess you're right. I just hate to see you go so far away, someplace where I won't even be able to have access to a video chat with you."

I'm silent, trying to hold in the suggestion, but then it comes out anyway. "You could go with me."

He doesn't speak as I bring the food to the table. I rush to fill the silence. "I'm sorry. I shouldn't have said that."

He glares at me. "No, you should. You have every right to want me by your side. It frustrates the hell out of me that I can't just say yes. Apart from the fact I'd be leaving behind everything I've built here with my practice, turning my back on family and friends who matter to me and that I'd be a useless appendage at your side, I can't even contemplate setting foot on a drone, let alone a spaceship."

We've been over this in all the conversations we had before I moved to Mars and filed for divorce. Wyatt's fear of flying is real, born of a childhood drone accident. He's tried all kinds of therapies to get over it, but none of them worked. I make up a taco, spooning the meat sauce—with real meat, not the synthetic stuff—and piling it high with guacamole, salsa and sour cream. I add a generous sprinkling of cheese, then offer it up to Wyatt. He takes it from me gratefully. In a soothing voice, I say, "I know, honey. That's why I shouldn't have asked."

"That's it, isn't it? I thought before, when we got the divorce, that that would be the end, but somehow we strung it out. With you going to live on Driskia, now it feels final."

"Yes. We're going to have to cut the cord eventually."

We don't say anything more for a long time as we eat. What else is there to say? I love Wyatt, but not enough to give up my dreams. I'm selfish that way, I know. No, hang on. I'm not going to do this to myself. It's not selfish to want to chase my dreams and to want to make something more of my life. Anyhow, it works both ways. He doesn't love me enough to overcome his fear of flying and go with me. Sacrifices are involved on both sides, sacrifices which neither of us are willing to make. So, it's finally time to move on and not look back.

Chapter 5

Wyatt

Tonight, I make love to Melinda in a frenzy of passion. She's about to slip through my fingers, but while she's here, she's still mine. I worship every inch of her lovely body, bringing her to orgasm after orgasm. I've had years to study her. I know how to make her come. I lick her pussy like it's my final meal, and I fuck her over and over again with my cock, hitting all the right spots to make her come for me. I fucking love this woman. I've tried so hard to get over her. It hasn't worked. She's in my blood and she always will be.

Now, as she sleeps tucked against me, I contemplate my lonely future. Apart from that one date with Callie, I've been alone the last three years, leaning on a handful of close friends, my brother and his family for company when life got too lonely. I know they think I should just get over Mel and get myself a new girlfriend. Eventually, I hope I will. Otherwise, my future looks very bleak. Mel's not coming back. Now that she's got the space travel bug, she's going to be exploring planet after planet, maybe returning to Earth for a few weeks here and there, but nothing more. I have to fucking accept that.

On the back of that thought, I remember what she said at dinner tonight. *You could go with me.* In that moment, I felt a spark of hope. Yeah, I should go with her. She's my girl, damn it! It might not be official anymore, but I don't fucking care about the legalities. Neither of us has moved on in all this time we've been apart. That must mean something.

I should go with her. I try to visualize myself on a spaceship and immediately, the nausea is there, overwhelming me yet again. *Shit.* I take deep breaths in and out, trying to chase it away. When it finally subsides, I'm left with a deep sadness. I'm losing the woman I love because I'm a coward. That's the bottom line.

Even knowing that doesn't change things. I can't wake up the following morning with a renewed sense of courage and be a better person. It doesn't work that way. No, I'm stuck being the chicken shit who can't fly and who doesn't deserve to keep the precious woman who has indelibly marked my heart. Maybe she will meet someone out there on a faraway planet who will make her happy. It guts me to think of it, but she deserves that at least.

In the meantime, we have three more days together before she's due to return to Mars. I'm not going to waste that time with arguments. No, I'm going to worship my woman every night and show her just how much I love her. And then after that, I'll just have to deal with the loss and get on with my life without her.

Chapter 6

Melinda

Friday morning arrives and with it, the moment of truth. As I make breakfast, I wait with bated breath for the call that will tell me where I stand with my candidacy. I'm just pouring out my second cup of coffee when my communicator rings. It's Peyton.

"Good morning," I say, picking up.

"Good morning, Melinda," she replies, then proceeds to get down to business. "I'm afraid Ven is out. It's been agreed that we will be sending Robert Schwarz, the European candidate, to represent the Earth Federation there. I'm sorry if that wasn't the news you wanted hear."

I hold in a sigh of disappointment. "Thanks for letting me know. So, what next?"

"Well, this is the other thing I wanted to talk to you about. You're aware of course that the Krovatians have agreed to allow a small delegation of Venorians and Driskians to live on their planet."

"Yes, but not humans, as far as I understand."

"That was the situation at first, however, the Venorians have spent some time vouching for us and the Krovatians have finally agreed to a human delegation on their planet, under special conditions."

I feel a rising sense of excitement. "What conditions?"

"We won't be allowed to have our own independent embassy, but they will permit us to have our people living in the same quarters as the Venorians, under close supervision. Now for the other good news. The Venorians have chosen Pravol and his new mate Treylor to lead their delegation, so you would be living with them."

That is good news.

"Does that mean you want me to lead the human embassy there?"

"Yes, Melinda. Your appointment has been approved and all we need is your confirmation. Are you in?"

"Yes, definitely," I respond immediately. I don't even have to think about it.

"That's great news. I think this may perhaps be an even bigger opportunity for you than the mission to Ven. We know so little about the Krovatians and there's so much valuable work to be done there."

We talk details a little longer then end the call. I put the communicator back down on the table and give a loud whoop, just as Wyatt enters the kitchen. "Good news?" he asks.

"The best. Guess what? It's not Driskia they want me to go to, but Krovatia."

Wyatt frowns. "I didn't think the Krovatians were allowing humans on their planet."

"Latest development. They'll allow a human delegation to live under the supervision of the Venorians, which is going to be led by our friends, Pravol and Treylor."

"Oh wow, that is good news."

He smiles now as he comes over and hugs me tightly. "Congratulations, Mel. I'm so proud of you. And I have to say, it puts my mind at ease to know you'll be living under Pravol's protection. That guy is like a rock."

"I know. And to be honest, I'm relieved too. I'll feel much safer being with them, and I know we'll work well together."

"Do you know who the other people are that are going with you?"

"One I know. Troy Summers, an engineer who was on the exchange program to Ven. The other is someone called Avery Walker, who I don't know much about except that she's worked her way up in the State Department."

"When do you leave?"

"I'll be going to Mars this Sunday, as originally planned. The Venorians will pick me up from there in about a month's time, which will give me a chance to wind things down and brief my successor."

"Any idea who that successor will be?"

I grin. "The one and only Lucas Rivera. I swear, this guy's been kicking at my heels, but I'm still a step ahead."

He kisses my forehead. "Looks like you got it all worked out. I'm happy for you, Mel."

I look up at him. "Do you have to be at work today?"

"Actually, no. I took the day off so I could spend time with you. What do you say we go down to the cabin?"

I kiss him gently. "I would say that's a very, very good idea."

So, that's what we do. My last two days on Earth are spent at the rustic but fully functional cabin in Virginia that Wyatt and his brother inherited from their parents. We don't talk about the future or argue. We don't rehash the past. We simply enjoy being together one last time. All too soon, it's time to say goodbye.

Chapter 7

Kirimor

It has been a long morning of visitors coming to put their cases before me and petitioning for my help. Some cases I deferred to their local sicors, the priests that serve across our planet. As the sicortar, I am the most senior of those priests and thus I only have time to deal with the most serious or most complex of matters. Those cases that receive my consent are noted down on my ledger with as much detail as possible by my faithful aide and friend, Sholinar.

On my receiving days, I spend the mornings seeing visitors before I retire back to my home for a lunch repast with my family—my four lovely drashas and our children. I am thinking longingly of lunch when Sholinar re-enters the room. "I have one final person to see you," he says.

I scowl. "Can they not wait another rotation? I have three more receiving days before I retreat to the temple."

"It is not the usual visitor, Sicortar. This young female has travelled from afar to see you. She would like to become your drasha."

That gets my attention. I have not had a new drasha since Cleotola joined my household six sun rotations ago. Sicors do not mate, but in order to fulfil our duties, we require drashas to service our needs. There is no limit to the number of drashas one may have. I know of one sicor who has eighteen of them. That is not to my taste, however. Of course, in my younger days, I sought pleasure in a large number of lovely drashas, but ever since the children came, I have settled down to just four and made them permanent members of my household.

Ordinarily, I would not consider adding another to our number. Indeed, I only accepted Cleotola into my home after the departure of Senjomena, who had been my drasha for many sun rotations before she decided she wanted more from her life than to service me. I bade her goodbye with a heavy heart. I had enjoyed not just her body, but also her lively, intelligent companionship. She now manages a large number of successful enterprises, and I am very proud of her achievements. Occasionally, she visits when her busy schedule allows. She has not mated, but she seems happy, and that is what matters most. There are many females in our society that find their true calling outside of mating and having children.

The only reason I am considering getting another drasha is because of Merostena. She has been with me the longest and is the mother of my two eldest children, Kiristen, who has just reached the age of manhood, and Kirimara, who is in her second year of college. I have noticed of late that Merostena has struggled to keep up with my needs. Holy sessions in the temple can be long and arduous, depending on the complexity of the cases I have to resolve. Servicing my needs during those sessions requires endurance, and I think Merostena is reaching an age where it is getting harder for her to keep up. To lessen the pressure on her, I am considering inviting another drasha into my household.

However, I have to be careful. My home is a symphony of harmony. I make sure there are no petty jealousies to poison the atmosphere. I will not tolerate in-fighting, envy or any negative energy in my house. All my drashas are filled with goodness and care for me, my children and each other with love in their hearts. Introducing someone new to our happy dynamic is a tricky thing. Before I accept a female as my drasha, I have to be sure she will fit in with my household as well as be able to service my needs in the temple.

Now, I look to my friend. "Could you not see her yourself, and begin the preliminary vetting process?"

"I could, but first I would like you to meet her. I have a hunch she could be the right person for you."

"Tell me a little about her."

"Her name is Pirofena, and she comes from the village of Pir in the southern sector of the planet. She is young, only twenty-two sun rotations old, but she is lively and spirited, as well as beautiful. I have a feeling she would suit you."

I take a deep breath in and out to banish my momentary irritation. Once I am restored to a calm equilibrium, I say, "Sholinar, you know that is far too young. Yes, I want a drasha that is young enough to keep up with me, but not someone who was so recently a babe. Why, she is the same age as Kiristen!"

His face takes on a mulish expression I know so well. It is the expression he wears when he is determined on a course of action no matter what. "That is why I want you to meet her first. I know she is young, but I trust my instincts and they tell me she is just what you need. Apart from Cleotola, your other three drashas are all close to you in age, and beginning to lag. You require an injection of young energy into your healing sessions in the temple because you and I both know the cases coming your way are as complicated and hard to resolve as ever before. I do not know how much longer you can keep shouldering this painful burden, Kirimor, and I hope that soon, a successor is found as the next sicortar. You deserve a break after such a long period of service to your people, but in the meantime, a young drasha brimming with positive energy is just what you need."

I regard my friend with love in my heart. The words he speaks are true. I have been sicortar now for twenty-three sun rotations, and the job does not get any easier. If this young female is as good as he says, then indeed she might be just what I need. "Very well my friend, show her in."

He bows and disappears, returning a short time later with the young female in question. She approaches, head bowed in respect and kneels before me. I examine her curiously. She is certainly pleasing to the eye. Her luscious silky black hair is swept up in a knot atop her head with loose strands cascading down her shoulders. I cannot see her eyes, which are cast down, but she has a finely formed face and full, kissable lips. Drawing my gaze down, I admire her plump little breasts, the perfect size to fit in my hand. Curiously, her body is unadorned, as if she wants me to see just her and nothing else.

I look my fill, enjoying the sight before me. Two things happen at once. My cock begins to twitch in appreciation, and her nipples, before my eyes, darken to a slate gray, then pucker up in invitation. She is aroused.

My, my, this is promising. A good drasha enjoys sex and has a responsive body. I do not want to be ramming my cock into a dry cunt at the height of my healing trance. In a thick voice, I say, "Pirofena, look at me."

She raises her gaze to mine, and I suck in a deep breath. Dark as the night and fringed with long lashes, her eyes are breathtaking. My cock is now fully erect. I want to devour this beauty and sink myself into her. I take a deep settling breath. Clearly, the lust will not be an issue, but I must still be thorough in my investigations. "Why do you wish to become my drasha?" I ask abruptly.

"It is my honor to serve you, sicortar."

"Yes, yes, I know all that. But why else do you wish to take this step?"

"All my life, I have known that was my purpose. From before I even learned to speak, I saw your image on the screens, in our prayer books, on our walls, and I knew I wanted to serve you. I have always been drawn to you."

"Most young girls dream of finding their mate."

"Yes, but not me. When my friends were dreaming of the latest males to have caught their fancy or the latest video star, all I could think of was you."

"What kind of thoughts did you have?"

"Dirty, dirty thoughts."

"Hmm," I growl. "Tell me more."

"I thought about your cock, a lot."

"My cock? You have not had the pleasure of seeing it yet."

"There was one image I found in which your loincloth was wet, and the outline of your cock was visible. I blew it up and saved it on my communicator."

I am amused. "You flatter me, Pirofena. As a sicor, my appendage is naturally substantial, but I am sure there are plenty of other cocks you could have fantasized about."

"Perhaps, but I fantasized about yours because it belonged to you."

I hold out my hand. "Show me your communicator. I want to see this image."

She pulls it out from its pouch at her side and swipes a few times before handing it to me. It is indeed a close up of me on a very hot day when my loincloth, drenched with sweat, had shown a tantalizing outline of my cock. "Naughty, dirty girl," I say, giving the communicator back to her. "Well, you are now in the presence of this cock. What would you like to do to it?"

Her eyes drop hungrily to my groin. "Sicortar, I would like to suck it into my mouth and swallow all you have to give me, then make you hard again so you can stuff it into my cunt."

"Spoken like a good little drasha."

"That is what I want to be, if you will have me."

"Has your cunt welcomed a cock before?"

"Many, many times, sicortar."

I raise my brow quizzically. She is quick to explain. "Those males meant little to me. I wanted to become well versed in the pleasures of the flesh so that I could please you."

"I see. Pirofena, if you were to become my drasha, I would expect you to join my household and be caring to all persons there, including my other drashas and children. I have no time for jealousies or ill-will. Do you understand that?"

"Oh, sicortar, if you would honor me with a position in your household, I promise to be worthy of it. I will love and respect all your drashas and children."

"Have you experience of caring for children?"

"Yes, sicortar. I help care for my older sister's baby daughter when she needs it."

"Would you like a child of your own?"

She takes a quick involuntary breath. "It would be my greatest honor to bear a child to you. Yes, sicortar, please fill my belly with your child."

I chuckle. "Not just yet, dirty girl. I already have five children, but another one would be a blessing indeed. However, I would need to be sure of you first."

She bows her head. "I understand."

I consider her in silence. I can see why Sholinar thought this girl would be right for me. I have not encountered quite such devotion before, but I think it is genuine. The only way to be sure is to look into her heart. I tap my communicator to call my friend. "Sholinar."

"Yes, sicortar?"

"Bring me the boral crystals."

"At once, sicortar."

The door opens and Sholinar walks in, holding the box of crystals in his hand. He places it at my feet, bows and withdraws. I open the box, riffling through the different boral crystals in there until I find the one I want. It is about the size of my thumb and colored dark pink. The crystals look innocuous, fooling the likes of the Venorians into thinking them to be pretty, harmless rocks. Nothing could be further from the truth. When combined with an energy source, the crystals are extremely powerful. However, they do not affect us in the same way as the Venorians. In them, they cause a shutdown of their neural receptors and eventually unconsciousness.

With Krovatians, the effect is different. It causes us to go into a trance where we can see the true aura of a person before us, easily identifying the negative and positive energies within them. Some Krovatians are born with a rare and special gift not only to be able to see these energies, but also to manipulate them. The gift becomes apparent in late childhood. For me, it happened when I was seventeen sun rotations old. Overnight, I went from a happy-go-lucky young Krovatian hoping to enter the technology college to one with a totally different path mapped out for my life. I became a sicor, leaving my family home to train at the local temple.

That first year of training was grueling. I had to learn how to absorb negative energy into my body and to neutralize it using the power of the boral crystals. Going into a deep trance, I would draw the foul energy towards me, letting it enter my chest and then clamping on it tight. Through deep meditation, I learned to crush its power and to break it down into harmless sexual energy, the by-product of which was a raging desire to fuck and to release cum.

It was quickly obvious to all around me that I had a great aptitude for this task. Sworn enemies, cruel and despotic individuals, and hardened criminals were all sent my way. After I had sucked in their negative energy like a vacuum, they emerged as new, practically unrecognizable. Within a few sun rotations, I was in much demand for my services as a sicor, and soon, I had expanded my skill to being able to manipulate energies from a great distance. Not many sicors graduate to that level of skill. It is why, at the age of twenty-six sun rotations, I was given the highest honor—that of becoming sicortar.

Although I am not in the temple at this moment in time, I always have an incense burner nearby. I draw it towards me now and place the boral crystal on it. As the crystal heats up, it begins to glow a brighter, almost purple color. I focus my gaze on the crystal and begin to chant a prayer to Taya, our goddess.

Oh mighty Taya, goddess of the universe, I worship and love thee. Grant me the grace to see with the wisdom of your eyes. Let the forces of the dark show themselves to me. Let there be no place for evil to hide or to reside. Shine your light, oh great Taya. Bless me with your goodness and your power. Shine your light and root out all darkness. I am your eternal servant, oh Taya.

Slowly, I raise my head and look to the girl before me. Her aura shines all around her, bright yellow with some flames of orange—radiant goodness, with a dash of fiery spirit. She is just what I need. I look carefully but see no hint of evil and no darkness, only light. Satisfied, I take a deep breath and exhale, coming out of my trance.

All this time, Pirofena has been kneeling with her head bowed, hands together in prayer. "Come here," I say gruffly. She looks up into my eyes, reading my desire. With a small smile, she brings her hands to the floor and begins to crawl towards me. She stops when she reaches my bent knees and waits obediently for my next instruction. "Take my cock out."

With soft, gentle hands, she pulls down my loin cloth and takes hold of my hard shaft. "In your mouth." She bends her head down and takes me into her mouth as far as she can. I press a hand to the back of her head and urge her to take more of me. "Deeper." I feel her relax her throat and take more of my thick length. I stroke her head. "That's it, baby girl. You are taking me so well. Now suck."

She clamps her mouth around my shaft and begins to suck, bobbing her head up and down with the effort. I drag my fingers through the loose knot of her hair, guiding her into the rhythm that best pleases me. "Good girl. That is it. Keep going." I begin to pump into her mouth, fucking the sweet moist depths. I feel my balls retract and I know I have not long to go. "Are you going to be a good girl and swallow me down?" Her eyes fly to mine, and I see her nod imperceptibly. My cock swells and with a loud groan, I come, releasing a stream of my cum into her mouth. She drinks it all down as promised and licks me clean. Once she is done, I pull out of her mouth. "What a good girl you are." She glows at the praise, smiling proudly, yet my sharp eyes also notice her squeeze her legs together. She too is in need of release.

"I think you have earned a reward, dirty girl."

I ease myself onto my back until I am lying supine on the floor mat. "Come and sit your lovely cunt on my face."

Slowly, she crawls over me until she reaches my face. She hovers above me for a moment, looking unsure. I place both my hands on her bottom, which through her loin cloth I can feel is soft and pillowy. With hunger in my eyes, I grit. "Let me taste you, dirty girl."

With trembling fingers, she undoes the ties of her loin cloth and lets it fall to the floor beside us. Her cunt is covered in a thatch of well-trimmed, silky black hair. Through it I can see her soft folds peeking out, a lovely shade of coral pink. Just beautiful. As I suspected, she is soaking wet with arousal. Gently, she lowers herself to me, and I take my first lick. Delicious. This girl is a rare delicacy indeed. Using my hands on her bottom, I push her further onto me and begin to eat her. With each lick of my tongue I hear her pant above me. "Oh. Ah. Oh yes, sicortar."

"Hmm," I vibrate my approval on her cunt, continuing with my feast. After a time, I dip my tongue into her opening and lick her on the inside. Her internal walls clench around me, releasing more of her tasty juices, which I swallow down hungrily. I can only imagine what she will feel like on my cock. Already, I am hard again and raring to go. But first, I want her to reach her own release. My tongue slips out of her and is replaced by my thick finger, which I curl to stroke her pleasure receptor. I search for and find the nub of passion above her opening and start to worship it with small flicks of my tongue. I can feel it swell under my touch and I know she is close. I enclose her nub with my mouth and begin to suck it, gently at first, then with increasing pressure, taking her over the precipice. "Ahh," she cries, a moment before I feel her pulse in release. I keep my suction until I feel her movements subside, then I carefully lift her off my mouth and lay her next to me.

Rising on my elbows, I watch her closely. Her cheeks are flushed; her chest rises up and down with each breath. Finally, her eyes flicker open. "Thank you, sicortar," she breathes.

"Dirty girl, you interest me," I say, running a finger to her breast. It puckers pleasingly under my touch.

"Do I please you, sicortar?"

"Very much so." I tweak her nipple between my fingers. "If I recall, there is one more thing you desired to do with my cock."

Her eyes go hooded. "Oh sicortar, please would you stuff your fat cock into my cunt?"

"Well, since you ask so nicely." I rise to my knees and swing her round to me. "Dirty girl, open your legs wide for me."

She does so with alacrity. "That's my good girl," I croon as I stroke my stiff shaft. "Is this the cock you want inside you?"

She nods vigorously. "Yes, sicortar. Please."

"Oh I do like a girl who says please." I lift her right leg to my shoulder, spreading her open for me. With my other hand, I guide my shaft to her entrance and push in slowly. She gasps as I fill her up. As a sicor, I am larger than most Krovatian men. That was the first clue that I had the gift, and which prompted my being tested for it at seventeen. I keep pushing in, not stopping until I am sheathed in her tight heat to the hilt. "Is that what you wanted, baby girl?"

"Yes, oh yes," she breathes.

I lean forward and capture her lips with mine. A lick of her bottom lip and she opens for me, allowing me to plunge my tongue into the sweet cavern of her mouth. She tastes divine. I kiss her long and hungrily, holding myself still in her cunt.

When I lift my head again, I growl, "Are you ready to get fucked like a drasha?"

"Yes, sicortar."

"It can get rough," I warn her.

"Please, sicortar. I can take it."

"When I am in a trance, the urge to fuck is so strong that I forget to be gentle."

"I am prepared, Sicortar. I will take whatever you give me."

"I am going to fuck you hard like I would in the temple, but as I am not in a trance right now, I will heed you if you say stop. Anytime it gets too rough, what do you say little girl?"

"Stop. But I know I will not say it. Sicortar, trust me when I tell you I can do this."

"We shall see, baby girl. Kiss me again before I start."

Her mouth meets mine in another scorching yet tender kiss. Then I release her lips and pull out until only the tip of my cock is still inside her. Leaning my hands on the floor on either side of her, I plunge back in with all my might. I hear her gasp. I plunge again, and again. Her gasps and moans greet my every thrust, but she does not tell me to stop. I begin to fuck her hard, getting rougher and rougher with each thrust. Glorious girl that she is, she meets my every thrust, welcoming me into her depth. Her tight cunt clings to my shaft like a second skin. I am so in tune with her that I feel the moment she reaches her climax, clenching her walls around me in spasm after delicious spasm.

But I do not stop. I keep fucking her through this orgasm and through the next, ramming her with my thick cock, filling her as she has never been filled before. She takes me, never telling me to stop. Sweat drips from my skin, mingling with the dewiness of hers, and still I carry on. I practically forget myself, as if I am in a trance. On and on I fuck her, never slowing down, never gentling. Then finally, my cock thickens, and I jerk out my release, gushing stream after stream of cum into her. As I fill her, she moans and gifts me with her fifth orgasm, a deep pulsing of her walls that drives another spurt of cum out of me. Spent, I collapse on top of her before remembering to turn us, so she lies on top of me.

We stay like this a long time. Eventually, I kiss the top of her head gently and say, "Baby girl, I do believe you have the makings of a fine drasha."

She sighs in bliss. "It is all I have ever wanted, sicortar."

I stroke my hands down her back. "We shall see. Sholinar will need to conduct further investigations, including meeting with your family, to ensure this is the right step for you to take. I will let him escort you back to your village after we have bathed, and you have eaten some sustenance."

"Yes, sicortar."

I kiss her again. "You have pleased me greatly, Pirofena."

Chapter 8

Kirimor

"**G**o in peace."

I have just bid Pirofena and Sholinar goodbye. He will be taking her back home and spending some time in her village, finding out everything he can about her. All my instincts tell me she will become my drasha, but I owe it to my family and to Pirofena, to make absolutely sure.

My communicator buzzes with a call. I glance to see it is Merostena and pick up.

"Kirimor dearest, are you not joining us for lunch today?"

I have been so distracted by Pirofena, that I lost track of the time. Contritely, I say, "I am sorry my dear. Something came up, but I am on my way home now."

"I will tell Dresolor to keep the food warm until then."

"Thank you, my sweet."

Quickly, I place my feet into sandals and head out to my transport. I receive visitors in my official rooms in the city, as I do not like strangers to enter the sanctity of my home. It is only a ten minute ride away in my solar powered drone, so hopefully I will not keep my family waiting too much longer for their lunch. In seconds, I have activated the engine and started the journey home.

I approach my compound shortly after. The secure and extensive grounds include the temple building, my house and some separate housing for my staff, including Sholinar and his family, Dresolor, our cook, and the groundskeepers. I land the drone neatly in the covered parking bay and jump out, eager now for some food after the exertions of the morning.

The early afternoon heat is stifling, but as I walk into the main atrium of my house, I breathe in the cool, fragrant air. I was personally involved in all aspects of the design of my home. Few buildings in Krovatia, except for mine, have cooling systems beyond solar powered fans, as befits our ethos of respecting the environment—an ethos that came about as a result of our history.

Our old planet had been cool, with skies as gray as the color of our skin. On arrival in the much hotter climate of Krovatia, and with no option to use our polluting cooling technology, many of our ancestors took to wearing as few clothes as possible. To other species, we appear a primitive race, going about in nothing but loin cloths, but that is far from the truth. We are happy though, to maintain the fiction that we are more technologically backward than we really are.

I have always felt though, that it could be possible to live in greater comfort without compromising our environment. In my spare time, I have tinkered with various technological inventions. After all, designing technology was what I had been planning to do with my life before I became a sicor. Over the last few decades, I have designed several different cooling systems that do not impact our environment negatively. When I was elevated to sicortar, I built this home and had one installed. There were a few teething problems at first, but I soon fixed them, and now, I have the pleasure of a cool, fresh environment for myself, my family and my staff. It is so cool in fact, that I shiver slightly in just my loincloth after being out in the heat. Quickly, I head to my chamber and wash my hands, before pulling on a loose shirt, lovingly embroidered by Jolpinesa, another of my drashas. Then I am rushing down the stairs to the dining room, where I am sure my family awaits me with impatience.

As I walk in, I am accosted by a flying missile in the form of my youngest daughter, Kiritela. I laugh and throw her up in the air before dropping her back into my arms again. "Pa, we're hungry!"

"I am sorry, my little star, but I am here now, so let us eat!"

I carry her with me to the low round table and sit myself down on the mat, keeping her in my lap. "And what delights has Dresolor made for us today?" I ask.

Kirilor, my middle son, pipes up, "He has made chilos. That is why we have been waiting for you so impatiently."

"Well son, in that case I am doubly sorry to have kept you waiting."

"Why were you late?" asks Kirimara, pouring me a glass of *nari*.

I smile my thanks at her. At twenty sun rotations old, she is a fine young woman, and I am amazingly proud of her. "I had a visitor late in the morning who had come from afar to see me. She is likely to become my drasha, so you shall meet her soon I am sure."

At this, all eyes turn to me. It is not every day that a new person is introduced to our household. Kiristen, my eldest, casts his serious eyes towards me. "What is her name?"

"She is called Pirofena. Sholinar has taken her back to her home in the south sector, and he is looking into her background, so that is why you may not see him for another rotation or two. If all his investigations show her to be the right fit, then I will invite her to join our household."

"What is she like?" asks Kirishar curiously. My third son is earnest and studious, with his face always buried in a book.

There is nothing for it but to impart the most salient fact. "She is lively and young, only twenty-two sun rotations old."

At this, Kiristen splutters. "But father, that is the same age as me!"

I look coolly at him. "I am well aware of that, Kiristen."

"Will it not be odd to have a drasha young enough to be your daughter?"

"She is an adult, Kiristen, and clearly not my daughter," I say firmly.

My eldest daughter looks at me inquiringly as she holds up a slice of chilos. "Did you check out her aura?"

"Of course. I would not consider bringing anyone into our home without doing so. Her aura is bright and there is no malice in her. She is also extremely devoted to me."

"As are we all," remarks Merostena.

I smile fondly at her. "I know, my dear, and I thank Taya every day for the blessing of having all of you in my life."

Kirimara takes another bite from her chilos and chews thoughtfully. "I think she may be just what you need, father. I look forward to meeting her."

"Is she pretty?" asks little Kiritela.

I ruffle her hair. "Very."

"Then I like her already."

Her brother elbows her. "We do not judge people on their looks, silly!"

"That is enough, Kirishar," I say sternly. "Apologize to your sister now."

He flushes and looks down at his hands. "Sorry," he mutters.

"You are quite right in saying that we should never judge people on their looks, but although Pirofena is very pretty, her beauty is also on the inside. I was struck by the brightness of her aura. I think you will all like her very much."

Jolpinesa, sitting on the other side of me, places a hand on my knee. "I am sure we will."

I kiss her cheek, then turn my attention to the food. As we eat, the conversation flows to other subjects. Kiristen is a little morose at the moment, for he is nursing a broken heart. He has a tendency to fall in love with every pretty male he meets.

"I thought he was the one," he says now in a sad voice.

I sip on my *nari* as I listen to his sister gently rib him. "That is what you said about Riloshar, who you dated before."

"You are young yet," his mother chides him. "Why not enjoy coupling with handsome males without convincing yourself each time that they are the love of your life? There is plenty of time before you need think about mating."

"That is what I try to do, but I cannot help it if I fall in love!"

"How was work today?" I ask him, deflecting attention from his broken heart.

He brightens up. "It was good! I was allowed to teach mathematics and science to a senior class." My son has chosen to become an educator and is currently in his final year of training.

"Did they behave for you?" teases Kirimara.

"For the most part. I had to break up a group of girls who were getting very chatty. I used my teacher voice on them and asked them to change places."

Kirishar sniggers, "What teacher voice is that?"

Kiristen levels a stare at his brother, then says in a clipped tone, "Kirishar, please stand and go sit over there."

I chuckle. "Not bad, my son. We will make an excellent teacher of you yet."

He smiles happily, then remembers something else. "Oh, and I had to send out a boy who was drawing pretty flowers on the breast of the girl sitting next to him."

Kirimara laughs. "I did that once to a girl. The teacher never noticed though, so I got away with it."

"It was a little awkward," continues Kiristen. "He had drawn circles around her nipple and was poking the pen right on her teat. They are only fourteen sun rotations old, much too young for that kind of thing!"

"Hmm, I think you have forgotten what it is like to be that age, Kiristen."

"Speaking of work," chimes in Cleotola, "what news have you of the aliens that are coming to live on our planet?"

"They will be arriving in another moon rotation," I say. "There will be a delegation of Driskians, Venorians and Humans."

"Will we get to meet them?" asks Kirilor.

"There will be a state dinner welcoming them to Krovatia. I may take two of you with me, but I am not choosing, so decide between yourselves and no arguing about it."

"They say Driskians are reptiles with green skin," says Kirishar with relish.

"If you plan to stare at them, then I am afraid I will not be taking you," I say.

"What do Humans look like?" wonders Kiristen.

"In appearance, I believe they are not unlike us, perhaps a little smaller in size, but their skin is a more earthy color, and they do not have a tail."

"I would very much like it if I could go with you," he says.

I look at my first-born fondly, then tease him. "I will take you, Kiristen, only if you promise not to fall in love with the first pretty face you see."

His lips quirk in amusement. "Then we have a deal, father."

The following morning, I come awake slowly and stretch my body lazily. That is when I become aware of a heavy weight on top of me. I open my eyes and look down, unsurprised to find Kiritela fast asleep on my chest, her tail wrapped around me and her mouth slightly ajar as she breathes in and out.

I am in the habit of sleeping alone, but of late, I have woken to company in the form of my youngest daughter. She wakes at night, probably to go relieve herself, and then on instinct comes to me, snuggling up to my comforting warmth.

I stroke her hair gently. In all honesty, I do not mind. Whenever I get mournful about my life, I think of my children—each and every one of them a blessing—and realize I cannot complain about my fate. Indisputably, I had other plans for my life when I was younger. I wanted to set the inventing world on fire, and I had vague ideas of finding a mate whose soul called to me. Instead, my path took another direction altogether. The work of a sicortar is burdensome and often lonely. Having to absorb evil and negative energy into my being is always painful and unpleasant. And the task of converting that evil into good is never easy. My lovely drashas help me with sexual relief when I am in the temple, and occasionally at home, but they are not my mates. They never will be. I offer them a comfortable life in my home and father children with them, but other than that they are free to pursue their own interests. Each of them has their separate private quarters, which I never enter without invitation.

On the positive side, I have more material riches than I could ever wish for, as sicortars are well compensated for the sacrifices they make. I am highly respected in my world and have a say in the decision-making at the highest level. But more than all that, I have my children. They truly are the joy of my life. In a society that discourages large families, it is a privilege to be allowed to have one. Another perk of being a sicortar.

I kiss the top of Kiritela's head, then shake her gently awake. "Wake up, little star."

"Mmm, don't want to," she mumbles.

I tickle her tail and she wiggles playfully. "Stop!"

"Then wake up."

"Alright, alright."

She sits up slowly and yawns.

"Go find your mama, so you can wash and get yourself ready for school. I shall see you shortly for the morning repast. Off you go little one."

She kisses my cheek sloppily and does as instructed. Then it is my turn to get out of bed and clean myself in the attached washing room. I pull on a fresh loin cloth and head out.

Later that morning, I arrive at my official rooms to begin another day of receiving visitors. As Sholinar is not here, his mate, Floritela, is stepping in to help. I smile at her. "Blessings, Floritela. Thank you for being here today."

"It is my privilege, sicortar."

"Have you heard from Sholinar? How is his business prospering?"

"I spoke to him just now. He is faring well. He thinks he needs another rotation to complete his investigations, but so far all seems well with the girl."

"That is good to hear. Let me go prepare myself, for I am sure our first visitors will be here very soon."

No sooner have I lit the incense burner and sat down on my mat to chant a prayer than I hear the door open. "You have a caller," says Floritela. "It is Denishar."

"Send him in."

The leader of the northern sector, in which I live, strides into the room and places a hand to my chest, then bows to me. "Blessings, sicortar."

"Blessings, Denishar. To what do I owe this pleasure?"

He settles down on one of the floor cushions before speaking. "It is about the boral crystals that were stolen by the Saraxians."

"They have been recovered, have they not?"

"Yes indeed, they are safely returned. However, I cannot help but wonder how the Saraxians got hold of them in the first place. It seems to me likely that they had assistance on this side."

"I thought this had been investigated and that the crystals had been stolen from our cargo ship on one of its missions."

"Something did not strike me as quite right about that story. Firstly, why would our cargo ship have been carrying the crystals? We do not trade them."

"I understand they were on board the ship not to be traded but because our representatives needed them to help establish the credentials of some new trading partners they were to meet."

Denishar's tail leaps up, a sign of his frustration. "If that is the case, then they would only have needed one or two crystals at most, not a whole crate of them. In fact, there is no mention on the ship's manifest that it was carrying such a large load of crystals. I have spoken to its commander, and he claims he only had two crystals in a pouch with him that were stolen. That does not tally with the large crate of crystals which has recently been returned to us by the Venorians."

I nod gravely. "No, it does not. I take it you have investigated this further?"

"I have, and I think I have enough evidence to suggest the boral crystals were stolen here on Krovatia, and not on board the cargo ship. It has taken some time, but I finally uncovered reports of boral crystals that went missing from a small temple on the outskirts of Krell, right near the border to the eastern sector. They were stored in a crate that was placed inside a locked room at night—not the most secure of systems. Anyone could have got to it."

"Did the local sicor check the energy signatures of those around him?"

"He did, as soon as he got some replacement crystals, but he could not find the culprit that took them."

"Is it possible that it was Saraxians who took them. Perhaps they flew in on a cloaked shuttle?"

"Doubtful. Our force field acts as a shield. No craft can land on our planet without it being lowered."

"If you are right, and it was a Krovatian who stole the crystals, have you established how they managed to pass them to the Saraxians?"

Denishar's craggy face frowns in concentration as he gives his tail a soothing stroke. "The crystals left on our cargo ship, of that there is no doubt. They must somehow have been smuggled on board. I have looked at the logs and shortly after the crystals were stolen from the temple, the ship had a consignment of medicines to the planet Flix on the other side of the quadrant. I imagine that the crystals were handed over at that point."

"Well, that should narrow things down surely. Either the commander of the ship or one of the crew is a likely culprit. Do you have access logs for the cargo ship?"

"I do. There are twelve Krovatians who could potentially have stored the crystals on the ship. I have sent you a file with information about them. Would you be able to do an energy scan on all these individuals?"

"Of course. I am in the temple in two rotations' time and will make it my top priority."

"Thank you, sicortar. I appreciate it."

He stands to leave, bowing once again. "Go in peace."

"Go in peace," I respond.

With Denishar gone, the rest of the morning flies by with a steady flow of visitors coming through my doors, each seeking help on some problem or other. I listen as attentively and patiently as I can to each one, yet it is with a sigh of relief that I finally bid farewell to the last of them. I stand, thank Floritela for her assistance, then head home to my family.

Chapter 9

Melinda

Back on Mars, I busy myself getting ready for my coming move to Krovatia. I clear out my things from the ambassador's office and crate up my belongings. Some of my stuff will remain here in storage on Mars and the rest will go with me. I am told Krovatia has a hot, tropical climate, so my warmer clothes can most probably stay behind.

Once Troy and Avery arrive, two weeks after me, we spend time getting to know each other and discussing our aims and strategies. Troy I already know, from when he was a candidate for the exchange program to Ven. One reason why he was selected then, and probably why he's on this forthcoming mission, is his uncanny ability to draw up complex schematics from memory. I know that he came back from his six months on Ven with an impressive portfolio of detailed drawings of the technology he saw while there. It's not quite espionage, as the Venorians were happy to show him around their facilities. However, I'm not sure even they were aware of quite what a talent he has to store information in his photographic memory and to then render detailed technical drawings.

Avery, I'm finding hard to pin down. I think it's going to take some time for me to work her out. She's competent, efficient, professional, but I'm not getting much of read on her actual personality behind the front she presents.

We're just wrapping up a meeting in which we've discussed our main objectives for this mission. First and foremost, obviously, we want to gather as much information as possible about the mysterious Krovatians—their culture, their history, their religious beliefs. Second, we want to explore trading opportunities, whether in the form of technology or in actual goods. Their planet is renowned for the huge variety of medicinal plants they grow, which could be of great value to us. And thirdly, we want to share with them aspects of our own history and culture, so that they get to know us a little better; perhaps even agree to open a Krovatian embassy on Earth. The more we discuss, the more excited I am at the possibilities.

My communicator buzzes with an incoming communication. It's from Treylor. I connect it to the big screen so that everyone present can listen in.

"Melinda, hello, this is Treylor. I was so excited to hear that you will be leading the Human delegation to Krovatia. I very much look forward to working closely with you. I wanted to send you some information we have gathered about the Krovatians. This may help you in your preparations. First of all, let us talk about dress code. As you know, Krovatia is a very warm and humid planet, so the less clothes the better!" She smiles mischievously. "In fact, the Krovatians only wear a loin cloth for clothes and nothing else, both the males and the females."

"Wow," I mutter, "that sounds a little primitive."

On the screen, Treylor continues with her discourse. "The reason for this is that they are a very eco-conscious society, and in order to protect the environment, they refuse to cool their homes with anything more than solar powered fans. So, with no air conditioning, I think over time they started wearing fewer and fewer clothes, until they got down to the bare minimum."

"Well, that's going to feel mighty awkward for us," I quip.

Troy chuckles. "Speak for yourself, Melinda. Having lots of naked male chests on display sounds like paradise to me."

On screen, Treylor is joined by Pravol, who places a possessive arm around her, palm planted flat on top of her chest. "We have agreed that you will not be showing this to the Krovatians."

Treylor quirks her lips in amusement. "I had thoughts of joining in their dress code, but—" She looks down at her ample chest and shakes her head. "It would not be practicable for me to walk around with these hanging down without support."

I laugh, though I notice from the corner of my eye that Avery is tightening her lips in disapproval.

"We Venorians are not shy about our bodies," continues Treylor. "After all, we like to bathe together, but even we do not walk about without clothes. I think it would make me feel very bare to do it. Now that Pravol is here, I will let him tell you what little we know about their history." She looks at her mate lovingly. He settles himself down next to her, keeping her hand in his.

"Greetings all," he now says. "So, let me tell you what I have found out about the Krovatians. Firstly, there is a reason for their eco-consciousness. The Krovatians originally came from another planet in a neighboring galaxy. However, they had to leave their planet after its environment was destroyed through over-population and pollution. Their ancestors travelled on their ships for many sun rotations before finding a new home planet to live on and they named it Krovatia, which means 'place of refuge' in their language."

I perk up my ears at this. What he describes has echoes in our own history, though thankfully we have not destroyed our planet—as yet.

Pravol continues, "I do not have the precise date when they settled on the planet, but we Venorians first made contact with them seventy-three sun rotations ago. As far as I understand, the small community of survivors who made their home on the planet vowed to start again and learn the lessons of the past by not polluting their environment. That is why all their energy comes from renewable sources and they discourage any processes that cause harmful by-products. They are very strict about this. I would say eco-consciousness is almost a religion to them."

He pauses before going on. "However, they also brought with them their established religious practices from their home world. They worship a goddess of the universe called Taya, and sometimes also an associated god, her son, called Dron. That is all I know, except that they have priests called sicors who use boral crystals in their temples, though I am not clear how or why they do this. We are keen to learn more about the crystals after what happened to us on our own planet, though of course, we will have to be careful around them."

"One of the Venorians coming with us on this mission is a scientist by the name of Hontar," chimes in Treylor. "He is a colleague of mine at the Institute for the Advancement of Science. He will be leading our research on the boral crystals, and as a precaution, he will be dosing us with a chemical called frekium, which stimulates our neural transmitters and counteracts the effects of the boral crystals on us. Hopefully, with the frekium in our systems, we will not be so vulnerable to a sudden attack of unconsciousness, though it has a side effect of making us more fertile." She smiles at her mate. "However, it is a risk we are prepared to take."

She addresses us again. "Well, that is all the information we have to share about Krovatia for now. We will be setting out in two rotations' time, so we should be with you by the end of the moon rotation. We very much look forward to seeing you again. Peace be with you."

She smiles at us, then ends the communication. I turn to my colleagues. "Well, well, well, that was interesting."

"I must say I'm intrigued," says Troy.

"What do you all think of this dress code? Any plans to go native and delight us with your marvellous near naked physique? I know how much you like to work out, Troy."

He flexes his arms. "I would love to, Mel, but it might be a tad too distracting for you."

I grin at him. I get the feeling Troy and I are going to get on. Avery, on the other hand…

"Well of course we won't be dressing like the Krovatians," she says now. "We're there to represent Earth and our ways, not go native."

"No, you're right, and I don't plan to. It will be strange though, to be surrounded by people wearing only loin cloths when we go about our business."

"That is where our professionalism will come to the fore," she says primly.

I smile at her. "I couldn't agree more."

Later that evening, I pace around my apartment, feeling restless. I know myself enough to realize what has triggered this mood. I miss Wyatt. Listening to Treylor and Pravol today, and seeing their happy domestication, was an unwelcome reminder of what I no longer have. For four weeks on Earth, Wyatt and I were together as if the divorce had never happened, and it was great—not just the sex, but the companionship too. Now, I'm having to go through withdrawal symptoms all over again. Only, for some reason, it feels worse this time.

I'm not regretting my decision. Exploring new worlds and developing human contact with alien races is what I want to do. Nothing comes without compromise though, and it does get a little lonely at times. I pick up my communicator and tap to open a novel I've been reading, settling myself down on my bed. I manage to get through a chapter, before I give up and put the thing down. Leaning my head back against the bed board, I close my eyes and take deep breaths, willing myself to relax. It's futile.

So, I call my ex-husband.

He picks up on the second ring, a delighted grin on his face. "Hey Mel, I was just thinking of calling you too. How are you, honey?"

At the sight of him, something eases in my chest. "I'm good. All packed and ready to go at the end of the month. How about you? Tell me your news."

"Nothing much to report. Oh, except I have a guest staying at the house."

"Oh?"

"Bear with me a minute. Let me go get her."

Her? What the fuck? I'm seized by an unreasonable jealousy. However, I barely have time to register my feelings before he's back, holding a large ginger cat in his arms. Stroking the top of its head, he smiles happily. "Meet Georgie. She belongs to the Meyers two doors down. They asked me to cat sit for them over the weekend. Isn't she a cutie?"

"The cutest."

Wyatt holds the cat towards the screen and says, "That's my girl Mel. See. I told you she was beautiful."

"You talk to the cat?"

"I do. You got a problem with that?"

"Not at all," I tease. "I'm sure Georgie makes for scintillating company."

"You know what they say about sarcasm being the lowest form of wit."

"They also say it's the highest form of intelligence."

"Touché."

He puts Georgie down and I see him settle himself back on the living room couch. "You watching anything?" I ask.

"There's a hockey game on, but I'm only half-watching while I read."

"What are you reading?"

"It's the final part of the Noviara trilogy."

Wyatt is a huge science-fiction fan, which makes it all the more ironic that he's staying put on Earth while I'm in Mars, about to go explore a new planet.

"Is it any good?"

"Yeah, I'm just finding it hard to focus tonight."

"Me too."

"You know the reason why."

I exhale. "Yes."

He stares at me with eyes as blue as a sunny sky. I gaze into them, feeling their pull across the millions of miles that separate us. His voice husky, he says, "Baby, want me to make it better?"

"Please."

"Take your clothes off, Melinda. Make it slow. I want to enjoy the sight of you."

I stand and do as he says.

Later that evening, I lie in bed physically sated, and talk to Wyatt until I yawn a goodnight and put my head down to sleep. As I drift off, I wonder drowsily if this is the reason Wyatt and I never cut that cord. These long, intimate and sexy calls have been my lifeline for the past three years on Mars, but soon, they'll have to stop. Once I'm on Krovatia, there will be no more Wyatt at the other end of the line.

Chapter 10

Wyatt

"Do two sets of each of these exercises every day," I say. "It won't take long, at most ten minutes of your time. Now that we've achieved mobility in your shoulder joints again, it's really important to start building up some strength there." I smile at Abby, a novelist who has been seeing me for her frozen shoulder these past few weeks. "I find it easy to do them while I'm watching the latest episodes of Melinda's Game."

"Wait a minute," she exclaims. "You watch Melinda's Game?"

I shrug my shoulders. "My wife's name is Melinda, so that's what got me initially intrigued. One episode in, and I was hooked."

She shakes her head disbelievingly. "Color me surprised. Ok, I'll do my best to remember the exercises." She gets off the massage table and starts to put her shoes back on. Suddenly, she stops and looks up. "Hang on. You do these exercises too?"

I grin. "I do! The work I do can be hard on my shoulders too, so I find it useful to do these regular strengthening exercises."

She drops her gaze to my torso. "Well, Wyatt. You're looking good on it. Shame you're married," she adds with a wicked grin.

I don't correct her. "So Abby," I continue, "I'd like to see you again in six weeks' time to check on your progress. Shall I book you in for your next appointment?"

"Sure."

I take out my communicator and open my appointments app. A minute later, we're all done, and Abby has left. I stretch my arms over my head with a grunt. It's 6 pm on a Friday and time for me to go. Quickly, I sanitize the table and wash my hands. There's a knock on my door and Lisa, a fellow chiropractor in my practice, pokes her head in. "You heading out?"

"Yeah. How about you?"

"Just got one more appointment."

I frown. There are three of us working here full-time and two others part-time, but tonight, there's just the two of us left in the building. "You want me stay put? I don't like the idea of you being here on your own."

"Nah, it's cool. It's one of my regulars, Nessa Brown."

"Sure?"

"Sure."

"Ok, I'll have the security feed on my communicator anyway, just for my peace of mind."

She smiles. "Go enjoy your weekend, Wyatt. I'll be just fine. You heading to the cabin?"

"Yes, it's been a few weeks since I've been there." *Since, I was there with Mel*, I add silently.

"Have fun."

"Will do." With a final wave and a smile, I head out to my car parked just a half block away. Overhead, the sky is humming with the sound of drones whizzing to various destinations. As ever, looking up at them, I wonder how on earth such busy air traffic can be maintained without collisions. On an intellectual level, I know. We have a state-of-the-art drone traffic system that ensures with incredible precision, that no two drones can ever collide, but on an emotional level, I still feel that fear and worry whenever I look up at the busy sky. I know I've been scarred by my personal experience. The image of that other drone coming straight at us is seared in my memory, stuck in slow motion. We were lucky, emerging unscathed from our crashed vehicle. The passengers in the other drone, not so. It was our accident, and many others, that precipitated the change in safety regulations, so I guess our trauma was not in vain.

The skies may be busy, but the streets are not empty either. There are enough people still wedded to their cars to maintain a healthy amount of traffic on the roads, though nothing like how it used to be a few decades ago. I get into my electric car and start the engine with a press of a button. It responds beautifully, purring like a happy cat. I stroke my hand affectionately over the gleaming wooden trim on the steering wheel. This pretty piece of equipment set me back by thirty thousand dollars, but it's worth every cent. I love it. It's my pride and joy—and another thing I would have hated to leave behind had I gone to Mars with Mel.

Yes, I'm that guy. The one who couldn't leave his car, couldn't leave his job, couldn't leave his friends and family, couldn't overcome his fear of flying… the one who let the love of his life slip through his fingers. *God damnit, Mel, why did you have to go?*

Last night, the two of us were lonely and missing each other like crazy. I was just about to cave in and call her when she got there first. Then we had mind-blowing communicator sex and talked late into the night. That's how it's been for us the last three years. We've maintained a piecemeal relationship, little crumbs here and there followed by long periods of drought. What the fuck am I doing, hankering after crumbs? Enough already.

With a determined exhale of my breath, I start the car moving. My overnight bag and fishing gear are already packed in the trunk, so I don't need to head home first. I dictate a quick text to my brother on my communicator.

Me: On my way out now.

Dylan: Ok, see you soon. We just got here.

I start up my "cruising in the car" playlist of songs, and for the next hour as I roll along the highway, I empty my mind and sing my heart away.

When I get to the cabin, I park the car next to my brother's drone. The front door slams open and Sam comes running down the porch steps. "Uncle Wyatt, come quick. We've got real burgers on the barbecue!"

"Real ones?" I ask, hugging my nephew and ruffling his sandy hair.

"Yep," he says, with a pop of the p.

"Well, let me just get my stuff out of the trunk, then we can go eat."

Moments later, I walk into the rustic wooden cabin and drop my bag in my room before hurrying out into the yard where the tantalizing smell of smoky meat draws me like a magnet. I spot my brother by the barbecue with my two nephews nearby, getting the table set for our meal.

My brother's face breaks into a wide grin on seeing me. I stride over and drop an arm over his shoulder. "What's this I hear about real meat burgers?" I ask.

"I figured you could do with some cheering up, so I splashed out for the real thing. Go get yourself a plate; they're all ready. Buns are over there."

"Thanks, Dylan."

I help myself to a burger and bun, as well as some broiled corn on the cob, then sit down at the table with my nephews, Sam and Nicky. Dylan soon joins us and for a while, we focus on the joy of eating real, delicious burgers. "Hmm, so good," I say, licking meat juices off my finger.

"Can't beat the real thing," agrees my brother.

"Why can't we always eat like this?" asks Sam plaintively.

"Because of global warming, silly," retorts his brother.

Dylan looks sternly at his ten-year-old son. "Nicky, that was rude of you. There's no need to call your brother names. Apologize."

"Sorry," he mutters.

Dylan addresses his younger son. "When I was a young boy like you, we ate meat all the time, but it started to cause problems for our environment. You see, cows like to fart a lot, and their farts have gases in them that aren't so good for our planet, so we needed to have fewer of them. We still get to eat meat, like we are today, but it's more of a special treat than an everyday food."

"Will we ever get to eat it all the time like you did? It's not fair you got to have it and we don't!"

That makes me chuckle. "I think you'll soon find out, Sam, that life isn't fair."

Dylan strokes his son's cheek gently. "I'll tell you something, son. I enjoy my burger far more now that it's a rare treat, than I ever did when I could have one every day. Sometimes having to wait for things makes you appreciate them more."

At this, a little voice inside my head can't help but ask. *Did it take Melinda leaving you for you to truly appreciate her?*

I'm not liking the answer to that question. God, what a fucking mess.

It's late evening and the boys are safely tucked up in bed. Dylan and I are lazing on the back porch, beers in hand. A light breeze ruffles my hair in the otherwise still and silent night. The dark sky is clear tonight, the backdrop to millions of shimmering distant stars. I gaze up at them, wondering which one of those tiny dots is the sun around which Krovatia orbits.

Dylan interrupts my train of thought. "So, how are you doing?"

I shrug. "Feels like I'm stuck in a time loop, dragging through all the same shit over and over again."

My brother takes a chug of his beer, wiping his mouth with the back of his hand. "Then break the cycle."

I raise my brow at him. "Just like that?"

"Just like that."

"Gee thanks bro. Why didn't I think of it?"

"Mock all you like, Wyatt, but you just said it yourself. You're stuck in a loop. Three years on from Melinda leaving, and you're still hung up on her. Unless you do something about it, you're just gonna be in the same place in another three years. Is that what you want?"

I huff and don't answer. After a while, Dylan gently prompts me again. "Break the cycle, Wyatt. You know the saying. Shit or get off the pot. It's crude but fitting."

I snort. "You calling me indecisive?"

"If the shoe fits…"

I ignore him and focus on finishing my beer, taking a long gulp of the cool amber liquid. I put the empty bottle down on the floor by my feet, thinking irritably about my situation. "So, you're saying I should start dating again, put Mel out of my mind? I've tried that. Didn't work."

"Well, you're going to have to make it work. Finally let go of Mel and actually invest in other relationships. Don't give me crap about it being impossible. There are other people out there who you could be happy with, but it's not going to happen as long as you're still stuck on your ex. Come on, Wyatt. Take decisive action."

"And what would you suggest, oh wise one."

Dylan ignores my smart talk and ploughs on. "For starters, sell the house and get your own place. Stop seeing her each time she comes back. Stop communicating. Just stop with everything and move on."

I busy myself peeling the label on the second bottle I've just picked up from the cooler.

"I can't," I mumble in a low voice.

"What's that you say?"

"I said I fucking can't!"

"Can't or won't?"

I look at my older brother in disgust. "Has anyone ever told you just how annoying a person you are?"

He sits up, puffing out his chest proudly. "It's part of the job description. Older brothers are duty bound to annoy their younger siblings."

"Yeah, well mission accomplished."

We sit in silence for a time, contemplating. But Dylan is nothing if not persistent. "So why can't you move on? What is it that's impeding your progress forward?"

I stare at the expanse of trees ahead, tall shadows in the dim light. "I love her. Plain and simple. If I could choose again who I want to spend my life with, it would still be her."

Dylan heaves out a long sigh. "Ok then, if moving on is not an option, do the opposite." At my look, he clarifies. "Whatever it is you need to do to be with her. Just do it."

I glare at him. "You know it's not that simple right?"

"Actually, it is. Just make a choice, Wyatt, and go for it."

"It would mean…" I sigh in exasperation. "It's not that easy."

Dylan grunts in annoyance. "I didn't say it was easy, only that it's a simple choice. Go be with her or don't. If you want her so much, just fucking get your shit together and do it."

"It would mean leaving everything behind. She's not coming back to Earth you know, not for a very long time."

"I know. Look, I'm the last one wanting to see you go. You're my only brother and I'll miss you, you little shit. Not to mention Sam and Nicky. But I'm also fed up with seeing you so damn miserable."

"It would mean flying, in space."

"I'm well aware."

I blow out a breath. "How do I fucking do it?"

"How do smokers give up cigarettes? How do alcoholics give up alcohol? They make a decision to do it. They get help and support. They take it one day at a time. You kinda have to do the same thing."

He takes out his communicator and swipes it a few times. "I've been waiting a long time to give you this. I think you might finally be ready. It's the name and contact of a guy who can help you with the flying thing. He comes well recommended. If you're serious about this, then give him a try."

"I've tried therapists."

"This guy is different. Trust me. If anyone can help, it's him. The rest is up to you."

I take out my communicator and stare at the info Dylan just sent me. Dwight C. Josephs. Counselling and therapy. I put the device back in my pocket.

"Thanks. I'll think it over."

"You do that. Just don't take another three fucking years over it."

"Message received loud and clear."

"How about another beer?"

Chapter 11

Melinda

I come awake suddenly and sit up, heart palpitating, skin clammy. It takes me a moment to get my bearings in the unfamiliar room. A few deep breaths, and it comes back to me. I'm on the Olar, a Venorian cargo ship that's transporting us three humans, as well as five Venorians, to our new home on Krovatia.

Regaining my composure, I command, "Athena, lights on."

Athena is a godsend, doing a million and one things to help me navigate my day-to-day life. When I boarded this ship, it connected to the Venorian data system and started acting as an interface, accepting voice commands in my language and communicating them to the ship's system. It also contains a brand-new real-time translator for the Venorian, Krovatian and Driskian languages, so that I'll be able to easily converse with my work counterparts.

Athena logs my data, from the personal, such as the dates of my period and ovulation, to all my work correspondence. It has a library of more books and movies than I will ever have the time to read or watch. It's my lifeline. I genuinely don't know what I would do without it. I don't know whose bright idea it was to call this magnificent piece of technology after an ancient Greek goddess of war—maybe it's to do with Athena also being a goddess of wisdom.

The lights come on and I blink a few times to adjust. Feeling thirsty, I pad out of bed to the small kitchenette in the corner of my room and pour myself a glass of water. I take in great gulps of the cool, refreshing liquid, letting myself slowly regain my equilibrium. I don't know what woke me—perhaps a bad dream. I've been unsettled ever since boarding the ship. I'm excited of course. Nervous too. And also, just ever so slightly discombobulated. I guess it's understandable. I'm taking a big step into the unknown and though logically I know I will be fine, part of me is terrified.

For the first time in my life, I will be living surrounded by alien species, with only two other humans for company and no immediate way to contact home. We have worked out a protocol with the Venorians whereby we can send communications through them to the planet Ven, from where they will be re-routed and transmitted to Mars and then on to Earth. We estimate the time lag for a message to reach its destination on Earth will be approximately six days and another six to seven days for the response to arrive. I guess that's not so bad in the grand scheme of things. Still, it's the most isolated and alone I've ever been in my working and personal life.

Returning to bed, I settle under the covers and dim the lights again, but sleep eludes me. I lie there for a while, trying to will myself into a relaxed state, but still can't find a way back to sleep. At times like these in the past few years, I've called Wyatt. *Well darn*. I can't do that anymore. Although, I can still record a message to send him.

"Athena, lights on and record video message to Wyatt."

I sit up in bed and position the communicator screen. "Hi, honey," I say. "I'm sending you this from my room aboard the Olar. It's my second night on the ship. As you can see, the space is comfortable, and I can barely even feel that I'm travelling at speed in space—the dampeners on these Venorian ships are amazing! Nothing like our own space technology. If you were here, with the portholes covered, I'm sure you wouldn't even realize you were in space. Anyways, it all feels a little strange, a little unnerving to be here… probably why I'm wide awake when I should be asleep! I'm told we're about a quarter of the way on our journey, so not long to go until I set foot on an alien planet. Exciting, right? How are things with you? Tell me about your week, your days. I want to hear all about it. I miss you."

I clear my throat. "I know, I'm going to have to get used to not being able to talk to you. I'm getting there. We should be able to still exchange video messages like this, even if it takes a few weeks to get a response. I hope we can continue to keep in touch. I'd like that. Bye for now, honey. I'll send something again when I get to Krovatia and tell you all about my first impressions. Take care. I love you."

"Athena, end message."

I get back under the covers and instruct Athena to dim the lights again. This time, after a little effort, I manage to fall into a fitful sleep.

My first glimpse of Krovatia is disappointing. On arrival into Krovatian airspace, we were intercepted by their security forces who boarded the Olar and checked our belongings, before taking us on board their shuttles to the land surface. The journey to the surface was a little bumpy as we broke through the atmosphere. When finally we came to a stop, I looked out through the porthole to see… nothing but a vast expanse of rocky desert. *Is this it?*

The Krovatian officers on board the ship, all dressed in combat gear—no loin cloth in sight—are polite but distant, giving us clipped instructions but not engaging in any conversation with us. All I know, is that we are being taken to a holding center where we will be scanned and processed. Now, as we come to a standstill, the officers open a hatch on the right-hand side of the shuttle and beckon us forward. We follow them, stepping out into the hot, barren landscape. *What now?*

They start walking towards a rocky outcropping a few yards in the distance. Unsure, I cast a glance towards my fellow humans and our Venorian colleagues. Troy shrugs his shoulders, looking as puzzled as me. Pravol, seeing the exchange, speaks softly, "I believe there is an underground space they are taking us to, but I do not sense any malicious intent. They simply want to ensure we pose no risk to them before allowing us into their midst. Let us follow."

We set to walking behind the officers. I was already aware that Krovatians have humanoid features and a light gray skin tone, but in our short video conversations with their leaders, I had not noticed the tail. Each of the five Krovatians escorting us has a long appendage peeking out from their uniform and swinging from side to side as they walk. I examine the female Krovatian before me curiously. Her tail—a slightly darker shade of gray than her face—bends flexibly forming a lasso shape before straightening again to simply hang down her body. I noticed her doing this earlier, when we were on the ship. Could this be a tell-tale sign of what is going on in her mind? Maybe when she feels nervous or excited, her tail flexes. That could be interesting. I make a mental note to log this idea in my next transcript.

By now, we have reached the outcropping of rocks and I see that Pravol is right. One of the Krovatian officers presses a button on his communicator and a door embedded within the rocks slides open. He motions us in, and we enter an enclosed rectangular space. My heartbeat picks up, but I'm determined to stay calm. Once we are all inside, the door shuts behind us and we start moving, a quick whooshing descent into the unknown. A few seconds later, we come to a stop with a light bump and the door opens to reveal a large open space before us with Krovatian officers busily working away at their consoles. Some of them look up and cast us curious glances before returning to their work.

Our escorts guide us forward down a long corridor until we reach a large metal door which opens again at the touch of a button on the lead officer's communicator. The room we walk into is on the small side, with no furniture except for some thick mats on the floor and a few cushions. There is a faint but pleasant aroma of some kind of incense, which stems from a small burner positioned in the middle of the room.

"Please, take off your shoes," the officer says, "and sit yourselves down on the mat. Sicortar shall be with you shortly. As he is the highest priest of our world, you must show him the utmost respect. Do not address him as he performs the holy ceremony. Just remain sitting until he is done."

He turns to address the Venorians. "Sicortar will be using boral crystals to scan you during the ceremony. I understand you have an antidote for its effects. Have you taken a dose?"

Hontar answers on their behalf. "Yes, we all took the precaution of taking a dose as soon as we reached your airspace. It will last for a full rotation."

The officer nods. "That is good. Then I shall go inform sicortar that you are ready." He turns to leave, followed by the rest of the officers except for two, who take position on either side of the door.

We all take off our shoes and sit ourselves down on the mat, which is surprisingly soft and springy. "A ceremony?" I whisper to Troy. "Any ideas?"

"Your guess is as good as mine."

"They talked of us being scanned," murmurs Avery.

Pravol, looking thoughtful, says very quietly, "I wonder if the Krovatians also have a telepathic ability, perhaps under the influence of the crystals." From the corner of my eye, I see him take hold of Treylor's hand in a reassuring gesture that brings a dull ache to my heart.

We sit for a while longer, waiting in silence. Although it is infinitely cooler down here than on the surface outside, I feel a trickle of sweat run down the middle of my back. I take a deep breath in, maintaining a calm demeanor despite the jangle of anticipatory nerves I'm feeling.

It's a good few minutes before we hear the sound of the door sliding open behind us. I raise my eyes and see the officers stride back in. They step aside and allow a tall, powerfully built man wearing only a loin cloth to enter the room. My eyes follow him as he steps imperiously forward and comes to a stop before us, legs in a wide stance, hands on hips. He peruses us silently, no hint of warmth in his forbidding expression. I steal a glance at him, taking in acres of pale gray skin decorated with swirls of tattoos that snake around his arms and make their way across his broad, muscled chest. My eyes flick down, noting the muscular thighs and a large, unmistakable bulge in his loin cloth. I take in a sharp breath. *Jesus, this guy is a priest?*

I force my gaze back up and meet his dark, glittering eyes that are fixed on me. For an endless moment, I'm caught in his stare. My pulse races, and I feel myself flush. *Who the fuck is this guy?*

Then I see him nod to someone behind me. An instant later, two beautiful women come forward, wearing only loin cloths, just like him. He indicates with his eyes where they should sit and they go to a mat set at the back of the room, gracefully kneeling on the floor. *Who are these women? Are they his assistants?*

I have no time to ponder this as the sicortar lowers himself to the floor beside the incense burner, placing his hands on his crossed legs. One of the officers comes forward, bearing a small box which he places at the sicortar's feet, then withdraws. The sicortar takes it and I see him select a dark pink stone, then place it on the incense burner. This must be the boral crystal I've heard so much about. As it heats up, I see it change color to a dark purple. I cast a quick look at my Venorians friends, just to check they are alright. Treylor meets my eyes and nods imperceptibly. Good.

Then my attention is back on the priest. His eyes are glued to the boral crystal as he begins to chant a prayer to the mighty goddess Taya, asking her to shine a light and root out all darkness. His prayer finished, he raises his eyes and observes us again, but this time, there is a difference in his gaze. It takes me a moment to realize he's in some kind of trance. His eyes stare, but there is a blank quality to them. As they come to rest on me, I feel a shiver of energy pulse down my spine. *What on earth is he doing? Is this how he scans people? What can he see?*

One by one, I see him scan each of us. When he comes to Avery, he pauses. He stares at her in intense concentration for what seems like forever, but she doesn't squirm. Instead, I see her drown in his gaze, deep breaths coming in and out of her. *What is going on?*

As he continues to focus his gaze on Avery, I look quickly to Troy. He shrugs, as if to say, "Hell if I know!" My gaze transfers to Pravol and Treylor. They shake their heads, confirming they too have no clue why Avery seems to be getting all this attention. I bring my focus back to the sicortar. He holds himself very stiffly, his eyes never leaving Avery. He almost looks as if he's in pain. Then I hear him emit a low growl. He takes deep breaths in and out, grunting with every exhale. *What is happening to him?*

His tail, which until now had been lying dormant on the floor, springs up, swirling with nervous energy. And there's something else. The bulge in his loin cloth has become a solidly erect tree trunk. *He's turned on?* On the back of that thought there's another. *My God he's big!*

My eyes stray to the two women at the back. They too are taking deep breaths in and out as they look devotedly at him. The one on the right, who seems to be only in her early twenties, slides a hand down to her crotch and begins rubbing herself through the loin cloth. I'm suddenly conscious of a wave of sexual energy bouncing around the room, all of it emanating from him, the sicortar.

He continues grunting deeply, eyes locked on Avery. With each grunt, I feel the sexual tension ramp up. My panties are growing damp, and not with sweat. I breathe in a male musky smell. It's him. Now I too am taking deep breaths in and out, inhaling that intoxicating masculine scent with all my might. My core throbs and clenches, and I have an urge to touch myself down there. I force my hands to be still, squeezing them into fists.

In front of me, the sicortar's grunting is getting louder and louder. Then, with a final exhale, he looks up and gestures with his hand, pointing to the door. The lead officer immediately comes forward and makes a motion for us to stand. I get to my feet awkwardly, embarrassingly aware of my aroused state. Quickly, we put our shoes back on and follow the officers out of the room. As I walk out, I can't resist a backward glance. With a shocked breath, I see the sicortar whip off his loin cloth with a loud bestial grunt and free his massive cock, erect and dripping with precum. As the door closes behind us, I catch a final glimpse of the young woman coming over to straddle that large cock. *Jesus, what did I just see?*

With rapid footsteps, I follow the group, my heart beating a staccato, as we are led to another room. This one is more spacious. Once again, there are mats on the floor—the Krovatians seem to have a liking for them—and a low table laden with plates of food and jugs of a pale peach liquid. The officer smiles, "Please make yourselves comfortable and have some refreshment. There are facilities in the room beyond, should you need to use them. Our checks have been successful, and transport should arrive shortly to take you to your new homes."

"Thank you," I say, then risk the question. "Is there a reason why the sicortar's attention seemed fixed on my colleague over here?"

He hesitates. "Yes, but I am not the person to explain it. Just know that the problem was resolved, and all is fine now."

"Problem? What problem?"

His gaze flies to Avery then returns to mine. "I-I do not know how to say. The sicortar is able to see your aura and absorb negative energy. He saw something that was not good, so he dealt with it."

"Are you saying he saw something negative in Avery?"

He struggles to find a suitable response, and Avery jumps in. "It's alright, Melinda, I'm fine. In fact, I feel more than fine. I'm not sure what he saw, but it feels like a big weight has been removed from my shoulders." She beams at me as I stare at her, nonplussed.

The officer, looking relieved, makes his excuses and hurries out of the room.

I look at Avery in concern. "Are you sure you're alright?"

"More than alright," she says cheerfully. "This smells good, and I feel ravenous. Let's eat!"

Reluctantly, I sit down and help myself to some food, which turns out to be delicious. Treylor, who has been silent up till now, shares her thoughts on what has just happened. "Well, that was very interesting. Was it not, Pravol?"

"Yes, Treylor mine. It confirmed my suspicion that the Krovatians, or at least their priests, have a telepathic ability. It is not quite like ours, which is based on touch, but I could feel him probe each of us in his trance."

"What do you think was this problem that had to be resolved?" asks Troy.

Pravol looks uncomfortable. "It is something that I picked up on previously in my interactions with you, but it is gone now, so it seems the sicortar was able to deal with it."

"Deal with what?"

Pravol is silent, so his mate is the one to speak. "We picked up some negative feelings from Avery towards you, Melinda—

but it is gone now. The sicortar must have somehow removed that negative energy from her." She turns to Avery and smiles. Lo and behold, Avery grins back. It's like she's a different person.

"I'm not sure I understand. Avery, did you have negative feelings towards me?"

She sighs. "I'm sorry, Melinda. I let my jealousy overrule me. Everything seems to fall into your lap so easily whereas I've had to work twice as hard to get where I am."

"That's not true! Nothing comes easy. Any success I've had has been down to hard work. Nothing has ever fallen into my lap."

She makes a placating gesture. "I know, and I'm sorry. That was how I felt before, but the feeling is gone now, believe me. That guy is incredibly powerful. What he did to me back there… wow! As I said before, it's like a weight has been taken off me. It feels great."

I stare are her, mystified. Treylor reaches across the table and squeezes my hand. "Do not fret about it, Melinda. Just accept that now, you have a colleague who is much more favorably disposed toward you than before. You can thank the sicortar for that."

"I guess. This is all so bizarre."

"I know," smiles Treylor. "Already, I have so much to report back to the authorities in Ven."

"Yes, I was just thinking the same."

Just then, a Krovatian officer walks in and tells us our transport has arrived. We hastily get to our feet and follow him, up the whooshing elevator to the surface where a large drone awaits us. And then, we're truly on our way to our new home on the planet of Krovatia.

Chapter 12

Kirimor

As a favor to Denishar, I have agreed to vet the alien newcomers in person. With my abilities, I could have just as well done the job from the comfort of my temple, but he insisted it was important for me to assess the possible risk they pose face-to-face.

I do not expect that I will need sexual relief from my drashas, as my job is simply to scan the aura of these aliens and check for any danger from them. However, just in case there is a need for me to neutralize them, I have brought Cleotola with me, as well as my latest drasha, Pirofena. I can sense her buzzing with excitement at her first official outing with me. I only hope she is not too disappointed when it is all over.

We arrive at the holding center, a secure underground structure located a quarter rotation's journey from the city. I am escorted with due honor and respect afforded to me, down to the room where the aliens await me. I have come across Venorians before, but I am curious to see these Humans. I step inside the room and walk to the center, slowly examining these new visitors to my planet.

I see five Venorians, easily recognizable from their stature and the bronze tone of their skin. Two of them sit close together—perhaps they are mates. The other three, two males and a female, sit across from them and withstand my scrutiny serenely. I do not sense any negativity from them, but my holy trance will soon tell me for sure.

I transfer my attention to the Humans. Curious creatures. They have an interesting flesh color, ranging from a pale, nearly white complexion in one of the females, to the dark brown skin on the male. He is well built, with a musculature that denotes regular physical activity, though of course, nothing compared to my great stature. Physically, these aliens seem not to be dissimilar to us apart from the skin tone, although none of them have tails, more is the pity.

As I gaze at them, I feel myself being observed intently by the final female in the Human group. Her eyes fly to mine, and for a few intense moments, we stare at each other. I sense avid curiosity in her dark brown, thickly lashed eyes. I do not miss the slight flare of her nostrils and the speeding up of her breaths. Well, well, I do believe this female alien is attracted to me. And well she should be. I am sicortar after all. I hide my amusement and signal my drashas to position themselves at the back of the room. Then, I start the holy ceremony.

Once the boral crystal is gathering heat on the burner, I chant my prayer and enter into a trance. As I suspected, the Venorians all display bright auras, with no hint of negative energy. These persons will not pose a problem to us, of that I am sure. Then, I turn to the Humans.

The male Human has a warm, bright aura. A good person. Satisfied, I move to the female who was scrutinizing me so intently earlier. I am met with bright shades of yellow and orange—another warm aura with no hint of negativity. There are also little streaks of pale green, possibly denoting anxiety and sadness. Perhaps it is anxiety at being on a strange planet and sadness at being away from her loved ones back home. I linger a little on her, feeling her warm energy pulse and reach out towards me. Hmm. An interesting female.

Lastly, I turn to the other Human female, the one with the pale, pale skin and rosy cheeks. Immediately, I stiffen. Oozing out of this female are streaks of muddy green, and sparks of dark blue. So much hatred and envy taking root in her small frame. I feel it drift out of her and, very interestingly, it all seems to be directed towards her female neighbor. I cannot let such evil fester. With an internal sigh, I set to work, drawing all that negativity towards me, sucking it into my chest and holding it down with all my might.

With a growl, I break it down, and let it dissipate. My breaths heave in and out with the effort, my cock engorges, and my balls fill with roiling cum. I grunt, my need for physical relief coming to the fore. I need to sink into my drashas, and I need to do it now. With one final exhale, I force myself out of my trance and signal to the officers that the ceremony is over. They quickly escort the aliens out, but I cannot wait any longer. Before the door is closed on them, I whip off my loin cloth and growl my need. Pirofena, proving herself to be an excellent drasha, comes to straddle me, and I ram my hard, dripping cock straight into her tight, hot heat. I fuck her hard, driving my erection deep into her over and over.

When I come out of a holy trance where I have had to suck evil energy, I am like a man possessed — all raging need. And so I fuck and fuck. When I have drenched her cunt with my cum, I move to my other drasha. I push Cleotola to her hands and knees, and with a still hard cock, I thrust into her from behind. My tail wraps around her tightly, imprisoning her in my embrace as I fuck her time and time again, showering her with the juices of my loins until finally, I am sated.

Exhausted, I pull out of her and collapse on the mat. I feel my drashas stand and go to the washroom. They return with a bowl of warm water and a washcloth. As I lay there, unable to move, they clean me gently and thoroughly. Thank Taya for my wonderful drashas. Once we are all clean, we nestle together on the mat, heads propped on the cushions, and slumber.

We awake sometime later and enjoy a repast before making our way back to my drone and flying home.

Chapter 13

Wyatt

I jog up the front steps and unlock the door, entering the quiet of my house. It's when I step into my empty home at the end of each day that I'm most assailed by loneliness. What good is a hard day's toil when all I have to go home to is this space, devoid of human warmth?

With a tired sigh, I slip off my shoes and head to the kitchen fridge, taking out a cold bottle of iced tea. I gulp it down, quenching my thirst. This July heat has been scorching. Quickly, I tap the controls on my communicator to activate the cooling system, then head up the stairs to my bedroom for a quick shower.

Once I'm clean and refreshed, I amble down in my sweats to the kitchen to prepare my evening meal. I don't have much of an appetite, so I make myself a chicken salad. Settled at the kitchen counter with my food, I tap my communicator to check for messages.

There's the usual slew of work mail and social media notifications. I ignore them and select the pulsing icon with the name "Mel". She has sent me a video communication, the second one since leaving Mars for Krovatia. I click on it and set my communicator to projection mode, so her video image is projected in 3D before me. She comes alive in front of me and starts to speak. The sweet sound of her voice acts like a balm to my tired, lonely, fractious self.

"Hi, honey, I've finally made it here." She stands and guides her camera around the room. I can see a large, low lying bed with a generous supply of plump, colorful cushions. The room is furnished in simple, clean lines. Apart from the bed, there's some shelving and a work space on one side, and a large closet on the other. Overhead, a fan is whirring, giving an old-fashioned feel to the room.

"So, this is my new home. It's a little rustic, but spacious and comfortable. All the amenities are there, except for a decent cooling system," she says pointing with her chin towards the ceiling fan. "It's not too bad though. The shutters keep the worst of the heat out, and the walls are well insulated. Oh, and there's also a shared central atrium with a cute little pool. Not suitable for swimming lengths, but great for a quick, cooling dip. Let me show you."

For the next few minutes, she walks around her new home, showing me all the rooms and the pool. Then she's back in her room and settling on the bed. She smiles her glorious, bright, heart-warming smile. "So, that's your introduction to my new home. I hope it sets your mind at rest. I feel really safe here, so please don't worry, honey."

She crosses her legs and leans back against the cushioned board at the top of her bed. "Let me tell you about the Krovatians. Well, as you know, they have gray skin, and yes they do go around wearing only loin cloths. And guess what? They have a tail! It's quite long and swings back and forth as they walk, but I've noticed that it can twirl about when they get nervous or excited. How fun is that!"

"When we first arrived on Krovatia, we weren't brought here but to some kind of secure place underground where they checked us out. Let me tell you, it was weird…"

I listen as she tells me about some strange ceremony with the head priest and how he sucked out the negative energy from her colleague, who apparently had been harboring festering jealousy towards her but is now a changed person. It all seems fantastical, exciting and a world away from my humdrum existence over here. For a moment, I feel a stab of envy. I'm the one who has always loved to immerse myself in science fiction novels, while her preference was more for historical fiction.

And yet, it's her that gets to go on this adventure to an alien planet, not me. A small, immature voice inside me screams, "It's not fair!" Filled with self-loathing, I try to quash it.

I get to the end of her communication and sigh, remembering my brother's crude words. *Shit or get off the pot.*

Fuck, he's right. I'm not liking who I am these days—a cowardly, indecisive guy who's envious of his ex-wife's good fortune. Fuck that. I bang my fist on the table. *Enough Wyatt! Get your shit together and stop being a fucking coward.*

I stand and take a deep breath. *Do it. Just fucking do it.* I pick up my communicator and request an appointment with Dwight C. Josephs. And then, before I lose my nerve, I send another message, this time to the White House, for the attention of Peyton Miller.

Chapter 14

Kirimor

I have been summoned to Denishar's palace to attend his first meeting with the leader of the newly arrived Humans. I am curious to properly meet the female who scrutinized me so curiously on the day I scanned them. I am also not a little intrigued as to why this female inspired such envy and jealousy in her fellow Human.

I land my drone and am shown to Denishar's receiving chamber. I step toward him for the traditional greeting. We place hands on each other's chests, then bow. "Denishar my friend, it is a pleasure to see you."

"And you," he responds. "Take a seat, please."

We sit facing each other on decorative floor cushions placed in the center of the room. As Denishar pours me a glass of *nari*, he remarks, "I invited you here today as a second set of eyes and ears for my first meeting with this representative from the planet Earth. You have already scanned them, I know, but I will be interested in your take on their prime motivations in coming here."

"I will be glad to share my thoughts and impressions with you."

"Kirimor, I supported you in your plan to open up our planet to greater dialogue with alien races. However, I must confess that I am not entirely comfortable with their presence here or devoid of suspicion."

"That is natural, Denishar, since we have not been used to having foreigners in our midst. I do not believe these people pose a threat to us, though you are right to be cautious."

"I have studied the information we have on them. Their race is not as technologically advanced as ours. However, there are parallels in our histories. They are facing great challenges in combatting the detrimental effects of harmful pollutants on their planet's environment, just like our ancestors did."

"As a spiritual man, I am interested in those parallels. Why is it that people, in worlds light years apart, can have so many things in common? It is one of the great mysteries of life."

"Indeed."

Denishar's communicator buzzes with an incoming call from his aide. "Sir, the Human is here. Shall I show her in?"

"Please do."

We stand as the door opens and the Human female walks in with a confident step, a warm smile on her face. "Denishar, it is a great pleasure to finally meet you in the flesh," she says.

"The pleasure is mine."

The female raises her hand and places it on Denishar's chest, as he does so on hers. I am pleased to see she is acquainted with our mode of greeting. A moment later, she steps back and bows. Denishar then introduces me.

"This is the sicortar, the highest priest of Krovatia. I believe you have encountered each other before."

Her eyes turn to me, and I detect a faint flush on her face. "Yes, we did on the day of our arrival, but we were not properly introduced. Sicortar, it is a pleasure to meet you. I am Melinda Garcia."

She comes to stand before me and raises a hand to my chest. There is a slight tremble to it, which only I notice. Looking deeply into her eyes, I place my hand flat on her chest, feeling her rapid heartbeat. The flush on her face deepens. As I step back and bow, I am surprised to realize that my pulse is also racing. My tail gives an involuntary sway towards her, brushing lightly against her ankles up to her knees. In an instant, I regain control and bring it back down.

"Melinda, the pleasure is mine." At the sound of my voice, her breath hitches ever so slightly.

We take our seats on the floor cushions, the Earth female—Melinda—to my left. As she gracefully crosses her legs and arranges the drapes of her dress, I lean a little towards her and inhale her fragrance. The notes of her aroma are different to those of my people. I scent something floral, maybe a tonic she has dabbed on her neck, and beneath that, the real essence of her. I breathe it in. There is a sweetness to it that draws me in, and beneath that, a unique female musk. I inhale and want more of that drugging essence.

My eyes focus on the graceful lines of her neck and the smooth, pale honey of her skin. My keen vision detects the pulse there that beats rapidly still. I feel a sudden urge to lick her right there and then to take that soft flesh between my teeth. My cock swells in anticipation. Goddess Taya! What is happening? I use the discipline honed over many sun rotations to force my breaths to slow and deepen. With an effort, I bring my focus back to the conversation.

Melinda is thanking Denishar for the warm welcome the Humans have received on our planet and is expressing her hope that this mission will lead to greater understanding and cooperation between our people.

"That is our hope too," replies Denishar. "I have learned something of your people's history, and it seems we have things in common."

"Yes, I have been struck by that too," agrees Melinda. "I was most interested to hear about how your ancestors were forced to leave your home planet after its environment became too toxic to sustain life. We on Earth have had similar challenges. The uncontrolled emissions of greenhouse gases over many decades has caused our planet's temperature to rise and created many environmental issues for us, such as flooding and more severe weather conditions."

That captures my attention. "Will this cause an unstoppable spiral that will result in your people needing to evacuate your planet?"

Her gaze finds mine. "I don't believe so. Climate change has created many challenges for us, but one of the defining characteristics of humanity is our ability to adapt and innovate. In the last three decades, especially after the Great Flood of 2069, our nations have come together, putting aside their differences to find workable solutions. We have been able to successfully mitigate the worst of the effects of climate change, though we still face many challenges."

"I believe it was our ancestors' inability to adapt that caused our great exodus, but we here on Krovatia have learned the lessons of our past well. Maintaining the delicate eco-balance of our environment is one of our most important guiding principles."

Melinda's eyes sparkle with interest. "I would welcome the opportunity to learn about how Krovatian society goes about maintaining this delicate eco-balance. We have so much to learn from you, but this isn't one way traffic." Here her face takes on a determined expression. "Despite not being as technologically advanced in the area of space travel, we humans have had great success in developing innovative technologies to help solve the problems we have faced, such as Artificial Intelligence. I believe we have useful information to share with your people about how we have tackled the environmental challenges on Earth."

I am mesmerized by the fire in her eyes as she speaks of her people's achievements. This close, I can see they are a rich brown with flecks of a darker bronze tone. They shimmer like a fine jewel in the light. I am also captivated by the undoubted courage this female exhibits. Here she is, on an unknown planet far from her world, meeting its leaders for the very first time, valiantly standing her ground and telling us in no uncertain terms that we have just as much to gain from this information exchange as they do.

I am so lost in my appreciation of her that I forget to reply. I stare into her face as her expression morphs, very subtly, from defiant confidence to mild hesitance. It is one of my great gifts as sicortar to command respect and awe with my searing gaze. I have, without being aware of it, been giving her the look that sends most others scurrying into submission. I expect her to bow her head in deference, but instead, she lifts her chin stubbornly and matches me stare for stare. What a remarkable female! No wonder she has inspired envy in others of her kind.

It falls to Denishar to answer in my place. "Indeed, Melinda, we look forward to such a fruitful information exchange. A good place to start would be for you to visit our Ministry for the Environment and begin a dialogue with officials there. I will instruct them to contact you with an appointment."

"Thank you, Denishar. I agree that would be a good place to start. However, we should not limit ourselves to just this. It would be useful if we could establish contact with all your government ministries in due course."

There she goes again, not limiting herself to what is being offered but asking for more. A fascinating female. Denishar inclines his head. "Of course, we will make arrangements for this. We would also like to invite you all to a banquet that will be held in honor of our alien visitors in a quarter moon's rotation."

"We greatly look forward to it, Denishar. Thank you."

"It is my pleasure and honor, Melinda."

He rises to his feet, the meeting over, and we all take our cue from him, coming to a standing too.

"Go in peace," says Denishar.

Melinda responds in kind, then she turns in my direction. Her face becomes a fraction rosier as she looks at me. "Go in peace, Melinda," I tell her, my eyes never leaving hers.

"Go in peace."

A moment later, she is ushered out. Denishar indicates that I should sit myself down again. "So, Kirimor. What did you think?"

I am not about to share my private thoughts about Melinda with him. Instead, I go with, "I believe there is potential here for some genuinely fruitful collaboration between our people. If, as she said, the Humans have found innovative ways to tackle their environmental challenges, then these are things that will be of interest to us. Let us develop the dialogue further and see where it takes us. We can of course, continue to be cautious."

"I think you may be right, my friend. I thank you for your presence here today and your wise words."

"It is always my pleasure and honor, Denishar." I stand to take my leave. "Go in peace."

"Go in peace, Kirimor."

On the journey back to my home, my mind is filled with thoughts of the Earth female. I cannot wait to encounter her again.

Chapter 15

Melinda

My first days on Krovatia are a bit of a blur as I adjust to being on a different planet. It's taken me a whole week to get rid of the space lag and bring my sleep patterns in line with the days and nights here. I've unpacked my belongings and set about making my new home feel like a home. Troy, Avery and I have spent time setting up our workspace and integrating our computer systems with the Krovatian ones. We've had help from a Krovatian liaison officer, a gentle young male named Desimar. He has spent countless hours with us, helping us with our tech needs and giving us valuable advice about how to get about in Krovatia.

After my initial meeting with Denishar, we have spent the last week showing our faces around the different government departments, as well as the Ministry for the Environment, getting to know the key officials and building up our knowledge base about this planet and its people. It has been weird going to work meetings and sitting across from half-naked individuals. I haven't quite got used to the sight of women walking about topless as if it's the most natural thing in the world. And maybe it is a natural thing and I'm the anomaly here, wearing layers of clothing that stick to my skin in the burning heat. I'm the one who feels awkward and overdressed.

As a concession to the local dress code, I have taken to wearing loose, sleeveless beach dresses, my legs bare and my feet in sandals. This is the most dressed down I have ever been in my entire working life.

We have been given a transport drone to use, but we never go anywhere unescorted. There is always a Krovatian officer with us, taking us wherever we need to go. It's for our safety, we're told, though I rather suspect it's the opposite. Until a level of trust between our peoples is established, we are going to be treated like suspicious aliens. I guess that goes with the territory. This is what our mission is all about, lowering those barriers and encouraging a mutually fruitful cultural and trade exchange.

I'm settling down to sleep in my bedroom when the bleep of the communicator tells me I have just received a message. I glance at the screen and see it's from Wyatt. *Wyatt.* The man I still love despite a divorce and light years' distance between us. I've not had time to dwell on him too much since I've been here, but now, with his name flashing on the screen, it comes back to me how much I miss him. This adventure to Krovatia would have been so much better if he had been here with me, and if we could have shared this experience together. I try to quell these thoughts as I tap the screen to open up the message and project his image.

The first sight of his beautiful face has my heart clenching. He's wearing a plain T shirt that hugs his chest, and his dark blond hair is rumpled sexily. He smiles, warmth radiating from his clear blue eyes. "Hi Mel, how are you, honey? I just got your message from aboard the Olar, but with the time lag, I'm guessing you'll already be in Krovatia when you get this."

His brow creases in worry. "I hope everything is alright, that you got there safe and that everyone is treating you right. Please, honey, let me know as soon as you can, even if it's just a quick message to say you're fine."

I blow out a breath in frustration at the impossibly long time it takes for our messages to transmit. I already sent him a communication a week ago, as soon as I arrived here, but by my estimates, he won't get it for another week. And in that time, he's going to be fretting. I reach out a finger to the projected image as if to touch him and reassure him. *It's ok, honey, I'm fine.*

He continues, telling me about his weekend trip to the cabin with Dylan and the boys. It's a strange feeling listening to him talk about his life back home—there's nostalgia, but also a sense of disconnection. That life isn't mine anymore, and although a part of me misses it, another, more powerful part is thrilled to be here. I wouldn't have missed coming here for the world. I tap the communicator to transmit my response, suddenly eager to share with him all the new things I've experienced on this planet.

I smile at the screen. "Hi, honey, I've just listened to your most recent message, and it kills me that you're sitting there worrying when all is fine with me, and I can't get the news out to you quickly enough. So anyway, this is me, a week into my life on Krovatia. I've been busy settling in. I've also met with some important officials and started a diplomatic dialogue. It all sounds very promising. Yes, they are a little distrustful of outsiders, but this is why this mission is so ground-breaking. I have a really good feeling about what we're doing here and what we can hopefully achieve."

I stretch my feet and relax on the bed while I think of the best way to describe the myriad fascinating things I've learned and observed in my time here. I grin, "Well, it's been strange going to meetings with people only wearing loin cloths. It's a bit disconcerting… I mean, sometimes you can't help your eyes straying to the naked chests on display, but then you look quickly away to avoid embarrassing them and yourself. The interesting thing is that although they are nearly naked, they have a ton of artwork decorating their bodies. I thought they were tattoos at first, but I've been told it's semi-permanent ink. Apparently, it's kind of a ritual for people to have their body art re-inked every few months, following the latest fashions. They take this very seriously here. When we went out the other day to the market with our escort, I saw several body art shops—I guess they're the equivalent of our tattoo parlors, but there's even more of them about than back home. It's like they're compensating for not wearing clothes by having elaborate designs inked on their bodies. I'm wondering if I should try it out for myself, especially if it's not permanent. What do you think?"

I reach out and take a sip from the peach colored drink by my bedside. I hold it out for Wyatt to see. "This drink here is something called *nari*. It's fruity, a bit sharp and lemony, but with a hint of sweetness too. The closest flavor I can compare it to is iced tea, but with more fruitiness. I love it, and it's like the national drink here. Everywhere you go, they offer it to you. I guess because it's so refreshing and cooling."

I tap my chin and try to think of what else to share. "Let me tell you a little about where we live. We're on a secure, gated compound which has been newly built for the alien diplomatic missions. There are a dozen houses altogether, this one I share with Troy, Avery, Pravol and Treylor. Next door is where the other three Venorians live, and the next two houses are occupied by the Driskians. The empty ones I guess are there for when the diplomatic missions expand, as I hope they will. I got invited over yesterday for a visit to our Driskian neighbors and met them all. Really interesting beings. Reptilian features, green skin, but otherwise quite humanoid in appearance. Their language, beneath the translation of my ear device, sounded like a series of hisses and clicks. That weirded me out a bit! At first sight, they were a little intimidating, but on closer acquaintance, they're not like that at all. Actually, they exude this great sense of calm and peacefulness. It's amazing that through this mission, I'm getting to know more about their race as well as the Krovatians. I'm hoping to go on an off planet visit to Driskia at some point in the future, but it's not going to happen just yet."

I take a breath to pause and gather my thoughts. "How can I describe the city to you? Well, it doesn't look anything like a city for one thing. There's the central shopping district, which has some interesting food markets and those body art shops I told you about. They're all located in a great big, well insulated building, away from the heat outside. There are bright rays of light that come through some strategically placed slats on the upper walls, so it doesn't feel dark and dim. The place is like a cross between an arcade and a mall, but the architecture is nothing like what we have back home. Lots of arched ceilings and little turret like rooms, and narrow winding internal streets. It's kind of cute. I've only been there once, but I'm hoping to do more exploring soon."

I take another sip of my *nari* drink. "But apart from the central shopping district, the rest of the city is quite spaced out, with little clusters of housing units interspersed here and there. The houses are all whitewashed and have very thick walls to keep the heat out." I scrunch up my face. "I'm not describing it very well. I don't want to make it sound like the people are living in primitive huts or anything like that. Even though there's a great simplicity to the design of the buildings, they are actually really cleverly built. And aesthetically, they're so interesting to look at. Lots of high domes and arches—I get the feeling Krovatians appreciate a feeling of space. Next time I'm out and about, I'll take some video footage so you can see what I mean."

I pause. "Anyway, I better wrap this up. The exciting news is that in a few days, we're invited to a state banquet where we'll get to meet and mingle with lots of important Krovatians, so I'm really looking forward to that. I'm not sure what I'm going to wear though. How formal can I get when my counterparts are going to be in loin cloths?" I chuckle.

"So that's all my news for now. I hope all is well with you. I miss you. Love you." I blow a kiss to the screen, then end the communication.

I was not kidding when I told Wyatt I had no clue what to wear to this state banquet. I need to mark the occasion with something more formal than the strappy beach dresses I've been wearing during the day, but none of the evening formal wear I have seems to strike the right note when I'm going to be in the presence of nearly naked individuals. I decide to ask my newly friendly colleague—still can't get over the personality change Avery seems to have undergone—for advice.

I walk to the end of the corridor to where her quarters are located and gently knock on her door. When she opens, I give her a rueful look, "Any clue what I should wear tonight?"

She laughs. "I'm having the very same conundrum. Come on in and see my final choices."

I step into her room for the first time and look around curiously. She has the same basic space as I do, but she's put a much more homey touch to the décor with some colorful throws on the bed and brightly colored rugs on the floor.

"This is nice," I say.

"Thanks. I wanted to create a space that felt like home, even if I'm light years away from Earth."

"That's what I tried to do too, but I have to say, you've made a better job than me. Did you bring these rugs with you from home?"

"That one over here I did, but the rest I bought from this market that Desimar told me all about. He took me there that morning when you had your meeting with the Ministry for the Environment."

"Oh, I didn't know. I'll have to ask if Desimar can take me there too one day. I could do with some of these decorative touches."

"I'd love to come along if you do." She leans over the bed and picks up two dresses. "So, which of these do you think?"

I examine the dresses. The first is a flowing maxi dress in a jade green silky material with a long slit up one thigh. The other is a sleeveless, form-fitting little black cocktail dress that comes down to just above the knee.

"Hmm," I say. "The black one is the most formal, but I think you'll be more comfortable in the green dress, so I'd go for that one."

She holds the dress to her in front of the mirror and considers. "I think you may be right. Well, decision made. Thanks. How about you?"

"Unfortunately, my wardrobe is comprised mostly of formal dresses, a little like that black one over there."

"Don't you have a sexy little number that you wear when you want to go out and get lucky?"

I look at her perplexed. "Er, no. I'm not in the habit of going out to get lucky."

"You're divorced right?"

"Yes?"

"And have been for a while?"

"Yes again. What does that have to do with anything?"

"Well, you're still relatively young and you're definitely single, so why not?"

I shrug. "Slim pickings on Mars, I guess."

"Hmm. So you don't have a single sexy, slinky dress that you would wear if you wanted to get someone's attention?"

I think about it. "There is one dress that I wore once when I went out with my ex for our tenth anniversary dinner date. It's quite revealing, which is probably why I thought to pack it after I heard about the Krovatian dress code. I haven't worn it in years."

She beams. "Come on, let's see it."

I hesitate, not yet ready for such level of camaraderie.

"Come on, Melinda." She hurries out the door and walks towards my set of rooms.

I follow on her heels until we reach my door. She steps to one side and waits for me to open. I give a mental shrug and invite her in. As we walk inside, I see her look around my space just as curiously as I was eyeing hers a few minutes ago, but she doesn't say anything or give me any fake compliments about the décor.

"So, where's that dress?" she asks instead.

I sidestep her and head towards the large walk-in closet, rummaging on the hanging rack for the dress in question. Finally, I locate it and pull it out. It's a low cut backless white dress with spaghetti straps in a soft satin fabric that falls to mid-thigh. At the front, there are two small pearl encrusted circular cut outs that cover my breasts and a sexy plunge of the fabric down the middle to reveal skin nearly to my belly button. It's more adventurous than anything I'd ever worn before, but on the high of going together for our tenth anniversary piercings on our most private parts, it seemed like the right choice. I remember Wyatt's reaction on seeing me in it. He growled and went all possessive caveman on me. The sex we had that night… one of the best.

I think back wistfully to that amazing night, and how I had no clue then that our marriage was nearly about to end. This dress holds so many memories. Probably why I've never worn it since. That and the risqué cut of the material.

"Holy moly!" Avery snatches it out of my hands. "Where did you get this amazing number? This is smoking!"

"I got it from a custom-made website called dress4you, do you know it?"

"No, but next time I'm home, I'll definitely be checking it out!" She holds the dress up again and then hands it to me. "I want to see you in it. I think this will be just the right thing to wear for the banquet."

I look at it doubtfully, but decide there's no harm in trying it on just the once. I take it to the bathroom and quickly slip it on, adjusting the front so it clings to the small curves of my breasts. I check myself out in the bathroom mirror before going back out to Avery's scrutiny. The dress shows off my light bronze skin, tanned to perfection this last summer, and my long, athletic legs. I twirl in front of the mirror and smirk. I look sexy and desirable—so not my usual look.

Back in my room, Avery takes one look at me in the dress and wolf whistles. "Wow, sexy lady! You are definitely wearing this. Please don't say no!"

I smile. "I'm not going to."

With Troy and Avery beside me, I enter the grand state room in the sector leader's palace, where the banquet is to be held. With us are our fellow aliens on this diplomatic mission, the Venorians and Driskians.

I have been to the palace once before, when I came to be introduced to Denishar—and met the charismatic priest—but that time I was taken to his receiving rooms, not this grand chamber we are stepping into now. Typical of Krovatian architecture, the ceilings are high and vaulted, creating a feeling of great space. Large decorative lights glint along the walls, above which are those clever slats that allow a fresh breeze to flow through the room. Massive fans, like horizontal wind turbines, whirl silently above us. It's warm, but pleasantly balmy rather than hot.

To one side, I see huge oval, low tables with flat, circular cushions on the floor to sit on. The tables are laid with beautifully decorated plates and glass goblets. On the other end of the chamber, a thrum of people stand in small groups, talking animatedly. On our entrance, the voices hush and eyes raise to study us curiously. Troy puts a comforting arm about my shoulders and Avery's as we find ourselves the objects of everyone's attention, and gives a reassuring squeeze. He's conformed to the local dress code tonight, dressed in a fancy loin cloth that shimmers in the light, and he's got temporary ink all over his upper body—beautiful decorative swirls and patterns which he got on a visit to a body art shop earlier this week. He looks hot and he knows it.

We move forward into the room, and an official, whose name I didn't catch, comes over to us with a slight smile. "Welcome," he says. "If you will come this way, you may pay your respects to our four sector leaders who are all here tonight."

We follow him to a raised platform in a corner of the room that I hadn't noticed at first, on which sit the four leaders, two males and two females. As we approach, we take it in turns to give the traditional Krovatian greeting, which we have all learned to do. First, we look deeply into the eyes of the person, then place a hand flat in the middle of that person's chest, above the heart. After a moment, we bow our heads and step back. I'm used to it by now, but the first few times, it felt bizarre to place a hand on a stranger's naked chest in greeting. It feels far too intimate a gesture, but the more I do it, the more I realize just how powerful this greeting is. It creates more of a connection with the person you are meeting than our limp shake of hands.

The first person I greet is Denishar, the leader of the northern sector, in whose palace we are. He smiles gently as I bow. "Melinda, it is good to see you again. I hope you have enjoyed your first week on our planet and settled in well."

"I have, thank you. I appreciate all that you have done to make us feel welcome here and the assistance we have been given." I nod my head towards Troy, resplendent in his shimmery loin cloth and body art. "As you can see, some of us have taken on the Krovatian lifestyle already."

Denishar peruses Troy from top to bottom and grins appreciatively. "I do see." His eyes return to me. "I hope next time it will be you, bare of these clothes and beautifully adorned in Krovatian body art."

"Ah, yes. We shall see. Perhaps."

He laughs at my confusion. "Please enjoy the evening's entertainment. We have some fine Krovatian food for your delectation and some Krovatian musicians will be playing songs for us as we eat. I hope this will give you a good introduction to our culture."

I bow my head again. "I look forward to it, thank you."

Then, I move on to greet the other sector leaders.

The evening progresses as I meet countless new faces and exchange pleasantries. The Krovatians are polite, welcoming even, but cautious about these visitors to their planet. It's strange to be the object of everyone's curiosity. I'm the outsider here, the alien. I'm reminded of a similar occasion just under a year ago when I presided over a formal dinner to welcome the Venorians who were coming to Earth for a six months cultural exchange. Then, the roles had been reversed. I had been the host, basking in the glory of having made first contact with an alien race, and it had been the Venorians who attracted all the curious attention.

A prickle on the back of my neck has me turn around suddenly. Dark, glittering eyes stare back at me. Him. He must have just arrived, as surely I would have noticed him otherwise. There he stands, a few feet from me, a tall distinctive figure in the crowded room. I haven't stopped thinking about him since that meeting in Denishar's office when he stared intimidatingly at me the whole time. No, I tell a lie. I haven't stopped thinking about him since that first day when he did that growly thing then whipped off his loin cloth. The sight of his massive oozing cock is not something I can easily forget. I flush now at the memory, and he smirks, as if he knows exactly what I'm thinking about.

I hastily turn my face away and resume my conversation with Krovatia's Chief Minister of Science, though I've lost the train of the discussion. I simply nod and smile, while I burn under the continued heat of the sicortar's stare. A moment later,

I feel the crowds around me part, and I know it's for him. I don't turn around. It's the Chief Minister of Science who breaks off what he is saying and addresses the highest priest of the planet with a pleased smile. "Sicortar, it is an honor," he says.

"The honor is mine," responds a deep, resonant voice that makes my insides vibrate. The two approach each other for the traditional Krovatian greeting, placing a hand on each other's chest, then stepping back with a bow. Then, the sicortar turns to me, the expectation clear. With a pounding heart, I step closer and put out a hand towards the hard, muscled expanse of his chest, my eyes locked with his. Before my palms can make contact with his skin, I'm seared by the touch of his large hand over the center of my chest, the fingers splayed wide. My breath hitches. And then, I'm touching my palm to warm, solid flesh, the skin surprisingly soft. I press my hand there perhaps a moment longer than required, enjoying the feel of his powerful body. Then, I step back and bow.

The sicortar addresses me, the deep voice sending a shiver down my spine. "It is good to see you again, Melinda."

"Likewise," I manage to croak. "It's good to see you, sicortar."

He brings his arm around a beautiful woman of an uncertain age who is hovering by his side. Her tail spins in circles, betraying her nerves. "This is my drasha, Merostena, and our son Kiristen."

His drasha? Is that a Krovatian term for a mate? It must be, as he's bringing her with their son to this formal event.

I notice a young man, with a striking resemblance to his father, standing on the other side of him. He grins and steps forward to greet me. We put a hand to each other's chests and bow, then he says, "It is a great pleasure to meet you. You are the first alien I have ever seen, and a very attractive one I must say."

At this, his father snorts. I laugh, glad of the opportunity to break the tense atmosphere. Kiristen gently pushes his mother forward. She smiles shyly and reaches out a hand to greet me. In a soft voice, she says, "It is an honor to meet you," then quickly steps back into the protective embrace of the sicortar—her husband? Mate? So who were those other two women with him on that first day? His mistresses? One of them was young enough to be of around the same age as his son. Is this a thing on Krovatia, for men to have both a mate and mistresses? If so, what a repellent practice.

The warm glow his presence had cast on me is quickly dispelled. My lips curl in distaste for an infinitesimal moment, before I compose my face into a mask of blank civility. If anything, his smirk grows wider, the bastard. I force my attention to what his son is saying. Something about being willing to act as a guide and show us the sights in the city. I smile at him warmly. Let not the sins of the father befall the shoulders of the son. "That is very kind, thank you. We would greatly appreciate it."

There's a gentle touch on my shoulder, and I turn to see Troy and Avery. We had gotten separated over the course of the evening. "Hey," he says. "How's it going?"

"Good, thanks. Let me introduce you to the sicortar, his drasha and his son. Everyone, these are my colleagues, Troy Summers and Avery Walker."

Avery gives a sigh of near adoration and approaches the sicortar to greet him. As she steps back and bows, she tells him, "I am forever in your debt, sicortar. Ever since that day, I'm like a new person—so much happier, as if a huge burden has been lifted off my shoulders. I've been waiting for an opportunity to express my deepest gratitude."

He inclines his head graciously. "I was simply doing my duty, but I am glad to see that it has had such a positive effect."

His son, meanwhile, is stepping back from Troy with a bow. He stares admiringly at my colleague's naked, decorated chest and blurts, "Oh my, you are beautiful."

Troy quirks a brow in amusement. "Er, thank you."

The young man flushes. "I am sorry. Sometimes words come out of my mouth without thought. It is one of my besetting sins."

Troy's face softens. "No apology needed. If I'm being honest, I was just thinking the very same about you."

"Oh." At this, Kiristen's tail flutters wildly in the air. I watch it in fascination.

Kiristen clears his throat. "Well, Troy. I was just telling Melinda that it would be my honor to show you around the local sights. In fact, if you would like, I would love to take you out to the water city tomorrow."

"The water city?" Troy asks, intrigued.

Kiristen nods eagerly. "Yes, it is a very popular place for Krovatians to spend their leisure time. It is formed of many interconnected pools of fresh water. I am sure you would enjoy it."

Troy smiles warmly. "That sounds like fun. I'm in. How about you Melinda, and Avery?"

"It sounds great," Avery says, "though I'd have to be careful not to burn my pale skin in the sun."

"That is not a problem," Kiristen assures her. "Our pale gray skin is also vulnerable to the ultra violet rays of the sun. That is why we have developed technology to protect ourselves. When you arrive at the water city, you will walk through a special spray that coats your body with one hundred per cent protection from the harmful rays."

"Well in that case, count me in too."

They both turn to me. I grin. "I wouldn't miss this for the world."

Kiristen smiles happily, his eyes still worshipful on Troy. "Great! I will come to take you from your quarters tomorrow morning at four beats past the sunrise."

I'm still grappling with the Krovatian concept of time. They measure it in "beats", which so far as I can gather, are each equivalent to around ten minutes. So, four beats past sunrise should be around forty minutes after sunrise. An early time to head out, but sensible if we're to avoid the worst heat of the midday sun.

"We look forward to it," I say. From the periphery of my vision, I catch a private exchange between the sicortar and his wife. He nods his head towards Kiristen and Troy, then gives her a meaningful look. She shakes her head in mild exasperation and the sicortar smiles, a twinkle in his amused eyes. I look quickly away.

Just then, the official in charge of the proceedings comes towards us, inviting us to take our seats for dinner. We follow him to our table, lowering ourselves onto the floor cushions with as much grace as we can manage. This sitting on the floor business is taking some getting used to. I'm just congratulating myself on managing this feat without flashing my underwear at anyone when I notice who has seated himself next to me on my right. Damn that devil priest of a man!

Despite my best efforts to ignore him, his close proximity sets my pulse racing. The scent of him assaults my nostrils—a musky aroma that's entirely too masculine and sexual. I've scented it once before, in that room when he did that growly thing to Avery, just before he whipped off his loin cloth and sank his cock in a woman half his age. Damn the man! This is one attraction I definitely do not want to feel.

He reaches across from me to a small round container from which he produces a steaming, lightly scented towel. Without invitation, he takes one of my hands and begins to gently cleanse it with the towel.

"Oh," I murmur. "I can do this myself, thank you," and try to grab hold of the towel.

He growls and bats the offending hand away, continuing with his task.

"Really," I say, "there's no need. I'm perfectly capable of cleaning my own hands."

Again, I'm met with a growl while he takes my other hand and wipes it clean. Then, without a word, he throws the used towel in a basket by his side and takes a fresh one out of the container. This time, I see him turn to his wife who sits on his other side, and cleanse her hands for her. Lastly, he uses a third towel to both clean his hands and wipe his face. I look discreetly around the table and notice the other Krovatian males doing the same thing. A few seats to my left, Kiristen is wiping Avery's hands, a studious expression on his face, as if he wants to ensure he does the task just right. *Okay.* So this must be some kind of Krovatian custom.

But that's not where it ends. Next, the sicortar reaches for a dish which contains some peculiar looking pale green balls. He takes one and brings it to my mouth. "Open," he barks. Of their own volition, my lips part and he pops the ball into my mouth. I bite into a crispy exterior, then I taste a delicious combination of fresh herbs and a soft type of flavorsome meat on the inside.

I chew the delicious food under his watchful gaze. "Mmm, thanks," I say. "These are wonderful. What do you call them?"

"They are called *mishu*. Would you like another?"

"It's fine, I can help myself. The dish is right here. There's no need—"

Another tasty green ball of *mishu* is popped into my mouth. While I'm busy chewing and swallowing, I see him plop a ball into his wife's mouth too. Well really, this is too much. Are females not supposed to eat for themselves on this planet? Again, I cast a discreet look around the table at the other

Krovatian guests. None of the other males seem to be feeding their female neighbors.

Encouraged, I decide to explore the food for myself. I reach towards a dish that contains what look like meatballs in a creamy sauce. The sicortar bats my hand away yet again. "Have patience!" he exclaims in a disgruntled tone.

"Really, there is no need for this. The food is right in front of me. I'm quite able to help myself without your assistance."

"Female, will you stop? I have no time for this nonsense."

I feel my hackles rise. "I do not wish to cause offence, but really sir, I am well capable of eating on my own." And I reach once more for the dish of meatballs.

An angry growl reverberates in my ears. A moment later, the sicortar's long tail whips up into the air, twirls into a lasso and slips over both my wrists, tightening around them in a choke hold. I can't believe this! The bastard of a priest has tied me up, with his darned tail of all things.

Keeping my voice low, I hiss, "Let me go now, or so help me God—"

At this, he laughs. The devil priest actually laughs. "You will do what? Call for help and shame yourself even further? What a glorious impression you will make on my people, and this on your first official appearance too."

I close my mouth with a snap, aware of the truth of his statement. I take a deep breath in to try to get my anger under control, then try again. "Sir, I am asking you kindly and politely to please release my hands."

He considers me for a few moments, then gives his answer. "No." Then he turns to his wife and murmurs something in her ear. She glances at me and nods. He kisses her cheek, then reaches for a side dish containing a mountain of pale, fluffy round little grains. He scoops some up with a large serving spoon onto his plate, then takes the creamy meatball dish and pours some of it over the rice-like grains on his plate. I sit and fume in silence, not wanting to cause a scene. I look to Troy, sitting to my left, for assistance, but his attention is entirely focused on Kiristen, sitting next to him. *Just great.*

I try to prise my hands apart, but my efforts are simply rewarded with a tightening of his tail around me. His fucking tail! If steam could come out of my ears, it would. I have never before been humiliated quite like this.

He ignores me and takes a long implement with two prongs, and begins to cut up the meatballs, or whatever it is those balls are. From another bowl, he takes some colorful diced vegetables and sprinkles them on top. To this mixture he now adds a little spoonful of some crunchy looking powder—maybe from some kind of crushed nuts—and finally, he scatters a few green herby leaves on top. He takes a small, curved wafer from another dish, and scoops a little of the mixture on to it, then brings it to my mouth. "Eat," he orders.

Out of sheer spite, I keep my mouth clamped shut, my eyes spitting fury at him. He bends toward me, putting his mouth to my ear. "Melinda. You will eat from my hands, that is a promise." He takes my earlobe between his teeth and bites gently. I go rigid in shock. The gall of this man! His wife is sitting right next to us, and there he is manhandling me. Unbelievable!

My eyes fly around the table to see if our little spat is getting any attention. A Krovatian female sitting across from me watches us with a smile, then she calmly begins to eat and converse with her neighbor, totally unaffected. So, no help coming from that quarter.

The sicortar brings the food to my lips once more. "Melinda, open."

I think quickly. My choices are, either make a scene or just let the annoying man feed me and deal with it afterward. Reluctantly, I part my lips. He slips the wonderfully aromatic food into my mouth, and I bite into it automatically. I'm not prepared for the explosion of delicious flavors on my tongue. The food is good, really, really good. I bite and chew, savoring the texture and mix of flavors that complement each other perfectly. I'm so entranced by it, that for a minute, I forget my anger and simply enjoy.

Next to me, the sicortar purrs in satisfaction. "That is my good girl." He takes a second wafer and makes another mouthful of food for me. This time, when he brings it to my lips, I don't demur but take it in hungrily.

Ok, so he may possibly be the most irritating male on the planet, and a cheat to boot, but this food… I think I'll suspend my annoyance just long enough to partake in the delicious feast. There will be plenty of time for a reckoning afterward.

For the next few minutes, I eat in silence as he feeds me, making the occasional involuntary moan of pleasure. He brings a glass of *nari* to my lips, allowing me a few sips of the refreshing drink, then feeds me something else, this time a type of rolled flat bread with an aromatic, spicy filling. Over the next half-hour, I eat everything he gives me, all of it utterly delicious. And I forget to be angry with him in my pleasure.

I notice Troy finally pry his attention from Kiristen to cast a puzzled glance at me and my hands still tied up with the sicortar's tail. He says something to Kiristen, who also glances at us, surprise and amusement on his face. I see him whisper something in Troy's ear, and Troy's chuckle. That's when I look down at my hands and realize the sicortar's tail is no longer imprisoning them in a tight hold. Instead, the knot around me has loosened and his tail is stroking my hands in a soft, rhythmic motion. I barely have time to take this in before the sicortar feeds me another bite of something delicious, a soft and gooey sweet thing. I can't help a moan at how good it feels.

The sicortar hums in his deep, gravelly voice, "Such a good girl, Melinda. It is a joy to see you eat. You have pleased me greatly." He kisses the soft, sensitive skin beneath my earlobe, and I quiver in response. Wait a minute, I'm supposed to be angry at him, right? But all I can do in this instant is breathe heavily and flood my panties. Great God, what is this man doing to me?

The man in question sniffs the air and grins broadly. "You are pleased too. That is good. Go in peace, Melinda." Then he stands, as does his wife, and walks away without another look.

I'm shell shocked, still not quite believing the events that have just unfolded. As I try to recover my senses, Troy sidles up to me. "Holy shit, Melinda, what was that about?"

I exhale a deep breath and try to get my bearings back. "If I knew, I would tell you."

Behind him, Kiristen approaches me shyly. "My father is a difficult man to impress, but I see you have made a great impression on him, as you have on me. I have been most honored to meet you, Melinda."

I smile back at him. "And I you, Kiristen. I look forward to our outing tomorrow."

"Me too. Go in peace." He turns to Troy, his heart in his eyes. "Troy, I am so joyful to have met you tonight, and I cannot wait to see you again. Go in peace."

"Go in peace," responds my colleague, with a warm smile. Kiristen gives us a final bow, then takes his leave.

We all stand and make our farewells to the other guests before heading back home, each of us quiet in the drone, reflecting on the curious turn of events this evening.

Chapter 16

Kirimor

I came to tonight's banquet curious to meet the alien visitors to our planet and also keen to see the Human female that so captivated me the last time. Melinda—what a sensual sounding name. It suits her.

I had no plans for seduction, but then I saw her contemptuous, snide expression which she quickly tried to mask. Nobody is allowed to disrespect the sicortar. Who does she think she is to look down on me? I decided there and then that I would, after all, seduce the female, and put her in her place.

I purposefully followed in her wake and sat beside her at the dinner table. I took great pleasure in tying her up with my tail and seeing her frustration and anger at being so imprisoned. I could not resist biting the soft flesh of her ear. And then I fed her luscious lips and watched her sigh and moan in pleasure. I smelled her arousal and walked away, mission accomplished.

Now, sitting in my drone on the flight home, with a cock that steadfastly remains rock hard, I am not so sure who it was that was doing the seducing. Merostena, sitting beside me, voices what she has no doubt been thinking all evening. "You are attracted to this Human."

I look down at the tent in my loin cloth and chuckle ruefully. "It would seem so."

"It has been a long time since you have expressed an interest in a female other than your drashas."

"The very longest time. Merostena, I have not looked for pleasure elsewhere since Kiristen was born."

My son rouses from his reverie to ask, "Why now, father?"

I shrug. "I do not know. When I scanned her, it seemed like her aura called to me. And tonight, I meant only to teach her a lesson for disrespecting me, but in the end, I got caught in her web just the same."

"I did not see her disrespecting you, father."

"It was only a fleeting expression of distaste on her face when she was introduced to us. I do not know why, but in that moment, the female looked extremely disapproving. I did not care for that expression."

My son is thoughtful for a while, then says, "Perhaps it was because the first time she saw you, it was with your other drashas."

I raise my brows. "I do not follow. Why would that be a problem?"

"Well," my son says, "I had an interesting discussion with Troy about his culture. On Earth, people do not as a rule have multiple partners. They have something called marriage, which is very close to a mating. I am guessing that she must have assumed that mother is your mate and that you were not being true to her when you brought your other drashas with you on that last occasion."

"Why would she think that?" I ask irritably. "I introduced Merostena as my drasha, not as my mate!"

"Perhaps she did not understand the term *drasha*, and thought it was a Krovatian word for being a mate."

I ponder this new information. I suppose it makes sense. It would explain the change in her demeanor when I introduced her to Merostena. I blow out a breath in frustration. I do not like to be misunderstood nor my morals to be impugned.

"You may be right, son. You are showing wisdom beyond your years."

He sighs. "If I am, it is only because I am in love, and sometimes the eyes of love make you see things more clearly."

I look at him in amusement. "Kiristen, I distinctly remember your promise not to fall in love with anyone at this banquet."

"I remember that too," says Merostena.

Our son puts a hand to his heart. "Father, mother, I know you have heard this before, but he is the one. I know it."

"Why should we believe you this time?" asks his mother.

"I agree it sounds like I have been flighty, falling in and out of love with every pretty face I see. But tonight was different. I cannot explain why. I just know with a deep certainty that I have met the person I want as my mate."

"He is an outsider, Kiristen, not one of us."

"The heart wants what it wants, mother. He is the one. I know it."

I gaze at my son in perturbation. "Kiristen, I do not want you to get hurt. You must know these Humans are only here for a short time, and then they shall return to their world. Please son, have a care for your heart."

He looks at me steadily. "As you have a care for yours?"

I snort. "I am not in love! Merely attracted to this Human. I may or may not decide to conduct a short relationship with her and explore this attraction, but that is all it will be. It cannot possibly be more."

"How can you be so sure, when it is the first time in over twenty sun rotations that you have felt an interest in someone other than a drasha?"

I stare at him nonplussed. He has a point. But then I gather myself and reply primly, "Because I will not let it happen. As a sicortar, you know I cannot have a mate, and therefore I cannot allow myself the indulgence of falling in love—at least not the wild romantic love you envisage." I put an arm around Merostena and kiss the top of her head. "Of course, I love all my drashas and my family, but that is different."

"So this Human female is just someone you will dally with, without it affecting your heart?"

"I have not decided yet what I shall do, but I certainly do not plan to fall in love. That would be extremely foolish."

"In that case, call me foolish, for I have fallen in love. Make no mistake."

I sigh, feeling every one of my forty-nine sun rotations. "For your sake, my son, I hope it is not so."

Chapter 17

Wyatt

My interview with Peyton Miller does not go well. She responded to my message with an invitation to meet online for a ten minute slot the following day. And so here we are. I have laid my request before her, and been met with a resounding no.

"I'm sorry, Wyatt, but travelling to Krovatia is just not on the cards. Even if Melinda had put in a request for her spouse—which technically you no longer are—we would have been hard pressed to provide a safe passage there. You must surely know that we are reliant on the Venorians for travel to that part of the galaxy. We do not have the technology on our own ships to go that distance."

"I understand, but I'm under the impression that Venorian ships now make regular journeys to and from Mars, so it would be possible surely for me to catch a ride with one of them and have them drop me off on Krovatia."

"Wyatt, let me be honest here. As far as we are concerned, you are an ordinary private citizen with no special privileges. We cannot be making passenger requests to the Venorians on your behalf. Perhaps if Melinda were to send us a communication, specifically asking for you to join her as her spouse, then we would consider it. But until then, I'm afraid the answer is no."

I look down at my hands, clenched tightly in my lap, and nod. "I understand. Thank you for your time."

She sighs. "I'm sorry to be such a downer. Give it time, Wyatt. Our space program is growing exponentially year by year. There may come a time, sooner rather than later, when we are able to make such journeys. Be patient."

"I don't have much choice, do I?"

"Take care, Wyatt."

"Thanks again for your time."

We end the connection and I sit back in my chair, eyes closed. Is this a sign that going to Krovatia is a really, really bad idea? A part of me welcomes the thought. I won't have to go into space after all.

I take a few breaths in and out and try to loosen the tightness in my chest. That's it then? The end of the road?

No!

Fuck no! I sure as shit am not giving up yet. I may have hit a road block, but I'll find a way to join Mel in Krovatia. Maybe I should bypass the White House altogether and go through my own Venorian contacts. I could get a message to Pravol and Treylor, asking for their help. Pravol, with his Venorian mindset about mating, has never fully understood my divorce from Melinda. To him, mates are mates for life. What more natural than for this human to try to get to his mate? Maybe Pravol could use his connections to help arrange my passage there and try to obtain permission from the Krovatian authorities for my arrival. In the meantime, there's the not so little matter of my space fright. I pick up my communicator and eye the appointment confirmation with Dwight K. Josephs. Next Monday at eleven am. I'm doing this.

I walk up the front steps of a red-brick townhouse in Lincoln Park and ring the bell. I wait a minute or two, then ring the bell again. I check my communicator. Yes, it definitely says Monday at eleven, and this is the address. I wait impatiently some time longer and I'm just about to turn around when I hear the door creak open. An older man, somewhere in his late sixties or early seventies, stands smiling absently at me. "Yes?" he asks.

"Mr Josephs? I'm Wyatt Garcia. I have an appointment with you today for eleven am."

His face clears. "Of course, of course. Do come in."

I follow him inside into a short vestibule crammed with overflowing bookshelves. He leads me towards a door that stands ajar and invites me into his office. It's a cosy room, dominated by a large desk and more bookcases full of paperbacks. He points to a brown leather armchair. "Do take a seat, Wyatt. Would you like tea or coffee, perhaps a soft drink?"

"Just water will be fine, thanks."

He goes to a small fridge, concealed within one of his bookcases, and pulls out a bottle of water for me. Then he takes a seat across from me at his desk and clasps his hands together.

"So, Wyatt. What can I help you with today?"

"I've been told you would be able to help me overcome my fear of flying."

"Fear of flying? Hmm."

He's quiet for several moments, and I start to get antsy. Is he waiting for me to say something else? Finally, he speaks. "So, tell me, Wyatt. How long have you been afraid of flying?"

"Since I was fifteen. I, erm, I was in a drone accident."

He looks at me enquiringly, as if he's expecting me to elaborate further.

I clear my throat. "So, yeah. After that, I developed a fear of flying."

He frowns. "Are you saying your drone accident was the reason for your developing this fear?"

Well duh! "Yes, obviously."

"It is not at all obvious to me."

"I had a terrifying accident while flying in a drone. After that, I was scared of flying. I would think the connection was obvious."

"So, before the accident, you were happy to fly. No fear at all?"

I look at him uncomfortably. "I wouldn't say that, no."

He twiddles his fingers and waits.

"Well, I've always been a nervous flyer. It's not something I ever enjoyed, but after the accident, I couldn't set foot on a drone again without getting awful nausea."

"I see. And you think the accident was the cause."

"It seems to follow, don't you think?"

"It could be entirely coincidental."

"You think?"

"I can't say for sure, only that it could be."

"If it is coincidental, then why was I able to get on a drone before it happened, but afterward I couldn't."

"Perhaps the accident provided you with the perfect excuse to avoid doing something you always feared doing."

"You think I'm using the accident as an excuse?"

He puts his hands up placatingly. "Wyatt, take a moment to look at this rationally. You tell me that you have always been fearful of flying, then you have a drone accident, after which, you no longer feel able to fly. Is it not also possible that a subconscious part of your mind seized on this event as a way to no longer have to do this fearful thing?"

"If it's an unconscious thing, then it's not under my control."

"Yes and no."

I look at him sceptically. "Please explain."

"If you had no control over your actions, Wyatt, then you wouldn't be here, wanting to overcome this fear. To a certain extent, you do have control. You have the motor skills to put one foot in front of the other. Physically, you can get into a drone; it is eminently doable."

Said foot starts tapping the floor agitatedly.

"But having said that," he continues, "it seems clear that you had a fear of flying long before the accident happened, and that fear is something that has felt beyond your control."

"Exactly," I say, "which is why I'm here."

"Why are you here, Wyatt?"

At my puzzled look, he clarifies. "Why now, after so many years, are you intent on overcoming this fear?"

"I—"

The words won't come out. Dwight C. Josephs watches me silently, waiting.

"I lost the woman I love."

Still, he doesn't speak, but just waits.

"She's leading our Earth mission to Krovatia. My ex-wife's name is Melinda Garcia."

"I see."

"She wanted me to go with her, but I couldn't."

"Couldn't or wouldn't?"

"You're beginning to sound like my brother!" I snap in frustration.

Still, he doesn't react, just waits for me to answer the question.

I breathe in deeply and exhale. "Both," I say.

He smiles. "Good, we're beginning to peel the layers away until we get to the truth. Let's focus on the wouldn't. Why wouldn't you go?"

"It would have meant leaving everything behind that had meaning for me. My family ties, my friends, the practice I'd invested several years in building up. I'd have had to drop all of that to follow her and be in her shadow."

"To be in her shadow. That's an interesting choice of words. Is that how you've felt."

I run my fingers down a rough patch of trim on the edge of the chair. "It makes me sound pathetic, envious. That's not the guy I want to be."

"No, I can see you wouldn't want to be cast in that role. But this is a space of honesty and no judgement. Speak, Wyatt, and tell me why you've felt in her shadow."

"We met years ago in college. Back then, I was top of the class, someone with prospects. I aced all my tests and was on track for a successful career in business or finance. That's the person Mel first met. Somewhere along the line, I've stopped being that person, and I've always wondered if deep down, she's disappointed that the man she married, the high achieving guy who was going places, is now just a plain old chiropractor."

"Have you ever asked her?"

I shake my head. "Even if I had, she would never have told me. She's not that kind of person."

"After years of marriage, you didn't feel you could trust your life partner with that question?"

I stare at a scuff on my shoes grimly. "No."

"Why?"

A pause. In my heart, I know the answer, but I've never verbalized it. "I think the job on Mars, and maybe also this one on Krovatia, was her way of leaving me without it looking like she was leaving me."

"You mean, it was her excuse to leave you, without having to explain her real reasons why?"

I nod.

"What if it's not what you think? You said she asked you to go with her to Krovatia. Perhaps she genuinely wanted you there with her. What if you allowed her to leave you because you didn't have the courage to have an honest conversation?"

"Well, that would suck even more than it already does."

"Yes, it would."

I run a hand through my hair. "Jesus!"

"Ok, let's regroup and focus on something else for the time being. Tell me, Wyatt, do you feel a lesser person because you're now a chiropractor and not a high-flying businessman?"

"Yes and no."

"Ok, let's explore this. Why does it make you feel like a lesser person?"

I sigh heavily. "This is a status-oriented city, and most of my former colleagues and friends, as well as my ex-wife, are in that high status world. To them, being a chiropractor is small fry. They don't say it outright, but I know they think it."

"I hear you, Wyatt. If that's the case though, and that's a big if, then perhaps it might be time to make new friendships and step away from that circle of acquaintances."

"The problem is that my ex-wife is in that circle."

"Ah… Other than that, are you happy being a chiropractor?"

"Yes. It's a much less stressful job, and I get a lot of satisfaction from helping people manage often very painful conditions. I get to go home at the end of the day knowing I've done good. I like that feeling."

Dwight smiles warmly. "I know what you mean."

He steeples his fingers on the desk, then asks, "So, if you want to move away from that circle of people that does not properly value what you do, and your ex-wife is in that circle, then why are you so hung up on getting her back? Why can you not move on and start afresh with someone who more closely aligns with the life you have now?"

I'm quiet, thinking it over. It's a question I've asked myself many times. I still don't have the answer, except—

"I love her still, very much."

"Enough to give up the life you have here and go be her shadow?"

I don't answer. Then, I shake my head again. "It's not what I want, but being here without her is a miserable existence too, so I guess it's the lesser evil."

"It seems a pity to live a life that you don't want just because it's the less bad option."

I raise a brow. "What would you suggest I do?"

He laughs. "That's not for me to say. But I would like you, before your next visit, to consider this question. Is there any way that you could go be with your ex-wife and not feel like you're in her shadow? Is there anything you could do out there on Krovatia that would bring you self-actualization? Don't answer me now; just think it over. How about you come see me again at the end of the week? I have some appointment slots on Friday."

"Sure, I can do that."

"Good." He smiles as he stands up and moves around the desk toward me.

I stand and shake his hand. "Thank you, Mr Josephs."

"Pff, call me Dwight."

"Thanks, Dwight, this has been—it's been a much needed conversation."

"I'm glad."

He leads me out to the front door, which he opens for me. "Take care, Wyatt. I'll see you Friday."

Chapter 18

Wyatt

*I*s there anything you could do out there on Krovatia that would bring you self-actualization?

Dwight's question haunts me the rest of the evening and for the following few days. He's planted a seed with that question. What if I were to go to Krovatia in my own right and not as Melinda's spouse? What could I do that would bring me self-actualization?

I got off the cut-throat business juggernaut I was on to retrain as a chiropractor, and I haven't regretted that move. I cut my stress levels in half and improved my quality of life immeasurably. However, I was less than honest with Dwight when he asked me if I was happy being a chiropractor. I enjoy it, sure. I love helping others and even more, I love being able to leave work behind when I go home. Melinda might thrive being on the clock 24/7, but not me.

Having said that, working as a chiropractor isn't entirely satisfying either. I know it doesn't utilize the full range of my abilities. I rose to the heights I did in my business life because I was damned good at it. I could put together profitable deals and negotiate the best of terms for my business. I could sniff out new opportunities like a bloodhound and go in for the kill before any of our competitors could get in on the action. Working as a chiropractor doesn't scratch the surface of what I'm capable of doing, and at times, it's painfully obvious that I'm only utilizing a small part of my abilities.

That's why my friends', and Melinda's, barely hidden disappointment at my decision to get off the business bandwagon stings. On some level, we all know that it was a cop out. Things got a little too tough that last year, too stressful, and my solution was to get out of the rat race and find something else to do—something vastly less complicated. I got burned out, reached my crisis point, and for the sake of my sanity, I had to leave that life behind. That was the right choice to make at the time. But now… I don't know anymore.

I'm certain I don't want to go back to my old work life, the one that burned me out, but not so certain I want to keep on being a chiropractor either. Dwight's question about what would bring me self-actualization has come at just the right time. What could I do that would utilize my talent and experience, without sending my stress levels through the roof? And how could I make that happen in Krovatia? My mind throws up lots of different metaphorical thought balls into the air, but I can't seem to make them juggle just yet.

My communicator buzzes with a message from Mike, an old school friend of mine. Our paths parted ways when he went to dance school, but we have still kept in touch. He's now the artistic director of the Washington Ballet. We have a standing date, once a month for dinner and—depending on the schedule—a performance at the ballet.

Mike: Still on for tonight?

Me: Of course.

Mike: Burgers, Mexican or Vietnamese?

Me: Vietnamese

Mike: Good choice. I've sent you an e-ticket for tonight's performance. I'll see you in the box.

Me: What's on the program?

Mike: Jesus, do you never keep up? It's Giselle, dumb ass!

Me: A classic, but it never gets old.

Mike: True that. It's also a debut performance for Nia Brown in the lead role. Remember she caught your eye as the courtesan last time you came to see Manon.

Me: Oh right. Yeah, I liked her a lot. Looking forward to it.

Mike: Gotta go. See you later.

Me: Later.

I drop my communicator on to the side table by my bed and begin to undress. As I do, I think about Melinda and how she's getting on in Krovatia. The latest message from her came this morning, recorded on the day of her arrival there. She showed me her new house and told me about some weird ceremony with a priest who somehow transformed the personality of her colleague, Avery. I sent her a message back, but I'm very conscious of the fact she won't be receiving it for at least another two weeks. I wonder what has been happening in her life over there all this time.

I head into the shower and take a quick wash, thinking about the other message I received today, this one from my good friend Pravol, the Venorian I got to know well in the six months he lived on Earth. After my last chat with Peyton Miller, I had contacted him, asking for help in my quest to get to Krovatia, emphasizing the fact that I needed to be with my mate—knowing how this would chime with him. His response arrived today.

Nodding gravely into his communicator screen, he said, "Hello Wyatt. As always it is a pleasure to hear from you. I am glad you are well and thank you for your enquiries into my wellbeing and Treylor's. We are both well thank you, and settled into our new home in Krovatia. I was also glad to hear of your wish to join Melinda here. It has troubled me greatly to see two mates such as yourselves separated, and I will of course do anything in my power to help you re-unite. I will personally forward your application for permission to enter Krovatia to the authorities here, and vouch for you. Perhaps you could write a letter explaining your purpose, and I will see to it that it gets to the right people."

He then smiled and continued, "As for the matter of transport, I also have good news. Martha, Krantor's mate, is on her way to Earth to visit her ailing grandfather there. She is travelling on one of our cargo ships—commanded by Treylor's cousin Rivlor. I believe Rivlor could assist in transporting you on her ship to Krovatia for a fair price which you will have to negotiate with her. I have taken the liberty to inform Rivlor that you are wishing to use her ship for transport and to share your contact details with her, so she should be in touch soon. I have also sent a communication to Martha, explaining your situation and asking if she can help put in a good word for you too."

He frowns then, looking uncomfortable. "However, Wyatt, I am uneasy about withholding this information from Melinda. I urge you to contact her and let her know your intentions. It would make me much easier in my mind if she was aware of all that you are planning. Please do let her know. I bid you farewell, my friend, and await your response."

Pravol is right. I shouldn't just spring on Mel unawares. I do need to tell her. However, I want to get all my ducks in a row first.

My heart quickens at the thought of what this could all mean. I could be on my way to Krovatia within a few weeks. The clock has begun ticking, with very little time left to overcome my fear of flying. On top of all that, I need to come up with a plan for what I'm going to do over there. My second appointment with Dwight tomorrow takes on a whole new dimension. We're no longer in the realm of possibilities but of reality.

Shit or get off the pot.

The time for indecision is over. I'm doing this.

I arrive at the theater just as the curtain goes up, and slip into the private box where Mike is already sitting.

"Hey," I whisper.

"Hey," he smiles. "Nearly gave you up for lost."

"Sorry."

Just then, the orchestra begins playing, and I sit back to enjoy the performance. Giselle is the story of a poor peasant girl who falls in love with a duke who masquerades as an ordinary peasant, hiding his true identity and the fact he's got a fiancée. Albrecht, the duke, has his fun and woos innocent Giselle, only for things to go wrong when he's unmasked for who he really is. This is when things get dramatic. Poor Giselle goes mad with grief, confronting the cheating, lying Albrecht, and eventually stabs herself with his sword. I've seen this ballet before, but Nia Brown, playing the role of Giselle, infuses it with renewed meaning. I watch spellbound as she goes from a sweet, trusting girl falling in love with the swashbuckling, handsome stranger, to a woman possessed with rage and madness as she confronts the man who's betrayed her.

I lean over to whisper in Mike's ear. "She's good."

He smiles smugly, "Yeah."

The first act comes to an end and the lights come back on in the auditorium. I stand and stretch my arms out. "Shall we go get a drink?"

"You go ahead. I need to go backstage and speak to a few people. I'll see you back here in the box, and we can catch up later at dinner."

"No probs."

I head out of the box, towards the bar area which is already filling up with people. I order a mojito on my communicator and collect it a few moments later. Standing by the bar, I sip on my drink, casually people watching. I love coming to the ballet. It's one of the art forms that I find the most helpful in getting me out of my head. In my most stressful times at my old job, coming to see the ballet once every month, thanks to my friend Mike, was one of the few times I could forget the ten million and one things on my mind and just immerse myself in the performance.

There's something magical about the music, the theatrics, the movement of graceful yet powerful bodies, that just gets me every time. And despite this ballet being set long ago in the 19th century, telling a quaint, old-fashioned tale about the betrayal of a poor peasant girl, there's an eternal truth to it about the human condition. Art, at its very best, does that. It transcends all barriers of time, language and race, and gets to the beating heart of who we are as humans. As you watch and experience emotions that you recognize, you realize you are not alone in this lonely world. You feel connected. That is what truly great art can do to you.

I came tonight, in a turmoil over what I need to do over the coming few days. And yet here I am now, calm and content, observing a parade of people chatter excitedly about the performance, exclaiming over how good the lead dancer was as Giselle and how much they enjoyed the first act. I feel a sense of connection with all these people who sat and experienced with me that marvellous piece of art. I can only compare it to that feeling you get in a rock concert when the band plays an anthem everyone sings along to, or a ballad that has all the gathered swaying to, holding up their communicators in lamp mode and creating a sea of lights. It's that great feeling of togetherness.

If I were asked to explain to an alien from outer space who we are as humans, then I would point to these great art forms. I would say, "Come and watch Ricky Charles perform 'One Day' in front of a live audience or come see a performance of Giselle, and then you will know what it is to be human."

Having witnessed Melinda's work over the years, I know most of the focus of diplomatic efforts is on trade, security and exchange of technology. Those are important things for us to focus on in our dialogue with different races, but if it were up to me, I would put the arts at the forefront of everything. What is the best way to build greater understanding with a new alien race? Let them experience our arts in all their varied forms. If, as I expect, they witness feelings and emotions that they recognize in themselves, then they will begin to feel a greater sense of connection with us as humans. We will no longer be aliens to them, but people with emotions just like them. And from that sense of connection, so many profitable new avenues could spring up.

As I stand here in a crowded bar during the intermission between each acts of the ballet, a prickle of excitement travels up my spine. A glimmer of an idea forms in my mind. Dwight had asked me a question.

Is there anything you could do out there on Krovatia that would bring you self-actualization?

I think I may well have an answer.

Chapter 19

Melinda

I can't sleep, thinking about the banquet and about him, the devil priest. What kind of fucked up person ties up a total stranger with his tail and force feeds her, all the while his wife is sitting nearby? I feel a sick jolt of disgust at myself for having gotten aroused by the whole thing. For still being aroused.

I reach a hand down and slide it through my wet, sticky folds. With a lubricated finger, I begin to stroke my clit, nudging the piercing and sending quivers through my body. I think of him biting my ear, his breath on my face, his overpoweringly masculine scent, his tail wrapped around my hands. I feel my core throb and rub the sensitized pierced hood frantically, aching for my release. With a cry, I come, my core pulsing repeatedly.

I let my hand fall away and catch my breath. I may have achieved physical relief, but I'm horrified to be getting off on memories of that bastard of a man. I close my eyes, and try to get some sleep.

I'm groggy the following morning as my alarm wakes me up just after sunrise. I stagger into the bathroom for a quick shower, then, knotting a robe around me, head over to the large eat-in kitchen and take out my precious supply of Colombian roast—I've brought enough coffee with me to last six months—and make myself my first cup of the day. This is one of my favorite spaces in the house. The work surfaces are made from a dark, beautifully crafted wood, giving a warm and inviting feel to the room. In the center, there's a large, rustic wooden table, thankfully at full height, so I don't have to crouch down on a floor cushion first thing in the morning. I realize the

Krovatians must have done their homework about our lifestyle and created a space which we would feel comfortable in.

I'm sipping the hot brew when Troy walks in, sporting yet another loin cloth, as if he was born and bred on this planet and not on Earth.

He sniffs the air. "That smells good. Enough for a second cup?"

I point to the coffee maker. "Help yourself."

He pours himself a cup and comes to sit opposite me. "Sleep well?" he asks.

"What do you think?"

He smirks. "I'm guessing you tossed and turned thinking about that gorgeous man's tail wrapped around you."

I laugh a little. "Something like that. It feels all kinds of wrong what he did last night."

Troy takes a sip of his coffee and sighs in pleasure. "That's good." Then he looks at me seriously and says, "You know Mel, if you wanted to explore this thing further with the hot priest, there's no reason not to. You're free and single. Go for it and enjoy yourself."

"No reason? What about the fact he's married and seems to be a cheater?"

Troy looks at me oddly. "No, he's not married."

"So, who was that woman with him, the mother of his son?"

"She's his drasha, not his wife."

"What's the difference?"

He laughs. "A pretty big one. A drasha is a form of concubine, Mel. He has several of them to, erm, service his needs."

"How do you know all this?"

"Kiristen is a fountain of knowledge."

"So he has a harem of women living with him to service his sexual needs?"

"Pretty much, yeah."

"And you think that makes him an attractive proposition for me?"

"I'm not suggesting you start a relationship, just have some fun. He seems like he knows how to give a girl a good time and he's packing a hell of a lot under that loin cloth."

"Yes, I saw. How about you? Thinking of having some fun with the son?"

He shakes his head. "Nah. He's gorgeous and sweet and lovely, but not the kind of guy for a fling. And he's young. Only twenty-two."

"He seems very enamored of you."

He scratches his salt and pepper stubble. Troy is something of a silver fox. "All the more reason to steer well clear."

Just then, Avery walks in, yawning loudly. "Morning all."

"Morning."

"You talking about the hot priest and the even hotter son?"

"What else?"

She comes to sit beside us. "And your verdict?"

"They're hot, but we're keeping our distance," I say.

She tuts. "Shame. I'd nail them both if I had the chance."

I hear a laugh behind me, and Treylor waltzes into the kitchen looking bright eyed.

"You are talking about the good looking sicortar and his son, are you not?"

I sigh. "Anyone else want to join this discussion?"

Pravol emerges through the door, raising his brows. "I take it you are all discussing the Krovatian priest and his handsome son."

"Naturally," I say with a laugh. On a serious note, I ask, "Did everyone notice us yesterday?"

Pravol comes to sit beside his mate and kisses the top of her head. "It was hard for anyone not to notice."

"Oh damn. What are people going to say about me?" I'm all too aware of the importance of my mission here. Please God I haven't messed things up on my first week on this planet.

Treylor places a reassuring hand on my arm. "Do not worry, Melinda. From what I heard, people are most impressed with you. The sicortar is not known for paying attention to females outside his household. They think you must be something special to have captured his interest."

I blush. "I didn't do anything. All I did was try to help myself to some food, but he wouldn't let me, and when I protested, he simply tied me up with his tail. I was spitting mad, I can tell you."

"Really? From what I saw, you were something the opposite of mad."

"Oh shit."

"Treylor is right. You do not need to worry," interjects Pravol. "Gaining the sicortar's attention has earned you considerable admiration among the Krovatians I spoke to last night."

"There you go," smiles Troy. "You've become a superstar already."

Treylor stands. "I am about to make some *joh*. Would anyone like some?"

Joh, I have discovered, is a hot Venorian beverage, similar to a chai latte.

"Ooh, yes please," clamor Troy and Avery together.

I stand. "No thanks, Treylor. I think I'll go get dressed. The hot young Krovatian will be with us in a quarter of an hour."

"What are you planning to wear to this water city?" Troy asks.

"My red bikini, if you really want to know."

"Both top and bottom?"

"Of course."

Troy grins. "Maybe go with the flow and leave the top behind."

I shake my head. "Not happening."

Treylor looks me up and down. "You have the body for it, Melinda. Firm little boobies, yes? Not like me needing all the support I can get to hold these big things up." She says this, pointing to her generous cleavage.

Beside her, Pravol grunts. "We have talked about this, Treylor. No showing of your breasts."

She tinkles a laugh. "Not me, no, but Melinda? I think yes. You too, Avery."

Avery surprises us all with, "Yes, I'm planning on only a bikini bottom at the pool today."

I raise my brows at this. "What happened to that talk about us representing Earth and not planning to go native?"

She has the grace to look shamefaced. "I was just being uptight. I'm not suggesting we do this all the time, but in a pool with everyone around us topless, I think we would stick out more with our tops on."

"We'll be objects of curiosity regardless. We can hardly be inconspicuous with our skin color and lack of a tail."

"I know, people will stare, but it will be one less way we look different."

"So, what do you say?" asks Troy.

"I don't know. I'll think about it. Better hurry all of you and get ready. We don't have long."

A few minutes later, a call comes through on my communicator from the security guard on patrol outside our compound, informing me that Kiristen has arrived. I ask the guard to let him inside, and we all make our way out the door, just as his drone, flying low, zooms to a stop outside our house.

Kiristen climbs out and rushes over to us with a smile. "Good morning," he says, placing a hand on Troy's chest in greeting. He steps back, bows, and greets the rest of us. "I hope you do not mind, but I have my younger brother and sister with me today. When they heard we were going to the water city, they begged to come, and I could not say no."

"Of course we don't mind," I say, peering at the window of the drone and catching sight of two young faces studying us curiously. We follow Kiristen onto the drone, which is large enough to accommodate about ten people. Once inside, I see a young girl, no more than four years old, and an older boy maybe twelve or thirteen years old. Their eyes goggle staring at us, the first aliens they have ever encountered.

"This is Kiritela," says Kiristen, pointing to his sister, "and beside her is Kirishar."

We smile at the children and say hello. As we settle into our seats, I ask Kiristen, "Why is it all your names begin with *Kiri*?"

"It is our family name. That is how we name people on Krovatia. First with the family name, then the given name. Our father is Kirimor."

Kirimor. All this time, I've thought of him as the sicortar, or the evil priest. Somehow, hearing his name makes him sound more human—well not human, but Krovatian. I'll rephrase. It makes him sound more like a normal being than some hallowed priest.

As these thoughts whizz through my mind, we're already on our way, flying to an adventure at the water city. Beside me, the two young children chatter animatedly, obviously excited.

"Kiristen," asks his sister plaintively, "will I be going on the tall waterway?"

Her brother regards her in concern. "It is very steep, Kiritela. Will you not be scared?"

"No! I can do it."

"Last time you screamed and cried. We had to ask to be fished out and it was very embarrassing," rebukes Kirishar.

"I promise I won't cry this time."

"What is this tall waterway?" asks Troy.

"We get pushed up high on log rafts, and once we get to the top, there is a long and steep descent down, lying on our backs in the water," answers Kiristen. "It is great fun, but a little too much excitement for very young children."

"I am not too young!" cries Kiritela.

He considers her for a moment. "It has been several moon rotations since we last went there, and I admit you are much grown since then. How about this? Once we are at the top, you lie on my belly, and I wrap you up in my tail?"

She nods vigorously. "Yes, please!"

"Very well."

As he says this, I feel the drone begin its descent. I look out the window and see before me an almost endless expanse of blue, dotted with the green of potted trees. It's like a massive oasis in the middle of a desert.

The drone touches the ground in a large drone park and Kiristen taps the engine off. He turns to us with a smile. "Ready?"

We all nod.

"Then let us go!"

We hop out and make our way towards the large entrance. We enter a whitewashed domed building, in the traditional Krovatian architectural style, and are greeted by a sales assistant standing at the counter. She looks at us curiously, but doesn't say anything except to ask how many entrance tickets we require. At this, Kiristen takes out his communicator to pay our entrance fees.

Troy stops him with a hand to his arm. "Kiristen, we can pay our way."

We brought a large supply of international credits with us, which we have changed to the local currency, so we are well able to pay. However, Kiristen refuses our offer. "No, you are my guests. Please, I insist." And he taps his communicator, completing the transaction.

The assistant ushers us through to a large foyer. She points towards a set of cabins up ahead. "You may remove shoes and clothing and place them in secure boxes over there. When you are ready, please walk into the sun spray room to get your protection. Ensure your eyes are firmly closed while the spray is in operation." She taps a map on her console to show us where we are. "This is the beginning of the water course. Follow the arrows to make your journey through the city. When you get to this sector here, you may pause your journey to get refreshments and use the facilities. Your entrance fee entitles you to an endless supply of free *nari* drinks and a choice of snacks to eat. Are you all confident swimmers?"

We nod. She looks at Kiritela. "And this young one?"

Kiritela pipes up indignantly. "Of course I can swim!"

The assistant smiles. "Well, then off you go and enjoy yourselves!"

We walk towards the cabins in question, and I quickly remove my beach dress, under which I'm wearing my bikini. My slim, waterproof communicator is tucked discreetly into a zipped pouch on the bottom part of my bikini. I place all my belongings into one of the boxes and lock it with my security code. When I head back out, I find everyone ready and waiting. Avery, as promised, is topless, baring pert white breasts which the young children are staring at curiously. Troy inspects me in my red bikini. "So, not going to let us see your gorgeous tits?"

I give him a look and shake my head.

Kiristen addresses me earnestly. "Melinda, may I say something? It would be an honor if you could trust me to be your companion and protector today. I will not let any harm come to you or allow any disrespectful behavior towards you. Please will you let us see just how beautiful you are under these coverings. Breasts are a natural and wonderful part of a female's body, and we admire their beauty greatly. Even though I am more partial to the male body, I enjoy and appreciate the sight of a fine female such as you." He places his hands on my shoulders, touching the halter neck ties of my top. "Please, will you let me remove this?"

I can't resist the earnest plea in his eyes. I guess I will stick out if I'm the only one covering my breasts. "Ok," I murmur.

He smiles sweetly, then carefully unties my top and lets it slip away. He takes a moment to study my bared breasts unabashedly. He looks back up at me. "It is as I thought. You are beautiful."

I glow at the praise. I've never been topless before, but there's no room for embarrassment or shame when all I can see is kind and honest appreciation of my naked form.

Troy wolf whistles. "He's right. These are magnificent tits you've been hiding. Even super gay me can appreciate the sight."

"Ok, so, moving on."

Troy winks. "Let's go!"

First, we enter the spray room, a large white cubicle with a red button on the wall which you press when you are ready. I shut my eyes and press it, feeling a warm spray of liquid all over my body. Within moments, the colorless liquid dries and adheres to the skin. Then, we're out the door and walking under a high arch, framed with tall palms whose dark green fronds cast a welcome shade in the heat of the day.

Before us is the start of the water course. It's a long, river-like pool that undulates and continues as far as the eye can see. This water city is massive, and it looks like we'll be going on quite a long journey in the water. Ahead of us, a small family of Krovatians are already jumping in with a splash and swimming away.

"As you can see," says Kiristen, "it is a very long water course which we shall be following. But do not worry. There are currents built into the water to assist us on our journey, so if your body tires of swimming, simply lie on your back and let the current drive you forward. There are invisible buffers on each side of the pool, so you do not run any risk of bumping your head. It is actually a very relaxing thing to lie back in the water and feel the current under you pushing you along."

He turns to his sister. "Kiritela, I am going to wrap my tail around your ankle the whole time. That way, I can make sure you do not get lost."

She's about to protest, but one look at her brother's set face changes her mind. "Yes, Kiristen," she replies docilely.

We approach the edge of the pool and Kirishar cries, "Let us all jump in together on the count of three. One, two, three!"

And we all jump in. The water is cool and fresh on my heated skin, making it come out in goosebumps. Looking around me, I see the pool is immaculately clean, with no hint of any debris or algae. Troy reads my thoughts and points to little filter vents that run all along the sides of the pool. "That looks like one heck of a filtration system. I'd love to take a look at the schematics."

Kiristen, paddling in the water beside him, answers, "I am sure we can arrange it, Troy. I will speak with the maintenance manager before we leave and ask if they can show us the schematics. If need be, I will use my authority as the sicortar's son to get them to agree."

Troy smiles, "Thanks, Kiristen, I can see you're gonna be a useful guy to have around."

I'm amused to see Kiristen blush a darker shade of gray at Troy's praise. Then, he points to the water ahead. "The initial part of the course, we shall be swimming, as there is no current until we reach that first curve over there. So, shall we go?"

"Let's go!" calls out Avery.

I see Kiristen carefully wrap his tail into a knot around his sister's ankle. The musculature in the tail must be flexible and strong enough to allow all these contortions. I think back to Kirimor's tail wrapped around my wrists last night. It felt strong and pliable, just like a rope, but the texture was incredibly soft. As I unthinkingly stroked it, I felt how smooth it was, with the tail ends covered in a mound of short, silky hair, almost like fur.

What things that tail could do to me in bed. I shake the thought away. I am not going to think about that man now. I plunge into the water and start to swim.

As Kiristen said, the current starts when we reach the first curve up ahead. All of a sudden, I feel a light whoosh under me, and before I know it, I'm hurtling along the river pool at great speed, not really needing to do much in the way of swimming to propel myself forward. I hear both children shriek in delight. And we're off, chasing down the water way.

My mind empties of everything except the joy of being out under a blue, sunny sky and feeling cool water lap at my body, the motion under me hypnotic and exciting all at once. It's not just the children shrieking. The adults, including me, are screeching out "oohs" and "ahs", and I even hear Troy in the din shouting, "Oh fuck yeah!"

Kiristen calls out to him, "Troy, watch your language! There are young ears with us."

I hear an "Oops!" from my colleague among the giggles of said children.

We continue along the river course for a good few minutes until I see a sheer drop ahead. I hear Kiristen shout with glee, "Get ready for the jump, hold your breath!" I see him yank Kiritela back with his tail and put his arms around her. Then we've reached the precipice, and I don't have time to swim away or avoid it. Suddenly, I'm in the air, falling down, and this time, I scream, in excitement but mostly fear. Oh God, oh God. Time slows as I fall to what feels like my certain death. My feet dangle uselessly in the air as I wave them about, trying to somehow break my fall.

And then I drop into the water with a mighty splash, going deep under the surface until I feel a great wave of energy propel me back up to break the surface and breathe again. I take great big gulps of air as I bob harmlessly in the gentle pool we've landed in. Adrenaline shoots through my body. In every pore of my skin, I feel the zing of blood rushing through me. Wow! That was terrifying, but amazing too.

Kiristen swims towards me, concern on his face. "Melinda, are you alright?" He pulls me to him and holds me tight against his large, warm body, stroking my back gently. "I am sorry if it gave you a fright. I thought you would enjoy the thrill of it."

He sounds so contrite. I pull myself together, taking a deep breathe to center myself, and say, "It was a thrill, and I'm glad now I did it, but I just need a moment or two to recover from the fright. I'm fine."

He holds me a few moment longer, crooning soft words of reassurance, until he feels me regain my balance. As he pulls away, he asks again worriedly, "Are you sure you are alright?"

I smile. "I'm fine."

Over his shoulder, I can see Troy holding Avery in a similar embrace, while the two children splash about happily, evidently unaffected by the massive plunge we just took. Maybe the older you get, the more fearful you become.

"You will be happy to know that the next part of the course is very gentle, with little or no currents. We will be winding our way through those narrow passages and having to complete a challenge to get past each hurdle. I think you will all enjoy this," Kiristen says, a tad uncertainly.

"I'm sure we will," I say, infusing confidence in my voice.

And enjoy it we do. There's plenty of fun and games as we wind through the spaghetti network of narrow water lanes and negotiate each of the challenges, some more silly than others. In one, we have to throw a ball through three sets of hoops. In another, we have to screech loud enough to activate the opening of the gate. In yet another, we have to answer a riddle—which clever little Kirishar promptly solves for us.

Eventually, we reach another wide pool where we see log rafts awaiting us. "These rafts will take us up to the top of that tall waterway." Kiristen points to a steep rock face, over which a water lane with a sliding mechanism for the rafts has been built. "We can ride two to a raft. I will take the first one with Kiritela. Kirishar, perhaps you can ride with Melinda, and the last one can be for Troy and Avery."

We all climb aboard the rafts, which rock slightly with our weight but remain stable. Once we strap the safety buckle on, the rafts begin to move, slowly making their way up the steep slope. I find myself practically horizontal on the cliff face and feel a tightening of fear in my gut. What if I fall off? Reason tells me that the safety buckle will hold me in place, but every instinct shouts danger as I'm tilted at a precarious angle. Is this fear how Wyatt feels whenever he tries to board a drone? Too late, I'm beginning to have a better sense of what he must have gone through.

Suddenly, a warm tail wraps itself securely around me. Kirishar speaks from behind me, "You are quite safe, Melinda. The buckle is very sturdy, and I have you tight in my hold." My fear ebbs away under the comforting hold Kirishar has on me. Fancy that. A twelve-year old boy comforting a forty-something woman. I turn my head to him briefly. "Thanks, Kirishar. That really helps. Keep on holding me, please."

"Of course. Do not worry."

I take deep breaths to calm myself as we climb higher and higher, our raft nearly vertical on the cliff face. Kirishar's tail tightens reassuringly around me as I grip the handle bar in front of me. What a difference it makes to have that warm comforting embrace. It doesn't eliminate the fear altogether but makes it bearable. Did I ever do this for Wyatt? Just hold him with empathy and comfort him through the fear? I'm filled with shame. I let my husband down badly in my barely hidden impatience at his inability to fly.

Finally, after what seems like hours, we make it to the top, a wide plateau of shallow water. I can see the endlessly long, curving water slides up ahead. A part of me wonders if I can ask Kirishar to ride piggy back with me like Kiristen is going to do with his sister. No, this part of the course I can do on my own. I just need a moment to regroup.

Troy comes over and puts an arm around me. "You ok?"

"Yeah. Just give me a minute."

"Sure. Take all the time you need."

And he holds me close while I breathe in and out, feeling like dirt for never having thought to do the same thing for the man I pledged my life to all those years ago. I'm drowning in shame. Why? Why did I never do those small, simple things that mean so much? Just hold him through it all and tell him it would be alright. Was it because I've been conditioned to see men as macho beings, as protectors who didn't need comforting or care? Every time Wyatt had a fit of nauseous fright at the prospect of flying, I felt disappointment in him for not being the strong, male protector I wanted as a partner. I hid that disappointment, but perhaps he sensed it. What a rubbish wife I was to him.

Tears prickle in my eyes, but I hold them at bay. This is not the time or place to have a crying fit. A few more breaths and I finally feel able to step back and smile at the concerned faces beside me. "I'm alright now, thanks you all."

"Do you feel ready to continue?" asks Kiristen. "If not, I can call for a drone to take you forward to the rest stop. It is located at the bottom of the tall waterway."

"No, please don't. I'm fine now. Let's go."

Troy goes first, lying flat on his back with his arms crossed on his chest, pushing off with a whoop of delight. Avery goes next, then Kirishar. His older brother looks across at me. "Are you ready to go now, Melinda?"

I nod and get into position, then with a deep breath in, push off. With the water churning around me, I fly down the slope, shrieking in happy surprise. This is fun, exciting and not a bit frightening. On and on I whoosh down the slide until I drop into the pool with a loud splash. I stand and shake the water out of my eyes, looking for my companions. I find them a little further ahead, waving to catch my attention. I wave back and swim towards them. A moment later, we're joined by Kiristen and an excitable Kiritela, chattering on about how much she loved the slide.

We make our way out of the pool and dry ourselves with fresh towels, handed to us by an attendant. Kiristen locates an empty table in the shade of a large palm frond and quickly guides us towards it. He taps on the computer console a few times to order our drinks and snacks, and we take the opportunity to sit back and relax after our adventurous journey through the waterway.

It's then I become conscious once again of the fact that I am topless. I'd forgotten about my state of undress during the excitement and thrills in the water, but now, feeling the curious stares of the Krovatians sitting around us, I begin to feel self-conscious. I cross my arms in front of my chest, then recognize the futility of that gesture and bring them down again.

Kiristen observes this and angles his large body in front of mine to shield me from the view of prying eyes. He smiles kindly. "Do not mind them, Melinda. They, like me, are full of admiration for your beauty." His eyes travel to my exposed breasts. "The coolness of the water has made your teats pucker up beautifully. And their dark color is in sharp contrast with the pale gold of your skin. It is no wonder others are staring. They cannot help admiring you."

I look down at myself and find that my nipples are indeed distended and hard, jutting out darkly against the creamy, pale skin of my breasts that have never before been exposed to the sun. I feel myself blush at the praise and the unashamed attention on my naked body. Such frankness is not something I'm used to.

"Thanks," I mumble.

Troy grins at me. "I second every word he said, gorgeous lady. You have nothing to feel embarrassed about. Flaunt it, girl!" He nods his head towards Avery, who is sitting entirely at ease. "It's not every day that I say this, but be more like Avery. Look at her, easy in her skin and proud of her body. You should be too."

I've never thought of myself as particularly beautiful, and my small breasts, though well-formed and pert, have not inspired much attention, except from Wyatt. It's a novel sensation to be the object of such unabashed admiration.

I'm distracted by Kiritela, who jumps into my lap and wraps her arms about me. "You are very pretty," she says.

I smile and hug her warm little body. "And so are you."

"I am hungry," she responds.

"Food will be here soon," Kiristen reassures her.

He sits close to Troy, and I see his tail flapping from side to side, stroking Troy's thigh. My colleague doesn't seem to mind in the least. Hmm, I wonder how long Troy is going to resist Kiristen's advances. I give it a week.

Our food and drinks arrive, and we attack it ravenously, the long swim having stoked our appetites.

As we are finishing up the last few bites, Kiristen says, "The rest of the course is pleasantly fun, but there will be no more heart-pounding thrills."

Thank God.

"First, we follow another river way, and this time, I suggest we all let the current take us forward while we relax on our backs and let our bodies digest the food we have eaten. After, that, we will arrive at the large wave pool—Kiritela's favorite, I think."

She yelps in delight, still tucked comfortably in my lap. I stroke the soft black strands of her hair that have escaped her braid. She refused to sit anywhere else but on my lap all through our meal, but I didn't mind. She's already charmed all of us with her endearing chatter.

"And then," continues Kiristen, "once we leave the wave pool, we come to the last part of the water city. It is where we play a game of bong."

"Bong?" asks Troy.

"Yes. It is great fun. We will split into two teams and play against each other. The object of the game is to catch the bong and throw it into the pit as many times as possible. One team defends the pit and the other tries to get the bong in. If the defending team stop the bong before it enters the pit, they get a point. If the attacking team gets the bong in the pit, then they are the ones to get a point. There are several bouncing platforms of different heights where we can position ourselves to jump up and catch or throw the bong."

He sees my confusion and smiles. "Do not worry, the rules will become clear when we begin to play." He stands. "Come, let us use the facilities and then be on our way."

The rest of our journey along the water course goes as described by Kiristen. Everyone, even the adults, have fun bobbing up and down in the large wave pool. Now, we come to the game of bong.

The pit is a round piece of netting on the surface of the pool, behind which are three platforms of varying heights, which we access by climbing up a rope-like ladder. I've been put in the defending team, along with Kirishar and Avery. I climb up to the top platform and as I go to stand on it, I realize that it's some kind of trampoline. Over the other side of the water pitch, Troy, Kiristen and Kiritela are bouncing on their own trampoline platforms.

An attendant releases the bong, a mid-size orange ball, into the air. It zooms about, as if it has a mind of its own. I see it approach Kiristen, and he jumps up high to bat it in the direction of the pit. If I don't do something, his team will score a point. I watch it closely as it approaches the pit, which is right below me, and with a mighty bounce on the trampoline, I reach out to bat it back towards the other team. Unfortunately, I lose my balance and topple into the water, to the sound of chortles from Kiristen's team. I resurface and hear Kirishar call out, "Good work, Melinda. You won us a point. Quick, get back to your platform!"

I splash my way back to the ladder and climb it as quickly as I can to get back into the game. Twenty minutes later, it ends — a victory for the opposing team, but we acquitted ourselves well, losing only by a margin of two points. I notice we've attracted quite an audience, as the bong pitch is set close to a lounging area for Krovatians to relax in once they've finished the course. As I climb out of the pool, ready for some R & R myself, I'm accosted by two male Krovatians. One of them smiles and says, "Well done, Human female! You did well in the game. Would you like to share a drink of *nari* with us?"

Before I have a chance to respond, a tail wraps itself around my waist and I'm dragged back against a hard male chest. Kiristen's arms drape protectively around me as he speaks in a clipped voice, "She is with me."

The two Krovatians take a step back. "Our apologies. We meant no offense," says the one who spoke to me earlier. They walk away hastily as Kiristen holds me tightly to him.

I hear Troy sigh dramatically, "Oh my, that was sexy! So domineering."

Kiristen releases me and faces Troy. "You think?"

Troy fans himself. "Oh yeah, babe, that was hot." Kiristen visibly preens under his gaze.

Ok, I give it less than a week.

"Thanks for coming to the rescue, Kiristen," I say. "That was very chivalrous of you."

"I promised I would protect you, Melinda, and I am a person of my word."

"That you are," says Avery. "That thing you did with your tail. Very hot!"

"Tails are very useful things. I am sorry that you do not have one."

I laugh. "Me too, Kiristen. I can see they come in very handy."

Just as I say these words, Kiritela's tail wraps itself around my legs. She leans in to me and yawns, "I am tired."

I stroke the top of her head. "Me too. I think it's time to go home."

"Come here, little one," says Kiristen, lifting his sister up on his shoulders. "Let us get our things and go."

A short while later, we're all trooping into the drone. Kiritela immediately settles herself in my lap, and less than a minute later, she's fast asleep. I hold her all the way home, then release her gently into her brother's arms. She doesn't wake as I press a light kiss to her brow.

In a hushed voice, I say, "Thanks, Kiristen, for a wonderful day out. I had a great time."

He smiles. "I am so glad."

I reach over and kiss his cheek, then climb out of the drone with Avery, leaving Troy behind to say his goodbyes in private.

Back in my room, I take a quick shower and pull on my sleepwear. I'm exhausted, but there's one more thing I need to do before I go to bed.

"Athena, record video message to Wyatt. Begin."

I position the screen and start to speak. "Wyatt, I owe you an apology. I've realized what a poor excuse for a wife I was to you. We went somewhere today and I felt real fear. It was dizzying, nausea inducing. And then someone, a young

Krovatian boy of only twelve years, wrapped his tail around me and told me I would be alright. That gesture of comfort meant so much, and I'm not sure I've ever really done that for you when you've been frightened of getting on a drone. Just held you and said it will be alright. And for that, I'm so sorry, honey. So sorry. I hope life is treating you well. I love you. Always... Athena, end message and send."

I slip under the covers and close my eyes. In no time, I fall into a deep sleep.

Chapter 20

Wyatt

Dwight C. Josephs sits across from me at his desk, his hands steepled together, regarding me quizzically. "I sense a change in you, Wyatt. Tell me, have you considered the question I asked you on your last visit?"

"I have." I beam at him.

His eyes twinkle in amusement. "So tell me, Wyatt, is there anything you could do out there on Krovatia that would bring you self-actualization?"

"I went to the ballet last night—a performance of Giselle. Have you seen it before?"

He nods. "I have, many years ago."

"Well, if you recall the story, it's all about love, betrayal, forgiveness and redemption."

He smiles. "The great themes of the human condition."

I point a finger at him. "That's right! And you know, that got me thinking. What would be the best way to foster greater understanding between ourselves and alien races?"

"The arts?"

"Bingo."

He regards me with interest. "And you have an idea for some kind of cultural exchange via the arts."

"Not only an idea, but a plan. I've even come up with a name and a brand—The Interstellar Arts Company. The company will stage a variety of different shows each year, showcasing the range of human arts, including ballet, opera, theater, music of all genres, movies, and visual arts."

"That's ambitious, Wyatt. How do you propose to do that?"

"I've sent an application to the Krovatian authorities through a personal contact I have over there, explaining my plan. I've also communicated with Martha Reynolds, who mated with the Venorian crown prince. She'll be arriving on Earth in three days' time on a Venorian cargo ship. I told her my idea, and she loves it. Through her mind connection with her mate, she's already obtained the go-ahead for me to travel to Ven with a troupe of performers. And transport will hopefully not be an issue either, as I'm soon to meet the commander of the Venorian cargo ship to negotiate terms."

Dwight raises his brows. "I'm impressed. But how will you put a show together?"

I grin. "I had dinner with my good friend Mike last night, who also happens to be the artistic director of the Washington Ballet. They're on a recess break after tonight's performance, and the dancers won't be needed back for rehearsals until October, when they begin preparing for their winter program. In the meantime, the dancers are free to do whatever they want, as long as they do not injure themselves doing it. I had brunch this morning with a group of principal dancers and soloists who are keen to be the first people from Earth to perform a ballet off planet. We're in the process of coming up with a program of ballets they could perform and recruiting the musicians we'll need to take with us. I'm also in talks with the Royal Shakespeare Company in the UK about the possibility of taking the current plays they are performing on tour with us. Oh, and I've made overtures to Ricky Charles's management about him doing some shows with us too. I read somewhere about his interest in travelling to other planets. I'm hoping he'll say yes. So basically, I'm working round the clock to get my program together and my artists signed up."

"Are you sure you haven't bitten off more than you can chew?"

I smile. "Putting together deals is what I do best, Dwight. I have no doubt I can do this."

He regards me solemnly. "There is still the other matter. To do this, you will have to fly."

I take a deep breath. "Yes, I know. And I'm determined to do it, but I'll need your help."

He nods. "I will do my best, Wyatt, but the rest is up to you. There is also something else you may not have considered."

I eye him curiously. "What else?"

"When you finally arrive in Krovatia, there is no guarantee that your ex-wife will still be single and willing to get back together with you."

"Ah."

I don't respond straight away, thinking through the ramifications. If I go all out with this, overcoming my fears and turning my life inside out, only to discover that Melinda has moved on, how will I feel? Not good, that's for sure. "I'll fight to win her back. She's too important to slip through my fingers."

"Wyatt, she is her own person and has the right to make decisions for herself. She may decide not to take you back. You need to be prepared for that."

"I hear what you say, Dwight, but we have a long history, and we love each other. Before she left, she asked me to go with her. There is every chance that I will win her back."

"And what if you don't?"

I sigh. "Then that will suck big time."

"Enough to make you regret having gone there?"

I think about this for a minute. "No, whatever happens, I have to give this a try. I'm doing this for me just as much as for her."

Dwight gives me a warm smile. "I'm glad to hear it."

"So, let's get started on this fear of flying thing. What do we do?"

"We? No, Wyatt, it's not me that has to do anything. It's you."

"So, what should I do."

He taps his fingers on the scuffed top of his desk. "It's very simple really. Take your communicator out and book a drone to take you back home. Then, when it arrives, you get in and let it fly you to your destination."

"Simple as that?"

"Simple as that."

"Will you come with me?"

"If you want."

"I want."

"Then I shall come aboard with you. However, you will need eventually to make such journeys independently."

"I will. One step at a time."

"Indeed."

"So, what kind of preparation should I do before I get on the drone."

He takes a sip of water from his bottle then puts it down. "Is there anything you think you should be doing?"

I look at him accusingly. "Dwight, I pay you to advise and guide me. You tell me."

He quirks his lips at that. "Very well, Wyatt, if you are looking for my advice, then here it is. You are well aware that drones are now one of the safest ways to travel—safer even than driving, if you read the statistics."

"I know."

"All you need to fly on a drone are the motor skills to step into it and out."

"I know that."

"So, there is nothing else left for you to do except decide. Will you go ahead with this, regardless of how terrified you feel?"

"Failure is not an option. I will."

He smiles. "Then there is little else you need do as preparation."

"No mantras I could be reciting?"

"Nah. Unless it's to repeat to yourself, 'I am doing this, I am doing this'"

"Shit or get off the pot," I whisper, almost to myself.

"What's that, Wyatt?"

I huff out a laugh. "Just something my brother said to me not long ago. 'Shit or get off the pot.'"

Dwight chuckles, genuinely entertained. "Not the language I would choose to use, but very apt none the less."

He looks at my communicator. "Ok, so let's do it."

"Now?" I ask.

"Why not now?"

"Isn't it a bit soon?"

"Wyatt, what was it your brother told you?"

"Shit or get off the pot."

"So, do it. Or give up and go home."

I pick up my communicator and laugh nervously. "I don't even have a drone app on here."

"It takes a few seconds to download one."

"Right."

I tap my screen and set up an app, then book a drone to pick us up in five minutes. I look up at Dwight. "It will be here in five minutes."

He smiles. "Perfect. Just enough time for me to get myself ready." He stands and walks out of his office, down the vestibule to a rack of coats by the door. He slips his feet into shoes and pulls on a light jacket. Opening the front door, he gestures to me. "Let's go."

We step outside just as the drone arrives, landing in a parking bay before us. My hands become clammy. My insides churn. "I think I'm going to be sick," I groan.

"That's alright, I have a bag right here," Dwight says briskly. He produces a paper bag from his pocket and hands it to me with a smile. "Any time you need to heave, feel free to do so."

It's not quite the response I expected, but I take the bag from him anyway, taking deep breaths in and out to try to quell the nausea.

"Shall we?" Dwight asks, pointing at the drone.

I nod and follow him to the vehicle. He opens the door and waits, clearly expecting me to get in first. Sweat rolls off my forehead and the sick feeling gets worse. I hold the bag to my mouth and retch. Deep breath in. Deep breath out. *I am doing this. I am doing this.*

I look at Dwight, who waits for me with a patient, friendly smile. "You know you can do this, Wyatt."

I nod. "Ok." I take another deep breath, and still clutching the bag to my lips, take a first step aboard the drone. *I am doing this.* Another deep breath, then I lift the other leg and climb inside the drone. I locate a seat and collapse onto it, breaths heaving. I retch into the bag again. Distantly, I'm aware of Dwight getting in beside me and shutting the door.

"Seat belt, Wyatt."

With shaky hands, I put the bag down and reach over for the safety belt, clipping it on.

"You're doing great, Wyatt."

I can't speak, clutching the paper bag in my hand and holding it to my face. Deep breath in. Deep breath out. I feel the engine rumble and then we're lifting off the ground. My heart sinks to the pit of my stomach. "Oh my God, oh my God," I mumble.

I feel a whoosh as we gain altitude and begin moving forwards. "Oh God."

"You're doing just fine, Wyatt."

I manage to look up into Dwight's kind brown eyes. I breathe, "I'm ok."

He smiles. "Yes, you are."

Throughout the ten minute journey to my house, he engages me in calm, soothing conversation. After a while, I'm able to respond in monosyllables. The nausea never quite goes away, but the paper bag is close to hand any time I feel the need to retch.

Then, it's time for our descent. As we lose altitude, I bury my face in the paper bag again, breathing in and out in shallow breaths. When we finally land with a light bump, I startle and shout, "Oh God!"

Dwight pats me gently on the arm. "That's it, Wyatt. Journey's over. You did it."

I did it.

"Thanks," I croak.

He opens the door and steps out. In a daze, I follow him out into the fresh air, taking deep gulps of it in. As soon as we shut the drone door, it flies off, ready to collect its next passenger. Dwight stands beside me with a grin. "Aren't you going to invite me in for a drink? I could do with a shot of something strong right now. How about you?"

I smile weakly. "That sounds like a good plan."

I walk up the steps to my townhouse and unlock the door, inviting Dwight in. He follows me to the kitchen where I reach up to take out a bottle of tequila. I hold it out to him. "How about this?"

"Perfect."

I pour out two shot glasses and we clink them together. "Here's to the beginning of my space voyages," I say, my voice still shaky.

"Happy voyages, Wyatt. I believe you're going to make a success of this venture, regardless of what happens between you and your ex-wife."

I down the shot, feeling the warmth of the alcohol seep all the way down to my toes. Setting the glass back down, I look at him resolutely. "I'll get her back, Dwight. Just you wait and see." *That's a promise.*

Chapter 21

Kirimor

I come awake to the familiar weight of Kiritela sleeping atop me. Leisurely, I stretch my tail and entangle it with hers, stroking her velvety tip with mine.

"Hmm," she murmurs sleepily.

"Blessed morning, my sweet little star."

"Blessed morning, pa."

Gently, I nudge her off me and bring her to lie against my side. "It is time to wake, little star, and get ready for school."

She snuggles against me. "It is so nice and warm here. I like it."

I rumble a laugh. "And I too, but it is time to wake nevertheless."

She yawns. "Pa, when will we see Melinda again?"

The children came back from their outing to the water city with the Earth female full of excited chatter about beautiful Melinda, how kind she was, the good game she played at bong, her fear when climbing the tall waterway and how Kirishar bravely comforted her, and of course, the fact that my clever son Kiristen managed to convince her to bare her lovely pale breasts. I am very keen to cast my eyes—and also my mouth—on these beautiful breasts. Ever since their expedition a quarter moon rotation ago, the question of when we shall see Melinda again has been a constant refrain on my daughter's lips. Little does she realize that I secretly ask myself that very same thing.

"We shall see," I answer diplomatically.

"If we invite her here, I can show her how to search for plo shells," she says plaintively.

"Perhaps. But now, it is well past time to get yourself ready. Off you go, little one, and I shall see you shortly for the breakfast repast."

With one final nudge of encouragement, she finally rises and goes to her mother's quarters to get herself ready for the day. I make my own morning ablutions, slip on a fresh loin cloth and shirt, then go down to the large dining room where my family gathers to eat the morning repast. My two sons, Kirishar and Kirilor, are already sitting with their mothers. Beside them sits my newest drasha, Pirofena. I go to each of them in turn to greet them with my customary morning kiss. As I take my seat, Merostena bustles in, carrying a basket of freshly baked *lam*, a savory bread that it is our custom to eat in the mornings. She places it on the table next to me, then wraps a loving arm around me. "Blessed morning, Kirimor," she says, giving me a sweet kiss on the lips.

"Blessed morning, my dear," I respond.

She sits herself to my right, as is her custom, and we begin to eat. A short time later, Kirimara walks in, her youngest sister in tow. She slides into the seat to my left and kisses my cheek while Kiritela scampers into my lap. "Blessed morning, pa," she murmurs.

"Blessed morning, sweet Mara. Have you seen Kiristen?"

She chuckles. "He has yet again spent the night with his new love, the Human."

Merostena clucks beside me, "Here we go again. How long will this one last I wonder?"

"His average is two and a half moon rotations," pipes up Kirilor helpfully.

"Given the state of his infatuation this time around, I would say it will be at least three moon rotations, if not more," states Jalimara, his mother.

"Or even longer," remarks Cleotola, walking into the room and coming to give me a kiss. "This Troy could be the forever one."

I look at her in dismay. "These Humans are only on our planet for a short time. It is unrealistic to talk about them in terms of forever."

Kirimara leans her head on my shoulder. "I know you worry pa, but I think if indeed Troy does turn out to be the one, as Kiristen claims, then they will find a way to stay together."

"I do not want to see him made unhappy."

"Neither do I, pa." She perks up suddenly. "On the subject of Humans, did I tell you that this Melinda that Kiritela keeps asking about will be coming to my university today to give a lecture?"

My ears prick up at this. "No, I had not been aware. When is she due to give her talk?"

"At nine beats before midday." She studies my face curiously. "Do you plan to come along too?"

"Possibly," I prevaricate. *Most probably*.

"Then I shall save a seat for you," smiles my insightful daughter.

I smile back. "Very well."

I spend the morning in the temple, going into a holy trance to scan the twelve individuals who had access to the cargo ship on which we suspect the boral crystals were smuggled. I have Pirofena and Cleotola with me, in case there is a need to aspirate any negative energy. In the event, they are not needed. My scans do not uncover anything untoward. On the contrary, I see good, positive energy in all the individuals—one of them indeed going as far as having a perfect bright aura with not a single spurt of negative energy. I send a communication to Denishar, informing him of the inconclusive results of my scans, then I glance at the time dial on my communicator. Ten beats to midday.

Hurriedly, I bid my drashas goodbye and go to my drone, programming it to fly to the university. A beat later, I walk into the large auditorium just as Melinda is beginning her lecture. She pauses at the disturbance, casting a glance up at me. I stand, hands on hips, capturing her gaze with mine. I see that tell-tale flush appear on her cheeks again. My chest rumbles in pleasure. Oh what a delightful female! Then I let my eyes travel across the audience to land upon my daughter's amused face. Slowly, as if I have all the time in the world, I strut towards her, lowering myself to the seat she has reserved for me. All this time, Melinda is silent, instinctively knowing that she must wait for the sicortar to sit before continuing with her speech. Once I am comfortably settled, I nod to her in signal that she may resume her lecture. In a slightly hesitant voice, she begins again.

I listen intently to her lecture, keen to learn all I can about her world. She pauses every now and then to take questions from the audience. I am displeased to see a number of students challenge her with questions that border on the rude, disparaging Earth for its lack of technology and wondering what possible benefits there could be for Krovatians to foster greater cooperation with Humans. I am tempted to step in and give these insolent pups a piece of my mind, but Melinda calmly diffuses their antagonism, responding with wit and charm to every question. I see her win them over bit by bit.

Towards the end of her lecture, she plays us video footage of the different types of cuisines on her world. People from different countries address us, showing us how they cook their most famous national dish. The last one is a blond haired man with startling blue eyes, who smiles at us and says, "Hi there, I'm Wyatt Garcia, and in case you're wondering, I'm Melinda's other half. Hi there, honey!" He waves at the screen and blows her a kiss. My hands clench at my side. This must be her mate. Her mate! Then on the back of that thought is another. Why is he not with her? My tail snaps forward into my lap, flicking back and forth in my agitation. Kirimara takes hold of it and strokes it soothingly.

On the screen, the male continues speaking. "I'm going to show you how to make a famous American dish called burgers…"

I watch as he forms a meat patty and cooks it on an open fire. While the meat is cooking, he jokes and chatters showing us how he splits a bread bun in two and garnishes it with some sauce and sliced vegetables, before sliding the cooked meat patty into it. He holds it up with a smile, "And here you have it. A burger." He takes a bite out of it and chews ecstatically. "Hmm, absolutely delicious." Then he puts it down and speaks to us again. "So, my Krovatian friends. I have a challenge for you. Send us your videos showing how you cook your favorite dish, and we will try to emulate them over here on Earth. We'll send you a recording of our efforts. Let's see how well we do. Looking forward to receiving all your entries. Take care and go in peace."

The moment the video ends, Melinda is bombarded with endless questions and comments about this male. "Your mate is very good looking!" "How handsome your mate is!" "What amazing eyes your mate has!" "Will your mate be joining you here on Krovatia?" "Does your mate have a brother handsome like him?"

Melinda holds her hand up for everyone to stop. "Yes, I agree, Wyatt is very handsome. However, we are no longer married, or in your terms, we are no longer mated. He is just a very good friend of mine now, that is all." I let out a hiss. They are no longer mated. *Good.*

As more questions are pelted in her direction, she holds her hand up again. "I am happy to answer questions about my planet, but please, no more about me or Wyatt." It takes a few more beats of questions before Melinda signals that her lecture is over. At this, I stand and walk over to her, placing a possessive hand on her shoulder. Energy pulses through her body at my touch. I address the crowd. "Thank you all for attending today's lecture. I have learned so much about Earth as I am sure have you. Please show your appreciation of Melinda on the count of three. One. Two. Three."

At three, the audience begins to hum together, a Krovatian way to express gratitude and appreciation. The louder the hum, the greater the appreciation. Melinda listens to our humming, a pleased but puzzled expression on her face. When the humming comes to an end, she places a hand to her heart and says, "Thank you all. It has been an honor and a privilege to speak with you today. Go in peace."

Everyone in the audience chants back, "Go in peace."

I stand beside her, my hand planted firmly on her shoulder as slowly, people begin to filter out of the auditorium. She remains still, feet rooted to the ground, her face beautifully flushed. A few hardy young students approach, as if to ask her further questions, but one look at my glaring face has them back away. My daughter comes to us just as the final few spectators make their way out.

"Melinda," I say, "this is my daughter, Kirimara."

"Oh, nice to meet you, Kirimara."

My daughter steps towards her, placing a hand on her chest in the traditional greeting and then bowing. "The honor is mine, Melinda. May I say how much I enjoyed your lecture. As pa said, we have learned much about your planet. It makes me hungry for more knowledge."

Melinda smiles. "Thank you, Kirimara, I'm so glad you found my talk informative. I hope in time, the people on our two planets will become much better acquainted."

"I hope so too. For too long we have remained closed off from others. I understand the reasons for this, but I agree with pa when he says it is time to open up communications with other friendly races."

Up until now, Melinda has been studiously avoiding my stare, but at this, she glances up at me. "Was it your idea to open up Krovatia to foreign delegations?"

I incline my head. "I may have had something to do with it."

"Then I thank you, sicortar."

"You may thank me, Melinda, by taking a ride with me."

She looks at me sceptically. "Where to?"

"You are here to learn about our ways, are you not?"

"Yes."

"Then I shall take you to a *drelan*."

"A *drelan*? What is that?"

My daughter interjects laughingly. "It is a place we go to when we wish to ease our bodies and minds. I am sure you will like it greatly. I only wish I could go with you."

"Mara, you are welcome to join us."

My daughter's tail swishes towards mine in affection. "Thank you, pa, but I believe you will enjoy this better without a third person with you, and also, I have work to do."

"I am always happy to have your company, dear daughter, but if you have work, then it must be done."

She smiles. "Let me be on my way. Go in peace, Melinda, pa."

"Go in peace," we both murmur.

I turn to Melinda, my tail looping around her waist. "Come with me."

She glances down at it. "Sicortar, I am happy to accept your invitation, but I must make it clear that I come with you only in an official capacity, to learn about Krovatian culture."

"Then come."

Again, she glances down at my tail wrapped around her waist. "So there is no need for this, whatever you think you're doing."

"Melinda, do not argue. Come with me."

She looks as if she is about to do just that, then decides against it and begins to walk alongside me. When we reach the auditorium door, I see a young Krovatian male lounging there in wait for us. He stands to attention as we approach. I give him my sicortar stare, expecting him to move away, but he stands his ground.

"Who, pray, are you?" I snap.

"Sicortar, I am Desimar, Melinda Garcia's official escort."

"You are relieved of such duty today, Desimar. Melinda will be spending time with me, and then I shall ensure her safe return home."

"But sir, I have been told—"

"I believe I have made myself clear."

"Yes sir."

I do not wait for any further response, walking Melinda out of the building in brisk strides until we reach my drone. She looks at it curiously as she climbs aboard. "This is an unusual design for a drone."

"It is my unique design. It is completely solar powered, but powerful enough to reach high speeds. And what is more, it is wonderfully cool inside," I say, flicking a switch to start the engine. Immediately, a cooling breeze blows in through the vents.

"You have a cooling system! This is the first air conditioning I've seen in my whole time on this planet. Is it allowed?"

I snort. "Nobody is going to question the sicortar. It is one of the few cooling systems on this planet, but let me assure you the technology is completely clean and has no negative impact on our environment."

"That is impressive. I'm sure there would be a lot of interest on Earth in such technology."

"This technology is for my sole use currently."

"That's a shame. Why so?"

I decide to be open with her. "A sicortar is not expected to meddle with such non-spiritual things. Perhaps one day, when I am retired from my official duties, I may pursue my other interests more openly."

"I see."

By now, we are up in the air and zipping through the sky towards a location on the outskirts of the city. Presently, she asks, "So, this *drelan*. What exactly is it?"

"As Mara said, it is place we go to ease our bodies and minds. It is set in a cave with hot therapeutic mud that we bathe in. I promise you will enjoy it."

"It sounds similar to mud spas we have on Earth."

"Yet more things we have in common. I do believe our peoples are going to grow closer in time as we realize that there are more things that unite us than divide us."

"I hope so. Such a belief is at the heart of the work I do."

"Then I believe your work will be successful, Melinda."

Her brown eyes fix on me. "I'm curious about the work that you do. What exactly is the job of a sicortar, if I may ask?"

"You may ask, Melinda. There are many aspects to the position, but fundamentally, I am responsible for the spiritual wellbeing of the planet. For our people to flourish, we must banish the evil energies that wreak harm and pain around us. Through the power I exert in a holy trance, I can search for that evil, extract it from people's thoughts, and break it down."

"That's what you did that first time? With Avery?"

"Yes, although I can also achieve the same result from a great distance."

"What exactly did you see in her that day?"

"She harbored great resentment against you. There was jealousy and a determination to bring you down in any way she could. She planned to discredit you at the first opportunity and have you sent back to Earth in disgrace so that she could take your place."

Melinda's eyes widen in shock. "Unbelievable!"

"It is true, I am afraid."

She shakes her head in disbelief. "And what about now? Is she—does she—still harbor such thoughts?"

"No, not now. I made sure to extract all that evil from her, and I checked her aura again just last rotation. You are still safe. However, her nature is such that such thoughts will eventually resurface. She will require constant vigilance, unless perhaps, you can arrange to have her sent back to Earth."

"Unfortunately, that isn't within my power—not unless she commits some kind of felony that I can prove."

"In that case, I will continue to scan her every quarter rotation to make sure she does not develop such wicked thoughts toward you again."

She touches a hand to my arm. "Thank you, I appreciate it."

"It is my duty, Melinda."

Our drone begins to lose altitude as we approach our destination. With a gentle nudge, we land in the drone park. I open the door and wait as Melinda climbs out. I see her look around curiously. From the outside, there is not much to see. The *drelan* is accessed through an internal passage which opens up into the large, cavernous space inside. I drape my tail around her. "Come."

She walks with me, no longer questioning the presence of my tail on her body. We reach the concealed entrance of the *drelan*, at the base of a jutting set of rocks. I activate our access code using my communicator, and a door slides open. Together, we enter. Inside is a long, gloomily lit corridor. Melinda glances about her uncertainly. "Do not worry. It is fine," I say.

She nods, and walks quietly beside me. After a few paces, we emerge into a larger space with high ceilings formed of stalactites. Discreetly placed urns provide illumination. In the center, a host sits at her console. She smiles upon our approach and stands. "Sicortar, it is an honor to welcome you this day."

"The honor is mine. This is my guest, Melinda Garcia, head of the Earth delegation to Krovatia. Please could you arrange for a mud bath for two with a body mind treatment."

"Of course." She taps on her console then looks up again. "It has been arranged. Please follow me."

She leads us to the end of the cavern and down a further dimly lit corridor until we reach a door that discreetly slides open for us. Inside is a smaller chamber of the cave, with two mud baths set into the ground. The mud is of a reddish brown color and infused into it are aromatic herbs. I see Melinda inhale deeply. "I like this aroma. What is it?"

"It is a mix of therapeutic herbs native only to this planet. They are expertly blended to bring harmony to body and mind."

The host nods her head. "Indeed, sicortar is correct. We have many sun rotations of experience in blending herbs for optimal effect on the body and mind. I will leave you now to your bath, but please press the button should you require any assistance, and of course when you are ready for your washdown."

"Thank you."

The host smiles and exits the room. Melinda turns to me, looking troubled. "So, this mud bath. How exactly is this supposed to work?"

"It is very straightforward, Melinda. We unclothe ourselves and enter."

"I—haven't got a bathing suit."

"You do not need one, Melinda. Take all your clothes off." Seeing her hesitation, I relent. "If you are shy about disrobing, I will turn my back and give you privacy."

"Please, I would appreciate it."

I turn around and give her my back.

"Thank you."

I wait patiently as she disrobes, until I hear the plop as she enters the mud bath. "May I turn back again now?" I ask.

"Ok."

I turn around and find her submerged in the mud to her neck. "You may place your head against this pillowy resting place," I say, pointing to it. I bend down to help settle her more comfortably. "How does that feel?"

"Good, thanks. The mud is lovely and warm, and I love this scent."

"I am glad. Now let me get into my own bath, and then I will start the treatment."

Quickly, I untie my loin cloth and remove it, placing it beside Melinda's discarded clothes. Her eyes widen at the sight of my cock, which has been semi-hard with desire for her since I entered the auditorium earlier today. "Look your fill, my lovely."

She turns her head away in embarrassment. "I'm sorry. I should have afforded you the same privacy you gave me."

I laugh. "Do not worry. I am not shy about my body." Slowly, I ease myself into my own mud bath and sigh in satisfaction. The thick, aromatic liquid wraps itself around me like a warm blanket. "Ah, that is good." Turning to face Melinda, I ask, "Shall we start the treatment?"

She frowns. "How do you mean?"

"At the press of this button, the treatment to ease your body and mind will begin."

She looks puzzled but agrees all the same. "Er, sure. Let it begin."

I press the button and lie back, keeping my head cocked sideways so that I can observe her reaction. The chamber fills with a soft, haunting melody, just as two pairs of hands begin to knead my body from shoulder to toe.

"What the fuck?"

At her shriek, I grin. "Relax, Melinda. It is only synthetic hands built into the bath. They have sensors that can expertly detect the contours of your body. Close your eyes and let the treatment work on your body and mind."

"You could have warned me!"

"I thought I did."

She grunts and closes her eyes. I watch as slowly, the expression on her face morphs from bewildered shock to serene calm. Satisfied that all is as it should be, I close my own eyes and relax back against my head rest, letting the treatment work its magic on my tired, aging body. The occasional pleasurable moans that I hear from Melinda tell me the magic is working on her too. While the kneading hands find every aching part of my body, the aromatic essences begin to work on my mind, sending me into a semi trance-like state of peaceful wellbeing. My mind empties of all worries and stresses, returning to a state of healthy equilibrium. The *drelan* is a place I frequent often for this very reason. I come here after a round too many of holy trances where I have had to bring evil into my body, and I let the healing power of the mud bath soothe away the pain of that toxic invasion.

After a while, the kneading hands stop and withdraw, replaced by a gentle current that ripples around me, working at revitalizing each nerve ending of my body. I feel myself drift away on a cloud of contentment. Time passes.

I come back to myself and breathe out deeply as I open my eyes. The cave around me is quiet, and the treatment session complete. Slowly, I sit up in my bath and reach for the call button to summon assistance for our washdown. Glancing across at the other bath, I see Melinda lying with her eyes still closed, a peaceful expression on her lovely face. I study it carefully, taking in the pleasing shape of her cheek bones, the small turned up nose and the long brown lashes that fan her eyes. "Melinda," I speak softly. "Melinda, it is time to wake."

Her eyes flutter open. She turns to me, looking disoriented. "How long have I been asleep?"

"I do not know. I too have only just come awake. It is time now for our washdown."

"Ok," she murmurs.

The door slides open and two attendants walk in. One of them walks towards my bath while the other goes to Melinda. "Sicortar, if you will let me assist you out of the bath?"

"Thank you." I stand, dripping thick brown mud, and take hold of the attendant's strong hand for balance as I step out of the bath carefully. A similarly mud caked Melinda does the same.

"If you will follow me," speaks the attendant. We let her guide us out of the cave, and walk behind her, leaving a trail of muddy footprints in our wake. A short distance down the corridor, we reach another door, this one leading to the wash room. The attendant points to the wash compartments. "Please enter the compartment and stand with your legs shoulder width apart. Place both hands flat against the wall."

Melinda hesitates for a fraction, but upon seeing me enter my own compartment and position my body in the required position, she goes and does the same in hers.

"Close your eyes please," says one of the attendants as the compartment door slides shut, enclosing me in.

I close my eyes, and immediately a jet of warm, soapy water gushes over me. It is followed by a set of automated soft brushes, built into the compartment walls, that begin to scrub me down. I let the brushes thoroughly clean every muddy nook of my body and scrape off the dead cells on my skin, leaving it smooth as I like it to be. Next door, I hear little squeaks coming from Melinda, as she experiences our wash compartment for the first time. Once the scrubbing is done, the brushes retract. A rainfall of water washes away all soapy and muddy residue, leaving us clean and fresh. The water stops automatically and our compartment door slides open again, revealing an attendant holding out a large fluffy towel. With quick, efficient movements, the attendant dries my body, then drapes the towel around my waist. She brings slippers and places them at my feet, wiping each foot dry with a fresh towel before slipping them on. "Sicortar, if you could follow me to the recovery room, I will rub oils into your skin."

"I thank you."

I see Melinda similarly robed in a towel, except that hers is draped over the whole of her torso, not her waist. A pity. I would have liked to have had a closer look at the pretty little breasts I glimpsed as she emerged, muddied, from the bath. "How did you enjoy the washdown?" I enquire of her.

"That was an interesting experience, that's for sure. This whole thing has been. Thank you for bringing me here."

"It is my privilege. But the experience is not yet over. Come and let the attendants oil our bodies before we go."

We walk to an adjoining room where two large mats are laid on the floor. "Please lie down on your backs and make yourselves comfortable," says one of the attendants.

We do as we are bid. The attendants crouch down on the floor beside us and begin oiling our bodies, starting with our arms and hands, then moving to our chests. I see the attendant with Melinda work discreetly under the towel, instinctively understanding that this Earth female is not comfortable with a display of her naked body. I am glad for that, as I do not want to cause my guest discomfort.

Once our bodies are oiled, my attendant comes to me bearing the loin cloth I had discarded earlier. I take it from her and quickly lace it on, then strap on my every day sandals. The other attendant has Melinda's clothes in her hand, waiting for me to give them some privacy. "Melinda, I will leave you now in the attendant's capable hands. She will bring you to me when you are dressed and your hair suitably dried, and we can then partake of a light meal together before we leave."

She throws me a grateful look. "Thank you, sicortar, I appreciate all that you have done for me today."

"As I said, it is my privilege. I am sure you will have much to write about in your next dispatch to your home planet."

"Yes, I will."

"Good. I shall see you shortly."

With this, I stride out, leaving her to get dressed without my wandering eyes on her. There will be time enough for that once I make her mine. With every beat that passes, I am more firm in my intention to pursue a dalliance with her.

She joins me in the post-treatment chamber a short while later, dressed in her Earth garb, looking bright eyed and fresh. She smiles when she sees I have ordered *mishu* for her. "Ooh, I've been wanting to try these again," she says as she comes to sit beside me.

"I thought as much. I remember your reaction to them the first time." I take a crispy green ball and bring it to her mouth. This time, she does not demur, but opens her soft, plump limps to take the food in.

She chews on it, moaning in delight. "Mmm, these are so good."

"They are some of my favorite foods too." I pour her a glass of *nari* and feed her some more. Females in my society generally eat by their own hands, but it is a sign of special favor when a male feeds them with his. I do not think Melinda fully understood how I was honoring her that first meal we had together at the banquet. Perhaps she still does not. Nevertheless, she takes the food from me uncomplainingly.

"So tell me, Melinda, how have you enjoyed your time on Krovatia so far?"

"I've loved it. Everyone has been welcoming and helpful, if a little cautious about us outsiders, which is understandable."

I nod. "We are good people. Living in peaceful harmony with each other and our environment matters to us greatly. That is why the work of sicors in weeding out negative energy is valued so much."

"Do you have crime on this planet?"

"We do, for it is not possible to monitor every single person's energies every single day, but not in anything like the amount we used to have on our old planet, before our ancestors moved here."

"Could you tell me a little more about that? I am curious about this exodus."

"It is a little before my time, so my knowledge comes from the history we were taught in school. Our home world was a beautiful planet, with lush forests, crystal clear lakes, fertile valleys and impressive cities filled with grand buildings. We were a technologically advanced people living a life of decadent luxury, but it came at a price. Every home, every drone, every factory producing the many things we loved to consume, created tons and tons of toxic pollutants. Some of our people sounded a warning about this, but they were ignored in people's greed for ever more goods and ever more comfort in their lives."

"Some of what you describe sounds eerily like events in my own home world," sighs Melinda.

"Yes, though I hope for your sake that what happened next in ours does not happen to yours."

"Tell me."

"It came to the point one day where the damage to our planet's ecosystem was so great that great swathes of it became uninhabitable. Many people lost their lives, as well as their homes. It eventually became clear that to survive, we would need to evacuate and find ourselves a new planet to inhabit. We sent out probes and spaceships to explore the outer parts of our galaxy, and eventually, they identified two possible new homes. One of them was a planet that was slightly cooler than ours, but with ample natural resources, including a large source of dorenium. The other planet also had many natural resources, but its climate was deemed too hot, so it was decided we would all go to the cooler planet. A convoy of dozens of ships took our ancestors there and we soon got started, creating a new colony."

Melinda watches me spellbound as I plop a final ball of *mishu* into her mouth. "Go on, I'm fascinated. What happened next?"

"The new colony, called Sarax, grew and became prosperous, but there were some dissident voices that said the lessons of the past had not been learned. We were consuming resources at an alarming rate and polluting this new planet just as much as we did our old one. Some people grew so disillusioned with what was going on, that a plan was hatched to take a group of us and start our own colony, this time on the hotter but habitable planet. There was much antagonism towards that idea from the authorities and many attempts to shut down this plan. In the end, a brave group of people fought a battle, liberating three spaceships and escaping Sarax with limited supplies to start a new life somewhere else."

"Your ancestors that came here, to Krovatia?"

"Yes, that is correct. My great-great-grandfather was one of them. Very early on in the colony, we established a charter with clear rules setting out our values. We would respect the environment of our new home and live in harmony with it and each other. We would cut our ties with Sarax and not allow their pernicious influence to sully this new project of ours. In fact, we would protect ourselves from all outside influences and focus on making a sustainable life for us and our children on this planet."

"So that's why you didn't allow foreigners on Krovatian soil."

"Yes, that is the root cause of it. However, over time we developed trading relationships with some friendly planets, so we did not totally cut ourselves off from the outside world. We did insist though, that such trade take place in neutral territory outside our planet, and all efforts were made to protect our way of life. While we undertook explorations of our new home, we discovered a repository of pink crystals which we decided to investigate and research. It was in the course of these investigations that we discovered the potent effect of boral crystals on us. We were able to enter into trances and read each other's auras for the very first time. And we also noticed that a select few of our people were able to go beyond simply reading the auras but also to manipulate them. Our ancestors decided to form a priestly body of people with such skills, naming them sicors. It was their task to ensure that evil thoughts, of the type that destroyed our former worlds, would not thrive here."

"And they appointed a sicortar to lead them?"

"Yes, the tradition became that the most powerful of the sicors would be afforded the title of sicortar."

"This explains a lot. Thank you for telling me. So, this means the Saraxians who attacked Ven last year were your kin."

"I do not think of them as my kin. Genetically, they are the same people as us, but in all other respects, we diverge greatly."

"I can understand that."

Our meal ended, it is time for us to depart, but I am strangely reluctant to do so. I have enjoyed this Earth female's company. "Melinda, will you do me the honor of dining with me again, perhaps next rotation?"

She pins me with fierce brown eyes. "In what capacity would we be dining together?"

"Melinda, you know quite well it would not be in an official capacity. I wish to conduct a romantic liaison with you. I believe you are attracted to me too, and this ex-mate of yours is out of the picture, is he not?"

She hesitates. "We are divorced, yes, though we still care for each other greatly."

"But you are free to pursue a new relationship."

She purses her lips. "Yes, though perhaps it's you who isn't."

I raise my brows at this. "How so?"

"The females I have seen with you—drashas you call them. They are there to service your sexual needs?"

"Yes, that is right. A sicor has sexual needs that exceed those of the ordinary person. It is right and fitting that we have drashas to help us with this."

"And you have fathered many children with them."

"Yes, you have met them. I still do not see the problem."

She casts me an annoyed glance. "It doesn't seem to me that you are free. In human terms, that would make you spoken for."

"It is true that I have not as a rule sought romantic liaisons outside my household. My drashas have fulfilled my sexual needs admirably, but that is all they do. I do not engage in intellectual conversations with them like I enjoy doing with you, nor do I romance them like I wish to do with you, beautiful, lovely Melinda. You enthrall me. Let me assure you, I live in my own quarters in the house and do not share my bed with anyone. I am free to be with you for however long our liaison lasts before we mutually end it, wishing each other peace and joy."

My tail flaps about then comes to rest in her lap. Without thinking, she begins stroking it. "I—I'm flattered, sicortar."

"Call me Kirimor."

"Kirimor, I'm flattered and I can see from your perspective that you think it's fine to both romance me and have sex with your drashas. But that's something that I as a human find very hard to accept. Even if this is a short term thing between us, I do not share."

"You would not be sharing me, my lovely. When we are together, you have my full and utmost attention, but of course I must do my work, and that necessitates that I fuck my drashas in the temple."

She shudders at this. "Oh God. Even you saying that makes me incredibly uncomfortable. I'm sorry Kirimor, but I cannot contemplate pursuing a relationship with you."

I sniff the air. "And yet your cunt weeps for me. I can scent your arousal, Melinda. You are alone here, with no male to sate your physical needs. Why deprive yourself of the untold pleasures I have in store for you?"

"Because I can't separate emotions from sex, Kirimor. It's not just a way to sate physical needs."

"No indeed, for us it would be a communing of both body and spirit. All the more reason not to deny ourselves. While you are with me, your happiness will be my top priority."

She looks away. "I—no, I'm sorry. Now please, could you take me home?"

I let out a breath. "Very well. Let us go."

In silence, I escort her to my drone. We fly to the home she shares with the other Humans without any further words. I land the craft just outside her front door and turn to her. "Melinda, my offer still stands should you change your mind. I am greatly attracted to you, both in mind and body, and would like to share pleasurable times with you if you will let me. Think on it."

She nods. "Go in peace, Kirimor."

"Go in peace, Melinda."

Once again, I have been summoned for a meeting with Denishar in his palace. I am guessing it is to do with the hunt for the perpetrators who stole the boral crystals. As my scan into those twelve individuals on the cargo ship proved inconclusive, we still do not know for sure how those boral crystals were taken off our planet and handed to the Saraxians. I know that Denishar has continued with his investigations, and perhaps, he has some new information now to share.

I am ushered into his receiving chamber. We place hands on each other's chests in greeting, then bow. "Denishar, it is good to see you."

"And you, sicortar." He points to a set of floor cushions positioned in the corner of the room, next to a fragrant water fountain. The sound of the water, gently trickling down in a never ending flow, is soothing and restful. It is the perfect place to sit and reflect, or meditate. I lower myself down on to a cushion and take a long, satisfying drink of *nari* from a nearby side table. Denishar sits on a cushion opposite me and also takes a drink. We repose in contemplative silence, letting the fragrance of the fountain waft over us and lull us into a state of deep relaxation. In this semi-conscious state, if both parties are willing, it is possible to communicate without words. I do not willingly enter into such a state with anyone but my closest and most trusted friends, of which Denishar is one.

We sit for a long time, deepening our trance and building a connection between our two minds. The advantage of communicating this way is that thoughts and ideas can bounce from one to the other at a rate much faster than words. It is one of the best ways of problem solving. At home, when I face a difficulty in my technical designs, I often invite Sholinar to share a trance with me so that we can work out how best to move forward in the creation of our latest inventions, for he works closely with me on all my designs.

At last, the bridge between our two minds is complete. I wait patiently for Denishar to begin. He surprises me with his first transmission.

"Have you ever wondered, Kirimor, what our lives would have been like if our ancestors had stayed with everyone else on Sarax and not insisted on creating a separate colony here on Krovatia?"

"No doubt we would have led a life of greater material luxury, wasting natural resources and creating yet more toxic pollution."

"No doubt, but other than that, have you not ever wondered what it would be like if we had not separated from our kin?"

"On occasion. It is no great matter to me after all this time. I know that I have distant relations on Sarax, but they are so distant now as to be akin to strangers."

"Same here. There is one family I have always wondered about though. It is the Prelo clan. You know of course that Prelonor and Preloshar were identical twins who went their separate ways—Prelonor deciding to remain on Sarax and Preloshar getting on the ship that eventually came here, along with our ancestors."

"I have heard the story, yes. I remember being puzzled that two brothers with the sacred bond of twinhood should take such different paths."

"Indeed. Another thing I have often wondered is whether some of our ancestors ever kept in touch with the family members they left behind on Sarax. After we had built our communication network that enabled us to link up with the Venorians and Driskians, it could have been possible for someone, without too much difficulty, to find a way to also communicate with the Saraxians."

"Surely such a communication would come to light? It is strictly against our laws to do such a thing."

"Some such communications were discovered and stopped. This was before our time, but I have looked at the privileged information logs and seen that there were several Krovatians indicted for sending out messages to Sarax. It was all hushed up of course, so this information is not in the public domain. Interestingly, one of the Krovatians convicted of this felony was Preloshar."

"Ah. What happened to him?"

"He served his time in a correction facility, then was released. He stayed under observation for many sun rotations, but was never caught communicating with Sarax again. He mated, lived to an old age and had a son, called Prelostor."

"You think he found a way to continue sending messages to his twin on Sarax without our knowing?"

"Difficult to say. He lived a model life as a citizen after his release. Maybe too model a life. He won awards for best eco-conservation three sun rotations in a row."

"And that makes you suspicious."

"I would not have thought about it at all, if not for the fact—"

"That his great-granddaughter is part of the crew of the cargo ship that smuggled out the boral crystals."

"Exactly."

"I scanned Prelonisha's aura carefully and found nothing alarming there."

"Think back to her aura. What was it like exactly?"

"It was a warm glow of bright colors. Not a single spurt of negative energy there."

"Too perfect. A model citizen."

"I see what you are getting at here. You are thinking that somehow she has found a way to mask her true feelings and masquerade as the perfect citizen."

"Is there a way to bypass your scan, Kirimor?"

"I have never thought so."

"Let us think about how that could be done. I am increasingly of the opinion that whoever stole the crystals and whoever smuggled them on board the cargo ship, is hiding in plain sight, somehow managing to evade our energy scans."

"I have been able to read negativity in even our wiliest criminals. Under the holy trance, nobody can avoid my all-seeing eye, no matter what subterfuge they try to use."

"Perhaps you are mistaken, Kirimor."

"You realize this calls into question all that I have believed and all the work I have done for the last twenty-three sun rotations as sicortar."

"I do realize, but when the evidence presents itself, one cannot ignore it. I am not saying your energy scans are faulty. Ninety-nine per cent of the time, I am sure you have been accurate in your assessments, and the work you have done for our planet has been invaluable. Do not doubt yourself on that. However, we must explore the possibility that, for a very small fraction of the population, your scans may not have been altogether successful."

"You think they have come up with some kind of barrier around their true aura?"

"I do not know. Think, Kirimor, if it were you wanting to fool an energy scan, how would you do it?"

"My scans look into a person's inner thoughts and feelings to sense if they are transmitting any negative energy towards those around them."

"Yes, and so?"

"The whole thing is predicated on what they themselves conceive as negativity. If someone has an evil intention towards another person, they know internally that what they are feeling is wrong. That internalized feeling is what I read."

"I understand, but how is this relevant?"

"What if the person doing or thinking of doing what by our standards is an immoral act, believes to the very core of their being that what they are doing is right and good? If their own conscience is clear, they will only transmit positive energy to me."

"So what you are saying is that our possible perpetrator is morally convinced that they are doing good by stealing the crystals?"

"Yes. That could be a way of shielding themselves from my energy scans. We have always believed that the theft of the boral crystals was done for financial gain. But what if it was done for other, more ideological reasons?"

"This is beginning to make sense of the puzzle. So now, let us explore the possible ideological motives."

"The theft of the boral crystals was used to attack the Venorians, not us. What possible connection could there be back to us?"

"Let us imagine that some of our citizens have been in continued contact with their kin on Sarax. Perhaps they see the easy lifestyle people lead over there and compare it unfavorably to our more eco-conscious life here."

"Perhaps, but how does that translate into wanting to assist the Saraxians in an attack on the Venorians?"

"What energy source do the Venorians have control over in their colony on the Utar belt?"

"Dorenium. As far as I know, there are plentiful deposits of the mineral on the Utar belt, enough to power Venorian space travel and industry for at least another century—if not more."

"And where else is there a massive repository of dorenium?"

"Here, in the southern sector of our planet."

"When our ancestors colonized Sarax, it too had great deposits of dorenium. What if, in their profligate lifestyle, they have squandered this resource and are now looking for other sources of dorenium?"

"It would explain the continued hostilities between the Saraxians and the Venorians, and their threat to us. But why would a Krovatian want to help them with that?"

"So, let us imagine that some Krovatians have continued to be in close contact with their kin on Sarax and are envious of the easy, luxurious life to be had there. Perhaps, they are wanting such luxuries for themselves over here. Perhaps, they have convinced themselves that it is the right of every Krovatian to live a better life with the energy intensive technologies that we refuse to use here. In which case, they might believe they are doing good by assisting the Saraxians to take control of the Utar belt and to possibly, in the near future, take control of Krovatia."

"What you suggest is very alarming, Denishar."

"I am alarmed and extremely concerned. I do not know how far the plotting between the Saraxians and such Krovatians has gone. We know only of Prelonisha, but there may be others working in conjunction with her that we have not identified yet. This is why I need you to somehow find a way to scan more accurately and identify those people whose auras are too perfect."

"There are a million people living on this planet, Denishar. I cannot begin to scan them all."

"No, but we may start with a scan of every high ranking individual. I will draw up a list and send it to you."

"It will still take time—time we may not have. What other measures will you take?"

"I am convening a meeting with the other sector leaders, but before I do, I want to make sure none of them are in on this. I doubt they are, but to be sure, could you scan each of them again for me?"

"Of course, I will get right on it."

"I am also going to deploy some trusted operatives to closely observe Prelonisha's movements and communications. Perhaps she will slip up and reveal her co-conspirators. I will also discuss our security measures with the sector leaders and review areas where we need to tighten things up."

"That is a good plan. I wish you luck with it."

"And you will get started on the scans of high ranking Krovatians as soon as possible?"

"Yes. It will mean going into more frequent holy trances than usual."

"Lucky for you, you have a young new drasha to help you out."

"So you have heard."

"Oh yes, the grapevine is full of the news that the sicortar has taken on a new drasha for the first time in many sun rotations, one young enough to be his daughter."

"Do not mock me, Denishar. I had my doubts when Sholinar first mentioned her to me, but she has turned out to be a fine addition to my household."

"I do not mock, Kirimor. I am happy for you and glad you have her now that you are going to be so busy. While we are on such matters, I am curious. What is the deal between you and that Earth female?"

"She intrigues me. I cannot tell you why. I am thinking of conducting a short dalliance with her. Will that be a problem?"

"No, you are free to find romantic adventure wherever you want. It is a cause for gossip though, and I also wonder whether she will agree to a dalliance with you. Her kind do not generally share sexual partners. If she knows about your drashas, she may not wish to be added to the list."

"Yes, I gathered that. My challenge is to convince her otherwise."

"The challenge may be greater than you think. You will also be interested to know that she has an ex-husband—similar to a former mate—who has applied for permission to join her here, no doubt with the intention of winning her back. He is the leader of a cultural arts performing group. He would like to bring the group here to share their Earth culture with us by performing drama, music and dance."

"I know of him. Will you be giving that permission?"

"As you know, I was very hesitant to agree to hosting the current delegations we have here. However, as you predicted, their presence on our planet has not proved to be a threat to us. On the contrary, my contact with the diplomatic representatives has taught me much about their races. I have found the information very useful. I must confess to being curious to see performances of their arts, especially as I have a personal liking for music and dance."

"So you will agree to their visit here?"

"Unless you have an objection?"

"My baser instinct is to say yes, I do have an objection. I do not wish for this golden haired, blue eyed male to come here and try to seduce Melinda again. But then my rational mind overrules the objection. I am quite certain that this male is no competition for me. If they were still mated, that would of course be a different matter, but then he would not have let her come here without him."

"You make a good point. Then, my friend, I do not need to wish you luck, for you will not need it I think."

"No, but you may wish me a happy and pleasant interlude with the Earth female."

"That I do. After all your hard work and sacrifice to your duty, you deserve the unique pleasure of romancing a worthy female—one that will stimulate you both in the bedroom and out."

"Thank you, Denishar. I believe she will do so. I have been much impressed with her feisty personality."

"As have I. Have a happy and enjoyable dalliance, my friend."

With our business concluded, we come out of our trance. I finish my drink of *nari* then stand. "Go in peace, Denishar."

"Go in peace, Kirimor."

I emerge into the mid-morning sunshine and head to my drone. I glance at the time dial on my communicator. There are still nine beats until noon, time enough to stop by the body art shop and update the ink on my skin. If I am to win over the stubborn Earth female, then I must look my best.

As I make my way to the shop, I focus my thoughts on her, rather than on the concerning news I have just learned from

Denishar. I do not want to think how many of the energy scans I have conducted in all my holy trances these past decades have been incorrect, though it is something I am going to have to examine in due course. Tapping on my communicator, I send a quick message to Sholinar, asking him to be available to me for a meeting after the lunch repast. I want to run this new information past him and see what he thinks.

For now, my thoughts are on Melinda. I must engineer another encounter with her and try to convince her to change her mind. Kiristen has been full of talk about how he wants to invite Troy over to our home for a meal with us. I am hesitant. I do not like strangers in my home, but Kiristen has been strangely insistent that this time, he has met The One. Could it be true? If so, then perhaps it would be right and proper to have Troy come over one day, and with him, Melinda? Or perhaps not. As Denishar has rightly pointed out, her kind do not usually share sexual partners. It may not be a good idea for her to see my drashas and be reminded that I fuck other women.

I need to get her all to myself, somewhere we will not be interrupted. My cabin, up in the mountains above our home, could be just such a place. It is where I stay when I visit the uplands, the part of my lands where I grow crops and breed animals. My groundskeeper Jenisor, and his two assistants, care for them on a daily basis, but I like to check in on their progress every now and then. I also sometimes visit the cabin when I want to get some peace and quiet on my own, away from my large, extended family. I do not do it often, for I love them and for the most part enjoy their company, but sometimes, my sanity requires that I get a break, and that is when I go to the cabin, where I can read at leisure, think up new inventions or play my favorite songs on my lanjo. Yes, the cabin is the perfect place to woo my delightful Human and trap her in my web—for only so long as she entertains me, and then I shall let her go.

I send another message, this time to Dresolor, my cook, asking him to stock up on food in the cabin and ensure it is ready for occupation. Now, the question is, how do I get her there? I decide the best way is for Kiristen to extend an invitation to the Humans. Once she gets to my home, I will manage to spirit her away up to the cabin. I smile impishly, greatly pleased at my machinations, as I land in the drone park outside the shopping arcade.

I hop out and speed away to my destination. I am a regular at this body art shop. I have known Dorinor, the artist, for many sun rotations, and I trust only him with the art on my body. "Greetings, Dorinor," I say, entering the shop. He is busy inking a female, drawing an interesting new pattern across her breasts. Hmm, I wonder how such a design would look on my Earth female. My mind skips to the possibilities, and I feel myself harden under my loin cloth.

Dorinor looks up with a smile. "Greetings, sicortar. I shall not be long. Please make yourself comfortable and help yourself to some *nari*."

The female's eyes, which had been shut, pop open. "Sicortar," she simpers. "What an honor to meet you."

I nod, putting on my most forbidding expression. I am in no mood for flirtatious females. I have enough on my plate with my drashas and the difficult, alluring woman from Earth. I help myself to some *nari* and sit on a cushion, with my communicator out indicating I am busy and not inclined for conversation.

Dorinor, may Taya rain blessings on him, understands and engages the female in conversation, keeping her attention focused away from me. In no time, he has finished the job and sends her on her way. He approaches with a smile, "Apologies for keeping you waiting, sicortar."

"No apologies needed, Dorinor."

"What are you thinking in terms of for your new inking?"

"I greatly liked what you did on my arms last time, so something in a similar vein. However, I would like a different design across my chest. Do you have any suggestions?"

"Take a look at these recent drawings. They are in keeping with the current fashion of concentric and interconnected circles—symbols of our love for our planet—surrounded by a wave of leafy looking swirls—which symbolize the bountiful nature around us. What do you think?"

I browse through the different designs, then point to the one I want. "This one I think, Dorinor."

"Good choice, sicortar. Please come through to my private workshop and we may begin."

I follow him down a corridor to the room in question, away from prying eyes. I lie on the reclining chair and quickly, he sanitizes my skin. Once that is done, he begins to paint me with the ink, all the while regaling me with the most recent gossip. Another reason why I like to visit Dorinor is the valuable information he has about what is going on in the city. I listen to the latest stories of love affairs, ruptures, new businesses and of course, the obligatory gossip about the aliens currently residing on our planet.

"It is said that one of the Earth females has made quite an impression on you, sicortar. Is that true?"

"Possibly. I enjoyed playing with her at the banquet. I may indulge in a little more play in due course. It will give her much to write about to her superiors on Earth."

Dorinor chuckles. "I am certain they have never come across a race like ours before. I hear they are fascinated with our tails."

"It works both ways. The golden color of her skin fascinates me, and her eyes are such a vibrant shade of brown. It is not something I am used to seeing."

"Indeed. I have seen photos in the news, and I agree, they are an attractive race. I was particularly struck by the other female, and the very pale cream of her skin. It would be such a perfect canvas for my body art."

I laugh. "Perhaps I can send her your way one day."

"I would greatly appreciate it."

Dorinor finishes the pattern on my arms and begins to ink my chest. In the pause while he adjusts his stance, I ask him, "Dorinor, have you come across any Krovatians that talk of living a more luxurious lifestyle and how our eco-conscious ethos is too restricting?"

"It is funny you should mention that. Just the other day, I was inking a young male and I heard a throwaway remark he said to someone on his communicator. Something like 'The heat lately has been so scorching. I live for the day when we can properly cool our homes again.' Then, the person he was speaking to must have rebuked him, for he changed the subject of the conversation."

He has my full attention. "Do you remember his name?"

"No, but I can look it up. It should be in my records."

"Please do and send me the information. Could you also let me know if you ever hear such talk again?"

"Of course, sicortar."

"Thank you."

A beat later, my inking is done. I stand and look at my reflection in the mirror, admiring the work. "Dorinor, you are genius. Thank you for this."

"It is my honor, sicortar."

"Go in peace."

"Go in peace."

Chapter 22

Melinda

I finish listening to the latest recording from Wyatt and replay it. The time lag between our communications is incredibly frustrating. I have been here on Krovatia for nearly a month, which means he must have sent this just after seeing that last apologetic message from me.

Wyatt's familiar face appears before me. He smiles, his wonderful warm smile, "Hey, honey, I got your message. Sweetheart, you don't need to apologize for anything. If anything, it's me who failed you. Me, who's been the coward. These last few weeks, I've done lots of soul searching too. I've decided the time has come to just get off my ass and stop being ruled by my fear, so I'm going to see a therapist Dylan recommended. I'm going to work through my issues and I'm hoping one day to get on a drone, and then maybe a space ship too. I'm trying, Mel, really trying to be a better person. So, honey, you have nothing to be sorry for. I'm sorry I let you slip through my fingers and fucked up our marriage. I wish… I wish I had done things differently. I miss you. I love you. Take care of yourself, honey."

I end the recording and wipe a stray tear. I'm so glad Wyatt is proactively trying to overcome his fears. So proud too. I just wish he could have done this a long time ago. Why couldn't he have displayed this determined attitude when I first went to Mars?

I start recording my response. "Athena, record video message to Wyatt. Begin."

"Hi, honey, this is great news! I hope this therapist you're seeing can help. I sense your determination and I know you can do it. I'm proud of you. Let me tell you what's been happening this end. I'm making good progress, building up my network of contacts. I've met all the sector leaders and top ministers. We're building a database for our records back home, with the names, pictures and descriptions of all the main players here, and we'll be keeping that updated. One of my main priorities is to improve and speed up our connectivity with Earth. I'm in talks with the Venorians to try to integrate our systems and create a more streamlined way to message you all. It still won't be the live chat we had back when I was on Mars, but I'm hoping the time lag between messages can at the very least be halved. Troy is putting a lot of hours into this, and I hope to have good news about this for you some time soon."

"Talking about Troy, here's a bit of gossip. He's dating a Krovatian guy and not just any guy, but the son of that head priest I was telling you about, the one who did that strange ceremony on the day we arrived. Crazy right? He's a lovely young man named Kiristen and they seem very much in love, though Troy still maintains it's just a fling."

I laugh. "We'll see about that! We've been invited to the sicortar's home for lunch tomorrow — that's the title of the head priest, sicortar. Think of this as Troy going to meet the parents, even though technically he's already met them. This will be the first time he sees them after he and Kiristen have officially started dating. Avery and I got an invite too, so we'll tag along and support him as best we can. I can't really decline an invitation from the head priest of the planet, can I? It's sure to be an interesting experience, visiting his home."

Not least after the proposal he made the other day. "I wish to conduct a romantic liaison with you." Fuck, why can't I get that out of my head?

I stretch my arms to the side sleepily. "Anyway, it's late and I best get some sleep. Take care, honey. I hope you are keeping well. Goodnight… Athena, end message and send."

I get under the covers. "Athena, lights out." Snuggling into my pillow, I close my eyes and drift off to sleep dreaming of dark glittering eyes and a soft tufted tail that wraps around me like a warm blanket.

Late next morning, Kiristen arrives in his drone to escort us to his home, where we've all been invited for lunch. He walks into the house and straight into Troy's arms. Troy pulls the young Krovatian roughly to him and ravages him with kisses.

"Guys, remember. We're here too."

They pull apart, breathless. "Sorry," mutters Troy, then drags Kiristen to him for another kiss, more gentle this time. Eventually, they come up for air, and Kiristen turns to us, face flushed an interesting shade of taupe.

"Please forgive my poor manners. Greetings, Melinda and Avery." He steps towards me and places a hand on my chest, then bows. He does the same to Avery. "Are you ready to go?"

"We are. Let me just get the plate of brownies I baked from the kitchen."

"You baked for us?"

"Yes, I wanted to share some of our food with you. It's a type of moist sweet cake called a brownie."

"I look forward to tasting it."

Quickly, I grab the carefully wrapped box of brownies and join them at the front door. "Ok, I'm ready."

"Then come along, let us go."

The journey to Kiristen's house takes no more than twenty minutes in the drone, but I can see from the window that we leave the city behind and fly over a very sparsely populated rocky terrain. After a while, I notice the blue of the coastline and a mountainous range close by. As we start our descent, I make out a compound of whitewashed buildings sitting near the edge of the cliff, overlooking the sea. Kiristen brings the drone down neatly into a parking space next to two other drones and switches off the engine. He turns to us with a smile. "Here we are. Welcome to my home."

As we climb out, the front door opens and a little figure flies out towards me. "Melinda!" cries Kiritela excitedly. I lift her into my arms and give her a big hug.

"Well hello, young lady. It's good to see you."

She wraps her tail around my waist and gives me a sloppy kiss on the cheek. I tighten my hold on her, giving her a big squeeze before lowering her back to her feet. I look up to see the sicortar watching me. Straightening my spine, I walk towards him. "Sicortar, it is an honor to be here." I go to place my hand on his chest in the traditional greeting, but instead, he pulls me to him, plastering my body to his. His tail snakes around me, binding me in his embrace and one hand buries itself in my hair, pulling my face to his. I feel his breath in my ear.

"In my home, call me Kirimor," he rumbles. He continues to hold me tight, rubbing his nose along the crook of my neck.

"Kirimor," I whisper, "let me go."

I feel his lips quirk in a smile. "Not yet."

He rains light kisses along the side of my jaw and down to the sensitive places on my neck. I try pushing him away, but his tail simply tightens its hold around me. "Kirimor, stop this. I don't know what you think you're doing, but let me remind you quite categorically. I am not interested in any sort of relationship with you."

He continues to nuzzle my neck. "Is that so?" He strokes his thumb along the pulse point at my throat. "Then why is your heart beating so frantically, Melinda? And why are your loins dripping with your arousal? I can smell you."

I squirm in his hold, shamefully aware of the truth of his words. "Let me assure you, sicortar, that I am here only in my official capacity as Earth's ambassador to Krovatia."

"It is Kirimor. And Melinda, I do not conduct official business in my home. When you step inside, you do so in a personal, not an official capacity."

"Then the personal capacity is my being here as Troy's friend and supporting him as he meets the parents of the guy he's dating."

"Troy has already met us. He requires no support."

"Nevertheless, that is the only reason I am here."

He grinds his hips against mine and I feel the nudge of his hard cock on my mound. "Liar," he breathes. But then he gives my neck one final kiss and releases me.

I step away from him, breathless, and realize we are all alone. Kiristen must have dragged Kiritela away with him. The sicortar sees my look and grins. "Did you think my son or your friends would protect you from me? No, my lovely. Here, it is I who rules. And protest all you like, but you will submit to me in the end. However, I am a patient man, Melinda, and I will bide my time. Come along now, let me show you inside."

He turns to go in the house, and after a moment's hesitation, I follow. We step into a wide atrium with the obligatory high vaulted ceiling, and I'm pleasantly struck by the cool, fresh air. By now, I have come to expect warm humid heat, only marginally cooler than the exterior. Now I come to think of it, Kirimor is wearing a long embroidered shirt over his usual loin cloth. Kiritela was also dressed, rather than wandering about half naked. In the chill of this air, that is unsurprising.

I look around, spying colorful artworks on the walls. Under my feet are tiles laid in an intricate mosaic pattern. The effect is bright, uplifting and yet also restful.

"This place is beautiful," I murmur.

Kirimor turns back with a smile. "Thank you."

He continues on his way, and I walk slowly behind him, looking about me and taking in the majestic beauty of his home. We walk under an archway, and I catch my breath. We have entered a large, circular room, one side of which is decorated with a variety of artworks and family portraits, and the other side decked in floor to ceiling glass windows with a dramatic view of the sea. It almost feels as if we are perched on the edge of the cliff, looking down at the endless expanse of blue below. It's breathtaking.

I stand, rooted to the spot. "Oh my," I whisper.

Kirimor looks pleased with my reaction. "This is my favorite place in the house. Come over and sit here. You will get an even better view of the sea."

I remove my shoes, placing them carefully to one side, and go over to the padded bench laid on the floor, overlooking the window. I lower myself to the comfortable cushioned seat and cross my legs, taking in the view. From here, the horizon where the sea meets the sky is directly at eye level. I'm so hypnotized by the glorious view before me, that I don't utter a word for several minutes. Kirimor sits silently beside me, letting me gaze my fill. Eventually, I'm aware of him pouring me a glass of *nari* and sliding it towards me. "Thank you," I murmur. "This is amazing, Kirimor. You are very lucky to have this."

"Yes, I am blessed."

We sit quietly, enjoying the peaceful beauty of the landscape before us, not feeling the need to talk. My anger and frustration from earlier has ebbed away. Now, I'm aware only of contentment and calm. I hadn't realized quite how restful the sicortar's presence could be.

The peace is shattered some time later by the clamor of voices as several people enter the room at once. I see Kiritela, accompanied by her older sister, Kirimara, who I met at the university when I gave my talk. "There they are!" cries Kiritela and launches herself into her father's lap.

He wraps her in his arms. "Were you looking for us, little star?"

"Kiristen and Troy and Avery are upstairs with Merostena, looking over old photo-videos of Kiristen. It is boring, so I decided to come looking for you, and then Kirimara said she wanted to say hello to Melinda, so I brought her with me."

By now, Kirimara has reached us, grinning broadly. In looks, she favors her mother more than Kiristen, but she has the sicortar's dark, expressive eyes. I stand and greet her the traditional way with a hand to the chest. We both step back and bow. "It's good to see you again, Kirimara."

"The honor is mine."

"Come and sit by us, Mara," says Kirimor to his eldest daughter. She lowers herself gracefully to sit to her father's right, resting her chin on his shoulder. "How was college today?" he asks her.

"It was a day, just like any other," she replies.

"No day is just like the other. What new thing did you learn today?"

She ponders the question. "I learned—that I should ask fewer questions in my chemical analysis class."

"And why is that? Questions are good."

"Yes," chimes in Kiritela. "I like asking questions."

Her father draws her in for a hug and kisses her cheek fondly. "So do I, little star."

"Only if the teacher is able to answer them," her sister replies. "I believe my endless questioning has become a source of irritation for him. He may start punishing me with lower grades."

"He would not dare! If anyone at college gives you trouble, you promised to tell me."

"And I will, but there is no trouble as yet. I only think it might be the more politic thing to be a little less inquisitive in his class."

"That is a valuable thing to be aware of," I interject. "No teacher likes to be shown up as lacking in knowledge. It's wise to respect the ego of others, especially if they are supposed to be in a superior position to you. Besides, if he can't answer your questions, then there's probably not much left he can teach you."

Kirimara beams at me. "That is exactly what I thought."

"What is it you study at college?"

"Natural science with a focus on the synthesis of medical plants."

"That sounds like an interesting course of study. Are you enjoying it?"

"Mostly yes, but this chemical analysis class, not so much."

"Kirimara is top of her class in nearly every subject," boasts her father proudly. "One day, she is going to be an excellent scientist."

"Do you plan to work in the pharmaceutical industry when you finish college?" I wonder.

"I am hoping to help develop new drugs to treat some common heart conditions." She hesitates. "Grandmother was taken from us too soon because of her heart. I am hoping to honor her life by finding more remedies for the condition that took her from us."

Kirimor strokes his daughter's hair, kissing her on the forehead. "Ma would have been proud."

"When did you lose her, if I may ask?"

Kirimor answers me with a sad smile, a suspicious looking glint in his eyes. "Three sun rotations ago. My mother had been a strong, sturdy woman, never ill a day in her life. Then, her heart gave up on her without a warning. It was a great shock to us."

"I'm so sorry for your loss."

He inclines his head.

Kiritela, with the innocence of youth, breaks the somber mood with a cry for attention. "Pa, can we go down to the beach with Melinda? I want to show her how to collect plo shells. She says she does not have anything like them at home."

He looks at me consideringly. "Is that so? Well then you definitely must show her how to find plo shells. We will all go down and have a swim in the sea together."

I shake my head. "I'm sorry to disappoint, but I haven't brought my swimsuit. Perhaps another time, Kiritela."

Kirimor eyes me with amusement. "That is not a problem, Melinda, as you well know. You may borrow one of Kirimara's loin cloths. You do not need to wear anything else."

He has me there. I'm sure Kirimor knows I went topless at the water city, so it would seem silly to be coy about my body now. And I did take all my clothes off at the *drelan*. But it's a world of difference having his searing gaze on my bare, unmuddied flesh.

He doesn't wait for my answer, turning to his eldest daughter. "Mara, my sweet, go find a spare loin cloth for Melinda to wear and see if Kiristen and our other guests wish to join us. I think Troy may have had enough of watching photo-videos of your brother by now."

Kirimara grins and flies off to do his bidding.

I'm still grappling with the fact the sicortar expects me to swim with him in nothing but a loin cloth. Damn!

Chapter 23

Kirimor

I hug my little star and kiss her soft cheek. "Kiritela," I murmur, "you are full of good ideas."

I had planned to take my time and weave my web of seduction slowly around Melinda. I did not lie when I said I was a patient man. But now that this opportunity has fallen into my lap, I will gladly embrace it. I look forward to seeing the stubborn Earth female uncovered, and I plan to get my hands on her every chance I get. My cock, semi-stiff since the moment I saw her today, rears up in anticipation.

I see her flounder for an excuse, knowing full well that after her escapade at the water city and the naked dip in the mud bath, she can hardly refuse to swim bare breasted. I release Kiritela so she can go up to her chamber and fetch the bucket she uses to collect plo shells. Alone with Melinda, I lean toward her and breathe, "Let it go, my lovely. Stop thinking of ways not to do this." I stand and hold out a hand to her. "Come with me."

She lets me pull her up to standing, still gazing at me uncertainly. Then I see her put on a determined expression. "It's just a swim, surrounded by your family, Kirimor." She points an accusing finger at me. "Whatever dirty thoughts are going through your head, you can forget about them."

"I am the highest priest in the land. I do not have dirty thoughts."

"Ha!"

I am greatly enjoying baiting my Earth female. "Perhaps the one with the dirty thoughts is you, Melinda. Tell me truthfully, how often have you thought about my tail holding you captive and wondered what else I could do with it in the bedchamber?"

She blushes hotly, and I know I have hit the mark. I let my tail roam up her side, stroking her contours softly all the way to her beautifully flushed face. I purr, "Oh my lovely, if you want to know what my tail can do, you need but ask."

Her breath hitches. She stutters, "Please, Kirimor, stop."

I wrap my tail around her neck, squeezing gently, but not enough to stop her breathing. Bringing my face up close to hers so she can feel my breath, I whisper, "You stop, Melinda. Stop fighting this. Sooner or later, you will be mine."

I sniff the air. It is as I thought. My Earth female is aroused. "Your body does not lie, my lovely. You are gushing down there." I place the flat of my hand against her mound, and she wriggles helplessly, unable to move away while my tail is choking her neck. "Oh, you are going to look so fine, stuffed with my cock while I choke you with this tail. You will spasm in pleasure like never before. So no, Melinda, I will not stop. Not until you admit you want this too."

I release her from my hold just as Kiritela bounds back in, carrying her bucket. Her older sister is not far behind. She goes to Melinda, holding out a loin cloth. "This should be a good fit for you," she says.

Melinda takes it and croaks, "Thanks."

"Are the others joining us?" I ask Kirimara.

"Yes, they will be down shortly." She looks at Melinda curiously. My Earth female's hand is clutching her neck where I imprisoned her with my tail just a short while ago. "If you will excuse me, father, I have some work to do, so I will not join you. I will see you all at the lunch repast—I have told Dresolor to hold it back until you return from your swim."

"We will not linger in the heat of the midday sun—just long enough for Kiritela to show Melinda the plo shells and for us to have a refreshing dip in the water. Tell Dresolor we shall return in three beats."

My daughter nods her head and takes off. Kiritela is holding out her hand to Melinda, urging her to follow. She leads my Earth female out of the sea view room and towards the elevator shaft I had integrated into my house, which takes us right down to the seashore. Melinda is strangely quiet on the short journey down, clasping the loin cloth in her hand and listening to Kiritela's chatter.

We emerge into a stone paved space shaded by two large palms. There are comfortable lounge chairs here, for when we want to relax outdoors and enjoy the fresh sea breeze. I turn to Melinda. "You may get changed into the loin cloth here and leave your things on one of these lounge chairs. Come join us in the water when you are ready." I open a large rectangular container and take out fresh towels and sun spray. "Do not forget to protect your skin with this. Simply spray two big puffs in the air in front of you, then walk under the mist. It will adhere to your skin automatically. Kiritela will show you how." I hand the spray to my youngest, who takes off her oversized shirt and promptly demonstrates how to use the spray. I follow suit, divesting myself of my shirt and getting sun protection on my pale gray skin.

"Thanks," responds Melinda, but doesn't move, obviously waiting for us to leave before she pulls off her dress. I decide to let her have her privacy, for now.

"Come, Kiritela, let us go. How about a race to the water?"

"Yess!"

We both run on the white powdery sand to the gently lapping waves on the shore. My daughter flies like the wind, so I do not need to exert much pretense to allow her to win. With a shriek of joy, she launches herself into the balmy water. "I won!"

I dive into an oncoming wave and catch up with her. "So you did, and your reward is…" I pick her up and throw her high in the air, letting her fall back into the water with a loud splash.

She screeches in excitement and swims back to me, wrapping her arms around my neck. "Again!"

So, I throw her up in the air once more. She swims back and clasps me around the neck again but is distracted by something over my shoulder. "Look pa, it is Melinda! Is she not pretty?"

I swing around to get an uninterrupted view of my Earth female making her way on the sand towards us. My appreciative eyes take in her long golden legs and the swing of her subtly curved hips as she walks. And her breasts. The children were right. They are indeed beautiful—just the right size to fit snuggly in the palm of my hand, delicately rounded pale flesh with puckered teats a shade of pinkish brown.

She walks, her back straight, shoulders wide, eyes fixed on me in challenge. "Very pretty," I rumble in answer to my daughter, not taking my gaze off Melinda. She dips her toes experimentally into the water, then reassured, splashes her way toward us. As she gets closer, she dives under the surface, emerging a moment later before us. She shakes the water out of her hair in delight.

"Wow, this is wonderful! Such clear water and just the right temperature!"

"Did you see me up in the air, Melinda?" asks my youngest. "Pa, throw me again."

So I oblige and throw my giggling daughter up in the air. She lands with a splash, shrieking with laughter. My heart fills with joy at her happiness. At this age, she is easy to please. I know her delight in these simple and innocent pleasures will not last forever.

Melinda laughs. "That looks like a lot of fun."

"Then you have a turn," I say gleefully.

"Yes, Melinda! Let pa throw you up in the air. He is very strong!"

My daughter is proving to be a formidable ally. I do not wait for my Earth female to protest. I grab her around the waist and pull her close to me, feeling those wondrous breasts nestle into my chest. I look into her lovely face, the melting brown eyes, cute little nose and soft full lips. I cannot resist a taste of them. I kiss her, running my tongue over the soft berry of her bottom lip. She holds out at first, but soon enough parts her lips with a sigh, allowing me entry. Oh yes, she can protest all she likes, but she wants me, just as much as I want her. My tongue brushes over hers, getting my first, delicious taste. The hands on my chest give up trying to push me away and dig into my flesh, the nails scoring my skin, marking me. I grunt and deepen the kiss. I know I should stop before I am past the point of no return. We are not alone. I indulge in one last taste of her, then without warning, I flex my muscles and send her flying backwards into the air. She screams in surprise as she falls back into the water with a loud splash.

Kiritela claps her hands in delight. "Did you like it, Melinda?"

My Earth female splutters and casts a glance at me before panting, "Sure. That was fun. Now, how about showing me those plo shells?"

As they wade out to the shore, I see Kiristen and his new love appear, followed by Kirishar and the other Human female. Absently, I study her bare form, noting the paler white skin of her breasts and dark pink teats. They are not unpleasing to the eye, but beyond noting the difference in appearance, they do not interest me overmuch. My eyes stray to Melinda, who is digging in the sand with Kiritela and looking for plo shells. Now *that* female interests me very much indeed.

My eldest son runs into the water, chased by the Earth male, Troy, who catches up and pulls him roughly to his chest, nipping him on the neck. Kiristen squeals delightedly. They frolic together, barely aware of anyone else's presence. I watch this scene unfold in fascination. I do not think I have ever seen my son act quite like this. Usually, he is the one that does the chasing, pursuing pretty boys with a remarkable persistence until he gets what he wants. Seeing him so under the spell of this man from Earth has me wondering. Could this, finally, be the one as Kiristen claims? My heart tightens painfully. I want only happiness for my son, but this outsider is sure to return to his home planet in due course and leave my boy heartbroken. Please Taya, let it not be so.

The Earth female, Avery, approaches me in the water and engages me in some chitchat about this or the other, which I barely register. My mind is twisted with worry over my son and the rest of my attention is fixed on Melinda, busily picking plo shells with Kiritela. As she laughs with my daughter and admires the dark pink shells, my chest tightens with a new worrisome emotion. I grunt a non-committal reply to Avery, then say, "Excuse me, I am going to go for a vigorous swim. I shall see you all shortly."

I do not wait for her response. I turn and dive under the surface, cutting through the water with strong, deliberate strokes. I swim far out into the sea, trying to empty my mind of all thought with the physical exertion. After a time, I stop to catch my breath, treading water and turning to see how far I have come. The house is a mere dot on the horizon. I feel a trickle of guilt for having strayed so far. Dresolor will have to hold up the lunch repast even longer than anticipated.

With a determined deep breath, I ready myself for the long swim back to the shore but stop as something large bumps me from behind. I whip around quickly in fright, then let out a relieved chuckle. Wise gentle eyes regard me in a large, dark gray body that bumps me again in friendly greeting. "Hello Turi, it has been a long time, my friend."

Turi nudges me again.

"Have you been spending time in the oceans of the southern sector?" I ask. "I have not seen you in a while."

Turi makes a low whistling sound.

"Did you find yourself a mate there?"

The creature emits a clicking noise, telling me no.

"I am sorry to hear that, my friend. Perhaps in the next season."

I give her a gentle tap. "I need to get back. They are waiting for me to eat the lunch repast. Will you give me a ride?"

Turi whistles her agreement. I settle myself on her ample back and hold on tight to the top fin, just in time as she surges forward, zipping through the water at top speed. Before long, we are close to the shore, which is empty of people—everyone now back inside. I thank Turi and slip off her back. With a snort of her spout, she disappears once more into the blue. I swim the remaining distance and step out of the water, making my way back to the house. The swim has done me good, and I have calmed my mind. I do not know what the future holds for my son, or for me, but I know this. I want Melinda more than I have ever wanted anyone in my life, and I am going to make her mine.

Chapter 24

Melinda

Kirimor has disappeared into the distance. I saw him speak to Avery as she bobbed about in the water next to him, her naked breasts jiggling in his line of vision. I'm a little shaken by the spark of fury I felt on seeing her so close to him wearing so little. A voice in my head wanted to shout, "Keep away! He's mine!" Ridiculous, I know. I have no claims on the hot priest, and no intention of following through with whatever it is he thinks we've started.

That I'm intensely attracted to him is self-evident. I'm not going to lie to myself about that. Even worse, when he has me in his clutches, my willpower deserts me and I turn to goo. As I admire the plo shells Kiritela and I have found, I try not to think about how good it felt to kiss him. I try not to think about that tail and how wet I became as he held me captive. I try not to think about his dark eyes that burn into my soul and promise untold pleasures. Most of all, I try to forget the look of pain in his eyes as he spoke of his mother's death, the look of pride on his face as he spoke of his eldest daughter's achievements, and his joy as he swung his youngest up in the air—because all these things represent chinks in the armor I need to form around myself when it comes to him. I cannot catch feelings for the sicortar, the man who has a harem of women at his beck and call to satisfy his every sexual need. Do I really want to add my name to the list?

Then, I saw him turn away from Avery and begin to swim out to sea. Where was he going? He cut through the water with powerful strokes, getting further and further away until he was barely a dot on the horizon. Now, as I try to locate him with my eyes, I feel a prickle of unease. Is it safe? I broach the subject to

Kirishar, who has joined us in our hunt for plo shells. "Kirishar, does your father usually swim out so far?"

He looks over his shoulder at the expanse of sea where Kirimor has disappeared from view and shrugs. "Sometimes. He says it helps him when he has things on his mind." His tail twirls up and strokes me gently on the arm. "Do not worry, Melinda. He is a very strong swimmer."

"That's good to know."

"Look at this one!" cries Kiritela, drawing my attention to her once more. She had dug out a large and unbroken pink shell.

"How beautiful! Definitely one to put into your bucket." I glance over at it. "We seem to have collected quite a few. Perhaps we should be thinking about going back inside. It is very hot out here."

A voice behind me says, "You are quite right. Let us all go back in."

Kiristen is there, arm in arm with Troy, and Avery not far behind. I can't resist asking her, "What did you say to the sicortar that had him swim away like that?"

"Me? All I did was praise this fabulous beach and thank him for inviting us to his amazing home."

Kiristen scrunches his face, trying to spot his father on the horizon. "He has gone very far. I wonder why." Then he too shrugs. "We should go back in and wash. Perhaps by then, he will have returned."

So in we all go. When we get to the paved patio space where I left my things, Kiristen points us to a side door I had not noticed before. "We can all wash ourselves here," he says. He opens the door and I see a large communal shower space, with overhead sprays and side nozzles built into the wall. He presses a switch, and warm water starts pelting us in all directions. It zings into my flesh, like a thousand acupuncture needles all at once. I squeal in shock, much to Kirishar's amusement. He shows me a button to press on the wall for soap, which foams out into my hand. I step away from the water long enough to scrub my body clean, then get back under the stinging rain to rinse it away.

In less than five minutes, we're all squeaky clean, and drying ourselves on the fluffy towels left on the lounge chairs earlier. I quickly put my bra and dress back on, and discreetly exchange my wet loin cloth for my panties. I keep casting glances out to the beach, hoping to catch sight of Kirimor. He still hasn't made an appearance by the time we get back inside the house and take the elevator up to the main level. As we exit the shaft, I see a Krovatian female who looks vaguely familiar. It takes me a moment to pinpoint why I recognize her. She's one of the two females who was with Kirimor on that first day we arrived on Krovatia.

She smiles easily at us but turns her attention to the children. "Kiritela, go quickly to your room and put on a fresh loin cloth as well as a new shirt. The one you are wearing is all wet. You will catch a chill soon. Go on, quick. You too, Kirishar."

Kiritela holds up the bucket. "Look ma, we got lots of plo shells."

"Indeed, but now you must go up and change."

"Yes, ma."

Kiristen hooks an arm through Troy's. "Come with me, my love. We can change to dry loin cloths in my room, and I can get you a shirt to wear. Our house is more chilly than most."

"I hope that's all you will do," I say dryly.

Troy huffs out a laugh. "No promises. Anyway, looks like lunch has been postponed until the sicortar makes it back."

The Krovatian female, presumably Kiritela's mother, looks up in surprise. "He is not with you? Oh dear, Dresolor will not be happy about that. I will go inform him now."

With a swish of her tail, she flits off to do this.

Kiristen smiles at me and Avery. "We will not be long, I promise. Please help yourselves to some *nari* and we shall be back very soon."

"No problem."

I head under the archway to that wonderful sea view room, Avery with me, and we settle ourselves down on the bench seat.

"That is one heck of a view," says Avery.

"Mmm," I nod. "Want some *nari*?"

"Yes please."

I pour us both a drink, and we sip it thirstily after all our exertions in the heat of the midday sun. "I don't know about you," I say, "but I've worked up quite an appetite. Hope the food is good."

"If it's anything like the spread we had at the banquet, it should be. Remember those delicious green balls? Now what were they called?"

"*Mishu.*"

"Ah yes, *mishu*. Those were good."

"I wonder where the sicortar has got to. Is it even safe to swim so far out alone?"

Avery raises a brow. "I'm sure he knows what he's doing. Nobody seems concerned about it." She sees my frown. "Hey, Melinda. Don't tell me you're falling for the hot priest?"

"Of course not!" I snap, then feel bad about having raised my voice.

"The way he grabbed you when we arrived... seemed like he was staking his claim."

"I'll admit he was getting a little frisky, but I'm handling it," I reply with confidence.

"Or you could go with the flow and enjoy."

"Avery, have you seen that bevy of females he keeps in his household for his sexual pleasure?"

"I've asked about this. He only needs them when he's performing his holy ceremonies—you know, like he did that first day on us. Apparently, the act of going into a trance and sucking in other people's negative energy has the effect of making him incredibly horny, so that's what they're there for. Don't think of them as his girlfriends or anything like that. They are literally there to service his needs as he performs his priestly duties."

I stare at her in astonishment. "You seem well informed. Who told you this?"

She looks smug. "I may or may not have grilled our friendly liaison officer, Desimar, about this."

"Why didn't you tell me this before? This kind of information needs to go into our reports."

"I've written it up. I can send it to you in time for your weekly report."

"Ok, thanks." I think about it a little more. "Even if that's what they are primarily there for, the fact is that he has several women living in his home who he has sex with, and who he has fathered children with. It's all just too messy a situation for me."

"Ordinarily, I'd agree, but look at the guy. Given the opportunity, I would not pass that up."

I remain silent. I'm so tempted to agree with her, but the idea of sharing a man with other women… No, I don't think I could do that. I've already developed possessive compulsions when it comes to the sicortar, as evidenced by my bout of jealous fury earlier against Avery. I don't think I could stand to share him with anyone. He has his harem of women, and I'm not going to be one of them. So, I need to retain my focus, harden my heart, and keep my lady parts well away from the dangerous priest.

Something catches my eye. I squint, trying to get a better view. It looks like a person, whizzing through the water at high speed. Is he riding some kind of jet ski? No, that's not it. I take out my communicator and use the zoom lens to get a closer look. It's Kirimor, and he's riding on some kind of large aquatic beast, holding on to its fin.

They slow down as they near the shore, and Kirimor dismounts, stroking the creature before it disappears from sight with a mighty whoosh. What on earth was that? I watch, dumbfounded, as the sicortar swims the rest of the way to the shore and starts walking back toward the house. I keep my communicator lens focused on him, ogling his strong, powerful body as he makes his way back here.

Beside me, Avery sighs. "That is one fine looking male, Melinda."

"I know," I whisper.

Chapter 25

Kirimor

We sit at the table, sharing our lunch repast. I have apologized profusely for holding it up. We make a large group—my five children, drashas and our three guests. Melinda sits far from me, on the other side of the table next to my middle son, Kirilor. I sense her trying to keep her distance, a cool expression on her face when she deigns to regard me.

It is the presence of my drashas that is doing this to her, for she was not like this with me before. But now, sitting surrounded by the five women that I fuck, it is something hard for her to ignore. I knew this would pose a problem, but I could hardly uninvite my drashas from the food table at their own home. I flex my arms and narrow my eyes.

The troublesome Earth female is just going to have to accept me the way I am. My drashas are there because I need to fuck them. It is just the way things are. This will not change things. I still fully intend to make her mine.

She looks up just then and sees the challenge in my eyes. Hers stare back at me coolly. I let my tail swish up in the air and point it in her direction, as a reminder of just what it did to her earlier today. She sees it, and a betraying quiver escapes her lips. *Good*.

"Some more *mishu*, sicortar?" asks a solicitous voice beside me. It is Pirofena, my latest drasha. She has settled well into my household, keeping her promise to love and serve everyone in my home devotedly. I know she has been very supportive in looking after Kiritela when her mother has needed a helping hand with her. And of course, she has fulfilled her duties as a drasha admirably, taking every single pounding I've given her during my holy trances. I have not gone easy on her, fucking her with all the need and abandon that my trances bring out in me. And she has not only taken it all, but she has enjoyed it too, climaxing on my cock time and again. Yes, I am most pleased with her, so of course, I smile benignly and reply in a teasing voice, "Only if you will feed it to me."

She hastens to oblige, lifting two dainty fingers holding the delicious green ball to my mouth. I part my lips to take the offering, and reward the pretty fingers with a lick of my tongue. As I do so, I glance across the table at Melinda. If looks could kill, then hers would be striking me dead this very moment. Her dark, fiery eyes spear me, flashing with fury. Then quickly, she drops her gaze and composes herself, returning to the cool ice queen of before.

Oh Melinda, you do not fool me. You want me just as much as I want you.

Her jealousy is revealing of how much she desires me, but there is no need for it. She has my full attention already, if she but knew it. My drashas are no threat to her. However, it is fun to poke the beast. Turning toward Pirofena, I drawl, "Mmm, so tasty. Almost as good as this." And I nuzzle her neck, giving it a quick nip that makes her emit a surprised, pleased moan.

My eyes cannot resist straying across the table, but this time, my frustrating Earth woman is resolutely staring down at her plate of food. I am almost disappointed until I see her left hand shredding the tablecloth. I watch her closely as she continues eating, face set in stone, while her fingernails unconsciously scratch the thin fabric covering the table. Except that now, instead of exulting in her jealousy, I am hit with a sharp stab of pain. The last thing I ever want to do is hurt Melinda. That same tight feeling in my chest returns. I still cannot put a name to it; the feeling is foreign to me. Not one of my drashas, not even Merostena, my longest serving companion, has ever made me feel like this. I am not sure I like the feeling.

I wait until the meal is over, then as they stand, readying to leave, I approach Melinda from behind and snake my tail around her.

"Kirimor! Let me go."

I bring my mouth to her ear. "Never."

A clearing of a throat brings my head up to see Troy, watching us a little nervously. "Erm, sicortar, thank you for hosting us for lunch. It has been a pleasure, but we need to be on our way."

I let my gaze settle on his, eyes never wavering. "The pleasure is mine, Troy. I will let Kiristen escort you and Avery back home. Melinda and I still have some business to conclude, and I will see her home later."

He tries one more time. "Melinda? You coming or staying?"

I tighten my tail around her. She could protest. She could insist on leaving now, and I would be honor bound to let her. I am not that much of a monster. The tail is merely reminding her that she belongs to me, and how much she likes what I do to her. She weighs her options quickly, then makes the right decision. "It's ok. I'll see you later."

He hesitates a fraction longer, but Kiristen tugs at his arm, nudging him away. "It is fine, Troy. My father is an honorable man. Let us go."

And with that, they turn to leave. I send a prayer of gratitude to Taya for my wonderful children. They have been most helpful today in my quest for Melinda.

Once they have gone, and with them the rest of my family to their various rooms in the house, she mutters under her breath. "Now will you let me go?"

Slowly, I unravel my tail from its noose around her. "Come with me, Melinda."

"Where are you taking me?"

"I thought you might like to see the rest of my estates."

Her suspicious gaze is tinged with curiosity. "The rest of your estates?"

I smile innocently. "When I became sicortar, I was gifted with this large tract of land on which I have built my house. It extends up into the mountain you see behind us. In those uplands, the climate is fresher and there are fertile valleys in which I grow a vast variety of crops as well as breed animals. Everything we eat in this household is grown on our land. I thought you might like to see it for yourself."

"I would very much like to. Do you mind if I film what I see on my communicator?"

"Not at all. Come now, let us get into my drone."

I curl my tail around her waist to lead her out. She stops dead in her tracks. "Kirimor, this is ridiculous. Can you please stop putting your tail around me like this. Believe me, I am quite capable of following you without being on a leash."

I hold back from blurting out the immediate thought that comes to me. *But I like having you on a leash.*

"Melinda, seeing as you have no tail of your own, perhaps you do not understand how it functions for us beings who do. My tail is as part of me as my hands are. When I wish to show special favor to the female I am escorting, I do so with my tail. Think of this as Krovatian gallantry. Now please, come with me."

She begins to walk with me but says tartly, "Strange then that none of the many officials I have met these last few weeks have wrapped their tail around me, let alone touched me with it."

"I did say it is a mark of special favor, my lovely. I do not put my tail on just anyone." With this, I tighten my grip on her, letting the tip of my tail stroke the underside of her breast tantalizingly.

"Kirimor," she breathes as the tip moves to touch one puckered teat straining against the fabric of her dress.

I do not respond but keep walking her to my drone, caressing her lovely teat and feeling her reaction. By the time we reach my drone, she is breathless, and not from any exertion. I open the door for her and help her aboard, then settle in beside her. Her face is flushed, but she does not speak.

"Melinda," I begin, my voice husky.

She does not respond, so I touch a gentle finger to her cheek. "Stop fighting this, my lovely."

Now she looks at me, her eyes flashing. "And what? Become one of your many women? Think again, Kirimor. This thing we have going on," she points back and forth between us, "is not going to happen, no matter how attracted I am to you. I. Don't. Share."

I start the engine and take us up in the air. Only then do I trust myself to speak. "This is who I am, Melinda. Accept it. I cannot change my life to suit you."

"I don't expect you to. That is why, we are not going to happen."

I switch tack. "Are you telling me, Melinda, that you are not also involved with another person? Remember, I checked your aura that first day you arrived. I detected sadness at the loss of someone dear to your heart."

"It's not the same."

"How so? Are you telling me there is not someone else in your life, someone important to you?"

She is quiet.

"So," I continue, "it is alright for you to have other people in your life but not me?"

"I do not have five other guys that I fuck on the regular."

"But you have that ex-mate of yours." We have reached my cabin and begin our descent.

"We were together for twelve years—sun rotations—but then we got divorced. It means that we parted ways and are no longer married, no longer mates."

"I see. In my culture, mating is usually for life, though we do on occasion have people who split from their mates."

We land outside my cabin with a light bump. I open the drone door and help Melinda out. She takes a look around us at the lush pastures before us and then to the rustic cabin. "This is beautiful. Do you come up here often?"

"Not as often as I would like. This is my place of refuge when I need to get away from everyone and just be myself. Come with me. I will show you around."

As I say this, I wrap my tail around her again. This time, she does not protest. We walk quietly down a path that follows the trail of a stream towards the enclosed pasture, which is dotted with drens, a small woolly animal that I breed. Melinda gazes at them curiously, taking out her communicator to capture some images.

"What are these creatures called?" she asks.

"They are drens, known for the tenderness of their meat and the silkiness of their coat. We use their wool to make soft but durable fabrics. Your bedding at home is most probably made with dren wool."

"Can I approach them?"

"Yes, but they are skittish animals and may run from you. Take it slow and do not alarm them."

I unravel my tail from around her waist and lead the way, taking very gentle steps toward a nearby dren grazing lazily. Once we are within touching distance, I quickly lace my tail around it and grab it by the horns. As it begins to thrash, I croon soothingly and use one hand to stroke its forehead. In a short while, it settles in my arms, and I murmur, "There, there, little one. No need to fret." Turning my gaze toward Melinda, I say quietly, "Come closer slowly. You may stroke its coat and the top of its head."

She does as I say, smiling in wonder at the silky feel of the wool beneath her fingers. The dren bleats in appreciation and her smiles grows wider. "Oh you cute thing."

"Do not get too attached, Melinda. This cute thing will one day be served on a dish at meal time."

"Ugh, don't remind me!" She ruffles its head and the dren bleats a few more times, happy to be petted and fussed by the lovely lady.

I chuckle. "It is the cycle of life. This dren is luckier than most of us. It gets to live a carefree, happy life in this beautiful valley until one day, it is put to eternal sleep. It will never have to face growing weak and infirm in old age. I consider that a good life to have led."

"I guess when you put it that way…" She gives the dren one final stroke then straightens to her full height.

Carefully, I release the creature, which gambols off into the distance. I return my tail to the place where it belongs—around my Melinda—and we walk on, going up a gentle hill that slopes toward another, heretofore hidden valley.

"Do you breed any other animals?" Melinda inquires.

"Yes indeed. Look over there. Can you see a set of outbuildings?"

She nods.

"That is where we keep the rest of our animals. There are jujos, medium sized feathered creatures that produce the most delicious eggs. And we also have a half-dozen bilos. They are larger creatures that produce the creamiest milk imaginable."

"Sounds similar to some of the farm animals we have on Earth."

"And also to the animals that were on my ancestors' home planet, light years away in another galaxy. I find it intriguing that civilizations and living things can develop in such similar ways so far from each other."

"Yes. For years before we made first contact with the Venorians, we always imagined alien species would be a lot more different to us then they turned out to be. Perhaps it shows we're all part of some grand master plan by some higher being."

I smile, "Indeed. All the different deities we worship could very well be a manifestation of the same higher being. I like to believe that in the end, all these spiritual paths lead to the same destination."

She gives a little laugh. "We have a saying back on Earth. 'All roads lead to Rome.' It stems from an ancient Earth civilization centered around a city called Rome, whose power expanded and created a great empire. The Romans were known for building a network of well-engineered roads in every corner of their empire, all of which led back to their city. In modern times, the saying is used to mean that you can use different methods to get the same result."

"I like that. We could amend the saying to, all roads lead to the same higher being."

"Yes, although it doesn't quite have the same ring to it."

I place a quick kiss atop her head. "Perhaps not. Keep talking, Melinda. I love to hear about your world. But first, tell me more about this ex-mate of yours. Why are you not mated anymore?"

"I'm beginning to think it's because I've been a bad wife to him."

"Wife?"

"Our word for a female mate."

"I see. Why do you think that?"

"My job was more important to me than the relationship. I left to become Earth's ambassador on the planet Mars. He stayed behind on Earth."

"A job will not keep you warm at night, Melinda. Nor will it nurture you with the love and affection we all need."

"And that is why you, sicortar, have devoted your life to a job that deprives you of a mate."

"I had little choice in the matter. Perhaps I am speaking from experience when I tell you a job is a poor substitute for a mate. And Melinda, call me Kirimor when we are alone."

She sighs. "You're not wrong, Kirimor. It's just…"

She takes a long time to continue, so I prompt, "Just what, my lovely?"

"I come from a relatively poor family. Neither of my parents ever went to college or got a decent education. All their lives, they have strived at menial jobs. I wanted something different for myself. It took a lot of single-minded determination to get to where I am. First, getting a scholarship to college, then clawing my way up the career ladder. It wasn't easy for someone with a background like mine. I suppose this struggle to make something of myself has come to define me as a person. It matters a lot to me that I'm not some lowly-employed, forgettable individual, but Melinda Garcia, someone who has made a name for herself."

"It is certainly an achievement to be proud of."

"Yet it has come at a price. I didn't think it would. Wyatt and I seemed like we were on the same trajectory. We met in college, and we were both high achievers, people going places. Then somewhere along the line, Wyatt got off that track we were on. He wanted an easier life, less stress, so he gave up his incredibly successful career to become a chiropractor—that's a type of therapist who works on your joints to relieve musculoskeletal pain."

"A very worthy profession."

"I didn't say it wasn't. He loves what he does and gets great satisfaction from helping relieve people's pain. But stepping off that conveyor belt to become a chiropractor created a mismatch in our lifestyles. He comes home every day at a reasonable hour while I'm constantly on the clock, in meetings, out and about.

Even before I left for Mars, we barely saw each other during the day. I could tell he wanted me to slow down, spend more time at home with him. I just couldn't get off that career path like he did, not after all the hard work and sacrifice it took to get me there."

"Even if it meant losing your mate?"

"Even if it meant that." She looks down at her feet, face sad. "It makes me sound like not a good person."

I stop and face her. "No, my lovely, just a flawed, complex individual, like all of us." I pull her into my arms and capture her lips in a gentle kiss. At least, that was the intention. But somehow, the kiss becomes a lot less than gentle as I ravage Melinda's lips, desperate for a taste of her. I feel her sigh as she allows my tongue to plunge into her mouth and tangle with hers. We feed on each other, our hunger stoked with every touch. Her hands come up to twine in my hair, pulling at the short strands as she kisses me back with just as much need as I am feeling. I lose myself in her, never wanting this kiss to end. With every touch, that crushing feeling in my chest resolves itself into a clear knowing. *Oh Melinda. My love.*

With a gasp, she pushes herself away, her breaths coming in and out in sharp pants. "No, Kirimor. Not this."

My tail rises to her face, stroking gently. "Yes, my love, this."

"No, Kirimor, we are not doing this."

She stomps away, but I quickly catch up and wrap my tail around her. She acknowledges the gesture with a slight falter in her step but doesn't stop. We continue walking, nearing the outbuildings that house my animals. I wave at my groundskeeper who approaches us with his slow, ponderous gait.

"Jenisor, how goes it today?"

"All well, sicortar. The bilos have been milked and we are just on our way to gather the dren into their enclosure before we return to our homes."

"That is good. This is Melinda, from the planet Earth. I will be showing her round then going to the cabin."

He bows his head respectfully. "Welcome, Melinda."

She smiles. "Thank you, Jenisor. It's good to meet you. I am most impressed with what I have seen so far."

"It is all due to the sicortar's great vision and leadership."

"And your hard work too, I'm sure."

"Ah, we try to do our best. Enjoy the rest of your day. Peace be with you."

With that, my grouchy, loyal henchman turns to go. Melinda watches him a moment as he disappears round the corner, then addresses me. "He seems very dedicated to his sicortar."

"As it should be."

She echoes with a laugh, "Of course, as it should be."

For the next three beats, I show her around my lands, though by mutual accord, we pause the personal discussion and focus simply on the beauty and peace of our surroundings. Melinda exclaims with wonder at what she sees and asks many questions. Her communicator comes out at frequent intervals to record her explorations, and I know that from a work perspective, our time here has been a fruitful one for her. It remains to be seen what is to be achieved on the personal front. As I guide our footsteps back to my cabin, I still hope to persuade my lovely Earth female to submit to me and become mine. The task, I know, will not be an easy one.

Chapter 26

Melinda

I'm conflicted as we reach Kirimor's picturesque cabin after our tour around his estate. I have no doubt he plans a seduction in that love shack of his. Part of me, the sensible, intellectual part, scoffs at the very thought of my giving in to the horny priest with a harem. The other part… well that's a different story.

It's not just the physical attraction, although my God that's intense. There's something else as well. Earlier, as we spoke about my marriage to Wyatt, I felt truly seen and understood. As we walked with his tail wrapped around me, I was strangely comforted. As much as I want to typecast Kirimor as a horny priest, I know there's more to him than that. There are so many facets to this intriguing man.

Then again, I'm also conflicted because of Wyatt. It's laughable really. Separated for three years and divorced for more than six months, yet I still feel married to him somehow. Why does it seem as if I'm cheating on him by being with Kirimor? Wyatt and I—we're done. I invited him to come with me to Krovatia, and he turned me down. I'll love him till the end of time, but he's not my husband any longer. I'm free to be with whoever I want.

Yes, but a priest who fucks five other women as part of his job? My head tells me to resist, resist, resist. And I will try my utmost to. Perhaps I should insist on returning home right this minute. That is the sensible thing to do.

But I won't. I want to spend more time with this man who makes me feel so good. I just have to make sure things don't get too heated.

We step inside the cabin, a large A-frame structure clad in dark wood, with a massive skylight window on one sloping side of the roof. The interior consists of one spacious open-plan room simply furnished with a kitchen area and low-set dining table on one side, and on the other, a low-lying bed positioned right under the window. At night, it must feel like sleeping under the stars. Next to the bed, leaning against the wall, is some kind of string instrument, and beside it is a cushioned bench on the floor, much like the one in his house overlooking the sea. Along with the bench is a small side table on which reposes a beautifully bound book, whose title is written in large Krovatian script. At the far end of the room, I notice a door, presumably leading to the bathroom.

It's obvious to me from one quick glance that this is not a place that Kirimor's extended family visits. This is exclusively his space.

Kirimor lets me walk in ahead of him and take a curious look around. He goes to the kitchen area and opens a cupboard built into the wall. From it he withdraws a rounded bottle filled with a pale yellow liquid and two sets of glasses. He places them on the side table, nudging the book aside.

"Take a seat, Melinda," he says in his low, gravelly voice.

I slip off my shoes and lower myself to sit on the bench. He joins me and pours the liquid into both glasses. I hear it fizz. "What's this?"

"It is Lom. It will make us feel mellow, without losing sight of our senses."

"Some kind of alcoholic drink?"

"No, as I said, it will not make you lose your senses. It has a chemical in its composition that affects your nervous system and brings a profound sense of calm. It also tastes delicious. Try it."

He sees my hesitation and laughs. "Melinda, I will not use any wiles to seduce you. This is just what I say it is. Something to make us both relaxed and mellow."

I take the drink from him and try a little sip. It tastes like sherbert, tart with a sweet, fizzy kick. Encouraged, I drink some more. Beside me, Kirimor sips from his own glass, gazing at me in amusement. "So, what do you think?"

"I like it. When does the mellow feeling come?"

"Give it a beat."

"Ok." I drain my glass and Kirimor pours me a second shot.

We sit in peaceful silence, enjoying the Lom. Finally, Kirimor speaks in a low, murmuring voice, "So, you parted from your husband, but he still matters a lot to you. Is that not so?"

"I love him. I always will."

"Do you think you may ever return to him and be mated again?"

"It's been three years, Kirimor. I think it's fairly clear that we're over."

He looks at me consideringly. "No, that is not what I sensed when I scanned you. It felt a lot more recent than that."

I play with the soft tassel on the armrest of my seat. "I—we still get together, whenever I am back on Earth."

"You still fuck?"

I raise my brow at his indelicate language. "Yes."

"And next time you return to your home planet, you will fuck him again?"

"I don't know. It depends on him too, if he's met someone else and started a new relationship."

"So far, in all this time, he has not started another relationship and neither have you. Is that correct?"

"We tried dating others at first, but it didn't feel right. Not for me, and I think not for him either."

"So what you are telling me is that you are still essentially mates, even though you are currently living apart."

I'm about to deny this, then relent. "Well, that's one way to put it."

He doesn't say anything more. After a while, I sneak a glance at him. His face is set in a deep frown. I don't like seeing it on him at all.

"Kirimor, talk to me."

He raises glittering eyes to mine. I catch my breath at the anger in them.

"So, Melinda, you have an ex-mate who you still love and fuck occasionally, yet you judge me for my drashas. What if I were to tell you that I too do not share? I do not share what is mine with anybody else. If I make you mine, then you will be all mine, no one else's."

"Bullshit! You're in no position to say that when you get to fuck other women all the time."

I watch him count to ten in his mind and pour himself another shot of Lom. "I see I shall require all the help I can get to maintain my temper," he grits out.

He drains the glass and puts it down. With a deep indrawn breath, he grunts, "I do not share my heart and soul with my drashas, Melinda. I simply fuck them in the temple when my holy trances render me unbearably lustful. It is a physical release, nothing more. My drashas live under my roof, but in their own private quarters. Every night, I sleep alone, Melinda. If I were to make you mine, you would be the only female in my heart and in my bed."

"You eat your meals with them and have fathered their children. I think it's quite a lot more than just a physical release, Kirimor."

"Yes, we eat together. I want my children to enjoy the company of both their parents. Why is that wrong?"

"I didn't say it was wrong. I was only disputing your claim that the relationship you have with your drashas is purely physical, and thus easy for me to overlook. It isn't."

"No easier than it is for me to overlook your mate back on Earth who is still in your heart."

"So, we both have baggage."

He sighs, "Yes, we do. Life is complicated, never simple."

We lapse back into silence. His tail snakes around my neck, the tip stroking my cheek gently. His large hands enfold mine. "And in the midst of all these complications, there are these feelings between us," he says softly. "I wish it were not so. I wish I could turn my back and let you go on your way, you and this ex-husband of yours. But I cannot, for you are now in my heart, Melinda."

He lifts my right hand and places it on his chest. My palm presses on warmth and firm muscle through the fabric of his shirt. I drop my head on to his shoulder, feeling a strange combination of sad, happy, peaceful and mellow. It must be the effects of the Lom kicking in.

"Kirimor," I breathe. "I have feelings for you too, but I can't let myself love you. It would just be a recipe for heartbreak."

"And yet my heart is yours, my love. Only yours. Is that not enough for you?"

"I can't get past the fact that you have sex with other women, Kirimor. I'm just not programmed that way."

"I see." He stares at our joint hands morosely. "Will you at the very least spend this one night in my arms? I will return you to your home first thing in the morning."

"Alright, but... I won't have sex with you."

He laughs sadly. "I am quite aware of that."

We stay like this for a long time. His thumb strokes the palm of my hand while his tail caresses my cheek. Eventually, my eyes drop to the book on the side table. "What's this book you have there, Kirimor?"

"This is a collection of revelations from our goddess Taya, put together by holy priests who received her wisdom over a millennium ago. I like to read them and meditate when I am here alone."

"Read me something from it."

"Very well." He picks up the book and leafs through it, settling on a page, then starts to read.

> *"Why," he asked, "does calamity befall me but not others? Where is the justice in that?"*
>
> *And Taya replied, "Do not look with envy upon others, for you do not know fully what path they tread. The rich, the blissful and carefree, the blessed in good looks and health—they may all appear to have greater fortune than you, but that is an illusion. What you see on the surface is not all that there is to be seen. Always remember. No person walks this life without calamity to endure and good fortune to enjoy. No person is given more calamity than they can endure and more good fortune than is just and fair. So do not look upon others but look to yourself. Nourish your soul and body so that you may endure the hard times, for hard times there will be. Cherish each moment of joy that comes, for surely in time you will be gifted with joy. Remember all this and you will have a life well lived."*

Kirimor closes the book and puts it back on the table.

"Wise words," I say.

"I like to read this passage to remind myself not to envy the good fortune of others or bemoan the hardships in my life."

"Do you need to remind yourself of this often?"

"No, not very. I have come to terms with the path my life has taken. It has taken me a long time to do so, Melinda. This life of a sicortar is not one I ever wanted."

"What did you want?"

He shrugs then draws me into his arms so my head lies on his chest, and threads feather light fingers through my hair. With the gentle, soothing touch, I become ever more mellow and content.

"I do not know. I was only seventeen sun rotations old when my gift was discovered, and I was sent to the temple. I wanted what most others wanted. A mate. Good friends. A successful career. I had ambitions to become a technological inventor. This last, I have managed to do in my own time. The cooling system in my house—that is one of my inventions."

I think back to what he said he wanted. "Why are sicortars not allowed to mate?"

"Melinda, it is not just your kind that believe in fidelity between life partners. In my culture, mates are faithful and exclusive. It would not be possible to have such a relationship and keep drashas."

"And drashas are a must if you are sicortar?"

He kisses the top of my head. "Yes, my love, they are."

"Because your holy trances make you horny? Why can't your mate be with you at such times?"

"It is difficult to explain. Unless you have experienced it, you do not know what it is like to go into a holy trance. In that state, I am able to see the most secret and wicked thoughts of the people I am scanning. With my gift, I can draw that wickedness toward me and absorb it into my being, but it is not a painless process. What my body goes through when I am taking that evil into me is hard to describe. It is like an internal shriek of agony. It takes supreme effort to clamp down on the evil and break it up. And then a reaction sets in. I become like a ravenous beast, needing to fuck all traces of that evil out of me. I can be rough, and I am insatiable. One female would not cope with all the pounding I need to give. Once, in the early days of my career when I only had two drashas, Merostena was taken sick, and I went into a holy trance with just Jalimara with me—Kirilor's mother. By the end of it, she could barely walk, and it took her many rotations to recover from the damage to her internal passage. I learned my lesson and have never since gone into a trance without at least two drashas with me. This meant, of course, that I needed to keep more drashas, as a backup."

"How long have you been sicortar?"

"I am now entering my twenty-fourth sun rotation in this role."

"And when do you get to retire?"

"Whenever a replacement is found. I hope it will not be much longer, but I cannot know for sure."

"There are lots of sicors. Why can't the most experienced of them step into your shoes?"

"Not all sicors have my gift. They can only draw evil from someone in the room with them, while I can do so from a great distance."

"But there are a few out there that have this gift?"

"Yes, there are three sicors that I know of that are able to do this. Two of them are very young, with little experience. The third, a person by the name of Melistor, is my best bet as a successor. He is currently stationed at a temple in the southern sector of the planet and has been sicor for six sun rotations. Ideally, he requires a little more time and experience before he is ready to attain my position. However, there is an important matter that I have been asked to focus my attention on, so I plan to contact him about taking on some of my duties for a while. We shall see how well he fares."

"What kind of important matter?"

"I am not at liberty to say."

I ponder this. "So, one day in the not too distant future, you will stop being sicortar. Will you then be allowed to mate?"

His arms around me tighten imperceptibly. "Yes, then I shall be free to mate. But who will want a tired old man?"

"Stop fishing, Kirimor. You know very well you are nowhere near a tired old man."

"I am nearly fifty sun rotations old, my lovely."

My fingers trace the solid wall of muscle on his chest. "That still leaves you with many good years ahead."

He chuckles, "We shall see."

The sun above us has begun to set when Kirimor rouses. "Are you hungry, my love?"

"I could eat."

"Then let me prepare you a light evening repast."

With athletic grace belying his fifty-something years, he gets to his feet in one go, holding out his hands to me. I take them, letting him pull me to standing. I follow him into the kitchen area and watch as he opens another hidden compartment in the wall, revealing a type of refrigerating unit. He pulls out a covered dish, which on closer inspection looks to be some kind of salad. A jug of sauce—presumably a dressing—comes out next. Kirimor pours it on the salad, then uses a two-pronged fork to mix it up. He looks up to find me watching him and smiles.

"These are fresh leaves and roots, shredded finely and garnished with slices of ripe fruit, all of it grown on my land. Try it. I think you will find it most refreshing."

He brings the dish to the dining table along with an implement that resembles a pair of large tweezers, and motions for me to sit. He take a seat beside me and with the tweezer-like implement, collects a mouthful of the salad, bringing it to my lips. "Open."

Obediently, I open up and let him feed me. The salad tastes fresh, vibrant and zingy. I savor it, just as he prepares the next mouthful for me. When I'm able to speak, I say, "We seem to have had this conversation before, Kirimor. You know I'm well capable of feeding myself."

The tip of his tail comes up to stroke my hands, reminding me of the last time I protested his attempts to feed me. "Melinda, do not argue with me on this. You will eat from my hands."

"Or else?"

He smiles evilly. "Or else, my lovely, I will be obliged to take appropriate action." With this, his tail wraps itself loosely around my wrists, not yet imprisoning me, but giving me due warning. He brings another mouthful of food to my lips, and I take it unprotestingly. Together, we finish up the salad, with him alternating between feeding me and himself.

I swallow my last bite and sigh happily. "Thanks, Kirimor. That was delicious."

With a pleased look, he stands, taking the empty dish back to the kitchen and quickly rinsing it out.

"Is there a bathroom I can use?"

"Of course, just through there," he says, pointing to the door at the far end.

I walk over to the door in question and open it. I find a spacious bathing area with a massive sunken bath and a Krovatian-style toilet bowl low down on the floor, together with a metal bar to hold on to while I crouch down. I know enough by now to take off my dress and panties before getting into the required position. These facilities are designed with Krovatians, wearing only loin cloths, in mind. I learned that the hard way in my first week on this planet. Once my business is concluded, I press the button on the side of the metal bar, and jets of warm water gush all over my private parts, cleaning me thoroughly. This is followed by a gust of hot hair to get me dry—no toilet paper required. I pull myself up to standing once more and go to place my hands in a recessed part of the wall. Warm soapy water flows over them, followed by the obligatory drying.

I get dressed and return to the main room, where I find Kirimor sitting on the bench and softly strumming the instrument that was leaning against the wall. He looks up at my approach but doesn't stop playing. I take a seat beside him and stretch my legs, crossing them at the ankle. The instrument sounds like a cross between a guitar and a harp, high-pitched and melodic. Kirimor continues to play for several more minutes, his face set in concentration. I watch him, admiring the hard planes of his jaw, the powerful straight nose and those expressive black eyes, always glittering with some emotion, be it passion, fury, lust or amusement. He's beautiful, the pale gray of his skin almost silvery in the moonlight.

The song comes to an end, and Kirimor puts the instrument away.

"That was beautiful. What is this instrument called?"

"It is a lanjo. I am proficient but not a master at playing it. I only do so for my enjoyment, up here on my own."

"Thank you for allowing me listen to you."

He smiles. "My pleasure, darling one. Come here."

He pulls me to him, tucking my head in the crook of his neck. I inhale his fragrance, musky and intensely male. His tail winds around my waist possessively. I'm enveloped in his large, powerful body, safe and content. If I'm not careful, I'm going to fall head over heels for this man. A man who is not free to love me, despite all his protestations to the contrary. Just this one night with him, then I'll keep my distance.

"I can feel your mind awhirl with thoughts, my lovely. Stop thinking; just feel."

"I was thinking about what you said earlier when you were telling me about your holy trances," I say, deflecting quickly. "I'm wondering what exactly you saw in us that first day."

"In Avery, so much envy and resentment for you. In you, I saw a warm aura that called to me in bright shades of yellow and orange, with trickles of pale green sadness and longing for someone—this ex-mate of yours."

"You could see all that, just from a quick scan?"

"Yes. I could have seen more if I had aspirated the energy into me, but I do not in general suck in anything other than the evil I need to dissipate."

I hesitate before asking, "And Troy? Anything negative there?"

He eyes me indignantly. "Do you think I would let anyone but a good man be with my son?"

"No, of course not. I was just checking."

"Rest assured that Troy has not even the slightest atom of evil in him. I have checked him several times, just to be sure. I will not let anyone bad near my son."

"You know they're madly in love, don't you?"

He grunts, "Obviously my family has a proclivity for Humans. I dread to think who next will fall under the spell of your kind."

"You make it sound like a bad thing."

"It is a bad thing when the female I love holds another male in her heart."

He's already alluded to his feelings, but hearing it out in the open makes me catch my breath. "You love me?" I sound like the type of female I despise, all needy and clingy.

His eyes burn with an emotion that warms me from the inside out. "Yes, Melinda, I love you." He places a large hand on my cheek. "And you love me. You are just too stubborn to admit it."

"I thought you said my heart belongs to another."

"It is possible to love more than one person, you know. But somewhere down the line, you are going to have to make a choice—him or me. I have already told you, I do not share."

"Neither do I, Kirimor. I won't make that choice until you are free to be faithful to one person."

He nods. "Then I shall have to be patient and bide my time."

"That's not to say I will necessarily choose to be with you once you are free to mate."

He looks at me wearily. "Playing games, Melinda? Do not."

I flush. Being coy, never showing your true hand, keeping the other side guessing—these are all skills I have honed over the course of my career. But he's right, there is no place for this kind of thing between us. "I'm sorry."

He stands and pulls me to him, holding me close. "It is late. Let us go to sleep." He leads me to the bed. "Give me half a beat to ablute in the bathroom. I shall be right back."

I sit on the bed and pull out my communicator. There's a message from Troy, checking in on me. I send a quick response, reassuring him that all is well. I smile when I see a second message, this one from Kiristen, also checking in on me but in a much more subtle way.

Kiristen: It was a pleasure to see you again today, Melinda. I hope you are enjoying your evening?

Me: Yes, thank you Kiristen. I am having a lovely evening.

Kiristen: I am glad. My father is a good man.

Me: Yes, I know.

Kiristen: Goodnight, dear Melinda.

Me: Goodnight, and thank you for your concern.

I smile as I put away my communicator.

"Who has put this smile on your face?" growls Kirimor.

"Kiristen was just enquiring about my evening, wanting to make sure all was well with me."

He smiles proudly. "I have brought him up well."

"Yes, he's a lovely young man. You can be justly proud of him. All your children, actually. They are so kind and respectful."

He comes to sit beside me on the bed. "I have been truly blessed."

"You are very lucky, Kirimor."

He pulls me into his arms and wraps his tail around my waist. I'm getting used to being held like this. "Did you never want any children of your own, Melinda?"

"We talked about it, Wyatt and I, but the time was never right. My job is all consuming."

"Any regrets?"

"Sometimes. But there's no point crying over the past."

"You could still have one, my lovely. It is not too late."

"What are you suggesting?"

"I am not suggesting, my love, merely stating. If you wish to have a child with me, I am more than willing."

I have a sudden urge to laugh. Kirimor senses my mirth and frowns. "You think this is a laughing matter?"

"No, but I can't help but laugh. This is the second time in as many months that someone has offered to father a child with me."

"Your mate on Earth?"

"Yes, last time I saw him."

"And you said no."

"I've told you, Kirimor. My career comes first. I wasn't about to shelve the opportunity to be Earth's first ambassador to Krovatia just to have a child."

"You do yourself a disservice, Melinda, when you talk about yourself like that."

"It's the truth. My job comes first."

"No, it does not." He puts a hand to my cheek, turning me to face him. "Do not lie to yourself, my love. I have seen you with Kiritela and Kirishar. You glow with maternal affection. You want a child, but you do not want one with Wyatt."

"And what? You think I'd want one with you? Why would I choose you over the man I've known, loved and trusted for decades? Hmm?"

"Because he is not the right man for you. I am."

"Ha!" I huff, not at all impressed with his smug tone. "Don't you think five kids is more than enough for one person?"

"It is plentiful, and I am truly blessed. But I am not averse to more. That is what I told Pirofena when she became my drasha not long ago."

I get to my feet, spitting with fury. "Don't tell me you've got her pregnant too?"

His tail pulls me back to the bed. "No. It is too soon, and I have to be sure of my drasha before I let that happen."

I struggle against his hold. "But you plan to have one with her in future? Is that it?"

His arms clamp around me tight, stopping my attempts to escape. "No, my lovely, not any more. Not now that I love you."

I cease my struggles but hold myself stiff. "See how it feels to have to share you, Kirimor? This is why there can be no us."

"No, I see that. We will have to wait until I am truly free. But in the meantime, I will not cause you any unnecessary pain by having another child with my drashas."

"How can you be sure that you won't, when you have insatiable sex with them?"

"I can scent a female when she is fertile, Melinda. On the evening of the banquet, I could smell the change in your body. It is probably why I was so aggressively flirtatious with you— or maybe not. It could just be the way I am around you. But anyway, what I am trying to say is that I know when any one of my drashas is fertile. At such a time, I make sure to keep her out of the temple. Each of my children have been planned, Melinda, not procreated by accident."

I sag against him. "I see."

He holds me tight, raining kisses on my head. "I never want to cause you pain, Melinda. Believe me."

"I do. I understand why your life is the way it is. But the thought of you being with them hurts. We're not even together and it hurts."

"The thought of you with Wyatt hurts me too. You are still in contact with him, sending each other loving communications, are you not?"

"Yes, we message each other every few days."

"And each time, he tells you of his love and you affirm your love for him."

"Yes."

"That hurts me, Melinda."

"I'm sorry. That was before all this happened between us."

"So you will stop?"

"I can't just cut him off without a word, but I guess next time, I'll tell him about us. Well, not that there is an us yet, but I'll tell him it's time to truly go our separate ways."

"There is an us, Melinda. It may not be a fully consummated relationship yet, but make no mistake, there is an us."

I open my mouth to deny, but he places a finger to my lips. "Do not lie to yourself or to me."

I sigh in defeat, and he drops his hand. "Ok. There is an us. Satisfied?"

"No, but I must make do with what I have for now." He pulls me to my feet. "It is time to go to bed. Take off these clothes, my lovely."

"I said, no sex."

"And I agreed, no sex. But if I am to sleep with you in my arms, it will be without the barrier of clothes between us."

"Won't that be too much of a temptation?"

"It will be the damnedest of temptations, but I can and will exert self-control."

I play for time. "You first then."

With a smirk, he lifts the shirt off his head and throws it to one side. Then, not taking his eyes off me, he unlaces the ties of his loin cloth and lets it slip down to the floor. I stare at his enormous cock, pointing straight up at me, the turgid flesh a dark shade of plum. A drop of precum oozes from the pink tinged tip. Oh what I would give to taste him.

He growls, "Melinda, if you place your lips on me, then consider our deal over. I will not be able to stop myself from fucking you."

I take a deep breath, trying to contain my desperate urge to do just that.

"Your turn now. Take off everything."

Slowly, I undo the buttons of my dress and pull it over my head, placing it carefully on the bench. I face him in just my bra and panties. He stands, muscled legs wide apart, a hand squeezing his cock. His eyes never stray from me as I undo the clasp of my bra and throw it over my dress. His chest heaves with each breath he takes. I pause, not yet ready to bare all.

"I said everything," he barks.

Slowly, I push my panties down to my knees, then step out of them. Naked, I face him, hands by my side. His eyes are glued to my pussy, and to the piercing.

"What is this I see?"

I look down at myself. "It's a piercing. Have you never seen one before?"

"Never down there." He looks up, eyes hard. "Who put this on you?"

"Wyatt and I went to a professional body piercer for our tenth anniversary. He got a matching barbell on his cock."

"You and your mate marked each other in your most private places?"

"Yes."

I swear, I hear him growl. "Take it off!"

"What?"

"You heard me. Take. It. Off."

"I—er ok," I mumble.

With shaking hands, I reach down and fumble with the piercing, undoing the clasp and pulling it off.

"Give it to me."

I hand it over and he puts it away in the pocket of his loin cloth. "Next time you adorn yourself with jewelry on your private parts, it will be mine and only mine."

"Yes, Kirimor."

He drops to his knees and places a palm to my now unadorned clit.

"This belongs to me now. Understand?"

I harden my heart and bend down to place my hand on his cock. "Not until this belongs to me and only me."

He huffs in annoyance. "You will not let any other male touch you or see you there. Are we clear?"

"Not until you promise that no other female will touch you or see you there."

"Woman!"

"Fair is fair, Kirimor."

"So help me Taya, if I catch you with another, I cannot be trusted with what I will do."

"Then you are going to have to find a way to keep this cock well away from your drashas. Get that sicor to take over and do it soon."

He breathes out in frustration. "I will try, Melinda, but I cannot promise."

"And I will try to keep my lady parts away from other eyes, but I cannot promise either."

"Earth female, you are exasperating!"

"Krovatian male, you are too!"

He stands and faces me, anger and frustration in his fiery gaze. Then suddenly, he starts to laugh. Not just laugh, but guffaw. I watch in amazement as he doubles up and emits a loud roar of laughter. Then he pulls me to him, and plants kisses all over my face while trying to get his laughter under control. Eventually he manages to pant, "My love, you are going to make an admirable mate."

"I'm not a sure thing, Kirimor."

"Oh yes you are. I will make sure of it. I am never going to let you slip through my fingers, precious, precious Melinda." Then he captures my lips and kisses me. We don't come up for air for a long, long time. Our naked bodies press to each other, his hard cock nudging my lower abdomen, letting me know just how much he wants me.

He pulls away with a loud grunt. "We need to stop, or so help me Taya, I will not be able to control myself."

We stand, breaths heaving, trying to regain our composure. Eventually, he puts a hand out and says, "Come to bed." He pulls down the coverlet and I get in, followed closely by him. He draws me to him, letting his tail wrap itself around my waist. "Sleep, my love."

After all the excitement of the day, I doubt I'll be able to sleep, but surprisingly, I do.

Chapter 27

Wyatt

The next forty-eight hours after my drone flight with Dwight are manically busy as I put together the program and recruit my artistic troupe for our first set of shows off planet. My communicator is never far from me as I make calls, take meetings, calculate budgets and find the funding I need to pull this project together. I feel energized and have a renewed sense of purpose. It reminds me of the high I used to get in the early part of my business career, before the art of the deal lost its shine in all the stress it induced.

So far, I have fifteen dancers signed up, a dozen Shakesperian actors, a small orchestra of musicians and a maybe from Ricky Charles's people. Costumes and sets are being prepared and packed. But there is one important thing I need to finalize—our transport.

Martha Reynolds arrived this morning aboard a Venorian cargo ship. We had a brief conversation before she headed off to Colorado to visit her family. And now, I am awaiting a knock on my door from the ship's owner and commander. In actual fact, the cargo ship is the property of various Venorian investors, but chief among these investors are the Lor clan, Treylor's family. Her father, Senlor, owns shares, as does her uncle, Stalor, and his only daughter, Rivlor, who is also the commander of the ship. Rivlor has agreed to meet me today and discuss business arrangements.

The doorbell rings and I sprint over to open it, breathless with excitement and anticipation. I stop dead in my tracks and stare at the person in front of me. Venorians are a larger race than humans, with tall, broad bodies and bronze-colored skin. The one who stands at my door is a veritable Amazon, perhaps six feet two in height. Long, powerful legs are encased in loose silky pants tied at the waist in a knot. A bare midriff displays taut abdominals, above which a short olive-colored tunic hugs the contours of ample, rounded breasts. My gaze travels up to meet large eyes the color of honey in a face framed by burnished gold tresses.

"Well, are you going to invite me in?" she asks in a deep, melodious voice.

"I—yes, of course. Come in."

I step back from the door to allow her in. "Rivlor?"

"That is me. And you are Wyatt."

She comes forward for the traditional Venorian greeting. Looking into my eyes, she places a hand to my cheek and brings her forehead to meet mine. A moment later, she steps back and barks out a laugh. Her eyes twinkle with merriment.

I flush with dismay. Of course, she's read my mind. One can control one's words and actions, but not one's thoughts. With hands on hips, she chuckles, "I am strikingly attractive. You are quite right to think so. And you…" She examines me from head to toe. "You are somewhat cute."

"Somewhat cute?"

"In that male Human way."

"Perhaps you've heard the human term, 'damned with faint praise'?"

She bursts out laughing. "No, but I like it! I am sorry. I do not mean to belittle you. Let us shake hands the Human way and begin our business."

She puts out her hand, and I shake it. "Welcome, Rivlor. Can I get you something to drink?"

"You have Coca Cola? I have developed a liking for it."

I smile. "Yes I do. Come with me."

I head toward the kitchen, Rivlor on my heels. Opening the fridge, I take out a bottle of Coke. "Would you like lemon with it?"

She considers a moment, then nods. "Yes, please."

I take out a bowl of sliced lemons and place a sliver into a tall glass, then pour the Coke on top. She watches it in delight as it fizzes. I fix my own drink and hand her the Coke. "There you go. How about we go sit in my study, then we can talk business."

She follows me, looking curiously around her as we go. When we pass by a montage of photos on the corridor wall, she stops and examines it. They are mostly photographs of Melinda and me over the years, as well as snaps of our extended families. She points a finger at a photo taken on our honeymoon. "It is her? The mate you wish to be with again?"

"How much has Martha told you about me?"

She makes a snorting sound. "Enough."

I'm not sure what that's supposed to mean, so I answer her original question. "Yes, that's Melinda, my wife. Technically, my ex-wife, but I'm hoping to change that."

She checks out Mel in the photo again. "She is good looking. Nice small boobies, just the way I like."

"Excuse me?"

"You know. It is good when I can hold a booby inside my hand and squeeze. Not like these."

She cups her substantial breasts to make her point. My eyes goggle, unable to look away from the movement of her hands on her chest. She sees my stupefied expression and smiles. "I like females. Males too, occasionally, when I need some cock. But let us talk business." With that, she walks smartly ahead toward the open door of my study. "In here?"

"Yes," I manage to say.

She finds a seat and settles herself on it, stretching her legs out and taking a long, satisfied gulp of her drink. She puts it down on the coffee table and says, "So, first I hear you are needing transport to Krovatia. Now, the story has changed, and you want transport for a large group of people? Explain."

"I have a business proposition."

"Yes?"

"I have set up the Interstellar Arts Company. We shall be performing shows on Krovatia, Ven, Driskia and any planet that will have us, showcasing the richness and variety of the arts on Earth. There will be dance, drama productions, musical concerts, art exhibits—all showcasing our diverse cultures and heritage. My plan is to put together different programs of entertainment throughout the year. We will travel and perform them for up to two months then return to Earth and organize the next program. I don't want to cut myself off from my ties with family and friends here, so a business like this will enable me to both see Melinda and return home regularly."

"And where is the profit in that for me?"

"I am willing to pay a reasonable fee for our transport and we can negotiate a share of the profits from the shows we put on."

"You think other species will be interested in seeing your art?"

"Yes, I do. If someone on your planet told you there was a dance show called a ballet, featuring beautiful, graceful and acrobatic performers from Earth, would you buy a ticket to see it?"

"It would depend on the price."

"Naturally. It would need to be affordable, but also high enough to cover our costs and profits."

"You would need permission to perform on different planets."

"I already have a permit from Krantor himself to perform my shows on Ven, and I am expecting a response any day from Krovatia to the application which Pravol submitted on my behalf. Both he and Martha Reynolds have vouched for me with the Krovatian authorities."

She sits forward, elbows on her knees. "And you wish my ship to act as your transport, shuttling you from planet to planet then back to Earth?"

"Yes."

"Wyatt, I make my money from the shipment of cargo, not the transportation of Humans."

I eye her coolly. "Rivlor, you can do both."

She sits back, giving a disgusted snort. "Ha!"

"I am willing to bet the humans you transport do not take up all the space on your ship, and you may still be able to fit a substantial amount of cargo. While we stay on a planet for two or three weeks for our performances, you are free to make some cargo runs of your own. It is simply a matter of working around our schedule and making some adjustments."

"And why would I make adjustments to my existing cargo runs which are already profitable enough?"

"Because this will be equally, if not more profitable, and crucially, it will be something that has never been done before. Think of how new and exciting it will be."

She laughs, a cackling sound in the back of her throat. "Of course, I will make great changes to my long established business all so that I can have more excitement in my life!"

Abruptly, she stops laughing and narrows her eyes. "Wyatt, there is one and only one reason why I run my cargo business. It is to make profit so I can sell up and retire within the next decade. I have plans to buy a stretch of land along the beach on the western shores of Lirisor, and spend the rest of my days eating good fresh food, swimming in the crystal clear waters, fucking beautiful young females—of which there are plenty on that island—and reading many stories; perhaps also writing some. Then, I will be at leisure to experience all the excitement I want in my life."

I stare at her. "That sounds like paradise to me."

She grins. "It is!"

I don't know what stupid impulse makes me ask the following question. "You have no plans to fuck any handsome men on Lirisor?"

"I will not say no if one comes my way. I like a good cock now and then."

"I'm sure most males would resent being objectified to just one part of their anatomy. There is more to us than just that."

She takes her time, running her gaze along my body. I'm surprised to realize that our banter has made me semi-hard, a fact that does not escape her notice. "Yes," she says, "there are many delicious parts to a male's body, but a cock is the most interesting of them all."

I breathe in sharply, trying to regroup. I can only ascribe my arousal to the fact it's been a long time since I've had sex, and to the explicit nature of our conversation. But we are here to talk business. And I'm not about to forget the reason why I'm doing all this—so I can be with Mel again.

"Well Rivlor, if profit is what interests you, then I believe we can do business together."

She smiles wryly at the shift in the conversation. "Very well, Wyatt. Let us explore this further. I believe it would be best to do so on my ship." She stands. "Come. Let us go there now."

I pale. "Go to your ship?"

She looks at me in confusion. "Where else?"

"Can it not wait?"

She puts her hands on her hips. "Look, Wyatt. Either you are serious about this business plan or you are not. I will be leaving in two rotations' time." She holds out two fingers to make her point. "There is no time to be lost. I have negotiations with other suppliers, so if you are not willing to come with me now, then there can be no deal."

"I am serious. It's just… I need time to prepare."

"Just bring yourself. No preparation is required."

"You don't understand. There are personal reasons why I need time."

She quirks an impatient brow. "What reasons?"

I take a deep breath and blurt out, "I have a fear of flying."

She is lost for words, eyeing me in shocked silence. Finally, she mutters, "Let me get this straight. You wish to start a business that involves you flying on a space ship, but you are fearful of flying?"

"Yes."

"Are you mad?"

I laugh mirthlessly. "No, just determined not to let fear rule my life."

"I applaud you for your bravery, Wyatt, but this seems like too big a jump to take surely."

"I can do it. Failure is not an option."

She looks at me sceptically. "In that case, come with me now. Show me you can do it."

I nod sharply. "Ok."

She picks up her empty glass and struts out of my study to the kitchen, where she rinses it out. I follow her with mine, and she takes it from me to give it a clean. Wiping her hands on a dish towel, she confronts me. "So, are you ready?"

"Yeah, let me just get a paper bag."

She doesn't bother to ask why I need it, but strides to the front door and waits for me there. I make a detour into the downstairs restroom and splash my face with cold water. My hands shake as I towel dry. *Shit, shit, shit.* I look myself in the mirror, then I say to my reflection, "You can do this."

Heart pounding, I walk out of the bathroom, grab a newly purchased stash of paper bags, then head to the door. Without a word, we step outside. The late summer sun casts a warm glow on my clammy body, as if to reassure me that everything will be alright. A drone awaits us on the other side of the road. We cross to it, my legs weak as butter. Rivlor holds the door open, waiting for me to climb in. Taking a deep breath, I step into the aircraft and busy myself with the safety belt, trying to keep myself distracted.

I feel her eyes on me, but I don't have the bandwidth to engage in any conversation. I hold the paper bag up to my mouth and breathe deeply. There is nausea, but not as much as before, thank God. I retch a little as the drone engine fires up. Soon, I feel the drop in my stomach as we rise into the air. *Just breathe.* Droplets of sweat bead on my forehead. *I can do this. I can do this.*

A cool hand is on my back, stroking gently. Rivlor croons in my ear. "Somewhat cute Wyatt, I think I would like to fuck you."

I gasp out a breath.

"Yes, I think you would like that too." Her hand travels up to ruffle my hair. "I want to see if that golden hair on your head matches the hair you have above your cock."

Breathe in. Breathe out.

"And I would like to see your cock. I think it is just the right size to fit in my mouth." More stroking along my back. "I want to taste your essence. They say Humans do not have a sweet nectar like a Venorian male, but in any case, I prefer sour to sweet, and I like my food well salted."

Unbelievably, my cock twitches at her words. I catch a hint of her scent as she leans over me, something vibrant and lemony, like the smell of freshly cut grass. She chuckles next to me. "Somewhat cute Wyatt, I like your smell too." Damn, I forgot she's telepathic.

She continues her slow, hypnotic strokes along my back. My face is still buried in the paper bag, breathing rapidly in and out. I feel a gentle touch to my neck as Rivlor runs her nose over the sensitive skin, inhaling deeply. "Oh yes, you smell good too, somewhat cute Wyatt."

I grunt into the bag, "How about you ditch the somewhat and just call me cute?"

She laughs delightedly. "Where would be the fun in that?" Her warm breath along the back of my neck has my hair standing on end. My cock stands fully erect, straining against the zipper of my pants. I'm breathing in and out quickly. All I can focus on is that teasing touch on my neck and the fresh scent of her skin. One of her hands slithers slowly down my arm, on to my lap. Will she? I gasp as I feel her inches from my cock. *Oh God!*

I thrust my groin up instinctively. My backside lands with a bump back on the seat. It's then I register that we've landed. In that same instant, Rivlor removes her hand and stands. "We have arrived," she says briskly and strides to open the drone's door. Nimbly, she climbs out while I take an extra moment to recover. I look down at the paper bag in my hand and crumple it up. Turns out, all I needed was a bit of sexual foreplay to distract me from my fear of flying. I stand and exit the drone on shaky legs. *Get a grip, Wyatt.*

We have landed at the space docking station, empty right now except for Rivlor's massive cargo ship. It's a concave structure encased in pale silver metal, triangular in shape with one long pointy end. From my limited knowledge, I know the ship tilts with the pointed end facing upwards for take-off and breaking through the atmosphere, then swings back to its horizontal position once in space. Up close, the ship is a giant beast, ferocious looking with its beaky point.

Rivlor taps a code on a console embedded into the widest part of the structure, and a door slides open sideways revealing a small hatch. She steps inside, and with a slight hesitation, I follow. The door slides shut behind us, leaving us shrouded in near darkness except for the light shining from Rivlor's communicator. She steps forward and places her hand on a wall pad. Immediately, another door opens into a second, wider hatch. We walk into it, and she tells me, "Stand there. The ship's security system needs to scan us before we are cleared to enter."

I do as she asks. A moment later, a purple beam of light above us performs the scan. It takes a few seconds for the computer to process the results, but then, another hatch door opens, this time leading into the interior of the ship. I follow Rivlor, too curious about my surroundings to feel any trepidation. We have entered a long corridor, the dove gray walls covered in some kind of plastic coating. As we walk down the corridor, we pass various sliding doors.

"These are our sleeping quarters," explains Rivlor. "There is a private chamber for myself and my second-in-command, a guest chamber which was most recently used by Krantor's mate, and a further chamber shared by the remaining three members of my crew."

It doesn't take a mathematical genius to figure out there are not nearly enough rooms to accommodate my large troupe of performers. There must be somewhere else where we will be able to bed down.

Rivlor glances back at me. "I will show you where your Humans can sleep." Her ability to read my mind is uncanny.

A few paces later, she stops in front of a door and presses her hand to the scanner. It slides open, revealing a large, empty space, about fifty feet long. "This is one of our cargo holds. It is ventilated, so it can be used for Human occupation. You will have to procure sleeping pods for each of your performers."

"What about washing facilities?"

"There is a large communal bath which we all use. Our chambers also have private rainmakers, so never fear, you can have privacy when you bathe should you choose." She points down the corridor. "The communal bath is down this way, and beside it are toilet facilities. It is not luxury living, but this is a cargo ship, not a passenger ship."

"I understand. What is the maximum number of people you can accommodate?"

She thinks for a moment. "Thirty-five. Maybe forty at a stretch."

My mind does the math quickly. We will have to reduce our orchestra to just a handful of players, or perhaps make do with recorded music. I'm already considering where I can shave off the numbers and how this could impact our ability to put on a good show. I reach for my communicator and start tapping out messages to several of my contacts, arranging an online meeting with them later that afternoon.

"Let's talk numbers," I say. "How much will you charge per person for a round trip to Ven, Krovatia and Driskia?"

"Including all meals, I want one hundred and twenty credits per person, plus ten percent of the profits you make on your shows."

I make a tsk sound. "I'll agree to one hundred credits per person and five percent of the profits."

She looks me square in the eye. "Wyatt, you want a deal, no? So do not waste my time with counteroffers. It is one hundred and twenty credits per person, plus ten percent of the profits."

"How about this? We make it one hundred credits per person, and I give you a greater share of the profits, say fifteen percent?"

"Fifteen percent of nothing is still nothing. How do I know your shows are going to be a success? No, I need to ensure my costs are covered regardless."

"Well then, can we agree to one hundred and twenty credits per person, but reduce your share of the profits to two percent?"

"Oh no, because if by some great miracle you do make a success of these shows, I want in on the profits."

"How about we keep your share of the profits at three percent for the initial run of shows and renegotiate further down the line?"

"Five percent and you have got yourself a deal."

"You drive a hard bargain, Rivlor."

"Do we have a deal?"

I put my hand out. "Let's shake on it."

She doesn't extend her hand. "There is one more thing you need to do before we can shake on it." At my look of enquiry she says, "Prove to me that you can fly in space without a problem. I want you to stay on this ship while we take an orbit around Earth. Get through that and we have a deal."

I let out a deep breath. "Ok, let's do it."

She taps a few commands on her communicator, then raises her honey eyes to me. "Come." Turning sharply, she steps out of the cargo hold. I walk behind her, beginning to experience twinges of anxiety. I try to clamp down on it, but my stomach continues to do weird somersaults.

Eventually, we reach a large set of doors which open to reveal some kind of operations room or cockpit. We are at the top, pointy end of the ship, framed by large windows which at this moment, show wide panoramic views of the Atlantic Ocean. Three Venorians, busy working away at their consoles, look up as we enter. Rivlor points to the one sitting at the front. "This is Shular, my second-in-command. Over there behind him are Vonlar and Romsal."

I nod weakly at them all. "Hi, I'm Wyatt Garcia."

Shular comes forward to greet me the traditional Venorian way. A moment later, he steps back, a frown on his face. I guess he must be reading my dread and anxiety. My suspicions are confirmed when I see him look toward Rivlor. "Are you sure about this? The male is terrified."

Ok, not just a little anxiety. More like full-on panic.

In answer, Rivlor makes a clicking sound with her tongue. The other two crew members, Vonlar and Romsal, take turns to greet me, and they too emerge from their brief foray into my mind with a frown on their faces.

"What if his terror induces cardiac arrest?" asks Vonlar in concern.

"Leave him to me; he will be fine." She sounds more sure of this than I am. Shit, where did I leave that paper bag?

Rivlor turns to the third crew member. "Romsal, get us the seat extension we use when parents strap children to them for take-off."

He rushes out to do her bidding. While we await his return, the other two go back to their consoles and resume their work. "I am programming our departure in one beat. Will that give you enough time?" asks Shular.

"Perfect. The longer we wait the more anxious he will be. Let us get this thing done."

I exhale deeply, trying not to hurl. I feel her hand stroke down my arm. "Wyatt, listen to me carefully. I am going to strap you to my body while we take off. You will be secure in my arms the whole time and I will keep you safe."

I nod, unable to speak.

Romsal returns with the seat extension, which he promptly attaches to one of the seats. "Ok Wyatt, come here." She leads me by the hand to the seat in question and arranges herself on it with her legs resting wide open on the extension. "Slide into my lap, with your back to me."

With shaking limbs, I do as she says, awkwardly sliding backwards into her lap. I feel her pin me with her legs and arms as she secures two sturdy straps around us. Dazedly, I realize my head is pillowed on her soft breasts. She's holding me like a mother would hold a child. There's no room for pride any more. That is long gone. All I can do now is survive this as best I can. I'm no longer a forty-one year old man, but a child, sniffling in fear and wallowing in the comfort of his mother.

"I'm scared," I croak.

"I know. It will be fine."

"Hold me."

"I will."

"What if the G-force is so strong you let me go?"

"I will not."

I feel a buzz under me as the ship powers up. I start to cry. "I—I don't think I can do this. Take me home."

"No."

"Please, Rivlor." I'm sobbing now. "I thought I could do this, but I can't!"

"You can."

My sobs get louder. Oh fuck, fuck, fuck. What have I done? Someone get me out of here.

"Wyatt, stop this."

But I'm out of control, screaming and sobbing, "Get me out of here!"

A sharp slap on my face silences me. I feel the burning sting on my cheek. I stop screaming and just shake in her arms, tears streaming down my face. The same hand that just violently slapped me is now stroking my hair. "Somewhat cute Wyatt, you will get through this. And when you do, I will reward you with the best fuck of your life."

"I asked you to stop calling me that," I snivel.

"I'll call you what I like. Now be a good boy for me and hold still."

The ship begins to tilt us backward. "Oh God, oh God!" I cry. We're now reclined fully on our backs.

The hand on my head slides down to stroke my face. "Shh, you will be fine." Soft fingers wipe away my tears. Beneath us, the ship's engine gives a loud roar. I tremble. She runs her thumb along my quivering bottom lip. "Open up, big boy." I don't question her, just do as she asks. She plunges her thumb into my mouth and some long forgotten instinct has me sucking on it. "Good boy," she croons.

I glow at the praise and suck harder. The roar of the engine becomes louder, a massive rumble reverberating through my body. I focus on the thumb in my mouth and keep sucking. The next few minutes are a blur of noise, vibration and force. Throughout it all, my lips are clamped around Rivlor's thumb as if it's a lifeline. I lose sight of where, who or what I am. I simply exist in this cocoon of warmth surrounded by loud rumbles, my only purpose to suck a thumb.

It takes me several minutes to realize we're sitting up straight again and that the loud roar has gone, replaced by a low humming as we cruise through space. *I did it*. I'm in space!

At around the same time, I realize I'm still sucking on Rivlor's thumb. Reluctantly, I open my mouth to let it out. It slides away, leaving a wet trail on my chin. We stay like this a moment longer. "Thank you," I murmur.

She pats my cheek. "I told you it would be fine. Now, come on. Let me unstrap you." With that, she efficiently unties the straps from around us. I shift myself forward until I'm able to stand, and she follows suit. The other crew members cast a look at us, the pity on their faces barely hidden. Well, that was an emasculating experience. I feel myself flush, embarrassment flooding in now that I'm no longer in a panic. Yeah, that's me. Wyatt Garcia, snivelling fool, who sucks on a grown woman's thumb. Jesus, can I sink any lower?

Rivlor must sense something of what's going on in my mind because she taps me on the shoulder and says, "That was brave, Wyatt. You did well. Now follow me."

I try to ignore the stares of the other people present, and walk after her on legs that feel like jelly. I follow her back down the corridor in silence until we reach a door, which she taps to open. "These are my private quarters," she says. "You may want to use the facilities and wash yourself."

Another reminder of what a fool I've made of myself. "Thanks," I mumble, and head in the direction she points to the washroom. Inside, I quickly relieve my full bladder and wash all the tear trails and snot off my face. I use a clean towel hanging on a rack to dry myself, then examine my reflection in the mirror. My eyes are still red-rimmed and puffy, but otherwise, I look like my normal self.

I let myself out of the bathroom and find Rivlor sitting on the edge of her bed. She observes me calmly as I come to sit beside her. "So, now do we have a deal?" I ask.

She smiles. "Yes, Wyatt, we have a deal. Can you be ready to leave in two rotations?"

"I'll be ready."

There's something else I need to ask. Should I go there? What the heck. "There's also the other deal you made."

"Ah yes. Anytime you want us to fuck Wyatt, just say the word."

"I love Melinda."

"I know you do, but you are attracted to me."

There's no point beating around the bush. "Yes, I am. Who wouldn't be? That doesn't mean I should act on it."

"How long have you and she been unmated?"

"It's been seven months, but we separated long before."

"And in that time, you have fucked others?"

"No, I've been faithful to Melinda all through the decades we've been together, and I mean to keep it that way."

She whistles. "That is a very long time. I cannot imagine it for myself, for I like to stay free to fuck whomever I please, but I respect you for it, Wyatt. We shall speak no more of this."

"Thank you."

"We need to head back. I am sure you have much to do to get yourself ready and I too have much business to conclude."

The feeling of dread makes an unwelcome come back. "Will the return to Earth's surface be as terrifying as the take-off?"

"No, it will be easier I think. And I will hold you, like I promised."

"Thanks, Rivlor. For everything."

"It is my pleasure."

Chapter 28

Melinda

I come awake slowly to a feeling of being surrounded by warmth. An instant later, I realize why. My face is burrowed in the crook of Kirimor's neck, breathing in his addictive male scent. I'm wrapped securely in both his arms and his tail. Further down my body, a powerful leg has me pinned tight to him. There is no escaping the sicortar's embrace.

Not that I want to. Despite the stickiness of our skin where we are pressed against each other, I feel snug and safe, the steady rise and fall of his breaths a comforting lullaby. I close my eyes and take a few moments to enjoy my closeness to this incredible man.

Yesterday, he said he loved me. He talked of becoming my mate. We've somehow bypassed the casual fling stage and gone straight into long-term relationship talk. I should be running for the hills. Instead, I seem to be running headlong in his direction. I've only known him a few weeks and already, I yearn for him.

It seems crazy. There are so many obstacles and complications, not least the harem of women he keeps in his household. I laid down the gauntlet last night. One hundred per cent fidelity or else no deal. The thought of him sinking his body into that young nubile drasha of his has me wanting to pull out my claws and scratch her eyes out.

He murmurs something in his sleep and shifts, tightening his hold on me. Even in slumber, he's staking his claim. This great powerful man wants me. And there's no denying I want him too.

What about Wyatt?

My mind strays to the man I've loved for more years than I can remember. I picture him in his last message, rumpled blond hair and bright blue eyes crinkling in his warm, familiar smile. My chest tightens in yearning for him too. I miss him so much.

Two very different men, and yet I want them both. I can't have my cake and eat it though. I have to make a choice, but I don't think I can. Not yet. Wyatt and I—we still feel like unfinished business. Can it ever be over between him and me? I can't imagine cutting the cord and severing our lives permanently. He's just too much a part of me. If he ever managed to overcome his fear of flying and join me here, I'd have a familiar partner who I could trust, and there would be no other women to sully the waters.

And then there's Kirimor. Undeniably, he makes me feel like no one has ever before. Could I walk away from whatever this is between us? Can he put an end to his career as a sicor and promise me fidelity? It's still too much of a long shot. As if he hears my thoughts, he grunts and slides his hand down my back, stopping at the dimples above my ass cheeks. His splayed hand pushes me into his groin, and his massive erection.

"I can hear your mind whirling with thoughts," he grumbles. "Stop thinking, female, and just feel."

"I'm feeling it, Kirimor. It's hard not to."

He chuckles and pokes me with his erection again. "Say the word, my lovely, and I'll slide this thick long cock all the way inside you. I'll give you a fucking like you've never had before."

"Not happening."

"No?"

"No."

He turns us so I'm lying on my back, his large body covering mine. He imprisons my arms above my head while his tail unravels from around my waist and snakes its way down to my mound. With uncanny precision, the tip finds my clit and begins to flutter.

"Ah!" I gasp.

"If you won't have my cock, then maybe you'll take my tail. Hmm?"

I don't get a chance to respond as his lips descend on mine, his tongue demanding entry. I suck it into my mouth greedily, revelling in the intoxicating flavor of him. He plunders my mouth, devouring me with his kisses. His tail, meanwhile, continues its massage of my clit, making my core throb and release the sticky juices of my arousal.

Kirimor bites my bottom lip, then sucks it into his mouth. I moan, lost in sensation. I lick his bottom lip then capture his tongue with mine again in a sloppy, wet, hungry kiss. I can't get enough of him. I rub my hips against him, wanting more. Suddenly, his tail is no longer on my clit. I barely have time to mourn its loss before I feel it slither down to my slit and push its way inside me. In it goes, and keeps going until—

"Ah," I scream as his tail finds my G-spot and begins to rub against it back and forth.

Kirimor captures my mouth again, sucking my tongue with his as his tail continues its unbearable friction deep inside me. I'm unravelling, coming apart. Logical thought is impossible. All I can do is lose myself in him. And then I'm there. My core pulses and throbs as a powerful orgasm washes over me. My internal passage spasms over and over, imprisoning his tail inside me in a choke hold.

With one final moan, I collapse back on my pillow. Kirimor pants above me, his tail still buried deep inside my pussy. I lift my lids and look straight into his fiery black eyes.

"One day, my lovely, you'll take my cock," he grunts. "But until then, I'll fuck you with my tail, and my mouth."

"Kirimor," I breathe.

"Hush, my love. Just feel."

And with these last words, he slithers down my body and pries my legs apart, opening me wide to his hungry gaze.

Slowly, he pulls his tail out of me, lifting it up in the air to show me how soaking wet it is.

He smirks, "There is one more passage this tail needs to enter, now that it is coated in your juices."

He whips it down again towards my slit, but this time it slinks past and comes to a halt at my back hole. His eyes fixed on mine, he begins to push it slowly inside. My mind is fragmented into a thousand tiny pieces. I can't think, only feel as instructed. Gently, but insistently, his tail gains entry into my tight back passage. I've barely processed this strange new reality before his mouth is on me, licking me all the way from my slit to my clit in long, powerful strokes.

"Oh shit, Kirimor!"

He groans in reply and continues to eat me as if his life depends on it. And his tail… Oh my blessed God his tail! It fucks me in a rhythm that matches his tongue on my pussy. But that's not all. One thick finger, then two, slide deep inside me, finding my sensitive spot and stroking me right there.

"Oh God!"

I'm being fucked by his tail in my ass and his fingers in my pussy, and it feels so damn good. Kirimor swirls his tongue around my clit, then sucks it deep into his mouth, the nub still throbbing from my recent orgasm.

"Kirimor!" I scream. "Kirimor!"

My hands clutch wildly at the sheets as my body writhes in unbearable excitement. He speeds up the pace of his licking and thrusting, building a fast rhythm that sends me into the stratosphere. I scream again as I come in sharp, endless pulses of my core.

I'm still panting when Kirimor comes to lie beside me, his tail slowly easing out of me. His face glistens with my juices and his eyes glitter as he grits out, "Melinda, you are mine. Do not ever forget it."

I remain silent, staring into his eyes, so he continues, "Each time your mind strays to him, I will drive you wild with pleasure and remind you who you truly belong to." He strokes gentle fingers down my cheek. "Tell me truthfully, Melinda, has he ever made you feel the way I just did?"

I don't want to admit it. Out of loyalty to my ex-husband, I say, "Wyatt knows my body inside out and how to make me come. Our sex life was great."

He smiles. "You haven't answered my question. And yet by omission, you have. No one else but me can make you feel like this, Melinda."

I'm coming down from my high now, and I harden my resolve. "We spoke of this last night, Kirimor. Until you are faithful only to me, there is zero chance you can make me yours."

He nods solemnly. "Understood. But while I untangle my personal affairs, you must do the same with yours. Close the door on your relationship with Wyatt."

I regard him mutinously, but then my sense of fairness reasserts itself. I am divorced, and my ex-husband chose not to accompany me on this mission to Krovatia. I am free.

"Ok," I say.

"Good. Now let us bathe together and eat. It is three beats past sunrise, and I am sure you have places to be today."

"I do."

He gets out of the bed and pulls me up with him. I follow him to the bathroom where he quickly fills the large tub with warm fragrant water and draws me into it, placing me on his lap. Tenderly, he runs a wash cloth over every inch of my body, then he massages my hair clean. I insist on returning the favor, tracing my fingers over every part of him, including that tree trunk of a cock. As my hands slides over the tip, he groans, "Melinda, have a care. There are limits to my self-control."

I give it one final squeeze, then move on. Once we are both clean, he lifts me out of the bath and dries me with a large fluffy towel. We get dressed, eat, then leave our little haven of love in the mountains. I climb into Kirimor's drone, and he flies me all the way home, landing in front of my doorstep.

As the engine stops, he takes my hand. "I love you, Melinda, and I want to make you mine as soon as I possibly can. Please keep this at the forefront of your mind."

I kiss him gently on the lips. "I know, and I will."

With this, he lets me go.

I enter the house and make my way past the central atrium to the corridor that leads to my quarters. As I pass the pool, I see Treylor climb out of the water. She catches sight of me and waves, so instead of continuing to my room, I make a detour and head towards the pool.

"Well hello, stranger," Treylor says, diffusing the rebuke with a smile. She wraps her magnificently voluptuous naked body in a towel and sits on a lounge chair. Venorians are used to sharing communal baths, and this shared pool is something of a communal bathing space in our household. On first moving in together, our Venorian friends asked if we minded them swimming naked, and we all told them we didn't. Live and let live is my motto.

Behind her, I see Pravol emerge from the water, and I wouldn't be human if I didn't notice the equal magnificence of his naked body. Truly, these two mates are a match made in heaven. He's tall, powerfully muscled, and nearly as well-endowed as Kirimor. These alien species make our own puny human bodies pale in comparison.

As he dries himself off on a nearby towel, I clear my throat and say, "Good morning all. How was your dip in the pool?"

"It was good," responds Treylor. "It was very hot last night, and we needed to cool off. Did you not feel the heat too?"

I flush guiltily, though I have nothing to feel guilty about. "I was somewhere else in the mountains actually, so I had a very pleasant night."

Pravol raises his brows at this. "You were with the sicortar?"

"Yes, how did you know?"

"We saw the three of you leave yesterday with the sicortar's son, but they returned without you."

"Ah yes, it's hard to keep things private when we all live together."

"I apologize if we are being nosy," says Treylor. "But I am very curious. Are you having a fling with the hot priest?"

At this, Pravol glowers. I'm not sure if it's because of Treylor calling Kirimor a hot priest or because he disapproves of my having an affair. Venorians mate for life, and as far as Pravol is concerned, my mate is Wyatt.

"A fling? Nope."

Treylor approaches me and puts her forehead to mine, a traditional Venorian greeting, and also their way of reading other people's minds. She steps back a moment later, a puzzled expression on her face. "I sense joy, excitement and conflicted emotions. What is going on, Melinda?"

"I—I've fallen for the hot priest, and he's fallen for me."

"So you are having a fling."

I shake my head. "No, I refuse to become his until he stops his relations with his drashas."

"I understand that is not feasible for a sicortar," says Pravol.

"So the solution is for him to stop being sicortar and pass the baton on to someone else."

"And he has agreed to that?"

"He says he will work on finding a replacement as soon as possible. We shall see how good his word is."

"And what about Wyatt?" asks Pravol, looking troubled.

"Wyatt and I are over," I say gently.

He looks like he's about to say something, but Treylor stops him with a hand on his arm. She says with a smile, "You are wise to wait before committing yourself, Melinda. Hold off until you are sure of your course of action. In time, hopefully things will become clearer."

I smile back. "Hopefully. I better run and get changed. I'm supposed to visit a recycling plant with Troy this morning. Have you seen him?"

"I believe he is having breakfast in the kitchen with his lover boy."

I giggle. "I see. Well, seeing as Kirimor has already fed me, I can skip breakfast and let the two lovers enjoy a romantic meal in peace."

"Kirimor? Is that the sicortar's name?" asks Pravol.

"Yes, it is."

"I see. Go in peace, Melinda."

"Thanks, have a great day you two, go in peace."

A couple of days pass as I continue my diplomatic efforts, going to countless meetings with officials and building our knowledge bank of Krovatian society. I do not see Kirimor, but he wakes me each morning with a call, asking after me, my plans for the day and always reiterating that he loves me. I force myself each time to ask him, "Have you had sex with any of your drashas?"

Each time, he looks at me sadly and shakes his head. Whatever this special matter is that is taking up his attention at the moment, it fortunately does not require his drashas to be present. I'm relieved, but also know it's only a matter of time before he gives me an answer I don't want to hear. I did prod him a little about this thing he's working on, and he eventually revealed that there appear to be some people that have somehow managed to bypass his scans by presenting an all too perfect aura. He is having to perform multiple scans on a range of high ranking individuals to identify these possible fraudsters, but as the scan involves him seeking out only perfect auras, there is no need to absorb negative energy or reach the horny state that requires a drasha to be on hand. In terms of finding a permanent replacement as sicortar, however, little or no progress seems to have been made.

This morning is no different from others, except for the fact that I will be travelling to the southern sector for a couple of days. The southern sector is the part of the planet with a massive rainforest. It hosts millions of species of plants, many of them of great medicinal value. The Krovatians have developed a huge pharmaceutical industry based on these natural resources, so I'll be interested to meet officials from this industry to seek out trade opportunities with Earth. I'll also be meeting the southern sector's leader, an older Krovatian female named Dorishena, and on top of all that, I've been invited to give a lecture at the university—a repeat of the one I gave at the university here.

Like clockwork, my communicator buzzes with a call from Kirimor. "Good morning, my lovely. Did you sleep well?" he croons into my ear.

"Very well thank you. How about you, hot priest? Sleep well?"

He does not react to my teasing about him being a hot priest, but simply quirks his lips in amusement. "Well enough, though I would sleep better with you by my side."

"Not happening. That night in the cabin was a one-off."

"No, it was the beginning of something special between us." His eyes twinkle. "However, it will not be long before you are in my bed again, Melinda."

"We'll see."

"So, I take it you are flying to the southern sector today."

"Yes, I'm looking forward to it."

"And are Troy and Avery accompanying you?"

"No, this time it's just me. Oh, and my official escort, Desimar, our liaison officer."

At this, he frowns. "I do not like the idea of you travelling alone with an unattached male."

"And I do not like the idea of you living in a house with lots of unattached females. Have you had sex with your drashas since I last spoke to you?"

His eyes gleam as he replies, "No, I have not. You are keeping me well leashed, my Melinda."

"Good."

"Make sure you keep well away from this Desimar."

"I am not planning to share a room with him, Kirimor. He's just escorting me there. That's all."

"It better be all, or I cannot vouch for his safety."

"Oh I do like it when you go all caveman on me."

He does not laugh. "I am deadly serious, Melinda. He lays one finger on you, and I cannot answer for what the consequences may be."

"Relax. Our relationship is purely professional."

He grunts.

"So, I better head out. Wish me safe travels."

"Always, my love. Go in peace."

I board the aircraft that is taking us to the southern sector. With me is Desimar, the liaison officer who was assigned to us when we arrived. He has been a constant presence in our lives over the last month, helping us get settled and guiding us on the ins and outs of living on this planet. I'm quite aware that his role also involves keeping an eye on us. The Krovatians have made no secret of their wariness and distrust of outsiders. For the most part, I've not minded having a minder. We've got nothing to hide, and I know it's going to take time to break the barriers between our peoples. That's pretty much what my mission here is about.

The aircraft we're taking is larger than a drone, about the size of a small commercial jet back on Earth. Unlike human jets which still run on kerosene—albeit much more energy efficiently than before—the Krovatian plane is powered by dorenium. I'm told this energy source is plentiful on the planet and considered eco-friendly enough to be used to power larger aircrafts, while the smaller drones that proliferate in the city are all solar powered.

This larger aircraft we're on is some type of regular shuttle between the different sectors of the planet, used by business people and dignitaries, as well as ordinary Krovatians. There are around sixty to eighty people on board by my rough estimation, and they look at me curiously as I pass them with Desimar to get to our allocated seats. The liaison officer places a reassuring hand on my shoulder. "Do not mind them," he whispers into my ear.

We reach our seats, towards the front of the plane and sit ourselves down. Like all Krovatian seating arrangements, they are set low on the floor and wide enough so we can sit with our legs crossed. I am beginning to get used to this floor sitting business. I've been doing yoga poses daily to strengthen my posture so that I can sit on the floor without slouching.

I make myself as comfortable as possible and tug the safety belt around me. Beside me, Desimar opens the tub which contains the now familiar warm, scented cloths, and takes my hands between his to wipe them clean.

I submit to the ritual with a smile as I examine my escort from under my lashes. He's somewhere in his late twenties, if I were to hazard a guess, with a fit, leanly muscled body covered in the obligatory Krovatian body art. His shoulder length black hair is braided in a fashionable style I've noticed on several other young men—the older Krovatian males seem to prefer to keep their hair cropped short. He's a handsome guy, and I'd be telling a lie if I said I didn't enjoy the attentions of such a fine looking and attentive escort. That's not to say I'd flirt with him or treat him as anything more than a colleague. Kirimor really has nothing to worry about.

"Thank you, Desimar," I say as he completes the cleaning ritual on my left hand and takes my right one.

"It is my honor."

"Have you been to the southern sector before?"

"Yes, many times. My family and I have vacationed there on several occasions. It is a very beautiful part of the planet. We stayed in cabins right in the heart of the rainforest, some of them built into the trees. We would go foraging for fresh herbs and wild berries, go fishing in the rivers and swim in the rocky pools filled with crystal clear water. Such wonderful times we had. If possible, I would love to show you around."

"That sounds amazing, Desimar. I would definitely like that."

A commotion ahead of us has me looking up. There is one more passenger boarding the flight, a person who seems to be attracting more attention than I did. At first, I don't see who it is, as he is preceded by his assistant, but a moment later, I spy long powerful legs. My pulse quickens. My eyes travel up those legs, lingering over the loin cloth that barely conceals the well-endowed appendage beneath. Surely it's not him. But as my gaze travels upwards, I meet a pair of black glittering eyes that burn into my very soul. Kirimor. His eyes travel to my hand, still held by Desimar as he wipes it clean, and his nostrils flare. He comes to stand before him and says in an icy, condescending voice, "I believe you are in my seat."

Desimar gets to his feet respectfully. "Sicortar, there must be an error. I am here escorting the Earth representative, Melinda Garcia."

"That is where you are wrong. Melinda is with me. You may sit behind next to my assistant."

"B-but—" At Kirimor's imperious stare, he quickly changes his mind. "Of course, sicortar, my mistake." With an apologetic look at me, he moves to the row of seats behind us and settles himself down next to Kirimor's assistant, someone I know goes by the name of Sholinar.

I turn to the person in question, ignoring Kirimor. "Sholinar, it's good to meet you. I have heard so much about you from the sicortar."

Sholinar looks at me in pleased surprise. "The honor is mine, Melinda. I too, have heard many good things about you, not only from the sicortar but also from all his children."

I beam at him. "They are delightful aren't they? Well, Sholinar, I hope you have a pleasant journey. I'm sorry to deprive you of the sicortar's company."

He snorts. "That is not a problem at all. I get enough of his company at home. Please, enjoy your journey."

"Thank you, I will."

Finally, I turn back to Kirimor, whose lips are set in a tight line of annoyance.

"Sicortar. To what do I owe this unexpected pleasure?"

He glares. "You know very well, Melinda."

"Keeping me on a tight leash?"

"The tightest possible."

He takes hold of my hand. "I said no one was allowed to lay a finger on you."

"I could hardly say no to a long established Krovatian custom, could I?"

"Now, you will not have to, for I shall be here beside you the whole time."

"Don't you have more important matters to see to as sicortar?"

"I do, and fortunately, these important matters align with my accompanying you to the southern sector. You shall stay in my quarters tonight."

"I believe we are booked to stay—"

"You will stay with me, Melinda."

"There's absolutely no point arguing this with you, is there?"

His eyes gleam. "Absolutely none."

I grin back at him. "Ok, well in that case, sicortar, may I say that I am delighted you have joined me on this journey."

He raises my hand to his lips. "Me too, Melinda, me too."

Chapter 29

Kirimor

I did not tell a lie when I told Melinda that I have important matters to see to in the southern sector. I had been planning to make this journey, but on hearing this morning that she would be setting out alone, with only Desimar for an escort, I was spurred into action. My mind will not rest unless I know she is under my protection. I do not know this Desimar, and I do not trust him with my precious Melinda.

I remove the armrest from between our seats and pull her to me, tucking her head into the crook of my neck. I feel her sniff me, taking deep inhales of my essence. I hold back a smile. My Melinda is addicted to my scent, much as I am addicted to hers. We belong to each other.

Softly, I stroke my fingers through the strands of her hair and hear her moan. "Ah, that feels good… So, what business do you have in the southern sector?"

"Can you not guess? It has to do with you."

She stills, then sits up to look at me. "You're going to see Melistor?"

"Yes, my love."

I pull her back to rest against me. "I plan to spend the morning with him tomorrow and see how well his skills have developed—hopefully well enough that he may accept stepping into my shoes very soon. And this afternoon, I shall come with you to meet with Dorishena and stay on to discuss business with her while you are taken on a tour of the different government departments."

"Oh. I'm not sure I like the sound of that. You know, that first meeting I had with Denishar, I felt you stare at me the whole time. It was quite intimidating."

I kiss the top of her head. "If I was staring, it was only with deep admiration. I marvelled at your courage and could not stop looking into your beautiful eyes. Their sparkle held me captivated."

"Was that what you were doing? It felt like you were glaring at me."

I huff out a laugh. "I am sorry, my love. I am so used to using my powerful sicortar stare to inspire awe and respect, that I forget sometimes that I am doing it. But please believe me when I say I was not glaring. On the contrary, I was enchanted. You put your hooks into me from that very first meeting."

She kisses my neck and mumbles into it, "And you put your hooks into me that first time I saw you during the holy ceremony."

"I smelled your arousal, Melinda. It made my cock all the harder."

"I saw it. I smelled you too. I could not forget."

My voice turns husky as I whisper, "It is your cock now, Melinda. I will make sure of it."

The naughty female puts her hand on it and squeezes.

"Melinda!" I groan. "Behave yourself."

In response, she gives it another squeeze, sending my pulse skyrocketing. I let her go and sit up abruptly. She looks back at me innocently. "Only keeping a check on my property," she says coyly.

"You will pay for this, my lovely. That is a promise."

Just then, the aircraft begins to accelerate in preparation for take-off, and we both fall silent. The rest of the journey is uneventful. I feed my Melinda a lunch cooked and packed for us by my cook, Dresolor. We talk some more, and I learn about her life back on Earth. She has a younger sister called Harper who is married to someone called Dan and has two children, a boy of six sun rotations and a girl of four, the same age as my Kiritela.

She asks me about the children, and I tell her of the latest happenings in my household. Kirilor's decision that he wants to become a designer of drones when he grows up. Kirimara's latest run in with her chemical analysis teacher—my daughter could not stop herself from pointing out an error in one of his analyses, much to his annoyance. Kirishar playing bong at school and coming home with a broken arm because he somehow fell off the platform and bumped into the neighboring platform's ladder. And finding Kiritela wrapped around me when I woke this morning.

She listens with rapt attention, her face betraying her emotions. She already cares so much about my children. I know Melinda was made for motherhood, and I am more determined than ever to make that a reality.

When finally, we arrive in the southern sector, there is an official government drone waiting to take us to Dorishena's palace, where she will meet us. The journey there is short, and before long, we are being escorted through the corridors of the palace. The architecture here is different to that in the northern sector of our planet. Where we favor domed ceilings and archways, southern architecture leans more towards clean, precise lines.

"Oh wow," Melinda says, walking beside me. "This feels very post-modern in style."

"Is that the Earth word for it? I like to describe it as cleanly symmetrical."

"That it is. I like it, though if pushed, I would still prefer the vaulted ceilings in the northern sector."

"I agree."

We are ushered into a chamber, Sholinar and Desimar walking in behind us, where Dorishena awaits us. I stride forward to greet her the traditional way. I look into her eyes as I place a hand to her chest, then step back and bow. "Dorishena, as always it is a pleasure and honor to see you."

"The honor is mine, sicortar."

She turns her attention to Melinda, who steps forward to greet her. "Dorishena, I am honored to meet you again."

Dorishena smiles warmly at her. "No indeed, Melinda, the honor is mine. I have been waiting for an opportunity to speak with you and find out more about your kind."

"Likewise, I look forward to a fruitful dialogue."

Dorishena indicates that we should sit, then turns to my aide and Melinda's escort. She greets them formally, and once we are all sitting, we get down to business.

Dorishena asks politely, "So Melinda, what are your impressions of Krovatia now that you have been with us for some time?"

Melinda sits with her legs crossed gracefully, her brilliant brown mane of hair, a little tousled after my ministrations on the plane, falling in gentle waves down her shoulders. She looks in her element. Once again, I am captivated as I watch her at work, talking with earnestness and determination about her mission here, parrying comments back and forth with quick wit and thoughtful intelligence.

I follow the conversation between these two strong, powerful females, occasionally interjecting, but mostly listening in admiration. Just as much as Melinda was made to be a mother, she was also made for this. I see the way she weaves her words cleverly to present her people in the best light and win the most concessions for her mission here. Melinda is keen to organize a visit of representatives from the pharmaceutical industry in her world to come to the southern sector and develop mutually beneficial trade opportunities. At first, she is met with the usual caution and resistance to outsiders' presence on our planet, but she ploughs on with determination. It is no surprise to me that by the end of the meeting, Dorishena has agreed to allow a small trade delegation from Earth to visit, pending the approval of the other leaders.

We rise to our feet, and Melinda thanks her host graciously. "Go in peace, Dorishena," she says as she makes to leave.

"Go in peace, Melinda."

I cast a glance at Sholinar, who has been sitting quietly and jotting down notes on his communicator all this time. He understands my look and follows Melinda and Desimar. He will keep an eye on her while I continue my meeting with Dorishena.

Alone with the sector leader, she guides me to sit in the corner, next to the fragrant fountain. "I thought we could meditate and speak through our minds, as we have much to discuss," she says.

"Of course."

We sit together on a set of floor cushions and let the fragrance waft over us as we listen to the gentle trickling of the water. After a quarter of a beat, we reach that state of deep relaxation where we can both enter into a mutual trance. I take some deep breaths in and out, focusing my mind on building a bridge with hers. Finally, we make the connection, and I wait for her to begin the conversation.

"You have completed a scan of the top ranking individuals on our planet, yet none have presented with that suspiciously perfect aura. Am I correct?"

"Correct. So far, our only leads are Prelonisha, who we suspect of having smuggled the boral crystals aboard the cargo ship. We have also discovered a young man who frequents my body art shop, named Norifen. I have gone on to scan the other members of his family but none of them had a suspicious aura. We know he was talking to someone on his communicator the day he was at the body art shop, but we do not know who that fellow conspirator is."

"I assume Denishar is having him closely watched?"

"Yes, both he and Prelonisha are under constant surveillance. Unfortunately, neither have put a foot wrong yet.

It almost makes me think we are mistaken in our suspicions. And yet, the evidence is to the contrary."

"No, something is definitely afoot. I have suspected for a long time that there would eventually be some pushback to our strict eco-conscious ethos. The possibility of an easier, more luxurious life was always sure to tempt some of our kind."

"So, while we wait to see if Prelonisha or Norifen present us with any further leads, I will continue with my scans, moving down the list to the lesser important dignitaries on our world. That is, unless you have a different suggestion for where I should be focusing my efforts?"

"I believe it is best to follow the trail started with those two individuals. Who do they encounter in their day-to-day life? Start there, and work your way down their own contacts. Eventually, we will flush out these conspirators."

"I believe you may be right. I will ask Denishar to send me the names of people who have interacted with Prelonisha and Norifen, and begin a scan of them."

"This will interfere with your usual duties as sicortar, will it not?"

"Yes, I have had to suspend my usual holy trances and just focus on the scans."

"Perhaps you should seek help. Have you considered consulting Melistor about this?"

"I have, and I am meeting with him tomorrow morning. I have other business I also wish to discuss with him."

"Oh?"

"Dorishena, you are aware that I have been sicortar now for twenty-three sun rotations. It is time for me to find a successor."

"I realize this day would come, but I did not think it would be so soon."

"I have personal reasons for wishing to expedite matters."

"Could that reason have anything to do with the beautiful Human, Melinda?"

"You are perspicacious as well as wise, Dorishena."

"It was plain to see that you only had eyes for her earlier on. But surely that is not reason enough to quit your post as sicortar?"

"It is, Dorishena, if I am to mate her. She refuses to share me with my drashas, and I am equally jealous and possessive of her. We must both be free to commit fully to the other."

"I see. This has come at an inopportune time, Kirimor, when you have mightily important work to do."

"Rest assured that I will always do my duty, regardless of my personal wishes, but I am hoping that with a little mentoring, Melistor will be able to step up to the position very soon. I will observe him tomorrow in a holy trance and guide him."

"Then I wish you luck, Kirimor."

"Thank you, Dorishena. Am I to take it that, should my request to step down as sicortar be presented to the four sector leaders, you would view it favorably?"

"As long as you present us with convincing evidence that Melistor is up to the challenge of being sicortar, then I will of course view your request favorably, as I am sure will Denishar. With the two of us on board, it should not be difficult to sway the other two leaders. However, I warn you, I will require proof that Melistor is up to the job."

"Understood."

Our discussion over, we both come out of the trance. I stand and bow, "Go in peace, Dorishena."

"Go in peace, Kirimor."

I wait for Melinda in the main atrium, sipping on a glass of *nari* and checking my communicator for messages. I update Denishar on my meeting and ask him to send me a list of known associates for the people under suspicion. Within a beat, he sends me back the information requested. I shall try to make a start on this tonight, as time is of the essence. Some instinct is telling me we need to root out these conspirators fast, before anything serious happens to our planet's security.

I look up to see Melinda approaching, followed by Sholinar and Desimar. I stand and go to her. "How did the rest of your meetings go?" I ask.

She beams her beautiful smile. "It went well, thanks. And you? Did you conclude your business with Dorishena successfully?"

"Indeed I did, and now I think we may take time to enjoy the rest of our afternoon. Come with me, my lovely."

She follows me into the tropical heat outside and climbs into the waiting drone. Desimar rushes forward, as if to accompany us.

"Thank you, Desimar, I can take it from here. You may go with Sholinar and we will see you in the morning, when the both of you will escort Melinda to her meetings."

"But sir, I am under strict orders to be with her at all times."

"Not when she is with highest priest in the land," I boom. "Go in peace, Desimar."

I close the door of the drone, not waiting for any further arguments. The engine starts immediately, and soon we are in the air, on the way to our destination.

"Where are we going?" Melinda wonders.

"I am taking you to a delightful place in the rainforest, where we shall be staying the night. It is another cabin, but this one is beside a natural rock formation with a clear pool of water."

"Oh! Desimar was telling me about this. He had planned to show it to me."

Melinda's words set my teeth on edge. "The more I hear of this Desimar, the less I like what I hear."

"He was only trying to be hospitable and show me the sights."

"Hmm."

She rests her chin on my shoulder. "Are you going to stay grumpy the whole journey?"

I quirk my lips. "Maybe, maybe not."

"What will clear the grumpiness away?"

"Perhaps if you were to come and perch your delightful bottom on my lap and place your arms around me, then you might be able to dispel my grumpy mood. Of course, if you wanted a guarantee of success, you could then decide to place your lips on mine."

"And that will definitely chase the grumpiness away?"

"Most definitely."

"Hmm," she says, as if considering the matter.

I raise a brow. "Melinda!"

She laughs, a delightful tinkling sound, and promptly deposits her pert backside on my lap. With a smile, she places her arms around me, and I immediately trap her in the noose of my tail. "Kiss me," I growl.

"Or what?"

"Or I shall die a thousand deaths until you do."

"Well, we can't have that," she whispers and brings her lips to mine.

All teasing is over as soon as our lips meet, hers soft and plump beneath mine. I kiss her hungrily, licking the seam of her lips and demanding entry. She parts them, and I plunge inside. Our tongues meet and lap at each other as we feast on the other's taste. Her kisses are like a drug, sending me into delirium. We are so caught up in one another that we do not notice we have arrived at our destination until we feel a slight bump as we land. We pull apart, breathless and panting, eyes burning with desire.

"Kirimor," she breathes.

"I know, my love, I know." I kiss her softly one last time, then shift her off my lap to stand and pull her up with me. "Come."

We get down from the drone which flies off, leaving us alone in the middle of the jungle. Melinda looks around uncertainly. We are in a small clearing surrounded by a thick band of trees. "Err, Kirimor, are we in the right place?"

I draw her to me. "Do not worry. Come. Let me carry this for you."

I take hold of her travel bag with one hand and hold out my other to her. She grips it tight as I guide her towards a small break in the trees, which reveals a hitherto unnoticed path. We pick our steps through it, walking for a quarter of a beat. Around us is silence, except for the normal sounds of the forest—a rustling here and there, the faraway cry of one of its creatures, the slither of a ground based animal fleeing our approach. Through our touch, I sense Melinda's pulse racing with anxiety. "It is fine, my love," I soothe her. "Just a short way longer."

A few steps later, we begin to hear the rushing sound of water. We quicken our pace towards it. In a short while, we find a narrow stream which we follow for another quarter of a beat. It widens the further we go. And then we see it. The stream falls in a rushing cascade into a medium-sized pool of crystal clear water carved by nature into the rocks. Above it, built into the trees, is a large wooden cabin.

Melinda stops and stares. "Oh my."

I enclose her in my arms. "Do you like what you see?"

"It's much better than I could ever imagine. The cabin even has a front porch to sit and watch the waterfall. Kirimor, it's gorgeous!"

"Come, let us explore."

I lead her around the edge of the pool until we reach the base of the trees. Hidden at the back of one is a narrow ladder that leads up to the cabin porch.

"You go first, my lovely."

She climbs up the steps gingerly, while my eyes follow her every move. We reach the top and stand together, surveying the view.

"It's beautiful," she says breathlessly.

"Come have a look inside."

I open the front door of the cabin and usher her in. It is not unlike my own cabin in the mountains in its simplicity, though much smaller in size. The room contains a large bed, a seating area and a small space for food preparation. Beyond that, a door leads to washing facilities. Melinda peruses it curiously. "It's cute. All the basics we need for our short stay. Is there food?"

"Of course, my lovely. I have taken care of that. Are you hungry?"

She smiles mischievously, "Maybe in a while, but first, I'd like to take a refreshing dip in that pool."

"I was about to suggest the same thing."

She takes her bag, which I've been holding loosely in my hands, and rummages inside. "Lucky I remembered to pack a swim suit."

"Err, my darling love. There is no need for such things."

She looks up, frowning. "What do you mean?"

"This place is entirely private. Nobody and nothing can come near without a warning on my communicator. We are totally alone, so there is no need for any clothing whatsoever."

"Ah." She flushes delightfully.

"We are familiar with each other's naked form, are we not?"

"Yes, I suppose we are."

"Then take your clothes off, Melinda."

"You first."

I smirk. "My pleasure."

There is not much to disrobe. I simply untie the laces of my loin cloth and throw it on the bed. My cock, already hard, stands tall and proud. Melinda stares at it, her lips parting. Then she resumes her customary self-control and looks into my eyes. "No sex, Kirimor. Not until you can promise to be faithful."

I so wish I could make that promise here and now, but I cannot. Instead, I say wistfully, "I know, my sweet." Then I add, "But there is much that we can do, short of having sex."

She stands, ramrod straight, looking me defiantly in the eyes. "Your tail?"

"My tail, my hands, my mouth. If you will allow me."

She considers, her breaths coming in and out quickly. "Alright."

"Take off your clothes, Melinda," I say gruffly.

In one swift move, she lifts her dress above her head and discards it on the bed, next to my loin cloth. Quickly, she removes her underwear, then stands proud, baring herself to me.

"You are beautiful," I say, my voice husky.

"So are you. I love looking at you." She looks towards the pool. "Shall we?"

"Before we go, there is something I wish to give you." I go to my loin cloth and withdraw a small pouch from the pocket. "I said not long ago that next time you adorn yourself with jewelry on your private parts, it will be mine."

I take out a new barbell, identical in size to the one I took from her, embedded on either side with a purple colored stone. "Let me put this on you, my love."

She stares at it, lips trembling, then nods. I kneel before her until her mound is at eye level. "Spread your legs, my lovely."

She does as I ask. With gentle fingers, I find the hood of her nub and thread the end of the barbell through the small, pierced holes, securing both ends in place. I look at my handywork, pleased with the result. The stones sit proudly above her pleasure nub.

"It's beautiful, thank you," she whispers.

"There is more," I say, taking something else out of the pouch. It is a pendant embedded with a row of more purple gemstones. "This goes around you like this." I thread it around her hips, so the stones lie flat against her womb, then close the clasp.

She looks down at herself. "It's gorgeous, Kirimor. Thank you. Are these boral crystals?"

I laugh, "No, my love, I am not planning to get into a trance each time I pleasure your body. These are vlor stones imported from Ven. They are known not only for their beauty but also for their healing and regenerative effect on the body."

"Oh," she says, sounding startled. "Thank you. I wish there was a mirror so I could see myself properly."

I take out my communicator and snap a picture of her. I look at it and smile. I know I will treasure this image for the rest of my days. I hand the communicator to her. "Look at yourself, my beauty."

She gazes at it and smiles. "I do look good in all that bling. Thanks, Kirimor. I love it."

I open a drawer and take out the sun protection spray. "We will both need this before we go out into the pool." I spray two shots into the air and walk under the mist, then hand the bottle to her. She follows suit. I hold out my hand to her, "Come, my love."

We make our way carefully down the ladder, then walk towards the edge of the pool. "It is quite deep," I say. "Shall we jump in together?"

She grins. "Yes!"

"On the count of three. One. Two. Three."

Hands still clasped together, we both jump in and screech at the contact of our bodies with the cool, fresh water. We emerge, spluttering, and I wrap my tail around her. We gaze at each other breathlessly and laugh together.

"Let us swim to the other end. It will warm us up." I loosen my tail's embrace, but keep it around her as we swim side by side to the other end of the pool. It is shallower that end, and soon, I am able to touch the bottom with my feet and stand, the water lapping at my waist. Melinda finds her footing and stands facing me, her beautiful breasts peeking above the water and tempting me, the teats firm and taut. I feast on the sight of her. "Melinda my love, you have never looked more beautiful to me than you do right now. You take my breath away."

Her breath hitches. And whatever self-control I may have had is gone. I clamp my mouth around the firm tip of her breast and suck with all my might. I squeeze her other breast with my hand, rubbing the teat between my thumb and forefingers. I am crazed with desire for her. My tail whips around, tying her to me, as I suck and bite and nibble on her delicious breast. She gasps. I switch my attention to the other breast, ravishing it with my mouth.

"Ah! Kirimor. Ah," she moans over and over above me.

The sound of her pleasure spurs me on. I take my time paying due attention to each beautiful mound, biting into the soft flesh then returning to suck on her glorious teats. Eventually, I work my way up her body, nipping the delicious flesh and burying my face in her neck, marking her with my bites, knowing that tomorrow, all will know she has been devoured and claimed. She moans again and I growl, "You are mine. Say it!"

"Ah, yes," she mumbles.

I bite her flesh again. "Say it!"

"I'm yours, Kirimor. Only yours."

A sound comes from me that is close to a howl. And then I capture her mouth in a wild and hungry kiss. She grasps me close and kisses me back, matching my hunger. Her body grinds against mine and I feel her aching need. With her in my arms, I march us to the edge of the pool, depositing her on the flat, rocky surface. Then I'm dragging myself out of the water and pulling her to her feet. "Come."

I lead her to a patch of mossy ground and lie down on it. "Sit on me, my lovely, let me pleasure you."

She kneels on my chest, hesitant. My tail flies up into the air, twirling in its excitement. "Let me put my tail in you, my love."

She nods her agreement and widens her stance, allowing my tail to sneak its way to her opening. As it begins to burrow its way in, she asks breathlessly, "Do you feel? In your tail? Like your cock?"

I understand her meaning. "Not as sensitive as my cock, but I do feel pleasure there." Then I'm plunging deep inside her tight, hot passage and finding her pleasure center.

She gasps. "Yeah! Right there."

"Good girl. Rub yourself on me."

She begins to bounce gently on me, letting my tail slip up and down inside her. Her beautiful breasts sway with each bounce and I cannot help grasping them both with my hands and squeezing their softness. I let her rub against my tail for a while longer, then grunt, "I want to taste you. Come sit on my face."

She shifts forwards, keeping my tail deep inside her, and approaches my face. I pull her down to me and kiss the moist, muskily fragrant flesh.

She moans above me. "Ah, Kirimor!"

My hands grasp her bottom cheeks firmly as I feast on her, licking from her slit up to her pleasure nub, tugging at the jewelry I put there. I feel her tremble in pleasure and pain, and lick her again, making sure to end it with a firm tug on the barbell. "Kirimor!" she gasps.

I do no let up, but carry on licking her over and over, delighting in her reaction. My tail continues its glorious friction of her inside passage, and as it tightens around me, I know she is close to completion. I take her nub into my mouth and begin to suck and flick it with my tongue, going at a furious pace, wanting only to help her reach her peak. And then I feel it. A pulsing deep inside her body, followed by a squirt of her juices all over my face. I am in heaven, lapping her deliciousness up, licking her through every shudder and throb of her climax. I eat her up, feasting on her tangy, musky flavor, never stopping until I feel a second wave of pulsing. She moans my name loudly, ecstatically. "Kirimor!"

Once she is spent, she collapses on me, her head on my chest. I hold her to me, running soothing hands down the length of her back. She pants, until at last her breaths become even. She plants a kiss on my chest and looks up. My face is still smeared with her juices. She touches it with her finger in wonder. "Kirimor," she breathes. "I have never come like that before, never gushed in that way. I'm sorry."

"Do not be sorry! I was never more honored than when you gushed your pleasure juices on me. I was in heaven."

She looks at me uncertainly, so I grunt, "If you are in any doubt as to how you made me feel, take a look at my cock."

She shifts to sit up and inspect my throbbing appendage which is oozing droplets of my nectar. She places a hand on me, though I am too large to fit in her grasp. She strokes her fingers up and down my length, spreading the sticky wetness. I groan in pleasure. "Melinda, my love. I am so close. A few more tugs and you will get me there."

She leans forward and begins to stroke me in earnest, each touch of her hand sending shivers of bliss down my body. And then, she brings her mouth to me, lapping delicately at my tip and I know it will not be long before I erupt. With an effort, she fits the top of my cock into her mouth and begins to suck.

"Ah, Melinda!" I groan.

She sucks me further into her mouth, the sweet moist heat driving me wild.

"Melinda, I am coming!"

She does not take her mouth off me, but keeps on with her sensuous sucking. I grind my groin up into her, desperate for her touch. I can feel my climax building. I know it will be substantial, as it has been a good many rotations since I had my last fuck. With a loud grunt, I climax, pulsing wildly and showering her with my nectar. She takes it all, swallowing my essence and licking all my juices clean.

I am still breathless when she finally looks up, a smug smile on her face.

"You are magnificent, Melinda."

"And you, Kirimor, are delicious."

I smile, and hold out my arms to her. She comes to me willingly, allowing me to enfold her in my embrace. "I love you, Melinda."

She kisses my lips softly. "I love you too, Kirimor."

Chapter 30

Melinda

Eventually, we rouse ourselves enough to swim some more, then we go up to the cabin where Kirimor sets about preparing our evening meal. Neither of us has felt the urge to get dressed again, so we potter around in the kitchen area, totally naked. I get distracted every now and then, ogling his beautiful body. Every time he feels my eyes on me, his cock twitches delightfully in response.

"Melinda!" he rebukes mildly, but I know he's secretly pleased.

"So, what are we having for dinner?"

He removes a packet of some kind of meat from a small fridge compartment built into the wall shelving. "These are some special cuts of bilos meat, produced here in the southern sector. Their bilos is different from up north, more tender and with a pleasing marbling of fat. I am going to cook them on an open fire outside on the porch."

"Can I do anything to help?"

"There should be a table cloth and eating implements in that cabinet over there, as well as a small folding table we can put outside. Will you set it up while I cook the meat?"

"Gladly."

While he starts the "open fire", some kind of barbecue pit, I busy myself, taking the floor bench seat out onto the porch and setting a low folding table in front of it. I find the table cloths, some plates, and more of those two pronged forks and large tweezers that I've seen used before. A glance inside the fridge finds a jug of *nari*, which I place on the table outside together with some glasses.

Preparations complete, I go stand beside Kirimor, observing his expert handling of the meat. His tail snakes around me, the only sign that he's noticed my presence. He cooks with single-minded focus, searing the meat on both sides, then placing it on a wooden board. He withdraws a sharp knife from a compartment beneath the board, and slices up the meat into thin, neat strips. There is a small bottle of some kind of sauce on the board, which he pours on the meat.

As he works, my eyes stray to his lower body. I can't help myself. I'm acting like a peeping Tom, but in my defence, I have never before seen such incredible power and beauty in a man. His cock hangs thick and low, nearly reaching the middle of his thighs. It swings a little from side to side as he moves, and my eyes avidly follow each pendulous swing. Beneath that delicious cock are two swollen ball sacs, their thin skin the color of a gray sky at sunset, a hint of pink dappling the gray. Sensing my gaze, his cock thickens and twitches. Kirimor grunts, but doesn't say anything. Suddenly, the lasso of his tail around me tightens, pulling me to his side. He bends towards my chest and bites my nipple, finishing off with a tug of his tongue, sucking the sting, then releasing it with a pop. He growls, "Let us eat, my lovely."

He plates the meat and passes it to me. I take it to the table, and he follows bearing two containers, which he places beside the meat. We sit together on the bench, legs crossed, and inevitably his tail finds its way around me.

"You're not going to tie my hands?" I ask with a smirk.

"You are going to be a good girl and let me feed you, Melinda. But of course, should you misbehave, the option is there to tie your hands."

"Maybe I'll need to misbehave then," I say, reaching out to lift the lid off one of the containers. Immediately, he slaps my hand gently away. His glorious tail unwinds from around my waist and trails down my body, starting with a soft stroke of my face. I nuzzle into it, grabbing the soft, furry tip with my hand and kissing it.

I hear a rumble in his chest, almost like a purr. "You like that, don't you?" I murmur. I enclose his tail in my hand and stroke my way down to the tip.

"Yes," he grunts. "Now be good and bring your wrists together on your lap."

I give his tail one final stroke then do as he says. He wraps it around my wrists, imprisoning my hands, but not so tightly as to hurt. "Now," he says, "let me feed you."

From the first container, he takes out some kind of salad leaf, a very pale pastel green in color. He places it on the plate, then using the tweezer implement, he grabs some cooked meat, smothered in the greenish looking sauce, and drops it on the leaf. He opens the other container and takes out some thinly grated crunchy vegetables and adds them to the mix. His hand returns to the container, coming back with sprigs of fresh herbs which he scatters on top. Then he expertly rolls the leaf and holds it out to me. "Eat," he orders.

Obediently, I open my mouth and bite into the rolled, stuffed leaf. "Mmm," I say, when I get the chance. "It's good. Lots of fresh flavors, some spice and a hint of lemon."

"It is called *loshi*," he replies. "Have some more."

I take another delicious bite. While I chew, he quickly prepares two more leaf rolls, one of which he gobbles in one big bite. The other, he brings to my lips. I open my mouth and eat it all up. Once we have finished eating the *loshi*, he goes inside and comes back with another container, this one with small syrupy cakes topped with a light, creamy type of frosting. He drops a cake into my mouth, and I lick the sticky syrup off his fingers.

"Hmm," he rumbles. "Good girl."

We finish our meal with a refreshing drink of *nari*, then work efficiently together to put everything neatly away. Once done, we come back out to sit on the porch. Kirimor plumps some cushions under my knees as I stretch out my legs and give a satisfied yawn. I lean into him, and he draws me against him, my cheek tucked into the fragrant crook of his neck. *I could stay like this forever.*

We sit, watching the sun set over the horizon and listening to the strangely hypnotic sound of the stream cascading water into the pool.

"Would you mind very much if I do a little work tonight?" asks Kirimor.

"What type of work?"

"I have been given a list of names of people who have interacted with two of our suspects. I need to scan them to see if any display a suspiciously perfect aura."

"How do you do that, with just a name?"

"I have the name and general location of the person. When I go into a trance, I let my mind wander to that location and call out that name. When someone who goes by that name responds—subconsciously through their aura—I fix my trance on them until I get a full reading of their aura."

He takes out his communicator and shows me the list of names. "I will methodically go down this list and see if there is anyone that catches my attention."

"Will it make you frisky afterwards?"

"Frisky?" he echoes in amusement. "I am always frisky when I am with you, my lovely, but you do not have to worry. As long as I do not absorb someone's negative energy, I am not at risk of turning into a rabid beast."

"Well, that's good to know."

"Will you mind if I start my scans now?"

"No, my darling, I don't mind at all. I'm curious to watch you and I've also got some notes I need to write up about today's meetings."

He looks at me oddly. "What?" I ask.

"You called me darling." His voice is a soft rumble.

I kiss his cheek. "Yes I did, darling."

For this brilliant piece of affection I'm rewarded with a hard, sizzling kiss that leaves us both breathless.

"Oh," I breathe. "I guess I should call you darling more often."

"I have no objection to that."

He stands and goes inside the cabin, re-emerging a moment later with the pouch that had held the jewelry. He produces a large boral crystal from the pouch and places it on the edge of the barbecue pit, under which red embers still emit radiant heat. I watch as the crystal darkens to a deep purple in color. Kirimor comes back to sit beside me, legs crossed as he begins to chant a prayer to Taya. Then he goes silent, and I know he's entered his trance.

I watch him curiously as he sits stock still, staring into space, his mind travelling to a distant place, calling out the name of the first person on his list. After a long while, I see him let out a deep breath and turn to me, no longer in a trance.

"No luck?"

"No, nothing of interest there. Let me go to the next one."

He checks his communicator, then once again, stares into space and lets the trance take him to the next person on his list. Another bust. He moves on to the next person, and then the next. After a while, I take out my own communicator and begin jotting down notes on my meetings today and starting to draft a report about my trip, to be sent to Earth in my next communication.

We work the rest of the evening peaceably side by side, both of us still naked, his tail securely wrapped around my waist. Around us, night falls. As it turns dark, a small lamp above us lights up automatically, emitting a warm, soft glow. Suddenly, Kirimor grunts beside me and exhales loudly.

"What is it, darling?"

He takes a moment before responding. "This last person... I sensed deep malevolence, of the type I have not encountered for a long time."

"Will you try to absorb that malevolence?"

"No, not tonight. Tomorrow, when I am with Melistor, I will let him seek this person out and see how well he does at neutralizing the evil. It will be a good test of his skills."

"So..." I hesitate. "You won't need to get sexual release?"

He takes my hand in his. "Melinda, as long as I am officially sicortar, I cannot promise sexual fidelity to you, much as I wish to. However, I pledge not to absorb evil energy or allow myself to reach a state of intense sexual need, unless it is absolutely imperative I do so. Tomorrow, I will guide Melistor and observe him in his trance, but I will not participate. If, however, he fails in the task, then I will not be able to put him forward as my replacement yet, and upon my return home, I will have to complete the task myself—and yes then, I will need sexual release."

My heart is heavy in my chest. I'm painfully reminded that loving Kirimor comes at a cost. "How likely is he to fail?" I whisper.

Kirimor huffs out a deep breath. "I think the prospects are good, my love. I do not want to tempt fate with false promises, but I am cautiously optimistic."

"That's good."

He stands and deftly removes the boral crystal from the barbecue pit using the tweezer implement. He drops it on the wooden board and leaves it there to cool. "I think perhaps, it is time to go to bed."

We each take turns in the bathroom, then slip under the covers in the large bed. Kirimor holds me close, his tail slipping around me. "Sleep now, my love," he murmurs.

Wrapped in the warm comfort of his body, I feel myself slip into a dreamless slumber.

Chapter 31

Wyatt

Our descent to the Earth's surface was not the most pleasant of experiences, but I'm proud to say I managed it a lot better. Yes, I clung on to Rivlor for dear life, and maybe I might have cried a tear or two. At least I didn't sob wildly or suck her thumb like a baby. I don't know if I'll ever live down the embarrassment of that particular moment in my life.

Back in my townhouse, I busy myself with the endless preparations for our journey. I barely sleep, at most a handful of hours. I whittle down my list of performers to a maximum of thirty-five people. This has involved some difficult decisions about who we take and who we leave behind. I've met with Lacey Holmes, the principal dancer leading our ballet troupe, to work out what ballets we could stage with just a dozen dancers. The big three-act ballets are out of the question, but we've included some pas-de-deux dances from our most classic ballets, such as Giselle, Swan Lake and Sleeping Beauty, together with some more contemporary abstract ballets.

The orchestra was another difficult decision. No way could we take with us a full classical orchestra, but I was keen to maintain some element of live music with our ballets. As a result, we've decided to take a trio of violinists, a cellist, some horn players and a percussionist. We're also including a pianist and somehow transporting a grand piano light years into space. The plan is to cleverly integrate recorded music featuring a full orchestra with our live musicians, all this under the expert guidance of Rinaldo Pucci, our musical director and conductor. When I think of how ambitious this project is, I'm almost giddy with pride and excitement.

The Shakesperian actors have confirmed they'll be performing Othello, as well as a twentieth century classic by Arthur Miller, called "Death of a Salesman". I once saw a Broadway performance of it years ago, and I'm looking forward to having it included in our program. I'm curious to see the reactions of aliens to two plays that so poignantly highlight the faults and fallibilities of the human condition. Perhaps it will chime with their own experience, or else it will fall flat. I'm all too aware of the risks I'm taking with this venture, but after what seems like a lifetime of playing it safe, I'm going all out. It's scary. It's exhilarating. It's amazing. I feel alive and reborn.

Best of all, Ricky Charles has finally confirmed he'll be joining us. At first, he balked on being told he could only take a maximum of four backing musicians with him and a roadie. What about his make-up artist? His PR reps? The backing vocalists? It took some persuading to get him on board and understand the limitations of the space on the cargo ship. I pointed out that creativity is the mother of invention. Couldn't his backing musicians double up as backing vocalists? And how about if the dancers, expert at doing their own make-up, also assist him with his? I talked him into it eventually. The guy's a bit of an asshole and a diva, but his talent is immense. Of course, he'll be taking the only available guest room on the ship, which means I'll be bedding down in a pod with everyone else in the cargo hold.

My final preparation, a little morbid, has been to write my will. In case I don't return from this journey, I want all my affairs in order. I'm leaving all my worldly goods to my two nephews. I've also signed over a power of attorney to my brother. Dylan will keep a check on my townhouse and ensure all bills are paid. My chiropractor practice is being sold to my other partners, but I've not quite burned all my bridges. If I wanted to, I could come back and start over.

First thing tomorrow, we leave on our epic journey. There is one more thing I need to do. I begin recording a message.

"Hey Mel, I hope life is treating you well. Honey, I have big news. You know I told you I was seeing a new therapist to get me over my fear of flying? Well, we did it. I successfully completed my first drone drone flight in years, but not only this. I also went into space for a short while. It was the most terrifying experience of my life, but I did it. So, now for my big announcement. First thing tomorrow, I'm leaving Earth and travelling to Krovatia on a Venorian cargo ship commanded by Treylor's cousin. I obtained permission to visit the planet with a troupe of artistic performers I've put together. I'm calling it the Interstellar Arts Company, and we'll be performing ballets and plays that showcase human culture."

I think about Dwight's words. *When you finally arrive in Krovatia, there is no guarantee that your ex-wife will still be single and willing to get back together with you.* With a deep breath, I say what needs to be said. "Honey, I hope with all my heart that we can find our way back to being together as a couple again. I love you forever and no divorce papers will ever cut you out of my heart. I want to be with you. I'm all too aware that this may not be what you want. I hope that's not the case, but I want you to know this. I am coming to Krovatia in my own right, leading my own business venture. I have no intention of imposing on you or cramping your style. I just hope, with all my heart, that I'm not too late and that I can make you mine again. I love you so very much. See you soon, honey."

I end the recording and send.

I barely manage any sleep as I toss and turn, anxiety and anticipation whirling in my fevered brain. The big day finally arrives, and finds me gathered with the rest of my troupe at the space docking station, surrounded by endless crates of supplies. I glance at them worriedly. I hope they will all fit. The ship door slides open, and both Rivlor and Shular step out.

They take one look at us and all our belongings, and stop in consternation. Rivlor comes over to me. "You are taking all this?"

I shrug. "Those crates over there contain all our sleeping pods. This here is our grand piano. And the various other crates contain instruments, costumes and sets for our shows. It's all stuff we are going to need."

She looks them over, hands on hip. "Very well. We will try our best to accommodate all this. Let us begin."

The next hour is spent in painstakingly transporting our crates, unpacking our pods, and trying to fit the grand piano in the narrow space allocated for our instruments. It's stressful grunt work. Tempers fray; people shout. That's until Rivlor shuts us up with a booming, "Be quiet!" She then proceeds to direct our efforts with the efficiency and skill of a seasoned war general. Everything has to be secured for take-off. When finally all is ready to go, we sit through a safety demonstration in which Rivlor lays down clear rules for us to follow throughout our journey on the ship.

And then it's time. We all get strapped in to our seats. I feel a fleeting wave of panic, wondering if I'll be expected to sit like everyone else. I cast agonized eyes at Rivlor, who quirks her lips in amusement and beckons to me. "Come here, Wyatt."

Relieved, if not a little sheepish at the curious looks I'm getting, I hurry towards her. She fastens on the seat extension and takes her position, legs opened wide. I manoeuver my body into her lap, laying my head on her chest. She tightens the safety straps securely around us as I try to calm myself with slow breaths in and out.

We begin our tilt backward, and my heart starts to pound double time. Rivlor's hands begin a leisurely stroke of my head, shoulders and chest. "You will be fine, Wyatt," she states. Her voice is nearly drowned out by the loud roar of the ship's engine beneath us. *Oh God, I don't think I can do this again.*

"Yes, you can," murmurs the mind reader at my back. She wraps both her arms around my torso and squeezes me tight.

And well yes, I manage to get through it. I don't think it's ever something I'll get accustomed to. After a while, I become aware that our seats have tilted back to an upright position and that others are unstrapping themselves and getting up to stretch their legs. That's it. We're in space, on our way to Krovatia. Before too long, I'll be finding Melinda, and trying to win her back.

◆◆◆

Our first few days in space are a period of adjustment for all of us. I'm not exact on the science, or on Venorian technology, but the spaceship manages to maintain gravity so we're not floating about in the air. It's not quite on a par with what it is on the Earth's surface, but near enough. Our steps feel a little slower and heavier when we walk, and it takes a bit longer to get back down to the ground when jumping up in the air. Not much of an issue for me, but for the dancers trying to maintain their training regimen, it has posed interesting challenges. In one corner of the dining hall, they have set up a barre to do their stretches and exercises on, but floor work involving pirouettes and jumps has proved far too tricky.

While the dancers try their best at maintaining their physique, the actors learn their lines and the musicians practise on their instruments. In between all this, we keep each other company, getting to know one another a little better, our resident rockstar, Ricky Charles, being the one prominent exception. He has kept mostly to himself, using the privacy of his own room as the perfect excuse not to mingle with us ordinary folk. However, his roadie, a guy named Wilson, has regaled us with lots of fun tales of their adventures on the road, making up for his boss's social ineptitude.

Of Rivlor, I have seen very little. Her duties as the ship's captain keep her busy, and mostly in the vicinity of the operations room which we do not frequent.

Being quartered in the cargo hold and sleeping in a pod doesn't afford me a huge amount of privacy. The pods are foldable structures made of durable plastic and silicone, brightly colored candy pink—someone's idea of a joke, I'm sure. Each pod, when erected, has space for a single bed, a small desk area and a storage compartment. I use the desk to work, sending out messages to my contacts on Krovatia, Ven and Driskia to arrange accommodation and confirm the venues for our shows. Our venue on Krovatia will be a lecture theater at the university in the northern sector, which has a large stage and auditorium. Pravol kindly put me in touch with the university authorities to start the ball rolling. I sit now to compose and send a message to the university outlining our requirements, the dates we plan to perform and requesting a price quote for our rental of the premises.

Then I stretch out my legs uncomfortably in the cramped space and listen to a message that has just arrived from my main contact on the planet Ven, a lady named Flidar, who also happens to be Treylor's mom. Flidar has scouted for possible venues that would suit our requirements. The Venorians do not have theaters, preferring to consume their arts in more intimate surroundings. The concept of a large theater with a stage is somewhat alien to them. It's funny to think that on their planet, we will be the ones considered alien, not them. I listen to Flidar suggest a possible venue for us. It's the lecture hall at the Institute for the Advancement of Science, where Treylor used to work before being deployed to Krovatia. I watch the video footage of the space that Flidar has kindly recorded for me, but my heart sinks. Unlike the Krovatian lecture theater, this space will not work for us at all. The stage area is far too small for dancers to skip and prance about on.

I sit back on my chair and sigh. If push comes to shove, we could consider setting up an outdoor stage, perhaps on some kind of sports field, if they have such a thing on the planet Ven. I start a new message. "Athena, record message to Flidar. Begin."

Smiling at my communicator screen, I speak. "Hello Flidar, I hope you and your mate are well. Thank you for sending me the video footage of the lecture hall at the Institute for the Advancement of Science. Unfortunately, it's not going to be a suitable venue for us. Our dancers need a larger stage to perform on. I am going to send you some video clips of ballet performances so you can get an idea of what kind of activities they will be doing and the space they'll require. If there is no suitable venue to be found, I'm wondering whether we could erect a stage outdoors, perhaps on some kind of sports field? I would be very grateful if you could look into this and get back to me as soon as possible. Thank you again for all your efforts on our behalf. Athena, end message."

Fingers crossed Flidar will be able to find something suitable for us soon, or else I dread to think what will happen. I'll have egg on my face for sure, having brought artists light years away from their home only to find they have nowhere to perform. And then, if and when that's sorted, I still have to sell tickets to our shows and ensure we have a paying audience. Abruptly, the ramifications of all I have to do start to weigh down on me. So far, I've been running on adrenaline, my efforts focused on putting this project together and getting it off the ground. Now that we are literally off the ground, the reality of what I'm undertaking is beginning to sink in. *What the fuck am I doing here?*

I stand abruptly, needing to get out of the confines of my pod and breathe some fresh air. Ha! That's a joke. I'm on a spaceship. No fresh air available. I step outside my pod, breathing heavily, and rush out of the cargo hold into the corridor. I have no set direction in mind, just a need to walk off my anxiety. What the fuck am I going to do if I can't find us a place to perform our shows? Oh my God why didn't I just stay home and continue with my nice, safe existence as a chiropractor? Why did I feel the need to make such a fucking grand gesture?

I'm striding forward in my agitation, uncaring where I go. That's why I end up barrelling into a tall, firm body, sending me falling down on my backside. "Wyatt," a voice barks. "Why are you running on my ship? Did you not listen to the rules?"

Rivlor holds out a hand to help me up. I stand and brush myself off, not knowing what to say. At last, I grunt out, "Sorry."

She frowns at me. "What is the matter now?"

I run my hand through my hair sheepishly. "It's nothing. Just another anxiety attack."

She examines me a moment more, then comes to a decision. "Come."

She strides off in the opposite direction, and I follow at her heels. We come to a door—her chamber—and she opens it with a touch of her hand to the wall scanner. I step inside hesitantly, not sure what we are doing here.

She points to the bed. "Go lie down."

My eyes flit to hers in confusion.

"Be a good boy Wyatt, and do as I say," she says in a clipped voice. "Go lie down on the bed, on your back, eyes closed."

The command in her voice is impossible to resist, so I do as she says, hesitantly making my way to the bed, slipping my shoes off and lying down.

"Close your eyes, Wyatt." I close them.

"Breathe deeply in and hold the breath." I take a deep breath and hold it.

"Now breathe out, and with that breath, let everything that is worrying you flow out of your body. Let it go." I breathe out, trying to empty my mind.

"Again." A cool hand touches my forehead as I take my next breath in and out. "Keep going, let your anxiety flow out with each breath."

I spend the next few minutes focusing on my breath, all the while feeling her cool hand on my face. She's using her telepathy to read my mind.

"Yes, I am."

So, what are you reading?

"You are worried about finding a suitable place for your shows on Ven."

Yes.

"You sent a video clip of the ballet dance to Flidar. May I see it too?"

Of course.

She removes her hand from my forehead, and I sit up. Taking my communicator out, I open a video clip of Sleeping Beauty, the scene where Princess Aurora skips merrily around the stage, gloriously happy at celebrating her eighteenth birthday. Rivlor watches it intently. On stage, Aurora is presented to four marriage suitors, each one of them holding out a rose.

"This is a very famous scene in the ballet Sleeping Beauty," I whisper. "It's called the Rose Adagio. The princess must choose one of these four men to be her husband. The dance sequence ends with her having to maintain her balance while each of the men spins her around. It's one of the most challenging roles for a ballerina."

I've put the screen on projection mode, so the dancers are displayed before us in 3D. Rivlor looks on, spellbound, as Aurora is spun around by each suitor, her bent leg up high behind her, then lifts her arms in the air to balance. She wobbles ever so slightly, and Rivlor gasps. Then she bravely maintains her balance while another suitor steps forward and holds out his hand. Finally, the fourth suitor spins her around, and this time, Aurora balances for a moment longer, waiting for the concluding beat of the music, before stretching her leg out ecstatically, and bringing it down to the clamorous applause of the audience.

I stop the video and smile at Rivlor, who is still wearing an awed expression on her face. "Your dancers will be performing this in your shows?" she asks.

"Yes. Not the whole ballet, but this Rose Adagio sequence."

"I would very much like to see it."

"You will. And you can watch the dancers while they rehearse it too. But we need somewhere to stage our shows."

She nods. "I understand now the kind of space you need. I think I may have a solution for you. First, let me contact my aunt Flidar with my idea."

"If you can help us with this, Rivlor, I'll be eternally grateful."

"Remember, I am set to make a profit from your venture too. I have a vested interest."

I smile. "How could I forget?" I sit on the edge of the bed and begin putting my shoes back on.

"Wyatt, I do not believe that your pod is a conducive space for you to do your work. Whenever you need to, come here and use this chamber. I do not mind."

"Are you sure?"

"I would not have suggested it otherwise. I will program it so you can unlock the door with your handprint."

"Thanks, Rivlor, for everything. I appreciate it."

"It is my pleasure, Wyatt."

Chapter 32

Kirimor

Like all sicors, Melistor is tall and powerfully built. He is not quite handsome, but his eyes glow with a keen intelligence and a gentle kindness. We are sitting across from each other in his brightly lit living room, sipping on a cool glass of *nari*. His home comprises a handful of buildings located on the outskirts of the city on a large tract of fertile land that cedes into the forest. From the window, I can see the clean lines of the temple building across from us. On the other side, a herd of drens are munching placidly on grass in a large, enclosed field.

On arriving here, I was struck by the palpable sense of peace and tranquillity. I know this is not accidental. As a powerful sicor, he has ensured that all around him is peaceful harmony—another sign that he is destined for the top job. He greeted me cordially and a lovely young drasha served us with refreshments. Now that we have finished exchanging pleasantries, I come to the reason for my visit. "Melistor, have you ever thought of becoming sicortar?"

He studies my face intently as he replies, "It would be natural for me to have considered the prospect, seeing as I am one of a few sicors with the requisite skills. However, I have not thought it imminent, or am I mistaken?"

"I would like to explore with you the possibility of taking over my duties as sicortar as soon as it is possible."

"I see. Is there a reason for the urgency?"

"I have met someone I wish to mate, but that is not a possibility while I am tied to my drashas."

"The Human female?"

I look at him in surprise. "How did you know?"

"News of your interest in her has spread far and wide. I merely put two and two together."

"I see. And as to taking over my duties. Do you feel ready to do so?"

He hesitates. "I had hoped for more sun rotations to hone my skills."

I nod. "I know, and I am sorry for that. But would it be possible, with my guidance and mentorship, to have you ready for the position?"

He frowns in concentration. "I believe it is possible, yes."

I blow out a relieved breath. "And you do not mind becoming sicortar?"

"It is a great honor and privilege."

"This life comes at a cost though. Not having a mate may seem unimportant when you are young and surrounded by nubile drashas, but with age, it becomes a lonely existence."

His eyes are full of gentle understanding. "I begin to see why the matter is urgent for you, but as for me… my circumstances are a little different. I have four wonderful drashas, but one of them, Filonesa, is my mate in everything but name."

At my look of surprise, he goes on to explain. "I have loved Filonesa since we were at school together. When my gift was discovered, she decided to stay on with me as my drasha and accept that I would require sexual release with other females. Her only stipulation was that she should be involved in the selection of the drashas, and that I should only have children with her. We are now parents to two young children, and we live together as mates. My other drashas are housed separately, and I only consort with them during holy trances in the temple. This arrangement works well for us. Could you not do something similar with your Human?"

"I am afraid not. She has demanded absolute fidelity from me, and more than anything, I wish to grant her this."

"Very well. In that case, I will try my best to help you grant that wish."

"I am deeply grateful, Melistor."

"How would you like to proceed?"

Over the next few beats, I brief him on the matter at hand, starting at the beginning with the theft of the boral crystals, and ending with my scans last night. He listens attentively, and when I come to the end of my tale, says, "So you wish me to scan this malevolent person and absorb his evil energy."

"Yes. I will guide and observe you as best I can."

He considers the matter, his brows knitted in a frown. "If the person is as malevolent as you say, then I should have at least three drashas with me during my trance."

"That would be advisable, yes. I suspect you will feel a greater than usual urge to fuck the evil out of you."

He gets to his feet. "Excuse me, Kirimor, while I go speak with Filonesa and ask her to ready my drashas for the ceremony."

He exits the room, returning half a beat later. "All are ready, Kirimor. Let us reconvene in the temple."

I rise to my feet and follow him out the door, down the path to the temple. There, I see Filonesa, the drasha who served our refreshments, and two other young women. They bow respectfully as we enter, and go take their positions across from us. Melistor opens a box of boral crystals and rummages through it, looking for the most appropriate crystal to use. After a time, he takes one out and shows it to me. "Think you this will suffice?"

I examine the crystal closely. It is a nice size and a good deep color. "Yes, this one will do nicely."

Filonesa approaches us with an incense burner, placing it at her partner's feet, then withdraws with a bow. I take out my communicator and show Melistor the name of the person we will be scanning. "You will find him in the northern sector, in the Dilka neighborhood." I open a map of the area and pinpoint where I located him last night. "Let your mind wander there and call out his name. Once you locate him, let all your energy focus on him and him only. Take time to study his aura and feel the malevolence leeching out of him. When you are ready, begin to aspirate the energy towards you. Focus on your breathing throughout and do not stop until the entirety of the evil energy has entered you. After that, you will need to exert supreme control to clamp down on it. This will be the hardest part. I will enter the trance with you and observe, without interference. However, I may provide some support if you struggle with keeping a tight hold on the evil once it is inside you. I can erect a stabilizing field around you to stop it creeping out of you. Are you ready?"

Melistor takes a deep breath and nods. I place the boral crystal on the burner and watch as it heats and deepens in color. Then, I begin to chant a prayer to our goddess Taya. Once I am done, we remain quiet while we each enter the trance. I watch him in my mind as he travels to the location and searches for our man. I spot our target quickly, but it takes Melistor a quarter beat more to locate him. That is not a problem. With practice, he will locate targets more rapidly.

I watch as Melistor focuses his attention on the individual, studying the vile aura of this man. I know the moment when he is ready. With a big, mighty breath in, he begins to aspirate the evil towards him. I shudder as I watch this malevolence approach us. It is of the darkest kind. Slowly, it begins to enter Melistor. I feel him tremble and shake, but he keeps going, absorbing every last trace of it into his body. Now, he needs to clamp down tight on it and not let it escape. I sense Melistor struggle with the evil power that has entered his body. He is unable to contain it.

With a deep breath, I come to his aid, erecting a stabilizing field around him that sends the vicious energy that is trying to escape back inside him. Through our mind connection, I speak to him, "You are doing fine, Melistor. Now take it one step at a time. Break up that evil, bit by bit. I will not let any of it escape you."

He starts breaking up each wave of evil energy. Some waves escape his body, but I send them right back with the force of my stabilizing field. I sense the effort he is putting into the task. It is draining work, but he continues bravely. I believe he will make a brilliant sicortar one day. I hold my position around him and wait patiently as he attacks each bit of evil that has entered him. It takes a long time to do, but eventually, the work is done.

I hear him growl ferociously as he comes out of his trance. He rips off his loin cloth, howling in rage, and falls upon the drasha closest to him. Without any preliminaries, he pierces her with his engorged cock and begins to fuck in rough, hard thrusts. Fortunately, the drashas were prepared for this eventuality and had rubbed lubricating ointment on themselves beforehand, else I would dread to think what pain they would be in. I hesitate, not wanting to leave while he is in such a raging state. However, Filonesa addresses me, "It is fine, sicortar, you may leave now. I can handle him. I have advanced martial training for this very purpose. I will ensure nobody gets hurt."

"You are sure?"

"Absolutely."

"Send him my regards, Filonesa. I will speak with him upon my return home. Go in peace."

"Go in peace, sicortar."

I make my way out of the temple, still perturbed after witnessing the depth of that evil. I had not thought such people existed on our planet any longer. The encounter has left me not a little worried.

I find my drone and climb aboard, programming it to fly me to the university, where Melinda is giving her lecture. I look at the time dial on my communicator. I should arrive a beat or two into her session. In actual fact, I make it there in half that time, walking into the large auditorium a mere half a beat into her lecture. She pauses and watches me as I make my way to the front and use my sicortar stare to send a young student scurrying away to a different seat. I see my Melinda roll her eyes at this, but sit myself down anyway. Once I am comfortably settled, I nod to her in signal that she may resume her lecture. With a wry smile, she begins again.

The lecture is a repeat of the previous one I attended, though this set of students is a little friendlier than the last, despite some challenging questions being asked. Once again, we end with the video footage of people from her world cooking their different types of cuisines, finally getting to her ex-mate, Wyatt. I grit my teeth as I watch him smile at the camera with twinkling blue eyes. "Hi there, I'm Wyatt Garcia, and in case you're wondering, I'm Melinda's other half." *No, you are not!*

"Take care and go in peace." On screen, the video ends, and as before, Melinda is peppered with questions about her handsome mate. With each question, I feel my face grow more and more thunderous. Melinda sees my expression and holds her hand up for everyone to stop. "Just to be clear, Wyatt is no longer my mate, but just a very good friend of mine."

I allow the students to question her for a beat longer, then stand and make my way to her. Placing a possessive arm around her shoulders, I thank everyone for attending and ask them to show their appreciation. Melinda smiles as she listens to the humming. She addresses them one last time. "Thank you all. It has been an honor and a privilege to speak with you today. Go in peace."

Th audience chants back, "Go in peace."

I do not want to linger here a moment longer. Taking her hand in mine, I lead Melinda out, ignoring the thrum of people flocking towards her with questions. I steer her through the crowd and out into the long corridor that leads to the exit. In no time at all, I have her bundled into my drone. A moment later, we are joined by Desimar and Sholinar. As soon as the door closes behind them, I set the drone to start our journey to the air field where we will be boarding the aircraft that will return us home.

I hold Melinda to me, letting my tail wrap around her. "Well done, my love. That was an excellent lecture. I was so proud of the way you fielded those difficult questions."

She smiles proudly. "Thanks, Kirimor. I think it went well. And yes, there were some tricky questions, but I've spent a lifetime learning how to think on my feet. I'm glad it stood me in good stead today."

"This has been a successful trip, but I am glad to be on our way home now."

"Yes, me too. I'm exhausted!"

"Then I will let you rest on the journey back, my lovely."

Soon, we land at the air field and exit the drone, only to climb aboard the large aircraft. Quickly, we find our seats and settle ourselves down. I reach out for a warm scented cloth and clean my Melinda's hands. I thank Sholinar as he hands me a container of freshly packed food, then feed my hungry girl. As she eats, she asks me about the success of my mission with Melistor. I fill her in on the day's events, adding, "I will invite Melistor to stay with me for the next moon rotation and train him further. By the end of that time, I believe he will be ready to take over as sicortar."

"I'm glad," she says.

"And just as soon as he is officially announced as sicortar, you and I are going to mate. I will not wait a moment later to make you mine."

"On Earth, it is customary to have an engagement period before one marries."

I claim her lips in a kiss. "Fortunately, we are not on Earth. Here on Krovatia, there is no such thing as an engagement period. When people want to mate, they mate."

"Surely you need to pop the question first?"

"Pop the question? I do not understand."

"On Earth, when a man wants to marry a woman, he gets down on one knee and asks her to be his wife."

My brows crease. "You want me on my knees, begging you to be my mate?"

"Begging, no. Asking, yes."

"Very well, my lovely. If that is what you want, that is what I will do, just as soon as we are alone."

"Not until you are free from your duties as sicortar and worked out new living arrangements."

I frown. "New arrangements?"

"Well, surely you cannot expect me to live under the same roof as your drashas, even after they stop being your drashas?"

I regard her in consternation. "I had thought you could live with me in my own private quarters."

"Kirimor, please don't take this the wrong way, but I don't feel comfortable sharing a home and daily meals with women you used to fuck. My home needs to be mine, not some shared harem with a load of other females. Some alternative arrangements will need to be worked out if you want me to live as your mate."

I stare at her. "You are seriously asking me to turf my drashas out of their home before you will agree to be my mate?"

She meets my stare defiantly. "No, I did not say that. All I said was that *I* will not share a home with them. Perhaps we need to think about having a separate place of our own."

I sit back, shocked to my very core. I had not thought my Melinda would ask this of me. She sees my distressed expression, and her face softens a fraction. "Let me ask you this, Kirimor. How would you feel if you had to share a home with

Wyatt in order to be with me? Would you like it if my ex-husband slept in a room down the corridor from you and shared each meal we had? Would you like to sit opposite the man who knows my body intimately and who put that piercing on my most private part? Would you be happy to have him in your orbit day in day out?"

Truthfully, no. I would not like that at all. I begin to see the problem, but not how I will solve it without gravely disrupting the life of my children and of my faithful drashas, who have served me so loyally for so many sun rotations.

I take her hand in mine and kiss it. "I see I have much work to do still, but I will find a way forward, my lovely."

She smiles. "Good."

I bring her head to rest on my shoulder. "Rest now, my love." She closes her eyes, and soon I hear her breathing deeply as she slumbers. I close my eyes too, but not to sleep. I have much to think about. Trust my luck to fall in love with a difficult, challenging woman! There are so many obstacles still in the way of my claiming her as mine. Some would ask if she was worth the trouble. Without hesitation, I would say yes. I recall the peaceful evening we had last night, just the two of us, working together in quiet harmony. I want more such evenings. Guiltily, I am aware that this will come at a price—a curtailment of my children's easy access to me. Or maybe not. Maybe, I need to think of an imaginative solution to my problem. It is not my children Melinda has an issue with. I know for a fact how much she already cares about them. It is my drashas that are the problem.

How do you solve a problem like my drashas?

Somehow, I will find a way. I may not have "amazing" blue eyes, nor hair the color of a golden sun, but I have a tail, a large cock and an addictive scent. I can give my Melinda sensual pleasure beyond her imagining. And crucially, unlike Wyatt

who had countless chances to keep her but failed to do so, I will
fight for the woman I love.

Chapter 33

Melinda

Kirimor sees me to my door on our return from the southern sector. He's been preoccupied since I laid down my ultimatum about his drashas. I don't know if that is a good or a bad thing.

I saw the shocked look of disappointment on his face when I made it clear I would not live among them, but I don't think my demands were unreasonable. I'm not going to sit through my meals every day with a nubile young woman making sappy eyes at him. It was painful enough that one time I had lunch with them. It's not that I want him to cut them out of his life—they are mothers to his kids and I respect that. I just don't want them in my orbit on a daily basis. Is that too much to ask? God, this is fucking complicated!

Kirimor slips his tail around me, drawing me to him. "Are you sure you do not want to come home with me, my lovely? I will miss having you in my arms at night. I can wait while you collect your belongings."

"No, Kirimor. I can't. We can't. Until things are settled between us, it's best if we sleep apart."

"Things are settled. I love you. You love me. We want to mate."

I kiss his lips softly. "You know they're not. You have a lot of untangling of your life to do before you can be with me. It's best you get started on it."

He grunts. "I want to be with you, Melinda. Every night I want to lie with you and wake up with you beside me."

"I want that too," I whisper.

He sighs. "I will make it my top priority."

"Goodnight, Kirimor."

He holds me to him, kissing the top of my head. "Goodnight, Melinda."

Reluctantly, he removes his tail and steps back. I watch him get back into the drone and fly off, before I go inside.

The house is quiet as I make my way back to my room. I put my bag down and slip off my shoes, then lie down on the bed, my hands tucked behind my head. So much has happened in the last twenty-four hours. It's only now I get to process. My hand slips down under my pants and touches the new jewelry on my clit, then back up to the pendant that's still draped across my hips. I've been well and truly claimed by the Krovatian high priest. Except, to win me, he needs to stop being a priest. I wonder how easy that will be. *Don't count your chicken until they're hatched, Melinda.* That's what my mama used to say. Wise words.

My communicator buzzes with an incoming message. It's from Wyatt. I open it and watch a projected image of Wyatt smiling at me. At the sight of him, my heart aches in pain and longing. Pain that finally, our paths are set to diverge permanently as I start my new life with Kirimor. And longing because, despite everything, I still miss my ex-husband like crazy. I wish there were a way to sever that connection, to end it all cleanly, but years of being together, of loving each other, has imprinted him on my heart.

"Honey, I have big news…"

I listen in amazement as he tells me about his first space flight and that he's coming to Krovatia with a troupe of artistic performers. When it ends, I replay the message, still not quite believing my ears. Wyatt is coming here to Krovatia.

A few weeks ago, this would have been the best of news. And then, things had to get complicated. I put my communicator back down and wipe a stray tear impatiently. Coming on top of everything else, this is just more than I can handle right now. I stomp over to the bathroom to brush my teeth and get myself ready for bed. The sad wistfulness of a moment ago has been replaced by a surge of anger. In my head, I'm ranting at my ex. *Why now, Wyatt? Why couldn't you have done this throughout all those lonely years I endured on Mars? Why, just as I've fallen for someone else, do you do this kind of gesture now? Your timing sucks. Big time.*

I get into bed, still smarting. Men! Who needs them? Here I am stuck in the middle between a man encumbered with a harem of women and another who thinks he can just pick up where we left off three years after separating. The way I'm feeling right now, I want to give both of them the boot. Stick to my career instead; that's never let me down. I force my mind to focus on work matters. Tomorrow, I need to start making overtures to the other sector leaders about a trade mission of representatives from our pharmaceutical industry to Krovatia. I worked hard to get Dorishena to agree to my plan. Now I need the other sector leaders to rubber stamp it and get the ball rolling. I'm not here on Krovatia to sit on my ass and wallow about the men in my life. I'm here to get things done. And I will.

Chapter 34

Kirimor

I spend a restless night. One night with Melinda has spoiled me for all others. Now all I can think about is the fact I desperately want to wrap my tail around her and have her in bed with me.

I wake to a warm little body nuzzled into my arms. Little Kiritela has found her way to my room again. I stroke her back fondly. My sweet little girl. I missed her the last two rotations I've been away. Then, my thoughts turn serious. If I do as Melinda wishes me to, then Kiritela will no longer live under the same roof as me, and I won't be here for her every time she wakes in the night and needs a reassuring cuddle. My heart baulks at the idea. There again, if I am being rational, this is just a phase that Kiritela will soon grow out of. She will not always need to come seek me out at night. Much as I love my daughter, it is not her I need in my bed at night.

I wake her with a light rub to her shoulders and a rumble in her ear. "Good morning, little star. Did you miss your pa?"

She stirs, yawning loudly. "Lots and lots."

"Tell me about what you've been doing while I've been away."

She turns on her side, opening her eyes and making a face at me. "We learned a new song at school. I wanted to sing it to you."

"Well, you can sing it to me now. What is it called?"

"It is called Oh Krovatia."

"Sing it to me."

She sits up, all traces of sleep gone, and begins to sing.

On and on we roam
Looking for a new home

I smile as I listen to the song all school children on our planet learn from an early age.

"Do you like it, pa?" my daughter asks eagerly.

"I love it, and you sing it so well." She preens at the praise. "Now my little star, it is time for you to go wash and get yourself ready for school. Give me a kiss before you go."

Kiritela drops a sloppy kiss on my cheek which I wipe discreetly away once she is out the door. Then I too get myself ready for the day ahead. There are yet more scans to do. I have to call Melistor and discuss next steps. And I have to start thinking about how to solve my drasha situation. But first, like the oxygen I breathe, I need to see my Melinda and speak to her. I pull out my communicator and call her.

She answers, sitting at a table drinking something hot and steaming from a mug. I learned from our previous interactions that this is an Earth drink called coffee that many Humans like to drink first thing in the morning. "Good morning, my lovely. How did you sleep?"

"I slept great. And you?"

I make a sad face. "Not so well. Someone was missing in my bed."

She huffs. "Kirimor, you have spent most of your adult life without me in your bed. I'm sure you can remember how to sleep in it on your own."

"I am sure I can, but I do not want to. Being with you, my lovely, has spoiled me."

She smiles, despite herself. "There is an Earth saying which says, patience is a virtue."

"It is the greatest of virtues. Unfortunately, I am not in possession of it at this moment."

She laughs, "You will have to be, old man."

I sigh. "Yes, I am an old man."

She rolls her eyes. Mine narrow. "Has something happened?" I ask. "You seem a little… brusque this morning."

She does not answer immediately, instead taking a sip of her beverage. Then she lifts cool eyes at me. "No, Kirimor, I just have to get to work. Denishar has agreed to meet me in three beats, so I have to finish my coffee and get going."

"Ah, that is good. I am sure you will get him to agree to your trade mission proposition. I will not keep you then. I wish you a most productive and positive day, my lovely."

She smiles as she ends the call. "Thanks, and you have a good day too."

Hmm. Something is definitely up. She is treating me like a business acquaintance rather than a lover. However, I shall get to the bottom of this. As it happens, I too have a meeting scheduled with Denishar this morning. Strange how fate seems to intertwine our two paths. Or maybe not so strange if we are fated to be together.

I make my way down the stairs to the large dining room where my family gathers to eat the morning repast. My children and drashas are already there, except for Kirimara and Kiristen. I greet them all with a kiss, as is my custom, then sit down as Merostena passes me a basket of freshly baked *lam*. "Blessed morning, Kirimor," she says, giving me a kiss on the lips.

"Blessed morning, my dear," I respond. "Where are Kirimara and Kiristen?"

She shrugs. "Kiristen has bedded once again with Troy, and Kirimara has already left for college."

I frown. "Did she at least remember to eat?"

"I made sure she took a roll of *lam* before she left."

"I wish she had waited. It has been two rotations since I have seen her."

"She will be back for the lunch repast, my dearest."

Merostena serves me a cup of *nari*. I mostly drink it ice cold, except for the mornings when I like to have it steaming hot. I take a sustaining sip of it, thinking of Melinda and her Earth drink, coffee. I am keen to sample it and see what is so special about it. I want to learn all I can about Melinda's Earth customs.

I sit quietly and half-listen to the usual chatter around me, my mind on the lovely female that has captured my heart. I did not like her cool manner with me earlier, but when I see her at Denishar's palace later this morning, I will make sure to remind her that she is mine now. And when I get her to myself, I will find out why it is she is acting this way. Something is bothering her, I can tell.

Merostena places a hand on my knee, stroking gently. "Kirimor, my dear, you seem distracted this morning. Did all go well on your trip to the southern sector?"

I force my focus back on the people gathered around me, smiling. "It went extremely well, thank you for asking."

She kisses my cheek. "Then what is on your mind?"

Now is as good a time as any to tell them all of my feelings for Melinda. "I am thinking of the female I have fallen in love with."

Her hand falls away. With a frown, she asks, "Is it that Human female?"

"Her name is Melinda, and yes, it is her."

"I love Melinda too," cries Kiritela excitedly. "When will I see her again?"

I hug my daughter to me. "I do not know, little star, but I hope it will be soon."

Her mother, Cleotola, sitting on the other side of me, runs a gentle hand over our daughter's head as she asks, "Will she agree to become your drasha?"

And here we go, the moment of truth. "No, Cleotola. She will not be my drasha. I am going to resign my position as sicortar just as soon as Melistor is ready to take over, and then I plan to mate her."

"Mate her?" cries Jolpinesa, shocked.

"What does that mean for us?" interjects Jalimara.

Merostena is silent beside me.

"It means, dear and beloved drashas, that I will be releasing you all from your duties. You will be free to live your own lives, even find yourselves a mate, should you wish."

"We have devoted our lives to you, Kirimor," says Merostena quietly. "How can we ever think of mating someone else? I had thought to end my days by your side."

I look at her sadly. "It is not to be, Merostena. I am so sorry, my dear."

She nods and looks down at her plate, not speaking.

"What will happen to us? Where shall we live?" asks Jalimara again.

"You will continue to live in this house. When I made you my drashas, I pledged to give you a home for the rest of your days. This will remain your home; nothing will change for you in that respect."

"Even I, who have been with you such a short time?" wonders Pirofena.

I smile at her reassuringly. "I made a solemn promise to your family that I would always take care of you, Pirofena. I will keep that promise. This is your home as long as you want it to be."

"Will Melinda be coming to live with us?" asks Kirishar innocently.

How to answer this question? I give as truthful a response as I can. "I do not know yet, but to begin with, I am hoping she will stay with me in the cabin until we have worked out more permanent arrangements."

Kirilor, looking troubled, murmurs, "Pa, are you leaving us? Will we not see you anymore?"

My tail reaches out to stroke his cheek. "My sweet boy, I will never leave you, and you will see me every day. I merely have to make new arrangements to make Melinda feel comfortable and at home here."

"What sort of arrangements do you have in mind?" asks Cleotola.

"I am thinking of developing the attic space of the house into a living area for Melinda and I. We had thoughts before of extending up there to make more room. Sholinar already has the plans drawn up. We can lift the roof up by a few more feet to give us extra headspace."

She considers this. "That could work. As your mate, it is understandable that Melinda will wish for some private space. I have read up about Human customs."

I look at her gratefully. "Yes. I want her to have this privacy, but also for all the children to have access to us whenever they wish."

"It will take time to complete such building works," states Jolpinesa.

"I will try to expedite the work, but yes, it may take a few moon rotations to get it done."

"And where will you be in the meantime?"

I sigh. "That is still a matter for discussion between Melinda and me. To begin with, I propose we stay in the cabin, as a way of celebrating the early period of our mating. After that, we shall see. Whatever happens, I will ensure I see you every day. Please do not worry about that. I will always be here for you all."

Cleotola tucks her head on my shoulder. "Change is always an adjustment, but I am sure it will all work out in the end. I wish you great happiness together, Kirimor."

One by one, the rest of my drashas wish me happiness, though I see that my oldest companions, Merostena and Jalimara, are struggling to hide their grief. I speak with all my children individually, making sure they are alright and giving them the affection they need. Finally, I leave for my meeting with Denishar.

◆◆◆

I arrive at Denishar's palace and am shown straight through to his receiving chamber. Denishar rises to his feet in welcome, a surprised Melinda by his side. I give my old friend the customary greeting, placing my hand on his chest then bowing. "Denishar, it is good to see you, dear friend."

"And you, Kirimor."

My tail whips up into the air and swings around my lovely Human, pulling her body towards me.

"Kirimor!" she protests.

"Hush," I say, bringing her face to mine and claiming her lips. I feel her try to pull away, so I tighten my arms and tail around her. I deepen the kiss, running my tongue along the seam of her lips, demanding entry. She is powerless to deny me. Her lips part, and I plunge into the velvety softness of her mouth. I kiss her long and hard, and when I do finally release her, she is breathless and quivering in my arms.

"I see you two need no second introduction," says an amused voice. I look up to find Denishar regarding us with a sparkle in his eyes.

"Melinda is to become my mate, just as soon as I am released from my duties as sicortar," I tell him.

My prickly female immediately takes issue with these words. "It is not a done deal, Kirimor. You're supposed to ask me first."

"Very well, let me ask you now in front of a witness."

"Kirimor! I am in a work meeting. This is not the place nor the time. And in any case, I said you weren't to ask me until you had untangled your life."

I brush gentle fingers through the soft strands of her hair. "Denishar is an old friend of mine, so I am sure he will forgive the interruption. You asked me to work out new arrangements with my drashas. I have. You will get your private living space, my lovely. As to the other matter. I have already set the wheels in motion to end my time as sicortar. Melistor will soon be coming to stay with me to continue his tutelage. I do not believe it will be long before he is fit to take my place. I am doing everything to untangle my life so I am free to be with you."

I remember what she told me about the way Humans get engaged to their mate, and I loosen my tail from around her waist so that I can get down on my knees. "So, Melinda, I ask you now in the presence of my good friend Denishar. My love, will you be my mate?"

She is flushed, her lips and even the tips of her fingers trembling. I wait patiently on my knees for her response, but she does not reply.

"Well, Melinda, what is it to be?" asks Denishar. "I can assure you there is no finer or more honorable person than Kirimor. Will you accept to be his mate?"

Still she does not respond.

I let my tail trail up her leg, stroking its way up her body to her face, where I let it brush against her lips. "Melinda, my love. My heart is yours and only yours for the rest of eternity. I swear a solemn oath that from the moment we mate, I will always be true to you. Please my sweet, be mine."

She takes the tip of my tail in her hand and kisses it. "Yes," she says, her voice breaking. "I will."

I sigh in relief then rise to my feet swiftly, bringing her into my arms. "It is settled now, my love," I whisper in her ear. "No more holding back from me. We belong together."

"Yes."

"May I be the first to offer my most sincere congratulations," booms Denishar jovially, reminding us we are not alone.

We turn to face him and say in unison, "Thank you."

"Now, with the matter settled, may we return to discuss our business?"

"Of course," says Melinda, resuming her cool, working demeanor. We sit ourselves down on the floor cushions, although I cannot resist snaking my tail around her luscious form again. "Denishar, I trust you have agreed to the proposed trade mission from Earth. Much good and many lives could be saved through the exchange of trade and expertise between our pharmaceutical industries."

"Indeed, Melinda has argued this very convincingly. I was about to give my agreement to her proposal when you walked in."

"Thank you, Denishar," smiles Melinda. "I believe this will be a mutually beneficial arrangement."

He returns her smile and says, "Nevestor, the leader of the eastern sector, will be visiting me next rotation, so I will be sure to discuss this with him. I do not foresee any difficulty in securing his agreement, but you will have to make your representations to the leader of the western sector, Lorifena."

"I understand," replies Melinda. "I will make arrangements to do so just as soon as I can. Thank you so much for your time today."

She makes as if to leave, but I stop her. "Stay, my lovely, while I conclude my business with Denishar. You do not have any urgent place you need to be?"

She hesitates. "No, but surely you don't want me here while you have your meeting."

"Oh, but I do. Perhaps you could work on your communicator for a short time while Denishar and I discuss matters."

"I can always wait outside, Kirimor, then you can speak more freely surely."

I gaze fondly at her. "That is very considerate of you, my lovely, but it is not a concern as you will not hear anything we say."

At this, she raises a puzzled brow. "How so?"

Denishar explains. "We will go sit by the fragrant fountain and let the aromatic essence help us reach a state of deep meditation where we can speak to each other in our minds."

Melinda looks at me in astonishment. "Does that mean that you're telepathic, like the Venorians?"

"No, not quite like them. I cannot read someone's mind through touch. However, when in a trance, I can build a bridge between my mind and Denishar's so we can communicate our thoughts rapidly. You can watch while we do it, though of course you will hear nothing of what we say."

"I'm intrigued. Well, if you don't mind, I do have work I can do on my communicator while you two discuss whatever it is you need to."

Denishar gets to his feet. "In that case, shall we make our way to sit by the fountain?"

I follow him to the corner where the fragrant fountain is, leading Melinda with me. I sit her beside me and wrap my tail around her. Denishar sits on the other side of the fountain, facing me.

Melinda watches us curiously. "So how does this happen?"

"We sit quietly, letting the scent lull us into a deeply relaxed state."

"What is this scent? Is it some kind of hallucinogenic drug?"

"It is the essence of a plant that grows in the rainforest of the southern sector. It works on our neural receptors in a not too dissimilar way to the boral crystals, letting us achieve that trance-like state. I do not know whether that constitutes a hallucinogenic drug. Other than allowing us to get into a trance, it has no lasting effect on our bodies."

"Will it have an effect on me?" wonders Melinda.

"I do not think so, although I cannot say for sure. If the boral crystals had little effect on you, then I suspect the scent of the fragrant fountain will not do so either."

She sniffs the air. "I can't actually smell anything. Is it working yet?"

The aroma of the fountain is strong in my nostrils, but I already know that our sense of smell is far more developed than it is in Humans. "Yes, my love. We can smell it. Now, we shall sit quietly and get into our trance while you work beside me."

"Ok," she says.

I take some deep breaths in and out, letting myself reach a state of deep relaxation. After some time, I begin to build a bridge in my mind towards Denishar. Finally, we make the connection, and we begin to speak in silence.

"I have grave news to report," says Denishar.

"What is it?"

"Dresishan was found dead in his home last night. Apparently of natural causes, but the circumstances make us deeply suspicious."

"It was always a risk, when Melistor cleared his mind of the pernicious evil in him, that someone would notice the change in him. However, we could not let that malicious energy prevail—we had to take action."

"Rightly so, but evidently, one of his conspirators noticed the change, or perhaps, having been cleansed of his evil, he sought to inform his conspirators that they should stop their activities—in which case, he became a risk to them. Someone evidently thought him enough of a risk to end his life."

"This also means the conspirators are going to be even more careful than before to lie low and not betray themselves to us if they know we are on their trail."

"Unfortunately, that trail has gone cold."

"It is a pity that Melistor cannot remember the details of Dresishan's malicious intentions that he sucked out of him. He was so focused on trying to maintain control over that powerful energy and not let it seep back out that he could not read it carefully for information."

"That is where your more experienced hand was needed, Kirimor."

"I am sorry. I had hoped that he would be able to give me some details once he had time to reflect afterwards, but that was not the case."

"And neither of our two suspects have done anything incriminating since we started watching them. So far, none of your scans of their known contacts have yielded any information either, except for finding the evil energy in Dresishan. We are currently looking into all his data to try to see if it yields any clues. Until then—"

"I will continue working my way through the chain of contacts for these three individuals. I am managing up to a dozen scans per rotation. Eventually, something will turn up."

"The fact that Dresishan has been eliminated suggests that whatever is being plotted may be close to fruition. I fear we do not have a great amount of time."

"Then I shall get Melistor to assist me with the scans. We will try to double the number and see if we can flush out the other conspirators as soon as possible."

"Kirimor, I do not have a good feeling about this."

"I agree, it is very concerning. I hope sincerely that we will find some leads soon."

"May Taya bless us with her light."

"May she hear our prayers."

"On to other matters. I must congratulate you. I never thought to see you mate, let alone to a person from an alien species. You do surprise me, Kirimor."

"Taya works in mysterious ways. I too never expected this, but I am so glad that Melinda crossed my path. I hope, Denishar, that you will help expedite matters when it comes to my passing on the duties of sicortar to Melistor."

"Do not doubt it. As soon as you declare that Melistor is ready, consider it done."

"Thank you."

"There is something else. Melinda's ex-mate and his artistic performers are due to arrive here within three rotations. They will need to be scanned on their arrival. Perhaps you will agree to do it?"

"Ah, that explains her grumpiness this morning. She must have heard that he was coming. Of course I will scan him and his performers, but have Melistor with me in case action is required to neutralize any of the individuals."

"So you have already begun your vow of fidelity?"

"I fully intend to be, although I know that I cannot make a vow as yet, not until I have been relieved of my duties as sicortar. If something critical were to come up, I would be duty bound to perform a holy ceremony and all that it entails."

"If so, I trust your Human will be understanding."

"I hope so, but with Melistor around, I do not foresee the need for me to perform any further holy ceremonies."

"And of your drashas, what will you do?"

"I have informed them of my plans and they will stay on in my home as before. However, I will make new living arrangements for Melinda and me in the house so we can have a private space for us to live in as mates."

"I wish you luck with this, my friend. You deserve every happiness."

"Thank you, dear friend."

We come out of our trance. I turn to see Melinda is hard at work on her communicator, totally unaware of the back and forth conversation that has been going on right beside her.

"My love," I murmur. She looks up at me. "Our discussion is concluded. Shall we go?"

"Oh yes, sorry." She gets to her feet and smiles at Denishar. "Thank you again, Denishar. Go in peace."

"Go in peace, Melinda, Kirimor."

Chapter 35

Melinda

Kirimor and I walk out of Denishar's chamber together. Strange to think that when I walked in over an hour ago, I was still for all intents and purposes single. And now, to coin an old-fashioned phrase, I am betrothed. No more doubts. No more holding back. As Kirimor said, the matter is settled now. It feels like a weight has been lifted from my shoulders. I'm free to love him as I want. No more holding back.

As per his usual, Kirimor wraps his tail around me as we head out of the palace grounds. "What are your plans for the rest of the day, my lovely?"

"I've been invited to visit the school where Kiristen works, but that's not for another hour and a half—that's nine beats from now."

"Ah yes, I recall Kiristen mentioning something about this. Then there is time, my love, to do something to mark our prospective mating."

We've reached the front entrance to the palace, where I see my escort, Desimar, lounging in wait for me. Kirimor sees him too and frowns. "Why is that male constantly with you?"

I huff. "Maybe it's to do with the fact your kind still don't trust us and feel the need to keep an eye on us."

"As long as I am with you, there is no need for that. I will inform him that he is no longer needed. He can keep an eye on the other Human female from now on."

I cast him an amused glance. "I'm not too sure he takes his orders from you, Kirimor."

At this, he draws himself up stiffly and pronounces with a touch of hauteur, "I am sicortar, the highest priest in the land. He will obey me."

Not for much longer.

By now, we are within hearing distance of Desimar, who rises to his feet as we approach.

"Sicortar," he says, giving him a bow.

"You are relieved of your duties with regard to Melinda, who is shortly to become my mate. You may escort the other Humans instead. Melinda will be moving in to live in our new home and I will be responsible for her."

"But sir—"

"I believe I have made myself perfectly clear."

"Yes sir."

Desimar turns to me hesitantly. "What about your visit to the school later this morning?"

To my annoyance, Kirimor answers for me. "I will escort her there. You may now leave."

He bows again and takes his leave.

"Well really, Kirimor, did you have to be so high handed with him?"

"Melinda, I do not think you realize that once you plighted yourself to me—as witnessed by the leader of this sector—your status in Krovatia changed. You are mine now and a part of my family. No more can you be considered a foreign alien."

"But I am a foreign alien. And what's all this about my moving to a new home. Nothing of the sort has been decided. I hope you don't think I'm moving into that great big house of yours with all your drashas."

His mouth takes on a firm line. "They are no longer my drashas. I have already informed them of this. If you paid attention, my love, you would know that I talked about us moving to a new home, not my existing one."

"What new home?" I ask in some confusion.

"My cabin in the mountains. We will live there as mates for now, until a more permanent solution can be found. I have plans to create a private space for us by building an additional floor to my house. I hope this is a suitable compromise, my lovely. We will have an entire floor to ourselves and you will not have to share your space with my former drashas, but my children will be able to come up to see us there whenever they want."

I stare at him, remembering that enchanted evening I spent with him in that cabin. All at once, I know that more than anything, I want to start our mated life there in that special place. As for his other solution, it's not ideal. I would still be living in the same house as these women who have such an intimate history with Kirimor, but it could possibly work. I do not want to cut him off from his children, ever. I have to make compromises too.

He sees me stare and his face creases into a worried frown. "You do not like my idea?"

I throw my arms around his neck. "I love you!"

His arms and tail tighten around me. "I love you too. So, I take it you approve of my idea?"

I smile up at him. "Yes."

"That is good. I had hopes that we could move in there tonight. There is nothing further keeping us from being together, my lovely."

I could baulk and put up obstacles, but frankly, I'm tired of fighting this. I'm all in now. "Yes, I would like that too."

"Very well, then this is what I propose we do. First, you are coming with me to a body art shop I favor and the artist, who I trust implicitly, will paint your body. It is customary for mates to wear the same designs on their bodies. Your body art will match mine so it is clear to all that you belong to me." He pulls gently at the sleeve of my dress. "This means, of course, that now you will dress the Krovatian way. No more wearing these to cover up your beauty. We will stop and purchase the finest loin cloths for you to wear, my lovely."

"Kirimor, I'm not sure I'm ready to bare myself like you all do."

"You are ready and you have already done so, at the water city. This will be no different. Let everyone see and admire that beautiful body of yours, my love. There is no shame in it. And let everyone also know that you are mine."

I'm silent, taking stock of things. If I'm honest, this hasn't come as a shock. I've been aware that living on this planet long term would entail me going native at some point. I just hadn't thought it would happen so soon. But Kirimor is right. I have already taken the big step, at the water city.

"Ok, but I still reserve the right to put on a dress when I go about my official duties. When I'm in meetings as a representative of humans, I'll dress as a human. Deal?"

He smiles. "That is entirely up to you, my lovely. Come, let us go."

He guides me to his waiting drone, and we fly the short journey downtown to the shopping arcade where the body art shop is located. We walk through the arched doorway, and follow the winding internal streets. We stop first, as promised, to buy some loin cloths, which Kirimor carefully inspects to make sure they are to up to his standards. With that out of the way, we continue to the body art shop.

The owner looks up from reading his communicator and gives us a beaming smile as we enter. "Sicortar! Such a great pleasure to see you again. Is it already time to renew your art?"

"No, Dorinor, I have not come for me, but for my Melinda here, who is shortly to become my mate."

"Your mate? You will no longer be sicortar?"

"I shall be handing over my duties within the next moon rotation, I hope. And as soon as I am free, Melinda and I will mate."

His eyes turn to scrutinize me. "Welcome, Melinda. May I be one of the first to congratulate you both."

"Thank you," I say.

"Please, come inside to my private art room."

He comes away from the counter where he was leaning and leads us down a short hallway to a door, which he opens and beckons us in. There is a large reclining couch next to a table full of pots and utensils.

"Please, Melinda, take a seat here. And sicortar, perhaps you would like to sit on the chair beside it."

We do as he says, while he takes out a large tablet and stylus, flicking the screen to a set of designs. "What are you thinking of, in terms of design?"

"I would like her body art to match mine as much as possible. See this delicate leaf pattern across my chest? I would like it replicated on her, going around her bosom and over her shoulders to join at the back. In addition, I would like you to swirl my name in a circle around her teats in that calligraphic style you use on mates."

"Of course, that will be no problem. Will you also have her name inked around your male teats?"

I've been blushing as they discuss my body, not knowing where to look, but now I raise my eyes to Kirimor, taking in his wide, muscular chest with its smooth pale gray skin and the flat, dark nipples. He meets my gaze with an intense stare of his black hooded eyes.

"Yes, I will have Melinda's name inked on me too."

"Very well, let us begin with you, Melinda. Would you please disrobe so I am able to see how the pattern will flow across your body?"

"Yes, of course," I mumble. I stand and start pulling my dress over my shoulder. Kirimor is at my side, taking it from me and placing it on the edge of the couch. He reaches behind me to unclasp my bra and gently pull it off.

"Melinda my love, you may as well take these off too," he says, pointing to my panties. "Then I can dress you in one of your new loin cloths."

I glance hesitantly at Dorinor, but he is tactfully looking away, sketching out a design on his tablet. Quickly, I pull my panties down and hand them to Kirimor, who in turn gives me the loin cloth he has chosen for me to wear. He helps me into it and ties the laces securely for me. Stepping back, he grins, "Oh yes, now you are beginning to look like a Krovatian! All that is left is to decorate your body. Are you ready Dorinor?"

"I am indeed. Please, Melinda, could you come and stand here while I work out the details of the design on you?"

I do as he says, and he holds out his tablet, taking a photograph of my torso. It appears immediately on his screen, and he quickly sketches a preliminary design over it. Kirimor looks over his shoulder, giving advice and guidance here and there. In a matter of minutes, the sketch is ready and he holds it out to me. "Would you be happy with something like this, Melinda?"

I glance at it in surprise. The body on the screen is me, but it's also not me. I'm amazed how a little body art can transform how someone looks. I take in the delicate leaf pattern that traces its way in an undulating fashion over my left breast, down the valley in between and up again over my right breast, before moving upwards toward my shoulder. I can also see the calligraphy that's been sketched less than an inch from my nipples, going all the way around.

"It's beautiful," I breathe.

Dorinor smiles proudly. "Thank you. How about you, sicortar?"

"It is perfect," Kirimor says.

"Oh good. Then please, Melinda, come and lie on the couch here while I paint the front part of the design on you."

I climb on to the couch and lie down, leaning my head back on it. Kirimor settles himself in the seat beside me, his tail gently swishing over the lower half of my body, avoiding the top half which is about to get painted. Dorinor picks up a very thin brush and dips it into the black-colored paint.

"I've always wondered how the art manages to stay on the body for so long before it has to be replaced," I say as a way to distract myself.

Dorinor smiles. "It is technology unique to Krovatians. This paint has special properties that allows it to sink below the surface of the skin and remain there for several moon rotations. Eventually, continued exposure to the rays of the sun will dissipate it. At that point, it is usual for Krovatians to return and have their next design inked on their bodies."

He begins very carefully to paint the pattern across my chest. Kirimor picks up the thread of the conversation. "When the time comes, my lovely, we will have our new art painted together. We will first discuss what we wish to have on our bodies and agree on the same design for the both of us."

"That sounds… very domesticated."

"It will become part of the rhythm of our lives as mates. Every three moon rotations, we will come see Dorinor for our new body art."

Dorinor grins as he continues painting the delicate pattern. "Sicortar has been coming to my shop for the last ten sun rotations. I have enjoyed the challenge of painting art to his exacting standards, but it will be double the joy to have your beautiful breasts as my canvas."

I flush, my whole body heating up, something that does not go unnoticed by either male.

Dorinor pauses his work and glances up apologetically. "I trust I have not offended you, Melinda. Please forgive me if I have."

"N-no," I stammer, "don't apologize. I'm just unused to having my breasts seen and talked about."

"They are truly beautiful, Melinda. You are blessed."

"She is stunning, is she not?" asks Kirimor proudly, his tail swishing over my thighs, and edging uncomfortably close to my crotch.

"Indeed, sicortar. You are a very lucky male."

"Thanks," I mumble.

We stay silent for the next few minutes as Dorinor completes the leaf pattern and begins the intricate task of writing Kirimor's name around my nipple. The flesh there is more sensitive, and when the paintbrush touches it, I can't prevent a little shiver going through me. Dorinor pauses, looking a little stern. "Please, Melinda, it is important that you stay very still while I paint you."

"I'm sorry," I say, trying not to squirm in embarrassment as I feel a corresponding wetness begin to seep through my nether regions.

Kirimor's eyes narrow at me as he catches the scent of my arousal. I very much fear that Dorinor is scenting it too. Damn it!

"It seems that my Melinda finds the touch of the paintbrush around her teats pleasurable, Dorinor. But she must be a good girl and stay absolutely still, no matter how much she enjoys the touch of your brush. Perhaps, if she manages to hold herself perfectly still, I might be minded to reward her very shortly."

"That sounds eminently fair, sicortar."

I can't believe these two are casually discussing my pleasure while I sit mutely between them. I grit out, "I can stay still."

"I know you can, my love," Kirimor purrs. "And I look forward to your reward."

I take a long breath, trying to slow my racing pulse. The next five minutes are agonizing as the brush flits close to my sensitive nubs, while I exert all my efforts on trying to control my reaction.

Finally, it's done. Dorinor places the paintbrush back on the tray, saying, "We need to wait a beat while it dries, before I can turn you over to do your back. I will leave the two of you alone, as I am sure sicortar wishes to give you your reward."

He stands and walks to the door, shutting it gently behind him. I heave out a soft sigh of relief. "Kirimor, that was so embarrassing."

He tuts. "No, no, you must not think that way. It is very common for females to become aroused when their breasts are being painted, and Dorinor is well used to it. Now let us focus on your reward, my lovely, for managing to stay still despite feeling so stimulated."

He unlaces my loin cloth and pulls it away, examining the wet patch on the inside of it with interest. "Part your legs," he growls.

By instinct, I obey the commanding tone of his voice, opening myself to his hungry gaze. He touches a possessive finger to the new barbells on my clit which he put there not long ago. I hiss at the contact. "So pretty," he croons. Dipping his finger further down where the moisture is leaking out of my slit, he brings it back to my clit, beginning to rub back and forth.

"That feels good," I gasp.

He adds a second finger to the mix, getting greater coverage of my sensitive areas and keeping up a hypnotic rhythm. His tail, which had been lying on my thigh, now slithers up towards my opening. With a quick stabbing motion, it enters me, sliding deep inside my pussy.

"Oh fuck," I moan.

"That is exactly what I am doing, my lovely, fucking you with my tail."

He pulls it back slightly, only to plunge it in even deeper.

"Oh my God!" I cry.

His two fingers start a more rapid movement back and forth on my clit, tugging at my piercing and sending tingles of pleasure pain down my body, while his tail fucks me in quick, sharp thrusts.

"Oh God! Oh God!" I repeat over and over. I can feel my climax building like a giant wave about to crash on the shore.

"Come for me, my lovely," he growls softly.

And I do. With a screech that can probably be heard all through the shop, I come, clenching my walls around his tail that continues to nail me mercilessly. When finally I quieten, he pulls his tail out of me with a wet squidgy sound and brings it up to my lips. "Clean me up and taste yourself," he rasps.

Without thought, I part my lips and allow the dripping tail to plunge into my mouth. I taste my sharp, slightly salty pussy juices as I suck it clean, running my tongue along the strong, flexible cord and the downy tip. When finally he judges it clean, he pulls it out again.

"Good girl," he purrs. Ridiculous as it may sound, I glow at the praise. He bends down to inspect my pussy. "This will not do," he says, looking up at me. "I cannot put the loin cloth back on a cunt that is so wet. I will have to lick it clean."

With that final statement, he settles on the edge of the couch and applies himself to the task of getting me cleaned up with his tongue. My core is still throbbing from that earlier mind blowing climax and his touch is like a candle to a flame, firing me up all over again. I squirm feverishly under him until he brings two large hands to hold me down. "Be still!" he adjures. Then he returns to his task, flattening his tongue and running it all the way up my pussy in long, slow, agonizing strokes.

"Kirimor!" I plead.

In answer, his cleaned tail comes up to stroke along my cheek before sneaking into the gap behind my neck and wrapping itself snugly around me. As he continues to lick my throbbing pussy, his tail tightens around my throat, not to restrict my airflow, but as a statement of his dominant possession. I can practically hear him urging me to lie still and be his good girl. I close my eyes and give myself over to him. In the far reaches of my mind, I realize this is what was missing in my relationship with Wyatt. Sometimes, not always, I wanted a strong, dominant man to hold me down and make me feel like it was safe to let go.

Feeling like I'm floating on a cloud, barely aware of my surroundings anymore, I let go. My second orgasm, when it comes, is a deep and never ending clenching of my internal walls. When it's over, I'm light headed and unable to move an inch. I feel Kirimor give me one last lick, then he's gently re-attaching the loin cloth.

A few moments later, there's a quiet knock on the door. At Kirimor's invitation, Dorinor enters. I'm too far gone for mortification, lying supine with my eyes closed.

"If I might ask you to turn and lie face down," says Dorinor.

Kirimor's gentle hands help to roll me over to my side and then to my front, where I place my face in a convenient breathing hole.

"Good girl," Kirimor says quietly.

I zone out as Dorinor begins his work on my back. The sensation of the brush painting delicate strokes on my skin is soothing and relaxing. I'm barely conscious of drifting off to sleep, until Kirimor gently nudges my shoulder. "Melinda, my love, it is time to get up. We are all done."

Slowly, I lift myself up with my arms and turn around to sit up. My eyes fix on Kirimor's chest, newly painted with my name in Krovatian script all around his nipples. He smiles. "You have marked me, my lovely. I am yours now and for all the rest of my days."

I look down wryly at my own marked chest. "And it seems I'm yours too."

He growls, "That you are."

He helps me stand and put my sandals back on. "Come now, my love, or you shall be late for your visit to Kiristen's school. I will take you there, but unfortunately I cannot stay as there are many urgent matters that require my attention. Kiristen will ensure that you are escorted safely back home so you can begin to pack your belongings. I will be along after sunset to help you transport everything to our new home."

I look at him dazedly. "So, it's really all happening tonight."

He kisses me tenderly. "Yes, my lovely, it is. Now that everything is settled, there is no point in waiting even one more night before we can live together as mates."

I decide there and then to go with the flow. Tonight, more than anything, I want to be in his arms, and truth be told, I never want to be alone again. This life together he's offering. I want it, and I'm grabbing it with open arms.

Chapter 36

Kirimor

My Melinda falls asleep as Dorinor paints the design on her back. No doubt it is to do with our earlier exertions. I sensed the moment she let herself go and submitted entirely to me. It was a beautiful thing—my strong, independent, fearless female handing over the reins and trusting me, not just with her pleasure but with her life.

My tail strokes the contours of her buttocks and over the soft skin of her thighs while Dorinor concentrates on his task. In a low voice, he states, "She is sleeping."

"Yes."

"On your last visit, sicortar, you asked me to tell you if I came across anyone else talking about living a more luxurious lifestyle and criticizing our eco-conscious ethos."

My ears prick up. "Yes, have you done so?"

"Last night, I was out partying with some friends. At the end of the evening, I felt a need for a sexual companion, so I located the companionship room at the venue we were in and went in. I sat drinking a glass of Lom, letting its effects make me mellow, and looked around at the males and females there. One person caught my eye—a nice strapping young male with beautiful artwork across his body. I approached him to take a closer look at that art, for I am always curious about competitors to my craft, and we got talking. I asked him where he got that lovely inking and he told me about a body art shop that has recently opened in the hilly quarter of the city."

I wish he would get to the point of his story, but there is no rushing Dorinor. He turns to dip his brush once more in the paint pot, then returns to his task.

"We continued our conversation, and my attraction for this male increased. However, the room we were in was very hot and stuffy. As I saw a trickle of sweat make its way down his fabulous body, I made a remark about the heat and how wonderful it would be if we could one day put pay to our strict eco ways so we could find companionship in more comfort. He laughed at that, dabbing at the sweat with a cold cloth and agreed wholeheartedly. Then he said something curious."

"What was it he said?"

"He said, 'Funny you should say that. The body artist you asked me about said something very similar just this morning as he painted me. In fact, he seemed very sure that such a day was coming soon, so perhaps we will not have to wait a lifetime for it.'"

"Anything else?"

"No, after that I suggested we head out to my place which was only a beat away, and take a dip in the cool water of my pool together. He agreed and came over to my place where we had a very convivial evening. When I woke up this morning, he was already gone, though he left a fragrant flower on my pillow as a mark of his appreciation."

"Did he give you any more information about this body artist?"

"No, only what I have told you, that he recently opened a shop in the hilly quarter."

"No name?"

"I am sorry, sicortar. I was too otherwise occupied with seducing him to investigate the matter more fully."

"No need to apologize, Dorinor. This information you have given me is very helpful. I will look into this, thank you."

Dorinor finishes painting Melinda, who is still fast asleep. He has me stand before him while he paints her name around my flat teats. I thank him for his efforts and pay him, giving him a little extra for the information he has conveyed.

"I thank you, sicortar."

"The honor was mine, Dorinor. Go in peace."

"Go in peace, sicortar."

He leaves the room, instinctively giving me the privacy I require at this moment. I take out my communicator and quickly message Denishar with this new information. I get a reply saying he will get his operatives to discover the name of this body artist as soon as possible so that I can scan him. There is also a message from Melistor, indicating he will arrive at my home shortly after midday. I have invited him and his family to stay at my house for the next moon rotation as I hand over my duties to him and train him further.

I send a response to Melistor.

Me: Good. There is much work to be done as we have found a new lead.

Melistor: I look forward to working with you on this and fulfilling my duty.

Me: Safe travels, Melistor.

Before I pocket my communicator and wake Melinda, I send one last message, this one to Dresolor, asking him to prepare the cabin for our long-term occupation, starting from this evening, including moving all my personal belongings there.

Me: Please make something special for our evening repast to mark this first evening in our new home together. Melinda greatly liked eating *mishu*, so perhaps you could include this. Also please ensure we have a good supply of Lom to drink.

Dresolor: Of course.

Me: Dresolor, could you also access the data on Humans and find out what they do when two of them mate? If there is any additional touch you can add to make our first evening in our home special, then I would appreciate it.

Dresolor: Leave this with me, sicortar. I will look into it.

Me: I thank you, Dresolor.

Satisfied that all preparations are underway, I go wake Melinda. Unfortunately, I will not be able to stay with her while she visits the school where my son works, but I am confident he will look after her well.

As we walk out of the body art shop and into the arcade, I sense the looks we are given. I am unmistakably the sicortar, known to everyone on this planet, so people are curious to see me walk hand in hand with a Human dressed in our ways and with matching markings to mine. There can be no doubt for anyone that sees us that I have claimed her as mine and that she is soon to become my mate. It also follows that I shall soon be stepping down in my role as sicortar in order to mate. The whispers follow us, and I know it will not be long before the rumors swirl around town and make it into the public news broadcasts. There will be no need for a formal announcement of my intentions, though I plan to ask Sholinar to draft one on my behalf anyway.

We climb into my drone and I program the aircraft to take us to Kiristen's school.

"The cat's well out of the bag now," murmurs Melinda.

"What is that, my lovely?"

"It's a human expression for saying that a secret is out."

"Ah yes. I was just thinking the very same thing. By evening, nearly everyone on this planet will know that I am shortly to mate you. That is how fast the rumors can travel."

"Do you mind?"

"Mind? Of course not? I want everyone to know."

"Yes, but it also means everyone will know you are stepping down as sicortar. Perhaps you wanted to prepare the public for this news in your own time."

I shrug. "I have already informed the important people who need to know. In any case, I will ask Sholinar to draft an announcement for tonight's public news broadcast."

She strokes my arm nervously. "So it's all happening. No turning back."

"Do you wish to?"

"No, of course not. It's just strange to be a public figure and have my personal life be the subject of general gossip. When I got engaged to Wyatt, it was a much more private affair."

I place a firm hand over hers. "I am not Wyatt, and together you and I are going to forge a new and different life together. There is no point making comparisons."

"It's impossible not to," she replies a little testily.

"You must try. Clear your mind of Wyatt and the life you had before. There is only one male you should focus your attention on and it is me."

She leans across to kiss me lightly. "Is that so?" she teases.

I am resolute and unbending. "Melinda, I have told you I will not share you. You are all mine now."

She runs fingers down my chest, touching her newly painted name. "And you're all mine too, so I will ask you to clear your mind of your drashas and the life you had before. This works both ways, Kirimor."

"My drashas are the very furthest thing from my mind," I grumble. "It is only you I think about."

"And you are all I think about too, but Kirimor, I can't cut Wyatt out of my heart. I will always love him, even if he's no longer my husband or mate."

That is not what I want to hear. My drashas, much as I respect them, are not in my heart. Separating from them has been more a logistical operation than anything else.

"You will see him when he comes to Krovatia," I state rather than ask.

"Yes, of course I will."

My hackles rise. She sees this and wraps her arms around me. "Kirimor, trust me. You have nothing to worry about. My mind is set and I want you as my mate for the rest of my days.

But that doesn't mean I won't be happy to see Wyatt again and spend time catching up with him."

I pull back, frowning. "What does it mean, catching up with him?"

I can see she is amused at my jealousy. She smiles as she says, "It means talking, a hug and a kiss on the cheek, but nothing more you pervy old man."

I am about to remonstrate but stop. "Very well," I say gruffly.

I pull her to me for a long, satisfying kiss. When I finally lift my lips from hers, they are plump and puffy from all my attention. Anyone seeing her now will know she has been thoroughly kissed and thoroughly claimed by me. At this moment, the drone lands and I let go of her briefly to open the door. Then, with her hand in mine, and my tail securely around her middle, I escort her down.

Kiristen awaits us at the main entrance to the school. He beams when he sees my Melinda in customary Krovatian dress, my markings painted over her body. He rushes forward and brings her into his arms for an embrace, his tail swirling around us in his excitement. "I am so happy and honored, Melinda, that you have accepted my father as your mate." He steps back to gaze at her admiringly. "The body artist has done an excellent job. You were beautiful before, but now you are extra beautiful and looking like one of us. Welcome to our family."

Melinda's face creases into a pleased smile, and I sense she is much moved. "Thank you, Kiristen," she says with a tell-tale flush on her face.

I pull my beloved son to me and hug him tight, showing my love and approval. "Thank you, Kiristen. I must leave you now for some urgent work. I hope Melinda enjoys her visit to your school. Please take good care of her."

"I will," he promises.

Then I untangle my tail from around Melinda and extract one final kiss. "I shall see you this evening, my lovely. Go in peace."

"Go in peace, darling."

Darling. I like that.

◆◆◆

Once home, I draw up my list of known suspects. First, we have Prelonisha, the crew member on the cargo ship who is believed to have smuggled the boral crystals aboard. Next, we have Norifen, the young man who made that inadvertent remark in Dorinor's body art shop. He is a medical student, working at a clinic in the hilly quarter of the city. Both he and Prelonisha have been closely watched, but so far their activities have appeared to be wholly innocent.

Then, we come to Dresishan, the person with the deeply malicious energy that Melistor sucked out. Before his death, he was a doctor, working in the same clinic as Norifen, which is why he was on my list of people to scan.

And now, we have this new suspect, the body artist who has set up shop in the hilly quarter. The one thing that links Norifen, Dresishan and this new individual is their location. It is a loose connection, granted, as thousands of Krovatians live in that quarter. But it is a lead, no matter how small.

I check my communicator as a new message arrives from Denishar. In it, he informs me that the body artist has been named and located. He is Leristor, and his body art shop is in the arcade on the southern reaches of the hilly quarter. I take out my boral crystals and light one up on the incense burner. Closing my eyes, I intone a prayer to Taya and enter into a trance. I let my mind wander to the location of his shop and call out his name. It does not take long to locate him. I focus all my energy on him, reading his aura. As I suspected, his aura is suspiciously perfect, with no hint of evil or negative thoughts. Another person in league with our other suspects. With a sigh,

I come out of the trance and send a quick message to Denishar confirming the results of my scan on Leristor. He answers back immediately.

Denishar: I will send out instructions to have him watched and make a list of all his known associates. Scanning them is your top priority.

Me: Melistor and I will work on this just as soon as we receive the list of names.

Denishar: Good. I sense we are close to uncovering the nature of this plot.

Me: I sense that too. I hope we can stop them before they succeed in whatever they are planning.

Denishar: May Taya hear our prayers. Please keep me informed of your progress.

Me: Of course.

While I await Melistor's arrival, I continue scanning the long list of people who have associated with our first three main suspects, but find nothing of note. At midday, right on time, I go to the front atrium of my house to greet my successor and his family. I have asked Merostena to be there too, so she can help Melistor's drashas and children settle in for their prolonged stay here.

"Melistor, it is good to see you again, and your family too. Come in."

I press my hand to his chest and he returns the gesture, then we both bow. "This is Merostena," I say, indicating my soon to be ex-drasha. "She will help you all settle in. In the meantime, work is pressing. Melistor, will you follow me?"

"Of course."

I guide him out to the temple where I like to do my trances. As we walk, I fill him in on the latest developments. He listens earnestly, then remarks, "The fact that three of our suspects seem to be located in the hilly quarter strikes me as significant."

"Yes, it is something we must consider."

"My geography of the area is not detailed. Is there anything of note there, perhaps something to do with our planet's security, that would explain why our suspects are concentrated in this one area?"

"I have had those very thoughts and have pulled up a large map of the area for us to scrutinize."

By now, we have reached the temple. We both remove our sandals and walk in, bowing in respect to Taya's shrine. I invite him to sit in my thinking nook, a cushioned area at the back of the temple. Once comfortable, I tap my communicator to display a map of the hilly quarter. I point to the south part. "Here is where Leristor has set up his body art shop, in this arcade." I move my cursor to a location north east of the arcade. "Here is the clinic where Norifen currently and Dresishan used to work." I point to the west of the quarter. "This is mainly a residential area."

"And what is this?" Melistor has identified a large building in the north east end of the quarter.

"This is the command center which monitors activity around our planet and manages the force field which shields us. They authenticate ships that request entry and lower the shield for them."

Melistor's tail starts wagging, betraying his excitement.

"You are thinking what I am thinking," I say.

"Anyone wishing to harm our planet would want to bring down that command center."

"Yes, but security is very tight. The airspace above it is protected by an internal force field, so no drones can land there. And the perimeter is highly secure too."

"Nevertheless, this must be an area of focus for our attention. Could we perhaps begin a scan of all personnel working at the center?"

"I will request the information from Denishar. I am not sure whether this enquiry will bear fruit though, as all personnel of high security areas are thoroughly vetted and scanned by me on their employment. I would have noted anything unusual in my logs."

"What if these people were 'turned' after their employment? How often are they re-scanned?"

"After their initial employment check, personnel are re-scanned every two sun rotations."

"So this means that someone employed then, could have since that time been brainwashed or convinced to join the group of plotters."

"Yes, it is possible. Let me contact Denishar now and request the names of all personnel at the control center." I quickly tap out a message to the sector leader then glance across at Melistor. "This means we have quite a lot of scanning ahead of us. We will pause now for our lunch repast, after which we will begin. Can you ensure your drashas are on hand in case we need to cleanse someone's energy?"

"Of course."

"Then let us go back to the main house for our meal."

We stand and walk side by side the short distance back to the house. On entering the atrium again, I see Melistor glance about him admiringly. "The aesthetics of your house are magnificent, Kirimor. Did you design it yourself?"

I smile proudly. "I did, yes, with the assistance of Sholinar."

"The vaulted ceiling gives a great feeling of space and the simplicity of the décor brings upon one a sense of calm and wellbeing."

"Yes, that was the intention. I am glad we have been successful in achieving that effect."

"I am honored to be your guest here, Kirimor."

"The honor is mine, Melistor."

I guide him to the dining area, where we find my extended family gathered and waiting for us, together with Melistor's drashas and children. I catch Kiristen's eye. "Did all go well with Melinda?" I ask.

He grins. "She charmed everyone at the school. And yes, before you ask, I escorted her safely back home where she is busy packing."

"Good. Thank you, Kiristen."

We all sit down around the large circular table. I reach out for the moist cloths and begin the usual task of cleansing Merostena's hands as she sits beside me. As I hold her soft fingers in the palm of my hands, I am struck by the thought that this will probably be the last time I perform this task on her. As I place them gently back down on her lap, I glance up at her face and see that she too is aware of this. Her bright eyes glisten with unshed tears. We do not say anything, but I take her hand in mine again and place a kiss on the palm before returning it again to her lap.

I look at my family sitting all around me. They are a little subdued after this morning's announcement and some are shy in the presence of our guests. Kirimara, my eldest daughter, breaks the uncomfortable silence, asking Melistor's drashas about their journey here, and soon, there is cheerful chatter all around me. I sit observing them, aware of a pang of sadness that this may be the last time I enjoy a meal with all of them. There again, I am also excited at the prospect of starting my new life with Melinda, and promise myself that we will host meals with my children as often as possible. Change can be uncomfortable and dislocating, but it is part of life. Nothing stays still.

At the end of the meal, I stop by the kitchen to thank Dresolor for the excellent food, and to ask him something else. "Dresolor, did you find out any data about how Humans mark the beginning of a new life between mates?"

He pauses in his task and says, "Yes sicortar, there are a few things I have learned. For example, when a newly mated couple first enter their new home, the male lifts the female in his arms as they cross the threshold of the door. It is supposed to ward off evil spirits."

"Ah, that is good to know. Anything else?"

"It is also customary for flower petals to be scattered over the bed. I have taken the liberty of collecting petals from our gardens and placing them in this container. Do you wish me to scatter them on the bed?"

I look at the container, filled with pink, red, yellow and purple petals. They do look very bright and colorful, and having them on the bed will infuse it with their fragrant aroma too. "Yes, I think that would be a good idea. Anything else?"

"Humans like to light candles to achieve a romantic effect in a room."

"Do we have any candles?"

"I have taken the liberty of procuring them. They are already scattered around the bedroom. All you will need to do is light them, but do make sure they are properly extinguished before you go to bed, to avoid the risk of fire."

"That is not a problem. And perhaps you could place the bottle of Lom there with some glasses, so we can partake."

"Of course, I will make sure of it."

"Thank you Dresolor. I want to make our first evening living in our new home as special as possible."

"I understand, sicortar. I have made the *mishu* and will bring it over to the cabin at sunset, together with a selection of other foods for your meal."

"Perfect. Thank you. Go in peace, Dresolor."

"Go in peace, sicortar."

Then I rejoin Melistor in the dining room and together, we walk back to the temple to begin our work.

Chapter 37

Melinda

It doesn't take long to pack my belongings. Apart from my clothes—which now that I'm going to be dressing like a Krovatian, will mostly hang unused in my wardrobe—I haven't brought that much with me from Earth. A couple of nick-nacks, my precious supplies of coffee, some favorite toiletries. Everything else of note is stored by Athena on my communicator.

There's a knock on my door, just as I'm finishing up.

"Come in," I call out.

The handle turns and Treylor walks in. She takes one look at me in my Krovatian get up and laughs out loud. "Oh Melinda, you are looking marvellous! Well done!"

"Thanks. This was mainly Kirimor's idea. He says in Krovatia, mates decorate their bodies with the same design to show they belong to each other."

"So the rumors are true. You are to mate with Kirimor?"

I beam at her, too happy to contain it. "Yes, just as soon as he can step down as sicortar."

"And what of Wyatt? You know he is coming here."

My smile dims. "Yes. It'll be a difficult conversation, but I've made my choice. I want to be with Kirimor." Then I give her a sharp look. "How do you know about Wyatt?"

"Ah, he contacted Pravol for assistance in getting transport here and permission from the Krovatian authorities."

"Why didn't you tell me?"

She looks at me apologetically. "At the time, we did not know you had started a relationship with the sicortar. We thought we were helping two mates to re-unite. Wyatt wanted to wait until he was sure he could fly and that permission had been granted before letting you know. We respected his wishes, though we did urge him to tell you."

I sigh. "He did, eventually. With the time lag, I only received his message yesterday."

"I am sorry, Melinda. Perhaps I should have spoken earlier."

"No, it's alright. What's done is done."

"If I may suggest…"

"What is it, Treylor?"

She comes to sit beside me on the bed. "I am thinking it may be kinder to Wyatt to let him know about your situation before he arrives on Krovatia."

"I don't know if that's possible with all the communications lag. I don't even know where he is right now."

"He is on a Venorian cargo ship owned by my family and commanded by my cousin Rivlor. They have reached this quadrant and are only a few rotations away, so you should be able to speak with him directly on our upgraded communications system."

"Directly? I wasn't aware we had gotten that far."

"It is a recent development, but we are now able to make calls to our home planet. I spoke with my brother, Prilor, just this morning."

"You mean I can just call him and he'll pick up?"

She smiles as she gets to her feet. "Indeed. I shall leave you alone while you do so. Go in peace, Melinda."

"Go in peace," I echo automatically, my mind focused on this latest news. I pick up my communicator, both excited and reluctant to put it to the test. *He's only a few days away from being here. He needs to know.* "Athena, call Wyatt," I instruct.

In moments, I hear a ring tone and then, miracle of miracles, there is a handshake at the other end and Wyatt appears on my screen. He grins excitedly. "Mel! How great to see you, honey!"

"Oh God I can't believe this! It's good to see you too."

He sits on the edge of his bed, in a room I don't recognize, and starts tapping on his communicator. "Let me put you on projector mode, Mel. I want to feel like you're in the room with me."

"I'll do the same."

An instant later, his form appears projected before me. I soak in his familiar, easy smile, the rumpled blond hair and twinkling blue eyes. "Oh Wyatt, you're a sight for sore eyes."

"And you too, honey."

I settle myself down on the end of the bed and adjust the communicator screen so Wyatt can see all of me. His eyes widen in bemusement on my semi-naked, inked form. "Holy shit, Mel. What have you done to yourself?"

I look down at the art on my body and grin. "It's called going native, Wyatt."

"You've been walking around town looking like that?" He looks genuinely shocked.

"Yep. It's no big deal. Everyone else is similarly dressed, so I don't stick out—at least not much."

"You've never even sunbathed topless on a beach. Wow. This is a lot to take in."

"This is the new, body confident me. Do you approve?"

He gazes at me in wonderment, then huffs, "Hell yes, sweetheart you look amazing! I just never thought this was something you would do, that's all."

"Well, I wouldn't on Earth, but it's different here."

"I bet!"

"So, I hear you're only a few days away from getting here and that you're coming with a load of dancers and actors to put on some shows."

"And that's not all," he says, looking smug. "I've also got Ricky Charles with me."

"No!"

"Yes! Can you believe it? I read somewhere of his interest in visiting other worlds and so I took a chance and contacted his agent."

"You have got Ricky Charles to come here to Krovatia to perform a concert?"

"Yep!"

I'm speechless. Ricky Charles is one of the biggest rock stars on Earth. I can't believe he managed to get him to come. Then on second thoughts I remember just how talented Wyatt was in the business world before he quit it. If anyone could do it, it's him.

I shake my head in wonderment. "Wyatt, that's amazing. I'm so proud of you!"

He beams at me. "Thanks, Mel. That means a lot."

Time to get serious. "Wyatt, it's incredible what you've achieved in a few short weeks. Overcoming your fear, setting up a new business, coming here. I am so proud and so happy for you, but there's something you should know."

His face falls. "What is it, Mel?"

There's no easy way to say it, so I just spit it out. "I've met someone here and fallen in love. We're going to be mated."

"Oh." He stares at me, bewildered and stricken. "How did this happen so quickly? You've been here less than two months. I thought we still had a chance."

"I'm sorry, Wyatt. I don't know what to say. Yes, it was quick. He's the sicortar, the head priest here."

"The one that sucked the evil out of Avery?"

"That's him. His name is Kirimor."

"Are you sure about this, Mel?"

"As sure as I can be of anything."

He rubs his eyes and looks away from the camera. "Fuck!"

"I'm sorry, honey. I hate to see you hurt."

"Mel, you deserve to be happy." His voice breaks. "I just wish it had been me." He puts his head in his hands. "Oh shit!"

A sob escapes him, then he looks up again quickly, taking deep breaths to try to keep it under control.

My own tears are flowing. "Wyatt, oh baby. I'm so sorry."

He wipes a tear away impatiently. "You have nothing to be sorry for! It's me who's sorry! I'm the idiot who let you go." He bangs a hand in frustration then sits, head bowed, for several long moments. Finally, he raises red-rimmed eyes. "So, what now?"

"You're still coming here, to put on your show?"

"Yes. I've got this far; I can't back out now."

"You shouldn't! Is there anything I can do from this end to help?"

He shakes his head. "It's all under control."

"Ok. Well, then I'll see you when you get here."

"Yeah." He takes a calming breath. "Mel, I love you. I always will."

"I know. I love you too, but it's time to let go."

He sniffs and nods.

"Bye, Wyatt. I'll see you soon."

"Bye."

Kirimor arrives just after sunset as promised. The minute I open the door, he wraps his tail around me and draws me to him. "Melinda," he rumbles, holding me tight.

I burrow into his large frame, breathing in that very male, musky scent of his. "I missed you too," I whisper.

"Are you ready to go, my lovely?"

"Yes, if you will help me carry a few things across to your drone."

"Of course."

It's the work of minutes to load up my belongings. While we're doing so, Troy emerges from his room, taking a moment to admire my new look. "Well, hello there gorgeous. That art looks mighty fine on you."

I feel Kirimor swell with pride beside me. "It does indeed," he concurs.

"Need any help with the bags?" Troy queries.

"No thanks, we're all done."

"If you've any room left on the drone, would you mind if I hop along with you? I'm spending the night at the main house with Kiristen."

"It would be our pleasure," responds Kirimor. I think he's grown rather fond of his son's boyfriend.

As we get on board the drone, Troy says wistfully, "It won't be the same without you here. I'll miss you."

"Given the fact you spend most of your time glued to Kiristen, I very much doubt it," I say drily.

"No, I mean it. It's just us three humans here, and Avery and I—well let's just say we're never going to gel. You're my human support group, Mel."

"It's not as if you're never going to see me anymore. The cabin is just a short ride from the main house, so you can drop in whenever you're there with Kiristen. And I'll be coming back here for our regular work meetings."

"Yeah, I guess so."

As the drone rises in the air, he adds, "Seeing as I have the both of you here, I might as well let you know something."

"What's that?" I ask, scrutinizing his impassive face for clues.

"I'm planning to propose to Kiristen tonight. I'd like us to get married the human way and have a mating, if possible."

I can't quite leap out of my seat as I'm buckled in, but I lean forward and high-five him. "Alright! That makes two of us."

A huge smile spreads on his face. "I'll have you know I was planning to do this way before the two of you declared your intentions."

Kirimor's tail releases me briefly to wrap itself around Troy in a possessive gesture. "This is joyful news, Troy. I am so proud to welcome you to my family."

Troy looks at him uncertainly. "So, you approve?"

"Did you doubt I would?"

"To be honest, I wasn't too sure how you would react to your son mating with someone from an alien race."

Kirimor quirks his lips in amusement. "Seeing as I too am mating with someone from an alien race—" Here he brings his tail back to curl around my waist. "—It would seem churlish of me to disapprove of you on that basis. Besides, the one thing that matters to me is what is in your heart. I have studied you carefully, Troy, and scanned your aura multiple times to be sure. I know your heart is pure and I know you love my son. That is enough for me."

Troy nods his head, his eyes glazing a little. "Thanks, Kirimor," he manages. "I appreciate that."

The drone begins its descent, landing a few minutes later in front of the main house, where we bid an emotional Troy farewell. Then we're rising swiftly in the air again, making our way up to the cabin, our new home—temporarily. We land shortly afterwards. Descending from the drone, I take a moment to admire the cabin. It stands nestled in lush green pasture, a tall A-frame building clad in thick logs of dark wood. It's not an imposing home, far from it, especially compared with the grand house below. But it has a rustic charm that calls to me.

Kirimor draws me to him with his tail. "We will soon build a new home for us, my lovely. In the meantime, I promise to make this cabin as comfortable as I can for you."

"I love this place. It's perfect."

"Then let us go in and begin our new life there."

I turn, wanting to grab some of my belongings, but he stops me. "I will fetch them for you later. Come."

He leads me forward, up the front steps of the cabin and opens the door. With a swift gesture that takes me entirely by surprise, he sweeps me up in his arms. "I believe it is a Human tradition for a male to carry his mate across the threshold," he says, walking inside.

I laugh in delight and hug him, nuzzling his smooth, warm neck. "Yes, it is."

Carefully, he sets me down, allowing me to take in my surroundings. The cabin's one main room has been decorated with vases of flowers and candles, which Kirimor now lights. They cast a warm, golden glow in the dark shadows of dusk. Something else catches my eye. I approach the large bed at one end of the room. Strewn all over it are hundreds of colorful petals, a confetti of pink, red, yellow and purple.

"Kirimor," I breathe. "This is lovely, and so thoughtful. Thank you."

He finishes lighting the candles and comes to me. "I wanted to make this a special night for us." He draws me into the circle of his arms and I burrow there, content. I feel the rumble of his chest as he murmurs, "Dresolor has prepared a meal for us. Are you hungry?"

"Famished."

"Then let us eat."

He goes to the kitchen area and returns with a tray loaded with several small dishes, one of which contains *mishu*, those green crispy balls with herbs and tender meat inside. He places the tray on the low table and sits me down next to him on the well-sprung floor seat.

"This looks delicious," I say, sniffing the air appreciatively.

In a repeat of our first meeting, he takes my hand and begins to clean it gently with a moist, fragrant cloth. I watch him, feeling unaccountably moved.

"The very first time I sat with you at a dining table, Melinda, I held your hands like this. I meant simply to toy with you. Then

I felt your soft skin and scented your intoxicating essence. You were wilful that night, refusing to allow me the honor of feeding you until I had to tie you up with my tail."

With those words, he brings his tail to my wrists and binds them together in an imitation of that first night. And like that first time, I feel a gush of moisture seep out of my pussy. His nose twitches.

"You were mad at me, your beautiful eyes spitting fire, but I scented your arousal, Melinda. I knew you wanted me. I felt your need of me, my lovely. It fired up an answering need in me. I have been your captive ever since."

He leans his head towards me and gently licks the outer shell of my ear sending tingles throughout my body. He continues in his deep, gravelly voice. "I thought all I wanted was a short dalliance with you, but I was fooling myself, Melinda. Deep down I already knew I was yours and you were mine." He drops tender kisses along the line of my jaw and down my neck, making me quiver.

"It will be my privilege, honor and pleasure from here on, to sit with you like this each night and share food with you." He takes a *mishu* ball and pops it into my mouth. I bite into the crisp skin and sink my teeth into the soft, flavorsome meat inside.

"Mmm, these are so good," I mumble.

"Then have more, my love," he says, feeding me another. He takes one for himself.

We eat the rest of our meal together, my wrists ensconced in his tail while his fingers bring the food to my mouth. Interspersed with this are hundreds of sweet kisses to my face, my lips, my neck, even the top of my head. I give myself over to him completely. Never have I felt more cherished.

"Kirimor," I tremble.

He brings his forehead to mine. I close my eyes, breathing him in. "I love you."

"And I love you, my lovely," he rumbles into my ear.

"Take me to bed."

"With pleasure."

He gets to his feet with athletic grace and lifts me easily into his arms as if I weigh nothing more than a rag doll. In three quick strides, he takes me to the bed, still decorated with petals, and deposits me on top of them. With little care for the newly purchased loin cloth, he rips it off me, then rips his own off just as carelessly. He dives in next to me, enfolding me in his embrace. Our legs tangle as he kisses me, sweeping the petals aside. His mouth on mine is hungry, demanding. His cock, pressing against my abdomen, is rock hard.

I dig my nails into his pale gray flesh, desperately seeking closeness to him. I kiss him ravenously, a new hunger now needing to be sated. I'm plundering his mouth with my tongue, nipping his soft, delicious lips with my teeth. My hands are everywhere on his body, squeezing the top of his shoulders, scratching my way down his back and kneading the firm globes of his ass. His hands are just as busy, mapping my body with powerful strokes. His tail whips about me in a frenzy, slapping against my ass and the back of my thighs in a wild, staccato rhythm.

"Kirimor!" I cry raggedly when we finally come up for air.

His voice is even deeper than usual as he grunts, "My lovely, I cannot wait any more. I need to be inside you."

"Please! Please!"

In one rapid move, he rolls us together until I'm lying on top of him. His cock is a solid, jutting rod between us as he settles me, legs wide, with a knee on either side of him.

"Mount me, Melinda. Take all of me."

I take hold of his shaft and guide it to my entrance. He's so huge I can barely close my fingers around him. I feel the large, rounded tip enter my pussy, stretching me impossibly.

"That is it, my lovely," he rasps. "Take me."

Slowly, I press down on his thick length, letting the slick, slippery walls of my pussy close around him inch by inch. I feel so incredibly full, and still there's more of him to take.

He groans in near agony. "Ah, so tight. Keep going, my lovely. Take all of me."

I moan. "I can't Kirimor. You do it."

With a feral growl, he digs his feet on the bed and pushes himself powerfully up, impaling me on the full length of his cock. We both cry out in an ecstasy of pain. I've never been filled like this before.

He holds me close, not moving in or out, giving me time to adjust to his size. His hands grasp each cheek of my ass, keeping me firmly in place while his cock takes residence in my overstretched pussy. His tail runs along my back, stroking me soothingly.

"How does it feel now, my love?" he issues in a ragged voice.

"Full. So full."

"Are you in pain?"

I check in with the lower parts of my body. Surprisingly, no. "No darling, I'm fine."

He sighs in relief. "That is good." He kisses my neck softly, sending a delicious shiver down my spine. "Do you think you could take a little movement now?"

"Yes," I breathe.

Gently, with his hands grasping the sides of my hips, he lifts me a few inches up, letting his cock slide out. A moment later, he thrusts back in. We both gasp.

"Again!" I cry.

Once more, he lifts me up, then slams into me again.

"Oh fuck. More!"

He thrusts into me once more. "Melinda," he gasps. "I need to fuck you now."

"Do it."

That's all the green light he needs. His restraint over, he begins to piston into me, his large hands holding me firmly in place. I close my eyes and give myself over to his powerful possession. Each thrust fills me to the brim, reaching a sensitive place deep in my pussy that makes my core throb. The pressure of his hands on my ass brings delicious friction to my clit, tugging at the barbell piercing he placed there not long ago.

The pressure builds. I can feel my orgasm approach like a massive tsunami about to hit the shore. "Oh God!" I moan. Still he fucks me, his thick shaft plunging into me in quick, hard thrusts, hitting that point deep inside. "Ahh!" I cry. My pussy walls begin to pulse violently around him as my climax surges over me, engulfing me completely.

I'm dizzy, my blood flowing towards my throbbing core. I collapse on top of him, but he's not done with me yet. With a growl, he lifts me off his chest and deposits me on my front. "Oomph." My breath squeezes out of me. Moments later, he's lifting me again onto my elbows and knees, and stuffing pillows under my chest to support my weight.

"I need to fuck you hard, Melinda," he grunts. "Let me."

I want that more than anything. "Please," I moan.

Then he's parting my legs and notching his cock into my opening again. In one quick lunge, he fills me with his thick length. I expel a breath, but already he's pulling out, only to thrust once more. In this position, his penetration is wonderfully deep. It's almost too much. He begins rhythmically pounding into me, untiring in his power and energy. I'm totally at his mercy, totally possessed, his large body wrapped about me like a warm, protective cloak. My core clenches again, my body priming for yet another climax.

"You take me so well," he groans. "You are mine, all mine."

As he continues to thrust, his tail snakes its way under me and finds my clit. It begins strumming back and forth like a bow on a violin, making my core sing with pleasure. "Oh God!"

The sensation of his stroking tail on my swollen clit takes me over the edge. I cry out as a second orgasm overtakes me, impossibly stronger than the first. I pulse around his cock, and with a loud groan, he thickens inside me and thrusts wildly, drenching me with his hot cum as he too reaches his climax.

Seconds pass. I'm in a blissed out daze, unable to think or speak. Kirimor has taken me to heights I've never experienced before. He holds me tight to him, his body enfolding mine, crooning words of love as I slowly come back down to earth.

He whispers gruffly, "You are mine, Melinda."

"Yes, Kirimor. All yours."

Gently, he withdraws and I feel a whoosh as his cum flows out of me. He touches it with a finger, pushing some of it back inside me. "One day, my lovely, my seed will plant a child in you. It is what you want, is it not?"

All pretense is gone. "Yes," I reply unhesitatingly.

"You are not in your breeding time, but I will scent it when your body is ready. Then I will fill you with my cum over and over."

"Yes." Then I say, "I may have left it too late, Kirimor. I'm forty-one."

"No, my love. You are still fit to breed. I know it and the pendant I put around your womb is having a regenerative affect. Do not worry about it. One day, you will become a mother."

He shifts us both so he's spooning me. "Nothing will make me happier than to fill your womb with my child, Melinda."

"You have so many already."

"I can have one more, a special someone who will be part of you and me."

"That would make me so happy."

"I know, my love. I know you."

"Yes, you do."

He holds me a minute longer, then murmurs. "Shall we remove ourselves from this sticky mess of petals and bathe before we go to sleep?"

"That would be an excellent idea."

"Then come with me."

He pulls me from the bed and walks me to the large bathroom, switching on the powerful shower that prickles my skin with its sharp, needle-like jets. He helps me wash, running a gentle hand along my sticky pussy to clean all the residue of our lovemaking. Once we're done, he switches the water off and dries me briskly. We use the ablutenizer, an amazing contraption for cleaning teeth, one of the many pieces of technology that I'm hoping to bring to Earth one day. I place my lips around the round spout and press the button to start the process. Warm liquid enters my mouth, followed by a set of automated brushes guided by a sensor, which thoroughly cleanse my teeth. Then he's leading me back to the bed, sweeping off the remains of the petals and lifting the covers for me.

We fit comfortably around each other and give ourselves to sleep.

Chapter 38

Wyatt

I left it too late. Too fucking late. I've goddamn lost the love of my life and it's all my fault. I throw my communicator against the wall of the cabin, but the plastic is unbreakable. It bounces harmlessly and lands on the floor. I want to break something. Anything. Smash something to pieces the way my heart is shattering. The pain is unbearable. I've lost her.

I stand, looking around me wildly for something to break. Rivlor's neat, uncluttered chamber doesn't afford me much scope. "Agh!" I roar. Then my eyes land on a ceramic ornament tucked on the top of a shelf. I pick it up, readying to throw, but hesitate at the last minute.

"If you value your life you will put that down."

I look across the room to see Rivlor, eyeing me coolly. Fuck! *What the hell is wrong with me?*

I put the ornament down quickly. "Sorry. That was stupid." I bend to pick up my communicator from the floor, then head to the door. "I'm sorry. I'll just go."

I make to leave the cabin, but she stops me with a sharp command. "Sit yourself down, Wyatt."

"Rivlor, I really am sorry. That was out of order." My voice becomes a croak. "I need to go."

"I said sit down!" I have never before heard Rivlor raise her voice. Without thinking, I do as she commands, sitting on the edge of the bed, looking down at the floor. I feel her come to sit beside me and her hand on my forehead as she reads my mind. Eventually, the hand falls away, and she sighs. "I am sorry, Wyatt. That is not the news you wished to hear."

Understatement. "No, it isn't."

"I too have had my heart broken, shattered into many pieces, so believe me when I tell you it will be fine. Time will heal."

"I can't imagine anyone crazy enough to break your heart, Rivlor."

"Ah, but he did. It was many sun rotations ago. I am over it now, though perhaps he is the reason why since then, I have gravitated towards females more than males."

I sniff. "We males of the species don't always acquit ourselves well, do we?"

"No, but females are no better. We are all imperfect beings."

"Truth."

We don't speak for several moments. Finally, she says, "Sometimes, it helps to talk about it. I want you to tell me about Melinda, from the very beginning of your story together. Come lie on the bed and place your hand in mine. I will build a neural connection with you so you can speak to me through your mind."

Already feeling much calmer, I crawl up the bed and lie down. She comes to lie beside me, then takes my hand, placing it on her naked mid-riff and covering it with hers. "Give me a few moments to connect to your thoughts."

I remain silent, breathing in her fresh, lemony fragrance. Is that her body wash?

She laughs quietly beside me. "It is my body wash. I am glad you like it. So, let us go back in time. Tell me in your head about your first meeting with Melinda."

I had just turned twenty-one. I was at a bar with some friends to celebrate. It was a popular place, not far from the university I was studying at. My friends and I, as foolish young brats do, decided to order some shots.

"Shots? What is that?"

It's small glasses of hard liquor which you swallow down in one quick gulp.

"Ah, I see. Continue."

The shots were brought over to our table, and my friends were egging me on to take my first one. I have to tell you, Rivlor, that I wasn't much of a drinker then. Nor am I now for that matter. Anyway, there they were, saying things like "Go on, Wyatt, take that shot." I was gearing myself to do it when I felt this presence beside me. I looked up from the shot glass to see this tall brunette with beautiful brown eyes smiling at me in amusement. "Cute baby face, sure you're old enough?"

"Ah, she thought you were cute too."

At least she didn't call me "somewhat cute".

Rivlor laughs. "I wanted to wind you up, and it worked."

Noted. Back to my story. I think I gave her an affronted look and said, "I'm twenty-one today." She just grinned back and said, "Well birthday boy, show us what you're made of." I knew in that moment, no matter how hard it was, that I was going to down all those shot glasses without hesitation. So, I did. Not taking my eyes off hers, I downed the first one, then the second and third. By the fourth, I was beginning to feel queasy, but I knew I couldn't back down. With an effort I downed the fourth and felt it burn down my throat. One more, I kept thinking. One more to impress the beautiful girl. So, I picked it up and swallowed it down.

"What then?"

I don't remember. I think I must have passed out. I woke the next morning in my room feeling wretchedly sick. Eventually, after I'd taken some pills and swallowed down a whole lot of water, I picked up my cell phone. That's what we had before they became known as communicators. On the screen, there was a typed message. It said, "I'm impressed. Well done Birthday Boy." She'd signed it with her name and left her number.

"I take it you called her."

I did. Asked her out on a date, but she said no, I was too young for her. She only dated older guys. But I was persistent. Wore her down until she eventually agreed to meet me for a coffee…

I spend the next few hours recounting my history with Mel. It feels therapeutic, going back in time and experiencing all over again the wonderful moments we had together. Then I get to the rocky parts, and that too feels good to talk about. I tell Rivlor about the near nervous breakdown I had working at my stressful job and how I felt I had to get away from it all to regain my sanity. I remember bits and pieces of conversations I had thought forgotten. Melinda's disappointment at my decision. Her attempts to make me change my mind, my hurt that she didn't realize how much I needed to get away from that toxic workplace. I think back to that year where I retrained as a chiropractor and how she threw herself even more into her work, how we barely saw each other. Something changed between us that year. In retrospect, that was the beginning of the end.

I finish my story, drained but also strangely calm. I lie there, eyes closed, my hand still tucked under Rivlor's, feeling the warmth of her taut abdomen beneath it. I drift off.

I come to sometime later. My hand is still right there, tucked under Rivlor's. With her other hand, she holds her communicator, scrolling down with her thumb. I can't make out the text, but I can tell she's reading something.

What are you reading?

I realize I've just spoken to her in my head. I open my mouth to verbalize my question, but she's already responding.

"It is a novel by one of my favorite Venorian authors."

What kind of novel?

"It is a kind of adventure set in a made-up foreign world."

On Earth we call this type of story sci-fi, sci-fi being short for science fiction.

"That is a good name for it. Yes, this is a sci-fi novel. I have always enjoyed this kind of story since when I was young. I think that is why I decided to make a career flying in space."

Sci-fi is my favorite type of book too. I've always dreamed of travelling in space, but I was too much of a scaredy-cat to do it. When Mel announced she was going to Mars, I was so envious. It's not something I'm proud of.

"Envy is a poisonous emotion to have."

I know. But I'm also proud of everything she's done. She's a strong kick ass woman, my Melinda. I love that about her.

"Yes, I can see that. You are attracted to strong females. One of the reasons you like me."

One of the reasons? Why else?

She chuckles. "You like that I am gorgeous and smell good to you. You like that I find you cute. You like that I see and appreciate you."

Yes to all those reasons. Rivlor, I like speaking to you in my head.

"It is a great Venorian attribute, is it not? A shame you cannot read my mind too."

If I could read your mind, what would it be saying?

"It would be saying, time to get up and get something to eat."

I sit up slowly, stretching my arms overhead. "I have taken up a lot of your time. Thanks again, Rivlor. It's helped a lot."

"I am glad you feel calmer. No more throwing things about, eh? That would make me most displeased."

I laugh shortly. "No, I won't do that again, I promise."

"Good. Let us go now and get some food. Listening to your story has made me very hungry."

I smile. "Let's go."

Chapter 39

Kirimor

Melinda has been mine for three rotations and everything in my life is bright and happy. Our home in the cabin is filled with love, laughter and passion. Last evening, we hosted my children for a family meal. Kiritela spent the whole time in Melinda's lap, wanting her attention. My children love her already. They have adjusted well to my move to the cabin. Being so close, and seeing me so regularly, I think they have been reassured that this temporary change in accommodation will not mean a distancing from me. I am still very much a part of their lives.

Melistor's apprenticeship is going so smoothly that we have agreed to shorten his training period. Next rotation, I will be officially stepping down as sicortar. Melistor will be invested in his new position on the same day, and I will be free to mate my Melinda. It will be a rubber stamping exercise, as we are already living as mates. And soon after, I will plant my seed in her, and we shall bring a new life into this world.

Everything is bright and happy, except for one thing. We have still not unmasked the plotters or discovered what it is exactly they are plotting. We have scanned and re-scanned all the employees of the command center, but have found nothing amiss. Now, we have returned our attention to scanning the known contacts of our group of suspects. We have made a start on the long list of people that Leristor, the body artist in the hilly quarter, has associated with.

However, this morning we are taking a break from such work in order to process the newly arrived visitors from Earth, including Melinda's former mate. They have been escorted down from their ship by our security personnel and brought down to the cavernous space underground where we await them. Altogether, there are thirty-five Humans. Melistor and I sit beside the incense burner, his drashas behind us. We watch as the Humans troop inside, looking a little apprehensive.

I put on my stern, forbidding sicortar face. Melistor, an apt student, wears a similar expression. The security guards instruct the Humans to sit in absolute silence while we scan them. I search their faces for him. I recognize him almost immediately—the blond locks of hair, the bright blue eyes. His gaze is upon me, focused and intent. He knows who I am, of that I am sure.

I stare back at him unwaveringly. This male is not my rival, for Melinda is undoubtedly mine. Nevertheless, I feel the need to impart a sense of power and superiority. My gaze is telling him clearly not to mess with me or mine. He blinks and looks away.

Melistor opens the box of boral crystals and selects the one to place on the burner. Although I am still officially sicortar for one more rotation, I let him take the lead in the proceedings. It is he who intones the prayer to Taya. Then both of us enter into our trance. I sense Melistor methodically scanning each Human, starting from the left and moving along one by one. However, my attention immediately goes to Him. I am keen to know what manner of man was once my Melinda's mate.

I scan him thoroughly. I see bright shades of yellow and orange—a gentle and warm personality with no hint of negativity. I should not be surprised. Melinda would not have stayed mated so long to someone who was not good. I also see little streaks of pale green, uncannily similar to Melinda's when I first scanned her. I summon the green streaks into me for a closer read. He is feeling anxiety at being in an alien land and having to put on a program of shows. There is also grief and sadness over the loss of Melinda. The man loves and mourns her. I can understand that. If I were foolish enough to lose her, I too would be beside myself with grief.

With a sigh of relief, I come out of my trance. I need not have worried about this male. In fact, it would behove me to extend the hand of friendship to him—that would please Melinda. I wait until Melistor completes his scans and the Humans are dismissed, cleared for entry to our world. Before they can all leave the room, I stride over to Wyatt and call his name. He pauses and turns to face me, a little nervous. I come to stand before him and say in my most gracious voice, "Welcome, Wyatt. I have heard much about you."

"You must be Kirimor," he mumbles.

"Indeed. May I greet you the Krovatian way?"

"Yes, of course."

I place a hand to his chest and look into his eyes. After a moment's hesitation, he does the same to me. Then I step back and bow. He bows back.

"May I have the privilege of escorting you to your lodgings? Melinda is at work there, and I am sure she is most eager to see you again."

He looks surprised but responds, "I'm eager to see her too. Thank you for the offer of a ride, if that's not too much trouble for you?"

"It is my pleasure, Wyatt. Come."

He follows, walking quietly beside me. We get into the elevator shaft, sharing it with a half dozen of the other Humans and two security guards. They sneak curious glances at me, but do not speak. Wyatt simply says to one of them, "I'll be hitching a ride with Kirimor to the house we're staying in. I'll see you all there. Could you ensure our equipment and bags follow us?"

"Sure, no problem."

"Thanks."

Then all is quiet again. We reach the surface, walking out into the barren desert landscape where the processing center is situated. My drone is parked a few paces away. I lead Wyatt towards it and remember something Melinda told me about him. "Are you still fearful of flying in a drone, Wyatt?"

He flushes an interesting shade of red. "You know about that?"

"Melinda tells me all."

"Oh right." Then he adds, "I'm a lot better than I used to be about flying, though I still don't enjoy it much. It's ok. I'll be fine."

"You will be fine, Wyatt. There is nothing to fear. My drone is perfectly safe."

He nods, though I can see his face is pale. His communicator rings, distracting him momentarily. As he picks up the call, I see over his shoulder that it is from a magnificent looking Venorian female. His expression clears. "Hey Rivlor," he says.

"Cute boy, tell me how you are."

"I'm doing good. We've finished being processed and are just on our way to our new lodgings."

"How was the shuttle flight? Are they treating you well?"

We stand in the shadow cast by my drone, while he continues his conversation with Rivlor, the commander of the Venorian cargo ship that brought him here.

"The descent to the planet surface was a bit rough, so I'm a bit shook up. I'll admit, I'm not looking forward to climbing into the drone that's right in front of me."

Her deep voice takes on a soothing, yet commanding tone. "I will stay on the line with you, Wyatt. Put me on projector mode and look at me the whole time."

I decide it is time to interject. "That will not be necessary. I will ensure he is fine."

Rivlor's eyes swing up, looking for the person who has just spoken. Wyatt adjusts his communicator screen so that she can see me. "And you are?"

"I am Kirimor, Melinda's new mate, and high priest of Krovatia. Wyatt is under my protection and I will see him delivered safely to his lodgings."

"I see."

She considers me for a long moment then turns to Wyatt, whose eyes have been following the power play between us in bemusement. "Cute boy, how do you feel about that? Tell me the truth. If you do not feel safe, I will come to get you right away."

Wyatt stares at me, standing powerfully before him with my hands on hips. Then he returns his gaze to Rivlor. "I—um, it's alright. We're cool."

"It is getting hot standing out here," I say. "Let us be on our way."

"Wyatt, should you need me, you must call," urges Rivlor.

"I will," he promises.

They end the call and I assist Wyatt to climb up into my snug, sun-powered drone. He looks around him doubtfully. "This is smaller than the drones I'm used to."

"It has the most energy efficient technology available in the entire universe, and it is entirely safe. I will ensure I get you there safely, Wyatt."

He nods nervously, not looking convinced, and straps himself in. I see him take out a paper bag from the satchel he is carrying.

"What is that for?" I ask in puzzlement.

"It's just something my therapist suggested to help me regulate my fear. I breathe into it, in and out."

"I see. And does it help?"

He smiles wryly. "A little. What really works is distracting conversation."

"Well, I am happy to converse with you during our journey." I start the engine and see him startle. He buries his face in the paper bag. "It is fine, Wyatt," I say, trying to sound reassuring.

This is the man who thought he could hold on to Melinda? No wonder she left him.

As we begin our ascent, I start a conversation. "So, Wyatt, I hear you are to put on some music and drama shows for us. I am very much looking forward to seeing them. Do you have a venue arranged? If not, I am sure I can be of assistance."

"It's sorted," he says shortly into his bag.

"Melinda is very excited about a singer called Ricky Charles. She tells me he is famed across your world for his singing."

"He's one of the best."

"I will be sure to bring her to see him perform. Anything to make my Melinda happy, I will do."

He huffs into his bag.

"She is mine now," I say gently. "You do understand that?"

He looks up from his bag, his blue eyes steely. "That is up to her to decide."

"And she has made her choice, Wyatt."

He does not back down. "I know, but let me tell you this, Kirimor. If you hurt her in any way, you will answer to me. I may look weak to you, but I'm stronger than you think, especially when it comes to Mel. You better treat her right. You do understand that?"

I laugh delightedly. "Have no fear, Wyatt. She is in good hands with me. I will love and cherish her to the end of my days."

"We shall see."

"Maybe you should think about finding yourself a new partner. What think you of this Rivlor?"

He scowls. "I will not discuss her with you."

"I think you like her."

He stares at me.

I continue undaunted. "She calls you cute."

I see the tell-tale flush spread over his face. Oh yes, he likes her. All the better. Hopefully, he will not keep hankering after my Melinda.

He smirks, "Perhaps it's because I am cute and charming. You should see the amount of fan mail I've received from Krovatian students who saw me in the video Mel played in her university lecture."

"Well, if we are talking of fan mail, you must know that as sicortar, I attract my fair share of attention. I let my aide, Sholinar, deal with it, but the list of adoring fans is long."

Wyatt eyes me in amusement. "Are we really comparing size? Next you'll be telling me your cock is bigger than mine."

I eye his groin then mine pointedly. "As to that, there is no need as it is patently obvious that I exceed you significantly in that department."

He laughs. "You really are going there! Dude, there's more to a guy than the size of his dick."

"I agree, size is not everything, but in the end, it comes down to this. Melinda has chosen the powerful male with the big dick over the cute and charming one." And with a flourish, I land the drone at our destination.

Chapter 40

Wyatt

I crumple the paper bag in my hand. Quite evidently, distracting conversation is a far more powerful antidote to my fear of flying than anything else. Volleying words with Kirimor has totally taken my mind off the fact we've been flying in this small, rickety looking drone. I can't believe the dude compared the size of our dicks. Maybe he's not quite so sure of Melinda as he pretends.

All of a sudden, I can't wait to be out of the drone and in her presence again. I need to see her, look her in the eye and hear her tell me the truth to my face. Kirimor opens the drone door and I jump down. We're parked in front of a set of identical houses, rendered in white with huge solar panels for their roofs. The door to one of them opens and there she is.

"Mel!" I rush forwards, lifting her off her feet in my excitement.

She laughs happily, wrapping her arms around me and holding me tight.

"I've missed you, honey," I say, kissing the top of her head."

"I've missed you too. I can't believe you're finally here!"

I put her down and smile proudly. "I made it, Mel. I conquered my fear!"

She places two hands on my cheeks. "I'm so proud of you. You're doing amazing things."

Then I'm hugging her again, wanting to feel her body against mine. She's not wearing much in the way of clothes, just a bikini bottom that looks a bit like a loin cloth. Her soft breasts press against me and I feel my cock twitch in response.

Before I have time to process this uncomfortable turn of events, a long powerful tail wraps itself around Mel, pulling her away from me. She grins and turns to Kirimor, putting her arms around him. I see her whisper something into his ear and he growls in response. Mel arches her neck to give him a long, open-mouthed kiss as he tightens his tail around her.

I watch, equal parts jealous and turned on. When they finally end the kiss, Mel's lips are swollen and glistening, like a ripe juicy berry. I'm seized by an urge to devour those sweet lips, but of course, that's off the table now that she's his. *Damn, this is going to take some getting used to.*

Melinda shines a loving smile over him. "Now could you please let me go so I can take Wyatt through and introduce him to everyone else? Then I need some alone time to catch up with him as promised."

Reluctantly, he withdraws his arms and tail, but stays close. "I do not like to leave you, my lovely."

She strokes his cheek tenderly. "I know, but there is important work to be done."

He sighs in agreement. "I will return to take you home at sunset. What plans have you for this day?"

"I cleared my schedule this morning so I could spend time with Wyatt. In the afternoon, I have a remote meeting set up with Lorifena. She's the last sector leader I need to convince about agreeing to a pharmaceutical trade mission from Earth."

"Very well, my love. Remember what we said."

"I remember. Don't worry." He kisses her one last time, then turns to me. "Go in peace, Wyatt," he mutters. Then he's striding away and climbing back into his drone.

We watch him leave together. "Come on, let's go inside to the kitchen and make you some coffee. Then we can sit down and talk." Mel threads her arm through mine and walks me inside.

We step across an atrium-like room which opens up into a small, enclosed yard with a rectangular shaped pool. Beyond that to the left, is a door which leads to a large eat-in kitchen.

Sitting at the table, sipping his coffee and reading from his communicator, is a tall bare chested guy with markings all over his body similar to what I've seen on other Krovatians. He smiles on seeing us and stands. "Hi there, you must be Wyatt. I'm Troy."

I shake hands with him, though it feels odd and inadequate as a greeting out here, with him dressed in just a loin cloth. "Nice meeting you, Troy. How are you doing?"

"I'm good. Looking forward to seeing Ricky Charles perform. I'm a huge fan."

I grin. "Who isn't? He should be settling in next door, so I'm sure you'll get to meet him soon."

"I'd go over there now and say hello, but I've got to head out. I'm just waiting for Desimar to arrive—he's our Krovatian escort, their version of a spy and bodyguard all in one."

"Oh right. Going anywhere interesting?"

"Yes, actually. It took me a while to wrangle the invite, but the Krovatian authorities have finally given me the green light to go visit their planet's control center. I'm curious to see the technology they use to maintain the protective shield around their planet. It's something we're going to need to set up on Earth at some point in the near future."

"Oh wow, that does sound very interesting. I wish I could go along with you. I've always been fascinated by that type of technology."

"I'm sure they won't mind one more human in the group. Wanna come?"

I hesitate, torn. "I was hoping to catch up with Mel. Plus, there's lots I should be doing to prepare for our shows."

"You sure? We'll only be gone two hours at most. The authorities have made it clear that we're not going to be lingering there too long, just have a tour, ask a few questions, then we're out."

"Oh well. You don't mind, Mel?"

She shrugs. "No problem, I'll come with you." She turns to Troy. "Where's Avery? I thought she was supposed to accompany you on this visit."

Troy makes a face. "She's pleaded some last minute indisposition and is lying in bed."

"Ok. Well in that case, give me two minutes to change into human clothes, and I'll come with."

"You don't go out in that getup?" I ask, pointing to her loin cloth.

"I do, but for official business, I prefer to be in human garb."

"Makes sense," I concur.

She smiles. "Come keep me company while I get changed."

"Sure."

With a nod at Troy, I follow Mel to her room, which is a few doors down the same corridor. Inside, she goes quickly to her closet and pulls out a floral patterned sun dress with thin straps. From a drawer, she digs out a bra and panties.

"Most of my stuff is now at my new home with Kirimor, but I've kept some human clothing here for occasions like these, when I need to go out on official business."

With no awkwardness, she strips off her loin cloth and I catch sight of something glinting on her mound. "What's that?" I can't help but ask.

She looks down at herself, then at me apologetically. "Kirimor insisted on removing the old piercing and replacing it with his own piece of jewelry. He's a possessive guy."

"Oh," I say, feeling deflated for some reason. She's marrying the guy. Of course he's got every right to want to mark her as his own. "May I see?"

She nods. "Sure."

I walk towards her and kneel, eyes level with her pussy. Where my piercing used to be is now a new set of barbells with purple-pink gem stones on each end. She's also got a pendant of those pink gem stones draped all around her hips. "Very pretty," I say.

I stand and let her pull on her panties, then the rest of her clothes. Once dressed, she faces me, expression cloudy. "I'm sorry, Wyatt. I know those piercings meant something, but it was time for a new start. I've made my choice, honey. I want to be with him."

"I know, Mel. You don't have to explain. Come on, let's go."

Chapter 41

Rivlor

My cute boy is safe. Krovatia is a friendly planet and this male, Kirimor, will protect him. I am certain of it. I am good at reading people. And yet, I am finding it difficult to leave him. I have a business to run and profits to make. It has been agreed that while the Humans stay on Krovatia for their shows, I can complete some short haul cargo runs, then return to pick them up for their onward journey to Ven. Really, there is nothing here to concern me. We must get going. Across from me, Shular waits patiently for my command.

"Engage the thrusters, and let us be on our way," I say finally.

He nods his head and follows my instruction. Our ship begins to move, gathering speed. I sit in my seat, heart pounding inexplicably. Something is not right. "Bring us to a stop and put us in cloaked mode!"

Shular casts a puzzled glance at me but obeys my command. Once we have stopped and hidden our presence with the cloaking technology that we use, he turns to me. "What is it, Rivlor?"

I return my old friend's gaze. "I do not know, Shular. It is a feeling I have that something is not right."

"You think the Krovatians will harm the Humans?"

"No. I do not believe so."

"Then what is it?"

"I cannot explain. Please humor me and let us wait awhile."

"Very well, Rivlor, but how long do you propose we wait like this?"

"I cannot say. Perhaps no more than a quarter rotation. I have a feeling something is about to happen."

Vonlar, his nephew and another member of my crew, speaks now, "I have every faith in your instincts Rivlor, which have never been wrong so far. If you think we should wait, then that is what we shall do."

We settle down to wait, for what I do not know. To distract myself, I pull out my communicator and begin to read. It is hard to maintain my focus on the story. Every so often, I stop to look at our sensor readings, but there is nothing new. With a sigh, I force my attention back to the story I am reading. It is by an author I like, so I should not be finding it so hard to engage with.

Suddenly, the ship lurches as a wave of energy hits us.

"What was that?" I rap out sharply.

"Something has just passed close to us. A cloaked ship I think," replies Vonlar.

We are hit with a second wave of energy.

"Another ship," states Shular.

Two more ships pass us, which brings the total to four unknown alien ships clustered just outside the force field that shields the planet of Krovatia.

"Who could it be?" wonders Vonlar aloud.

"It cannot be a friendly presence," I say dryly. "Going on recent history, my money would be on the ships being Saraxian."

"The Saraxians are kin to the Krovatians. Why would they want to attack them?"

I think about it. "Perhaps it is because Krovatia has a commodity they desire and are in short supply of."

"Dorenium," mutters Shular.

"They will not get through the force field," observes Vonlar. "Krovatians have some of the best security in this quadrant."

"That is very true," I say. "Perhaps they know something we do not."

Shular looks at me quizzically. "What are you thinking, Rivlor?"

"Could there be Krovatians working on the inside with their kin, the Saraxians? The ties of family bonds can be strong and it is only seven decades since Krovatia was colonized. It is not impossible that some of the settlers stayed in touch with their kin on Sarax."

"You are thinking that someone on the inside will cause the force field to be lowered and allow the Saraxians entry?"

"It is a probability," I say, taking hold of my communicator. Using the secure, encrypted line that we established between our people who came to live on Krovatia and our home planet, I make a call to Pravol.

He answers me straight away. "Rivlor, good tidings to you. Is all well?"

"There is a concerning situation, Pravol. We are on the edge of the force field protecting Krovatia, in our cloaked state. We have just felt four cloaked ships pass us, presumably unfriendly."

"Saraxians?"

"That is my best guess."

"They will not be able to get through the force field. It is one of the best in the galaxy."

"Unless there is someone on Krovatia working with them. Can you open a secure communication with the Krovatian authorities and inform them of what I have seen? I do not want to hail them myself, in case we are intercepted."

"Of course, I will do so straight away."

"Pravol, if that force field is lowered, then I shall fire in that direction with all the fire power I have in my possession. I should be able to take down one ship, maybe two, but the other two would get through."

"Understood."

"One more thing. Whatever happens, please look after Wyatt. Is he in the house with you?"

I see Pravol turn to his mate, my cousin Treylor, and ask, "Have you seen Wyatt?"

"He left with Troy and Melinda just two beats ago."

"Do you know where they were going? We have to bring them back to safety with us."

"Oh my holy lord Lir! They have gone to visit the command center."

"Is that the place which controls the force field?" I snap.

"Yes! I need to contact the authorities now, Rivlor."

"Understood."

I end the communication and stand, feeling agitated. Turning to Shular, I say, "Get our weapons online. Make sure we are ready to fire as soon as the force field is lowered. Prepare to do evasive manoeuvers as soon as we fire."

"Understood."

I send a prayer to Lir. *Please keep my Wyatt safe.* And then I force myself to wait, not taking my eyes off that force field.

Chapter 42

Kirimor

It is with difficulty that I tear myself away from Melinda. I trust her, and I know she will keep her promise to me. I am not worried about her being alone with Wyatt. And yet it bothers me to leave them. Something feels off kilter. I am not sure why. I try to shake the thought away and focus my musings on the work that needs to be done.

My drone lands back home, in front of my temple building, where Melistor is already hard at work scanning the contacts of our latest suspect, Leristor, the body artist in the hilly quarter. I have a feeling that soon, we are going to find answers to our many questions about what is going on.

I remove my sandals and enter, going to sit at my usual place beside the incense burner. Melistor is deep in a trance, the boral crystal on the burner emitting the required energy field for this to happen. Melistor's drashas are sitting close by, heads bent in prayer. On sensing me, they lift their heads and bow them again respectfully. I put my hands together and intone a silent prayer to Taya, then I too focus on the boral crystal to enter into my own trance.

Once in my trance state, I am able to communicate with Melistor. "How goes it, Melistor?"

"So far, nothing to report. I have scanned two of Leristor's associates and I am now searching for the third, a person named Desimena, who came into his shop for some new artwork one rotation ago. I do not have an address for her, so I am searching out each part of the hilly quarter, calling her name."

"I will assist you. Which parts have you not done?"

"The north east and east quadrants."

"Very well, I will search for her in the east quadrant."

I focus my attention on that part of the city, hovering over each building there and calling out, "Desimena!" After a few efforts, I finally get a response. "I have found her, Melistor. You go on to the next person on the list while I scan her."

Then, using the skills honed and practised over several decades of being sicortar, I bring my focus to Desimena and read her aura. Everything perfect. Nothing out of place. Another one of our suspects. I come out of my trance to send a communication to Denishar, informing him we have found yet another suspect. *Desimena*. Who is it I have met recently of the same family designation?

Then it comes to me. Desimar. The liaison officer who has been escorting the Humans everywhere they go. It could be a coincidence, but on the balance of probability, I do not believe so. Was he not scanned before he entered the security services? I search my logs of scans I have performed in my time as sicortar, entering his name. I hit a match from three sun rotations ago. I scanned him then and found nothing amiss. There are no notes beside his name, so nothing called to my attention then. Could it be that he got "turned" after going into service? At any rate, he urgently needs to be re-scanned. I need to find out where he is so I can locate him in my trance. The quickest way to do this is to call my Melinda.

I tap the icon with her name on the corner of my screen, but she does not answer. Curious. I try calling her again, and still no answer. Becoming agitated, I call Denishar, but he too is busy and does not pick up. By now, Melistor has come out of his trance beside me and looks askance at my agitation. I explain the situation as quickly as I can.

"Perhaps Kiristen will know," he suggests. "Troy will have told him where is going today and surely Desimar would be escorting him."

"Yes! You are right."

I put a call through to my son. Luckily, he answers on the first attempt. One look at my face tells him something is wrong. "Father, what is it?"

"We urgently need to locate Desimar, the male escorting our Humans. Do you know where Troy plans to be today?"

"Yes, he has been very excited about it. He is going to the command center in the hilly quarter—"

"Fuuuuck!" I cry.

"Father?"

"Thank you, son. I will speak with you later."

Hurriedly, I sit back and begin the process of re-entering my trance. I hover over the command center and call out his name. Sure enough, he is there and responds almost immediately. Once I have him located, I begin my scan. I am hit with powerful evil vibes. I shrink back in horror. Seeping out of Desimar is wickedness more intense than I have ever seen before. Something terrible is going to happen today at the command center. I am sure of it. And Troy is there, at the heart of danger. What about Melinda? I come out of my trance.

Where is Melinda?

She was going to stay at home today and catch up with Wyatt. Surely that is where she is still. Then why is she not answering my call? I pick up my communicator and try her again. Still no answer. I call Troy. No answer from him either. I am dizzy with worry. My Melinda is in grave danger. She must be with Troy. It is the only thing that explains why she is not answering. I must get hold of Denishar and inform him at once. I try calling him again, but still he is unavailable. Time is of the essence. Something must be done now. There is only one thing for it. Desimar must be neutralized. I glance at Melistor, considering him briefly but dismissing the idea. The level of evil I have just encountered requires experience only I have.

Sending a quick prayer to Taya, I enter into my trance again. I call out to Melistor. "I need your help!"

Immediately, he focuses his attention on me. "Kirimor, what is it?"

"Danger, evil, the most wicked of hearts. It is Desimar, the person escorting the Humans, and they are at the command center today. I need to neutralize him right away. The level of evil I have seen in him is such that I will need you to act as a second, sending back any evil waves of energy that escape from me."

"Of course."

"There is no time to lose. Let us start."

We send our focus to the command center in the hilly quarter and both locate Desimar at the same time. I feel Melistor's gasp beside me as he reads the evil in him. A moment later, he sends me reassuring words. "I am with you, Kirimor. Do what you must."

And so I begin. With supreme focus, I aspirate the malevolent energy towards me. I feel it entering my body, contaminating me with its foul maliciousness. I breathe deeply, allowing it all to become part of me. I am full to overflowing with evil energy, and still more keeps coming my way.

"I will catch whatever more there is," murmurs Melistor. "Deal with what you have captured inside you, then I will neutralize the rest."

Relieved, for I do not believe I can take in more of this wickedness, I concentrate on clamping down hard on it so it does not escape me. It sits there, in my gut, in my chest, in every part of my body—toxic evil, coursing through me. Then, with all the power I can summon, I begin breaking it down, bit by bit. It is almost like an old fashioned sword fight, a battle with the evil followed by a spear into its heart to bring it down. It is an endless, abhorrent task. The only thing that keeps me from sinking into despair is the knowledge that I must do this to save Melinda. The thought of her keeps me going through this grueling, arduous labor.

Finally, it is done. There is no more evil energy inside me. I give out a low, ragged breath and slowly come out of my trance. It is done now and I must trust that Melinda is saved. As I re-enter reality, I feel the post-trance madness begin to take a hold of me. My cock is rock hard and desperate for release. I howl in pain and frustration. No! I must not.

"Aghh!" I stand and whip off my loin cloth in one violent move. Then I put my hand to my cock, trying to jerk off the deep-seated need. Oh Goddess. I need. So much. My hands clench around my length, trying to appease the need, but it is not enough. I howl again. Around me, I hear worried voices and I know they are discussing me, but I cannot focus on the words they are saying. I groan in pain. I need.

Behind me, someone is grunting. I whirl around in fury. It is Melistor, pounding into his drasha. I cry again in pain as I see him fuck. I need it too. Of Goddess how I need! My hands pull at my cock violently, trying to settle the ache. All it does is make me ache more.

I need to fuck and purge this evil out of me. I need a moist cunt to sink myself into and rut. A soft breast to bite. But I must not. Melinda.

"Aghh!" My rage knows no bounds. I pound my fists on the wall, screaming my fury. Then it is my head I am banging. Maybe this pain will erase the other pain and quench that need. I bring my head to the wall again. There is a red stain there—my blood. I am about to launch myself at the wall again when strong arms restrain me.

"Kirimor! Stop!"

I howl in response and try to fight him off. It is Sholinar, I know. My friend and aide, but right now my enemy, stopping me from what I need to do.

"Leave me alone!" I scream.

"Kirimor, you need to fuck. Nothing else will ease your pain."

I cry out again in rage and frustration. Sholinar ignores my screams and with a strength I did not know he possessed, brings me down to my knees on the floor, holding me in a tight lock with his arms across my chest. Over my head, I hear him instruct someone. "Quickly, mount him."

"No!" I scream, but Sholinar's grip on me is like iron.

Then a soft cunt is sheathing my cock. Pirofena. It feels so wrong and yet so good. I grunt again. Sholinar murmurs into my ear. "We are here to help you, Kirimor. Let Pirofena take the edge off your pain."

Without my volition, my hips rise as I thrust up into that glorious cunt. Its moist walls close around me and I lose all control. Suddenly, the hands around me are gone and I am lying on top of Pirofena, fucking her with abandon. I close my eyes, picturing Melinda. It is her I am fucking. No one else. "Melinda," I chant to myself as I pound into that welcoming cunt. I clutch a soft breast in my hand and put my teeth to it. I am beside myself, pummelling my cock into that tight channel and biting into inviting flesh, marking her breasts and her neck, guided by my beastly urge. With a loud groan, I reach a powerful climax, spurting jet after jet of my seed. When I am done, I collapse on top of her, unable to move.

I come back to consciousness and find myself in my own bed up in the cabin, all alone. Memory returns and with it, all that I have done. A pain so strong crushes my chest. *Melinda*. I scrabble around for my communicator. I call her, but she does not respond. What does it mean? Is she hurt? Dead? In desperation, I call Sholinar. He picks up immediately.

"Melinda!" I cry.

He understands my question. "She is fine, Kirimor. None of the Humans at the command center were hurt, and your prompt action stopped Desimar from bringing down the force field and destroying the building. You saved the day, Kirimor!"

"But Melinda," I repeat.

"I do not know how to say this to you, Kirimor."

"Out with it!"

"She arrived at the house and ran to the temple to find you. I think she knew you would be in need and she wanted to be the one to help you. When she got there, she saw you rutting with Pirofena. She watched you, evidently upset, then she turned and ran back out again. Another Human was with her. He escorted her to their house."

I groan again. "How long ago was this?"

"Kirimor, you have been asleep one whole rotation."

"Agh!" I cry out in frustration. "I must get to her at once."

"You need sustenance, Kirimor. I shall send Dresolor up with some food. Then you may go find her. Also, Denishar would like to see you as soon as you are able to go."

"I will go to him as soon as I have seen and spoken to Melinda."

"Of course. Eat first."

I grunt in reply and end the call. Jumping out of bed, I stride purposefully into the bathroom and wash. In the mirror, I notice the gash on my forehead that has been bandaged. I touch it, remembering. That is the awful thing about it all. I was not fully in control of my actions, but I remember every damnable thing that happened—including fucking Pirofena. Not just that. I also remember something else, something that intensified my beastly urge to fuck. I scented her, and she was ripe for breeding.

I finish washing and put on a fresh loin cloth, then with a heavy sigh, I pick up my communicator again. Pirofena answers on the second ring. "How are you doing? Are you hurting?"

"Only a little, sicortar. I shall be fine, thank you for asking."

"Pirofena, I know. Has it taken?"

She is silent for a moment or two, then in a low voice, responds, "Yes."

"You are certain?"

"Yes, I have scanned my body for a new life. We are to have a child."

The words are like a hammer to my doom. Eventually, I shall welcome and love this child, but for now, I am angry and hurt.

"Why?" I cry.

"Please do not be angry with me. It was Sholinar. He called, demanding a drasha come to the temple right away. Sicortar, you were in such pain and agony. We had to help you."

"I am no longer sicortar," I grind out.

"No, perhaps not, but to me you always will be."

"Could not another drasha have done the job? It must have been obvious to everyone that you were in your breeding time."

"Merostena insisted it had to be me. She said someone young and strong was needed to withstand the violence of your needs."

Merostena. It is all beginning to make sense. She saw an opportunity to drive a wedge between me and Melinda, and she took it.

I try to hold back the angry words. I know it is not Pirofena's fault, nor Sholinar's. They only did what they thought was right. Had they not stepped in, I do not know what would have happened to me. Perhaps they did the right thing, saving me from self-destruction. Yet their actions have had devastating consequences. My Melinda. How do I tell her about this child? How can I do so without causing her unbearable pain?

"Take care of yourself, Pirofena. We will talk again some other time."

"Go in peace, Kirimor."

"Go in peace."

I end the call and put my head in my hands. There is a knock at the door. "Enter!" I shout.

Dresolor steps inside, carrying a steaming tray of food. "This is for you, sicortar."

"Call me Kirimor. I am no longer sicortar."

He smiles. "It will take time to adjust. I still think of you as sicortar."

"Thank you for the food, Dresolor."

"It is my honor."

He places the tray on the table and leaves. I go to it and force myself to eat enough to sustain me for the day. I am sure it is delicious, but all I can taste now is misery. My meal over, I put the tray away, then go out to my drone, programming it for the journey to the house where Melinda used to live. With a heavy heart, I watch through the window as the drone rises up into the air and flies toward her. I know, coming up, is the most difficult conversation I will ever have. I send a prayer to Taya to help me. *Please, let Melinda forgive me. Please, please, let her come back to me.* I do not hold out much hope though. I know my Melinda.

Chapter 43

Melinda

Desimar looks up in surprise as Wyatt and I climb into his waiting drone after Troy. "Melinda. I did not expect you to join us on this excursion." His eyes turn to Wyatt. "And this is?"

"Desimar, please meet Wyatt, my ex-mate."

His smile is cautious as he approaches Wyatt for the traditional Krovatian greeting, planting a hand on the middle of his chest then bowing. "Welcome, Wyatt. You are to come with us today? Have you been granted permission?"

Wyatt is about to babble an excuse, so I speak up for him. "Our invitation from the command center states that permission is granted for three humans from Earth's delegation to visit today. Well, here we are, three humans from Earth, coming to represent our planet."

Desimar looks doubtful, but then shrugs. "In that case, let us be on our way. We have strict instructions to arrive eighteen beats after sunrise."

Wyatt comes to sit beside me on the drone, strapping the safety belt around him. His face has gone pale and all at once, I remember how I felt, weeks ago at the water city, when we climbed the tall tower in our flimsy rafts. I bring his head to my shoulder and encircle his larger hands in mine as best I can. "It's ok, honey."

"I know. I'll be fine; don't worry."

"Hold on to me. I'm here with you all the way."

He tucks his face into the crook of my neck and brings one of his arms around my waist, holding on to me tightly. I'm relieved he shows no hesitation in seeking out comfort from me. The Wyatt I knew before would never have done that. He was too imbued with the conditioning, passed down from his family and the social expectations around us, that men should show no weakness. This, however, is not weakness but strength. It takes strength to overcome your fears like Wyatt has done. I kiss the top of his head and whisper, "I'm so proud of you."

He responds with a tightening of his hold around me, then I hear the flutter of his voice in my ear. "I love you."

"I love you too."

Over his head, Troy and Desimar watch us, the one with sympathy, the other with curious interest. The drone engine starts and soon, we're up in the air on our way to the hilly quarter of the city, where this command center is located. Throughout our flight, Wyatt stays huddled close to me. I stroke his rumpled blond locks, my heart full. How is it possible to love two such different men so much? I want to spend the rest of my life with Kirimor, but I haven't stopped loving Wyatt. Life is so damned complicated. I try to put such thoughts away as our drone begins its descent and lands at our destination.

The command center is a large circular building with the typical Krovatian whitewashed exterior and a rooftop loaded with solar panel tiles. There's also something more—an arch of fluorescent blue light hovering above the building.

"What's that?" I ask Desimar, pointing to it.

"It is a force field that secures the building so that no harm can come to it."

"How is it powered?" wonders Troy.

Desimar's expression is blank. "As to that, I do not know exactly. Once we are inside, you may ask our guide."

"Definitely," agrees Troy.

By now, Wyatt has unplastered himself from my side. A little shamefaced, he murmurs in a low undertone so only I can hear, "Thanks."

I squeeze his hand in response, then weave my fingers through his. "Let's go see this place."

At the main entrance, two security guards check our credentials and search us with their scanners. After that, the entrance gate lifts to allow us inside an indoor courtyard where we go through a second round of checks. Security is tight. I feel a tingle of excitement and nerves at being allowed into this fortress. I'm sure Troy, with his ability to reproduce detailed technical drawings from memory, will be obtaining a load of valuable information today for us to relay back to Earth. I can't resist smiling a little at the thought—another positive notch on my belt as the leader of this diplomatic mission.

A Krovatian female, dressed in uniform, comes to greet us. She steps towards me first and places her palm on my chest, and I do the same. We step back and bow. "Welcome to the command center," she says. "I am Manolora, and I will be your guide today."

"Good to meet you, Manolora. I am Melinda Garcia, head of the human mission to Krovatia. This is Troy Summers, our lead engineer, and Wyatt Garcia, our cultural attaché." I make up Wyatt's job title on the hoof. He raises an amused brow at this but says nothing.

Manolora smiles at them and extends the traditional greeting. Once that is done, she beckons us forward. "Follow me."

She leads us up a set of stairs, then down a short corridor, explaining, "I will take you first to my quarters, where we can start with the briefing, then I will take you to the heart of the command center, where our specially trained team manages the force field above our planet."

"Thank you," says Troy. "I am very much looking forward to seeing this."

"Yes, I can understand that. Our security system is one of the best in the universe."

We arrive at a set of double doors, which Manolora opens with a scan of her palm. We enter a rectangular room, furnished simply with floor seats and a side table, along with a tall lectern with a computer console.

"Please, take a seat," says Manolora.

As we do so, Desimar hovers uncertainly by the doorway. "Excuse me," he says apologetically. "I think something I ate this morning has disagreed with me. Is it possible for me to go to an ablution room?"

Manolora gazes at him with sympathy. "Of course. Let me show you where to go." She smiles at us. "I will not be long. Please help yourselves to a drink of *nari*."

She exits the room with Desimar, returning less than a minute later. Going to her console, she taps a few keys and projects on a large screen in front of us a briefing video with instructions on do's and don'ts for our visit. We watch in polite silence and then all of us sign a declaration that we have understood the conditions under which we are allowed to tour the command center. As we are finishing up, there is a ring on the door, and Manolora opens it for Desimar.

I glance at him kindly. "Ok there, Desimar?"

"Yes, thank you. I am much better now."

He pats his stomach, but my eyes stray to a bulge in his loin cloth that wasn't there before. Is he aroused? That seems strange after a bout of indigestion. I quickly look up, not wanting to be rude. Nobody else seems to have noticed, thank goodness.

"Good," says Manolora. "Then we can be on our way to the operations room, the heart of our command center. Please remember to follow all our rules. No touching of any object or approaching any of our personnel."

"Understood," we chorus.

We follow her outside and walk further down the corridor to a set of elevators, which she summons. The door opens with a whoosh when one of them arrives, and we get inside. Manolora palms the reader to get it moving, and in moments, we are descending rapidly, my stomach plummeting. We land with hardly a bump, and the door slides open quietly in front of us.

We exit the elevator into a cool, white vestibule. In front of us are glass windows and a door, behind which I see a half dozen Krovatians in uniform, working at their consoles. I notice that the center of the room is dominated by a strange contraption that projects the blue, fluorescent light we saw earlier through an opening in the roof above it. This must be the force field. I'm curious, wondering whether this is what protects the building or whether this is the thing that is protecting the entire planet. I'm sure Troy has a million questions too.

We approach the door, where there is a security guard, standing to attention. He nods at us gravely, and taps a code to let us enter the room. The glass door slides open and we're in. The Krovatian nearest the door glances up from his console and smiles, before returning to his work. Manolora leads us in with another injunction to stay close to her and not touch anything. "This is our operations room. There are always six personnel on continuous rotation ensuring that the force field around our planet is working as it should. They also let our cargo ships or shuttles in and out when needed, after extensive security checks. Our system is second to none. Over here is where it all happens." She points to the curious blue light in the center of the room. "This—"

She's interrupted by a sharp sound. Startled, I turn to see Desimar holding a laser gun and pointing it right at us. Behind him, the security guard lies dead on the floor, brought down by the laser blast. The Krovatian who smiled at me a moment ago steps bravely forward, hands in the air. "I do not know who you are or what you want, but please stop. If you are here to bring down the force field, you will fail. Our security protocols will block all forced attempts to bring it down. Be sensible, and put down your weapon now."

Desimar's eyes gleam as his face takes on an unfamiliar, maniacal expression. "I think not," he says, and shoots the Krovatian down. I gasp and shift closer to Wyatt. Our hands find each other, squeezing tight, trying to both reassure and seek comfort.

Desimar grins in satisfaction at his handywork. He addresses us all, his gun still pointing in our direction. "I do not need to override your security protocols to bring it down, you fools. I can simply destroy this entire place. All around the building are my associates, each packing on their bodies a massive dose of high-caliber explosives. At precisely twenty-one beats after sunrise, they will all detonate them."

One of the Krovatians standing at his console responds, "No amount of external explosives can force their way through the force field. Your attempt will fail."

Desimar smirks. "Again, you are mistaken. There is one way to do so. If at the very same time, I detonate the explosives I am carrying—" Here he glances down at the bulge in his loin cloth and continues, "then the powerful surge of molten energy from the internal explosion will travel up this shaft and join forces and combust, creating the perfect storm we need to bring down this entire edifice."

The Krovatian pales, but retorts, "This is a suicide mission. You will perish along with all of us."

"Ah, but my name will live on eternally in the history books as the saviour of Krovatia!"

He's mad. Absolutely raving mad. And he's going to get us all killed.

Wyatt and I exchange glances. They say at moments like these, your entire life flashes in front of your eyes. That's not really true. I'm not thinking backward but forward. A thousand thoughts cross my mind. That if I'm about to die, then there's no one I'd rather be with than Wyatt. I'm also angry. What a wasted effort for Wyatt to overcome his fear of flying and come all the way here, only to die on the day of his arrival. I think of Kirimor. How will he react to news of my death? Will he be alright? I think of my family back home, mom, dad, my sister. What will happen to Krovatia if the force field is destroyed? Will it be invaded? Will the people I love be safe? I think of little Kiritela and my heart pinches in pain.

Desimar takes out his communicator and checks the screen, all the while holding his gun fixed towards us. "One tap here," he boasts, "and this place will turn into a raging inferno." He smiles at me, "Only a quarter of a beat until it's time. Say your prayers, Melinda." Then he sends a warning to one of the Krovatians in the room, "Do not even think of heroically tackling me to the ground. You take one step forward and I will detonate." He holds his communicator up threateningly, and the Krovatian backs away.

We all stand, frozen in place, our eyes on Desimar and the detonator in his hand.

This is it. There's no way out of this.

Then something very strange happens. Desimar's eyes go glassy, as if he's not really seeing us. He stares into space, and a slow angelic smile forms on his face.

Is he praying?

The smile turns into an expression of ecstasy.

What is going on?

Suddenly, he becomes alert again, looking straight at me. "I am so sorry," he says. Then very carefully, he places the communicator down at his feet and lowers his weapon. In seconds, the Krovatians are on him, holding him down and placing the detonator safely away. In that same instant, the building is rocked by a series of shudders and loud bangs. It takes me a moment to work out that Desimar's associates must have set off their explosives outside. Will the force field hold?

I walk into Wyatt's arms, wanting to be close to him. The building around us vibrates but holds strong. "We're going to be ok. We're going to be ok," I chant under my breath.

"What the fuck happened to him?" demands Wyatt in a shaky voice.

That's when it hits me. His evil energy must have been sucked out of him. Only one, maybe two, people could be responsible for that. "Kirimor," I whisper.

"Kirimor did this? You mean the evil sucking thing?"

"Yeah, I think so."

"Holy shit!"

A swarm of Krovatian guards are suddenly all around us. "Please come out, hands on your head," they bark at us. We're escorted out of the operations room, a shaken Manolora leading our group, her tail waving about frantically. As we move along, I have another realization. If Kirimor did this, then the after effects of his trance will drive him into a sexual frenzy. I need to get to him as quickly as I can.

People swarm around me as the Krovatian security forces direct us out of the building.

I need to get to Kirimor.

As we emerge outside, I'm stunned by thick black smoke, and stumble on some rubble. Wyatt steadies me with a strong arm. Together, we move hastily away from the burning detritus outside the command center. A few yards down, we come upon a wall of drones and security forces. They usher us through towards medical personnel, who take us into temporary erected tents and check us over.

I turn to Wyatt. "I need to go. I have to get to Kirimor."

"Right now?"

"It's urgent Wyatt. He needs me."

Something in my face convinces him of the urgency. "Ok, let me see what I can do."

Wyatt goes out of the tent and I see him accost the nearest security guard. He has a short conversation with him, flashing his sweet smile and using his irresistible charm. A minute later, he's back. "Ok, the guard has agreed to take us to the sicortar's house."

I glance at Troy. "Ok if I leave you?"

"I'll come with you. I need to be with Kiristen."

"Ok, let's go."

The guard is as good as his word, guiding us towards a parked drone a few feet away. We climb aboard quickly and strap in. Moments later, we're up in the air. Wyatt holds my hands, and I'm not sure who's doing the reassuring, him or me.

All through the journey, I keep a constant prayer, "Please God, don't let it be too late."

Troy uses his communicator to inform Kirimor's staff that we're on our way, and to let us through their security system. Then we're landing outside the house, a stone's throw from the temple. I wrench the drone door open, not waiting for the others, and run toward the temple building. I push inside and come to a sudden halt.

In front of me is a sight that will forever be etched into my memory—a bloodied Kirimor lying on top of that nubile young drasha. I stare in disbelief as he pounds her violently with his cock and bites her breasts. On and on he fucks her, viciously, violently. When finally he reaches his climax, he gives a thunderous roar, bucking into her wildly. Then he collapses, spent, a grimace on his semi-conscious face. I watch all this in stunned silence, immobile.

An arm comes around me. "Let's get out of here," mutters Wyatt.

I let him lead me out, barely able to put one foot in front of the other. Distantly, I hear him speak with Troy and the security guard, but I can't make out the words. He bundles me into the drone, and we lift off.

◆◆◆

The dream is vivid. Kirimor is running about like a raging bull, cock pointing to the sky, and crying out, "I need! I need!" I see him from a distance and try to make my way to him, but there are too many obstacles ahead of me.

I call out to him, "I'm here, Kirimor. Take me!" But in the chaos of his madness, he doesn't hear me. Instead, he rushes about heedlessly, smashing his fists on the furniture around him. In a fit of fury, he hammers his head to the wall, making the blood gush from his temple. In raw anguish, I hear him scream, "Melinda!"

I come awake with a start, heart pounding and sweat soaking my back. It takes me a moment to return to reality — the dream felt so real. *Kirimor*. His desperate cries still echo in my head.

Slowly, my heart resumes its normal beat as I lie in bed, remembering the events of that dreadful day. Beside me, Wyatt sleeps, snoring lightly. He's shared my bed, platonically, for the last two nights. He's held me and shown me love, helping me to lick my weeping wounds. Thank God he's here. I don't know how I would have coped otherwise.

From Kirimor, there's been no word, not that I'm ready to speak to him just yet. Through Kiristen, I've learned that he's been passed out in bed, recovering from the trauma of that holy trance and its aftermath. I don't know what I'll say to him when he eventually wakes and comes to see me, as I know he will. What do you say to the man you love, the man who saved your life, and the man who fucked another woman to do so?

A hand strokes down my arm. Wyatt drops a kiss on my shoulder. "I can hear your thoughts from here," he drawls sleepily.

I turn and accept his embrace, fitting my body to his warm, familiar one. I inhale the scent of him, the hint of woodsy cologne and his own male essence that I know so well. It smells like home.

"Sorry," I murmur. "I can't stop thinking about him."

"Perhaps it's time you talked. Do you know if he's woken yet?"

"Not sure. It should be today, I would think."

"Mel—" he pauses, searching for the right words. Drawing me close to him, he drops kisses on the top of my head. "If Kirimor hadn't done what he did, you and I would both be dead."

"I know."

"So maybe you shouldn't think of this as him betraying you, but him saving you. Can you find it in you to overlook what came next?"

"I don't know, Wyatt. I'm trying to. I want to. It's just… I can't forget what I saw and how it hurt me."

He sighs and holds me closer. I stroke my hands through his dark blond hair and thank my lucky stars for having Wyatt in my life still. In all the years we've been together, he's always been true and faithful. And what did I do? I threw it all away. I know it, just as surely as I know what a mess I've made of everything. I knew the risks of getting involved with Kirimor and his drashas. I tried to hold out and resist him for as long as I could, but then I gave in too soon and got burned.

I nestle into Wyatt's comforting body. Finally, he pulls away and strokes a hand along my cheek. "I love you, Mel. I know things are rough for you right now, but I promise everything will work out fine in the end."

"We'll see. Anyway, we better get up. You have rehearsals to get to and I have a meeting with Troy and Avery."

"Yes ma'am." He gives me a quick kiss then jumps out of bed and runs to the shower.

◆◆◆

We're sitting in the kitchen, sipping our first coffee, when Kirimor arrives. He walks in, escorted by Pravol who must have seen him arrive and opened the door for him. Our gazes meet over the top of my coffee cup, a somber expression in his dark hooded eyes. I put my cup down shakily.

Kirimor comes forward wordlessly. He's a little paler than usual and there's a bandage around his temple, but he still oozes overpowering masculinity. His tail jumps into the air and wraps around me. As it ties itself securely around my chest, Kirimor chooses to address Wyatt first. Placing a large hand on his shoulder, he booms, "Wyatt, are you well?"

"Ah, yes. Thank you I am."

Kirimor continues to survey him carefully. "They did not hurt you at the command center?"

"No, I'm uninjured thankfully."

"And your business here, how is it going? Do you need any assistance with it? Do not hesitate to ask, and I will do everything in my considerable power to help you."

Wyatt smiles uncertainly and says, "Thanks, Kirimor, I really appreciate that. We're happy with the venue and about to start rehearsing this morning. Tickets for our shows are meant to go on sale later today, and any help you can give to spread the word would be really appreciated."

Kirimor bares his teeth in a semblance of a smile. "Consider it done. I will get my aide, Sholinar, to contact you shortly so you can share with him the information you have about your program of shows. He will then make it his business to spread the word far and wide across this planet. There will not be a single empty seat in the audience for your shows."

"Thank you so much, Kirimor," Wyatt says, looking stunned. "This is more than generous of you. And thank you for saving our lives."

"No thanks needed. This is my honor and duty."

Kirimor finally turns his attention to me. "Melinda, come with me. We need to talk."

I'm half minded to kick up a fuss and say no, but I'm a mature woman and I know he's right. We do need to talk. I nod wordlessly and stand, Kirimor's tail still tied securely around me. "We will go to the cabin," he states.

Again, I'm about to demur, but I want our conversation to be private, and there are too many people around in this house. "Ok."

He leads me out to his drone, never releasing his tail's hold on me. Wordlessly I climb in and watch him start the engine. The flight to his home is short and silent, neither of us wanting to start this conversation in mid-air. I think of all the things I want to say to him. Where do I start?

The drone lands gently outside the cabin. As I catch sight of it, my heart lightens. This is such a happy place, already filled with many joyful memories. No wonder Kirimor wants me here for this talk.

We step out of the drone and walk together towards the front door. He opens it and ushers me in to the bank of seats at the end of the room, positioned with a view of the lush green valley outside. In the short time I lived here, I loved seeing this view every morning with my coffee.

We sit, still not talking. I focus my gaze on the green grass outside. "Melinda, look at me." My eyes fly to his. Caught in his regard, I can't look away. "Melinda, I know you are hurt. I hurt that you are hurt." His deep voice reverberates in my heart. "But know this one important thing, my lovely. Until the end of time, you will be mine and I will be yours. The bond we have cannot be undone. Even if you decide to journey light years away back to Earth, you will still be mine, always. I will never, *never*, invite another into my bed or into my heart."

I know he means every word. I believe him. And yet. "I saw you fuck her!"

"I know."

"You bit her breasts and spilled your cum into her!"

"I know"

"It hurt! It still hurts every time I remember it."

"I know, my love."

"Why couldn't you have waited a little longer? I was on my way to you."

"I tried. I knew I had to get through it alone. It drove me so mad I was banging my head to the wall. I was not going to fuck anyone if I could help it."

"So, what happened?"

"My rage must have worried those around me. Maybe it was the fact I was hurting myself and gushing blood. In the end, Sholinar restrained me and forced me to my knees. He is much stronger than I realized. He locked me in his arms and ordered Pirofena to mount me."

"That's not what I saw when I arrived."

He sighs. "No, it isn't. You see, once her moist cunt wrapped around my cock, I lost control. But there was also something else that caused me to go over the edge."

"What's that?"

He takes a deep breath before saying it. "I smelled her and she was in her breeding period. The aroma of a female when she is ready for breeding is indescribably intoxicating to a male."

My heart pounds like a hammer in my chest. "What are you saying, Kirimor?"

"She was in her breeding period, and when I emptied my seed into her, I bred her."

Pain lances through me. "She's pregnant?"

"Yes, it is confirmed."

I breathe in and out in loud gasps, trying to control my escalating anger and grief. I can't speak for the pain. His voice is rough with emotion as he says, "I am so sorry, Melinda. I never wished to cause you this pain."

"You were supposed to have a child with me!"

"Perhaps we still can—"

"No! Don't even say it! It's too late for that. It's too fucking late!"

"No, it is not. I know how much you want a child. As soon as you enter your breeding period, we can try for one."

"No! That would be your seventh kid, Kirimor. Even by your standards that's far too many. And it won't take away the fact that your child is growing in her belly as we speak. What will you do about that?"

"There is not much I can do except love that child and raise it as I have raised the rest of my children. Pirofena already lives in my house, under my protection. She will get all the care and help she needs."

"And what about me?"

"Perhaps you will love that child too, the way you love my other children." His words may hold truth, but right now, I very nearly hate that child for existing when I wanted one of my own with Kirimor. I can't even begin to think about having a relationship with him or her.

"This is too much to take, Kirimor."

"You can take it, Melinda, because you are strong. We will get through this together."

I wipe a tear furiously and get to my feet. "No, I don't think we can." I go to the closet and open it, taking out my belongings. The loin cloths I leave behind. I'm not going to parade myself topless with Kirimor's markings on me. With determined focus, I pack the most important of my things. The rest can be sent across later.

"Melinda, do not do this."

I ignore him.

"Melinda!"

I finish my packing and glare at him. "Kirimor, whatever we had together was destroyed the minute you fucked your drasha and put your seed in her. This is not something I can come back from. Ever!"

I storm out of the cabin and over to the waiting drone. When I get there, I realize I still need Kirimor's help to fly back home. He follows after me, bellowing, "Melinda, you are making a foolish mistake. You belong to me!"

I gaze at him icily. "I belong to no one. Now please, have the courtesy to take me back."

His tail whips around me furiously, lashing me to him. With powerful hands, he holds my face and captures my lips. I try to kick against him but he holds firm. His tongue probes my mouth, demanding entry, but I deny him. He simply redoubles his efforts, licking the seam of my lips over and over until I give way and part them. He plunges in, kissing me roughly, hungrily, like a starving man faced with a banquet. His familiar, masculine taste overwhelms me. Soon, I'm kissing him back just as desperately. It's only been two days, but God how I've missed him!

His hands roam about my body, moulding me to him. In one swift move, he rips my panties away, baring my pussy to his ravaging fingers. He palms my mound, then plunges a searching digit inside me, testing my readiness for him. It emerges wet and dripping. Next moment, he's lifting me and pressing me against the cool metal exterior of the drone. I wrap my legs around him instinctively as he presses into me, filling me as nobody else has ever done. With each thrust of his cock, he snarls, "You. Are. Mine."

With mindless abandon, he fucks me against the drone. I welcome each thrust, gasping at the powerful intrusion. "You are mine, do you hear?" he cries again, then he's fusing his mouth to mine, possessing me in every possible way. I'm swept away in a rip tide of passion and need. The pounding of his cock inside me ignites every nerve cell in my body. My pussy throbs as the blood flows straight to my core. His tongue strokes roughly against mine, sucking me into him while he thrusts deep into my body and my soul. My climax is a massive pulsing wave of pleasure, taking me unaware. I clench around him, pulse after powerful pulse, and then he too is going over the edge. With a loud roar, he plunges one last time and showers me with his cum.

He pins me to the drone as we slowly come back to our senses. With it returns the reality of my situation. This passionate joining changes nothing. He's still having a baby with that pretty girl who's at least twenty years younger than me. It's a gnawing, aching pain that won't leave me.

Finally, he lifts his head and stares at me with his dark eyes. "You belong to me, Melinda, and you know it."

I sigh. "I'm not going to argue with you over this, Kirimor. I love you and perhaps you're right, the bond we have cannot be broken. But I'm too hurt to be with you and I'm leaving. Now."

His nostrils flare, but all he says is, "Very well. Let us go."

He pulls out of me, looking in satisfaction at the cum that streams down my leg. Keeping his tail around me, he lets me climb aboard the drone, then starts the engine. We're silent again on the journey home. As we begin our descent, my spirits sink low along with the drone. This is it. After this, who knows when I'll see him again.

We land on the ground, but neither of us moves. We sit a moment longer in silence.

"Melinda. That cabin in the mountains is your home. I will arrange for you to receive your own drone and it will be cleared to pass through my security system. Whenever you wish to return, all you have to do is fly it to the cabin. Day or night, I will welcome you by my side, my love. I am yours, for eternity. Do not ever doubt it."

I nod mutely, then open the drone door and climb down. Without looking back, I go to my front door, unlock it with my code and enter.

Chapter 44

Kirimor

One quarter moon rotation has passed without my love by my side. I obtain daily news about her from Kiristen who gets it from Troy. I have even spoken to Wyatt, under the pretext of asking after his shows. As promised, they have all sold out, and later tonight, I am taking my sons and daughters to a concert by a famous Earth musician called Ricky Charles.

I sit on the bench facing the mountainside view, idly strumming on my lanjo. Melinda loved spending her mornings here beside me as I played my music, enjoying the sight of endless verdant hills. My heart pinches in pain. Wherever she is right now, she is hurting too, I know. How do I ease this pain? What am I to do to get her back? I cannot undo the thing that is causing her to hurt the most—that baby growing in Pirofena's belly.

There is a knock at the door. "Enter!" I call out.

Kiristen walks in, and spotting me on the bench, comes to sit beside me. I continue playing, and he sits listening, not talking, until I put the instrument down. "What is it, son?" I murmur.

His tail twitches and flutters over my legs. I bring my own tail up and tangle it with his in a gesture of comfort. Sometimes, such gestures are more powerful than words. We sit there for a long while, our tails joined in solidarity. Eventually, he speaks. "Mother is desperately sorry, pa. She wonders if or when you will ever forgive her."

I give a long exhale of displeasure. For this past quarter moon rotation, I have made the cabin my home. I have avoided even going inside the main house, except when absolutely necessary. I have found it difficult to talk to Merostena after the role she played that fateful day.

"She hurt me deeply and betrayed my trust."

"I know, pa."

"With deep feminine intuition, she struck at Melinda where she knew it would hurt her most—her childlessness. She knew what sending Pirofena to me in her breeding time would do. She banked on the fact it would drive Melinda away, and hoped it would restore me to them as before."

"All this, I know. Undoubtedly, she has done wrong. She knows this and is sorry."

I nod wordlessly. I hope in time, I will be able to overcome my hurt and distrust of my old companion. But not right now.

"All this will take time, Kiristen. Right now, my priority is Melinda. Healing her hurt is what matters to me most. Your mother will have to wait."

"I understand."

"What news do you have of Melinda?"

"She will be at the concert tonight."

"I thought as much. Hearing the excited way she talked about this Ricky Charles, I know she would not want to miss his show."

"Troy too is full of anticipation. I am excited to see what the fuss is all about."

"We must be prepared for the fact that this man's music speaks to Humans more than us. However, I am going with an open mind."

"Great art should transcend all barriers."

"That is true, my son."

He kisses my cheek. "I shall see you later, pa. Go in peace."

"Go in peace, my beloved son."

I think of Melinda as I wait patiently in the drone for each of my children to get on board. She is never far from my mind. I am in the larger craft as we are all travelling together. This one can easily fit the seven of us, including Troy, who has moved in with Kiristen permanently. Soon, there will be one more. I have seen Pirofena only briefly to ask after her health, but the baby seems to be growing healthily. It is much too soon for us to discover its sex or for a bump to show on Pirofena's belly, but already, I love this child and look forward to the day when I can hold him or her in my arms. No matter the circumstances of its conception, this child is a blessing and will be loved. I only hope Melinda will see it this way one day, when the hurt has faded.

Kiritela runs up the steps to the drone and rushes toward me. "Pa!" I hold out my arms for my little star. She wraps her slim tail around my middle, planting a sloppy kiss on my cheek. "Little star, how was your day?" I ask tenderly.

"It was ok." This little jargon she has learned from being around Troy, who uses it a lot in his speech. "I have been waiting all day to go and see the Humans perform their music."

"And now we are going."

"Will we see Melinda there?"

My little star misses Melinda greatly. She keeps asking when she will come back. Unfortunately, I have not been able to give her a satisfactory answer.

"I hope so."

The other children troop inside the drone. Kirilor, my middle son, comes to sit beside me and repeats his younger sister's question. "Will Melinda be there?"

It is a testament to Melinda that all my children are already so deeply attached to her. She is made for motherhood. I still do not fully understand why she and Wyatt did not have a child of their own. It pains me that she refuses to have mine. I give my son the same answer. "I hope so, Kirilor. I have missed her very much."

Kirishar, always so earnest and thoughtful, pins me with a glance. "Will she ever forgive you, father?"

That boy understands far more than he should. I honor his question with a considered response. "I do not think it is a matter of forgiveness, Kirishar, but more a matter of hurt. I think it will take some time for it to stop causing her so much pain. I believe time is a great healer, but I am impatient and want her back as soon as possible. I must do something to help ease that pain and show her how much she is loved."

"What do you propose?" asks Kiristen, just as our drone rises into the air.

"I do not know, my son. It is taxing my mind greatly."

"Some kind of grand gesture should do the trick," agrees Troy. "She's aching to be back with you, but that whole baby thing is what is holding her back. It's not easy to see a woman half your age carry the child you so desperately wanted to have yourself."

"What kind of grand gesture could I do? I am not a theatrical person prone to that kind of thing. I would do anything in my power to bring her happiness. But what?"

Troy shrugs. "You're asking the wrong person. The most romantic thing I've ever done is get down on one knee and propose to this one here." He brings an arm around Kiristen and draws his body to him, kissing the top of his head.

Kiristen sighs happily. "It was very romantic, my love."

It is bittersweet to watch these two together. They are so happily in love—a sad contrast to my misery.

Kirimara ponders the issue then states, "Pa, you are a public figure still. Could you not do something on the news broadcasts perhaps? Make a public declaration of your love in front of everyone. Would she like that do you think?"

I think about it. "It is a possibility. I am not sure if that would sway her."

"You could take her on a ride in the ocean with Turi," suggests Kirishar helpfully.

"Have Dresolor cook her a feast with her favorite Human foods," thinks Kirilor.

Kiritela wraps her arms around my neck. "Sing her a song, pa. You sing so well."

Her older sister laughs. "That is not a half bad idea."

As the drone begins its descent to our destination, I say, "Thank you all. You have given me much to think about."

I sit in the auditorium of the university lecture hall. As a former sicortar, I have been afforded pride of place at the front with my family. My eyes search the audience for Melinda, but there is no sign of her or Wyatt. To occupy myself, I read through the program about Ricky Charles. According to it, he is a country rock singer from a town called Nashville. I am not sure what country and rocks have to do with music. Could it be he sings odes to the geology of the country? We have a tradition here on Krovatia of composing poems to celebrate nature, so perhaps it is something in the same vein.

The lights dim and a hush comes over the audience. To my right, I spot some movement. It is Melinda arriving with Wyatt. As she takes her seat, she feels my eyes on her and looks up. We stare at each other across the short distance. Then she looks away and sits down.

A spotlight illuminates the center of the stage. Into it struts a man, holding an instrument close in looks to a lanjo. I sit up. This could be interesting after all. He smiles at the audience and addresses us, "Hello Krovatians. It's an honor to be here. Here's a song I wrote." And he starts strumming on his lanjo-like instrument. His voice, when he begins to sing, is deep and melodious. His song is about the joys and anxieties of first time fatherhood. I listen to it, smiling at a lyric which reminds me of myself when I first held Kiristen in my arms. I glance across at Melinda. Her eyes are fixed on the stage, her hand rubbing her chest through the thin material of her dress. *Oh my darling love, how I wish I could ease this ache.*

The concert progresses, this time with other musicians joining in to create a cacophony of loud sound. It takes a while for my ears to accustom themselves to it, but somehow, I find myself swaying to the beat of the music. I listen intently to the intelligent, insightful words Ricky Charles sings. He is talented. I can see that. Every so often, I cast my eyes towards Melinda. Several times, they cross paths with her eyes on me. I cannot help myself from mouthing, "I love you." Her eyes widen, then she looks away again. But then, as if she cannot help herself, she looks to me again. I mouth the words once more, "I love you." I see her breath hitch as she stares at me. Finally, she looks away again. This time, she maintains self-control and stubbornly refuses to look my way again.

There is a lull, then Ricky Charles addresses the audience. "This last song tonight is one that has great meaning for me. It's about a time I did something that hurt someone I love. I wrote the song with the hope that one day, the hurt would heal enough for her to forgive me. The song is called 'One Day'."

Melinda and Wyatt rise to their feet and hold out their communicators with the flash light on. *Curious.* I see other Humans in the audience do the same. As the music starts, they sway from side to side with their lights casting a glow, like stars in the night sky. Soon, other Krovatians take the hint, and they too stand with their communicator lights on. Troy gets to his feet and holds out his light. Kiristen too. Within a short time, we are all on our feet, swaying our lights back and forth. And then, Ricky Charles starts to sing.

I know you hurt, my love I hurt too…

The song continues, detailing the rupture between the lovers and the hope that one day, they will re-unite. When the song finishes, the audience spontaneously breaks out into loud humming. I realize there are tears on my cheeks. I gaze across at Melinda. Tears streak her face too. We stare at each other for an endless moment. Then it is gone. The lights come back on in the auditorium, and the concert is over. People start filing out, a rumble of voices as they exclaim about the performance. Melinda and Wyatt disappear from my sight.

"That was amazing," enthuses Kirimara.

"I loved it. Especially that final song," agrees Kiristen.

I look at my son. "Kiristen, I think I know what grand gesture to make."

He smiles. "I'm glad."

Chapter 45

Melinda

We're back from the concert, which was a great success. All day, Wyatt has been stressing about it. The soundcheck was a disaster. The sound system wasn't working properly. Ricky Charles stormed off and had a hissy fit in his dressing room. Wyatt finally managed to talk him out of his funk. At one point, it looked as if the whole thing would never get off the ground. At the last minute, it came together. We got to our seats just as the lights dimmed, and I saw Kirimor. I couldn't look away. His eyes looked so sad. He mouthed, "I love you" to me several times. I wanted to say it back, but I didn't.

Now we're in my room, and Wyatt is pacing about excitedly, still on a high from the success of the evening. He's on a call with Rivlor, telling her all about it. I hadn't realized he had formed such a strong friendship with the Venorian commander of the cargo ship. She's also an investor in his venture, so I guess she has a right to know how it went.

He grins into the camera, "You should have seen the auditorium light up with thousands of communicator lights for the last song. It was magical."

Her deep, melodious voice responds, "I hope to see it for myself when he performs on Ven. Cute boy, I am glad it went so well."

Cute boy?

Wyatt finally ends the call and undresses. We haven't been intimate since he came here. He sleeps in his boxers and I wear a tank top and panties to bed. I don't know if Kirimor and I will ever get back together, but I know that Wyatt and I are finally over, much as I love him. We should have cut that cord long ago. Now, I want more than anything for that love we had to morph into deep and lasting friendship. I think we're on our way there.

He goes to the bathroom then comes back and gets into bed beside me. I turn and lie on my side, facing him. "So, it's cute boy is it?"

He blushes. "It's not what you think. Just a private joke we have going. Rivlor has been a very good friend to me, nothing else."

"You're free to make it into something else, if that's what you want."

He gives me a pained look. "You're what I want, Mel. Is there really no hope?"

I touch his stubble roughened cheek. "It's time to go our separate ways, honey. Being with Kirimor has made me see that."

He blows out a long breath and stares at the ceiling. "I know. I'm beginning to realize it too."

"I know it's a cliché, but I think we can become just good friends."

"What, when I stop finding you hot and wanting to fuck you?"

I laugh. "When you put it like that…" On a more serious note, I ask, "When was the last time you had sex with someone else? Truth time."

His face takes on a sober expression. "Last time I put my dick in another woman was a week before I met you, twenty years ago."

I sigh. "That's a long time."

"Yeah. Mel, you've been the only woman in my life since I met you."

"I'm sorry it didn't work out."

"Me too."

I trace a finger along the golden hair on his arm. "In all that time, haven't you been attracted to others and wondered what it would be like to have sex with them?"

He quirks a brow. "Mel, I'm an ordinary human, not a saint."

"So, just think. Now that we've finally cut that cord, you're free to explore those other possibilities. Act on any attraction that comes your way without any guilt."

"I guess so. We'll see."

"So, Rivlor?"

"I meant what I said. We're just friends."

"Would you like it to be more?"

He exhales loudly. "Mel, I am not having this conversation with you. Don't fob me off on others to make you feel better about dumping me."

"Was that what I was doing? I'm sorry."

He sighs. "I'm sorry too. Come here. Let me just hold you."

I roll over into his arms. We stay like this a long time. "I'll always love you, Wyatt."

"I'll always love you too."

Next morning, I'm in the kitchen, sipping on some coffee, when Kiristen walks in. I smile at him. "Hey, how was it for you last night?"

"It was amazing. This Ricky Charles is incredibly talented. I feel honored to have been in the audience."

"I'm glad."

"Melinda, there is someone who wishes to speak with you."

I put down my coffee cup and look at him enquiringly. "Who would that be?"

"My mother. She is sitting by the pool. I told her to wait there."

"Why does she want to see me?"

"I will let her speak for herself, but please Melinda, will you give her a little of your time?"

"Sure."

I stand and follow him out of the room, towards the small central yard. I see her sitting on a lounge chair in the shade. As I slide open the glass door, Kiristen stops me with a hand on my arm. "I will give you privacy for this talk. Please tell ma I will wait for her in the drone."

"Ok."

I step outside and make my way towards Merostena. She stands at my approach, and I greet her with a palm to her chest, followed by a bow. "Merostena, this is a surprise. What can I do for you?"

She gazes at me sadly. "I have come, Melinda, to explain things to you and beg for your forgiveness."

Puzzled, I gesture for her to sit down and take a seat on a nearby lounger. I wait for her to speak. She's silent for a few beats, then gathers the courage to look me in the eye. "Melinda, it is a very shameful thing to admit, but I have harbored jealousy of you ever since you caught Kirimor's eye. You see, I have loved him many, many sun rotations, but I know he has never returned those feelings. I took comfort in the knowledge that I was his lead drasha and the mother of his two eldest children, that I was his companion for life even if he did not feel romantic love for me."

She clasps her hands in her lap. "Then you came along, and it was clear that Kirimor had fallen head over heels in love with you. When he announced that he was stepping down as sicortar and releasing us from our duties as drashas, I felt bereft. I am ashamed to say I felt anger towards you for taking him from us. Then came that day when he went into a holy trance and came out of it in a mad sexual rage. He was beating himself up against the wall and raging. He kept saying your name over and over. Sholinar became concerned that he was going to seriously injure himself and ordered me to bring a drasha to him. I saw my chance. All morning, I had scented Pirofena, and I knew she was in her breeding time. Cleotola wanted to put herself forward for the task, but I insisted it had to be Pirofena. I nearly dragged the poor girl to the temple in my haste. You see, I knew in my heart that having Kirimor breed her would drive a wedge between you and him. It was very wrong of me. I know that. I am so sorry, Melinda. I would like to ask for your forgiveness, and if you are unable to give it, then at the very least forgive Kirimor. He is heart sick for you."

Throughout this speech, I've been listening, horror stricken. So this happened on purpose, not by accident. This woman sitting in front of me purposely put a dagger into my heart in a fit of jealousy.

Can I ever forgive her? I take a deep breath in and try to center myself. Do I want to hold on to hate and resentment? No. It will only poison my life.

"What you did was very wrong and very hurtful. You achieved your ends, but somehow I doubt it brought you what you wanted."

"No," she agrees, "it did not."

"I will forgive you, Merostena, but I don't think I can forget. I will ask you please, henceforth, to stay out of my life and stay out of my business."

She nods in acquiescence. I stand, the interview over. She stands too. "Go in peace, Melinda."

"Go in peace. Kiristen awaits you in the drone."

She inclines her head and turns to go. I watch her leave, then I set about the usual tasks of my day, my heart heavy.

Chapter 46

Wyatt

I'm sitting in the auditorium, idly watching a rehearsal for our first night of ballet performances. My communicator is never out of my hands as I send and respond to messages. We still have a run of performances to do in Ven and Driskia, and ten million and one things to organize. I'm so focused on my task that I don't notice a person take a seat next to me until he flicks his tail in my direction.

I look up and see Kirimor. My rival. My nemesis. The man who captured the heart of the woman I love. But also the man who saved my life. I shouldn't forget that. Instead of a scowl, I simply give him a cold look. "Kirimor, what can I do for you?"

"Wyatt, I want to congratulate you on the success of your venture. I thoroughly enjoyed the Ricky Charles concert, and I hear good things about the dramatic performances you put on these last few rotations."

"Thank you."

He looks across at the dancers on the stage and frowns. "Does it not hurt them to dance on the tip of their toes?"

I laugh. "A little maybe, but they are used to it. They wear special shoes called pointe shoes that give their toes support."

"I see."

He is quiet as he watches a couple of dancers perform a pas de deux. Finally, he turns back to me. "Wyatt, there is something I would like to ask you."

I raise a brow. "Yes?"

"I would like to make a grand gesture to show Melinda how much I love her."

My expression cools. "And?"

"And I would like your help to make that happen."

I snicker. "You want me to help you win back the woman I love? You're kidding, right?"

"I am deadly serious."

"Why the fuck should I be helping you?"

"You are under no obligation to help me. However, if you truly love Melinda, then perhaps you would wish her to be happy."

I look away, a lump in my throat. It has been hard seeing Mel so sad the last few weeks.

Encouraged, he continues. "I know I can bring her much happiness. Wyatt, she belongs with me. Each day that we are apart is a miserable, unhappy day for the both of us."

I huff out a breath. "So what do you want me to do?"

"I would like you to convince Ricky Charles to accompany me in a special rendition of 'One Day', just for Melinda."

"You want to serenade her? How? When?"

"On the last night of the ballet. We have tickets for the performance, and I want you to make sure Melinda is there in a prime seat. At the end of the ballet, I would like to come onstage with Ricky Charles and for him to say to the audience that he is here on a special request to sing a song for a beautiful lady named Melinda. And then we shall sing it together — although it would be preferable if I spend some time with Ricky beforehand to rehearse it so it is as perfect as possible."

I stare at him dumbfounded. Then I start to laugh. "Can you at least sing?"

He puffs out his massive chest. "Of course I can sing."

"So, you'll do your song, then what?"

"Then, I shall get down on one knee and ask Melinda to marry me. That is how it is done in your culture, is it not?"

"Yeah." I look away, not wanting him to see my eyes glaze over. I blink several times to regain control.

"Ok," I say.

"You will do it?"

I pick up my communicator and call Ricky Charles. He answers on the third ring. "Hey Ricky, how you doing? That's great. Listen Ricky, I have an interesting proposition for you…"

Five minutes later, the deal is done. Kirimor puts out his hand and I shake it. "I meant what I said that first day. You hurt Mel, and you'll answer to me."

He nods gravely. "Never again, if it is in my power. All I want is to make her happy."

"Ok then."

Chapter 47

Melinda

All night, I toss and turn, unable to get Merostena's confession out of my mind. If I can forgive her, then surely I can forgive Kirimor too.

The truth is, I forgave him a long time ago. Thinking on the chain of events, I don't know that he could have done things any differently. He acted honorably throughout. He always made sure not to promise fidelity so long as he was still sicortar. I knew the deal. In an emergency, he would have to act in accordance with the duties of his position. It sucks that as a result, Pirofena became pregnant with his child.

I bunch up my pillow for the hundredth time.

So, he's going to be a dad again, and the baby won't be mine. I should get over myself. It's not the end of the world. I love all his kids. They have already charmed their way into my heart. Little Kiritela. Earnest and serious Kirishar. And all the rest. This sweet innocent baby won't be any different. He or she will be a part of him. How can I not love that child? Of course I will.

So, Mel, what's the hold up? Just get over your pride and go to him.

It takes a long time, but I eventually fall into a fractured sleep. I wake up in the morning heavy eyed. Wyatt slumbers peacefully next to me looking positively angelic. I poke him in the arm. "Hey, Wyatt. Wake up."

He groans and turns to sleep on his other side. I poke him again. "Wake up, I need to talk to you."

"What is it?" he mumbles.

"I'm going back to Kirimor."

That wakes him. He sits up, rubbing his eyes sleepily. "Say that again."

"It's time I get over myself and go back to Kirimor. I'll take the drone and go to him after breakfast."

"Wait up, wait up. What's the big rush?"

"Wyatt, when you realize you want to spend the rest of your life with somebody, you want the rest of your life to start right away."

"Isn't that a famous quote from an old movie?"

"It is, but it's also very true."

"Ok right, but maybe take some time to think it over. How about you wait until after the performance tonight? I know Kirimor has got tickets to go."

I consider it. "No, I still think it's better if I go to him now. Think about it. We could go to the ballet together as a date if we're back together again."

"Mel, I really think you should wait."

I frown at him. "Wyatt, are you still harboring a hope that you and I might get back together? Is that it?"

He blows out a frustrated breath. "No, that's not it at all. I just think the timing is off. Best wait until the evening to see him."

I narrow my eyes at him. "Wyatt Garcia, what aren't you telling me?"

He holds his hands up innocently. "Nothing. Just stating an opinion."

"Well in that case, I beg to differ from that opinion. I'm going to him straight after I've had my coffee."

He huffs. "If that's what you want, then do it."

I stand and march to the bathroom. "I will."

A half hour later, I climb into the drone and program the journey to the cabin. I tap my fingers impatiently throughout the short journey. Now that my decision's been made, I can't wait to see him again. The drone lands, and before the engine even has a chance to shut off, I'm out of it and scrambling towards the cabin. I open the door and step inside. "Kirimor!"

I'm met with silence. It doesn't take me long to realize he's not in. I pace about restlessly. Should I just wait for him here? Or should I call and find out where he is? I hold my communicator indecisively. Perhaps I should call. I'm about to tap his name when there's a knock on the door. A moment later, Kiristen walks in. He stops in his tracks when he sees me. "Melinda! I did not expect to see you here." Then his face breaks into a grin. "I am so glad you came." He rushes over to me and holds out his arms. I walk into them and feel him hold me tight. "We've missed you so much. Pa will be so happy when he finds out you are here."

I step away and ask, "Where is he?"

"He has had to go on a last minute trip to the eastern sector to look at some parts for a new machine he is building."

"Oh. Will he be back for the ballet tonight?"

"Yes, I believe he plans to go straight to the university and meet us there. Will you be going too?"

"Yes, I wouldn't miss the final night's performance."

"Perhaps I can escort you there?"

"Would you mind? I know Wyatt needs to go there extra early, but I'd rather not."

"It will be my privilege. I will come and get you with my brother and sisters and Troy. They have all missed you and will be so excited to see you."

I smile. "I've missed them too."

"Then it is settled."

Reluctantly, I follow him out the door. With a murmured "Go in peace," we each get into our separate drones and fly out.

Ok, so the rest of my life won't start quite as soon as I wanted. Patience. Only a few hours more and I'll see him at the ballet. Perhaps I should wear that dress again, the one I wore at the banquet. Or not. Maybe I should go dressed in just my Krovatian loin cloth. My lips quirk into a crafty smile.

Chapter 48

Kirimor

Trust my challenging Earth female to scupper all my plans. I had to beat a hasty exit from the cabin when Wyatt called telling me Melinda was on her way. What I would have given to have seen her! But I have made my plans.

I have spent several rotations in preparation. There is a feast of delicious Earth dishes—plus a plate of *mishu*—being prepared by Dresolor as we speak. Yesterday, I finally managed to locate Turi after a long swim in the ocean. She whistled her agreement when I outlined my plan.

And of course, I have spent many beats with Ricky Charles, practising the song. I believe our harmonious rendition will impress my lovely female. I very much hope so. I have also, with Wyatt's assistance, procured her ring size and had a beautiful golden ring, set with a vlor stone, made especially for her. All is ready and now, I await the moment impatiently.

Kiristen has been told to make excuses to Melinda for my tardiness. She believes I am still stuck in the eastern sector, unavoidably delayed. In actual fact, I am backstage, among the dancers and musicians that will be performing tonight. I watch in amusement as Wyatt paces back and forth, stressing out about this, that or the other. That male certainly has a nervous disposition. He needs a calm, soothing presence in his life, like that magnificent Venorian female that called him cute.

The curtain goes up. I watch the performance from the wings. From the looks and sounds of it, it is going well. Wyatt comes to stand beside me and instinctively, I wrap my tail around him. "Relax, Wyatt. All is going well. It is I who should be nervous, not you."

I release him from my grasp as he raises a brow. "And you're not?"

I shrug. "Perhaps only a little."

"Well it helps to know she wants you back."

I make a happy rumbling sound in my chest. "That it does."

The curtain goes down on the performance. The dancers take their bows amidst the loud hums of appreciation. I take out my communicator and send a one word message to Kiristen. "Ready?"

He responds with a thumbs up, another new habit inspired by Troy. I look over at Ricky Charles, standing on the other side of the wings, and nod. Seeing the signal, Wyatt has the curtain rise again. Holding a guitar in one hand —that is what that lanjo-like instrument is called—Ricky Charles struts onto the stage. An excited murmur goes through the crowd. Then they hush in anticipation.

"Good evening, everyone. My name is Ricky Charles and I'm here tonight by special request to sing a song for a beautiful lady named Melinda. Someone you all know is here to sing the song with me. Kirimor, please join me onstage!"

I know my cue. Without hesitation, I walk onto the stage and join Ricky Charles. I turn to him. "Thank you, Ricky, for agreeing to this very special request." Then I face the audience, unable to locate Melinda in the darkness of the auditorium, but trusting that she is there. "Melinda, my love, this song is for you."

Ricky Charles begins to strum the first chords on his guitar. It has been agreed that I will sing the first part alone, then he will join me on the chorus in a beautiful harmony. I take a deep breath and begin to sing as if my life depends on it.

I know you hurt, my love I hurt too
I know what I did, what I did, what I did was
wrong
but I can't take it back. All I can hope is that

The song continues until Ricky Charles strums the final chords, then silence falls. I address the darkness of the audience. "Melinda, my love, please come up here."

There is some slight scuffling, then I see a tall form stand and make its way towards the stage. As she approaches, I see her face for the first time, wet with tears. Stumbling a little, she climbs the steps onto the stage and walks towards me. She stops a few paces away, her eyes welling with emotion. I fall to one knee. "Melinda, love of my life. If the past half moon rotation has taught me anything, it is that life without you is devoid of joy. If you will let me, I would like to spend the rest of my days by your side, filling both our cups with overflowing joy and happiness."

I take out the ring and proffer it to her. "Melinda, will you do me the honor of becoming my wife?"

She takes a step closer, then another, until she stands before me. Her lips tremble. Tears flow. Gently, I repeat the question. "Melinda, please will you marry me?"

"Yes," she croaks.

I take her hand and slip the ring on her engagement finger — I made sure to research which finger that is. Then I stand and pull her into my arms. Around us, the auditorium explodes into loud hums. I capture her lips with mine and kiss her for a long, long time. Finally, I pull back and say, "I love you."

She smiles through her tears. "I love you too, so much."

"I never want to be parted from you again."

"Me neither."

"Good." I kiss her again. As I do, I feel the curtain fall again, shielding us from the audience's view. Someone pats me on the shoulder. I look up into Ricky Charles's grinning face.

"Congratulations you two."

"Thank you," Melinda says. "That was the best surprise ever. Thanks for agreeing to do this with Kirimor."

He salutes me. "It was an absolute pleasure. I wish you both a very happy future together."

"Thank you, Ricky", I say. He nods and walks off.

Then it's Wyatt's turn. He points at Melinda and laughs, "Gotcha!"

She looks at him bewildered. "You knew?"

"Why else was I so keen to stop you from going to Kirimor's this morning."

She shakes her head. "I can't believe you helped him with this."

His smile is wry. "I can't either, but Mel, it's good to see you smile again. Be happy."

She sniffles and hugs him tight. "Thanks, Wyatt. You're the best."

"Nah, Kirimor is, but I'll take an honorable second place." He gives her a final pat on the shoulder, nods to me, and takes his leave.

"My lovely, it is time to go. We are to have a special celebration dinner with our family."

"Our family?"

"It is yours now, as much as mine."

"I like that."

"Then let us go."

◆◆◆

I come awake with a happy sigh feeling a welcome weight atop my body. I shift us sideways and snake my tail around her thighs. She makes an adorable grunting sound. "Blessed morning, my lovely", I murmur.

"Mmm."

"I have one more surprise for you."

She lifts one eye open. "What?"

"If I tell you it will not be a surprise. Let us get up and have that morning cup of coffee you love so much."

"Ok."

I sit up and get out of bed, striding towards the food preparation area in the cabin. I start making the coffee, as I have learned to do. A short time later, Melinda joins me, sniffing appreciatively. I pour her and myself a cup. We take our first sip of the hot brew.

"Ah, that's good," moans my lovely Earth female. She takes another sip, then puts the cup down. "So now, tell me what's the plan."

"We are going down to the beach for a swim."

"That's nice."

I smile and drink some more of my coffee. It is not quite as satisfying as a hot cup of *nari*, which is my usual preference in the mornings, but I am getting to appreciate the taste of it. "I was thinking, my lovely, about our future living arrangements. I believe, after all that has happened, that it would be preferable for us to live in this cabin permanently rather than build a private apartment for ourselves in the main house. What do you think of extending this place so there are rooms enough for the children, should they wish to sleep here?"

"I think that's a great idea. I've always loved this place. I think I would definitely prefer to live here."

"Then that is what we shall do." I lean over to kiss her. "Now, put on a loin cloth and let us go down to the beach."

A beat later, our drone drops us off on the edge of the powdery white sand. I take her hand in mine. "Come, my lovely."

Together we walk into the clear warm sea until it is up to Melinda's shoulders. "Mmm, this was a lovely idea, Kirimor."

"There is more." I whistle three times the agreed signal. Melinda looks on, puzzled. A moment later, I see Turi's dark gray form approach us.

"Oh, what's that?" cries Melinda.

I pull her to me. "Do not fret. It is my friend, Turi. She is come to give us a ride."

Turi nudges us gently and looks at us with her intelligent eyes. "Melinda, meet Turi."

She smiles in wonder. "Hello, Turi."

Turi whistles in response.

"She is telling us to climb on board," I say. I lift Melinda on top of Turi's back, then climb aboard behind her. With another whistle, Turi dives forward and begins whizzing through the waves. Melinda shrieks with joy as we travel at high speed in the water, feeling it splash our faces.

"This is great!"

I smile as she cries out again in excited pleasure. We travel like this for a few beats, enjoying the wind in our faces and cutting through the waves at top speed. Eventually, Turi loops around and returns us to the beach where we started. We get down, laughing joyfully.

Melinda strokes Turi's smooth back. "Thank you, Turi. I had such fun!"

Turi whistles in response.

"Thank you, old friend. Peace be with you." With a final whistle, Turi dives in the water and disappears into the distance.

Melinda beams at me. "That was incredible! Thank you for thinking of it."

"Actually, I must give credit to Kirishar. It was his idea."

"Then I definitely need to thank him."

I pull her to me. "Happy?"

"Very happy."

"Good." And then I kiss her.

Epilogue

Melinda

Ten years later

As our aircraft approaches the western shores of Lirisor, we all look out the windows, eager for our first glimpse of this island paradise. Kirimela is the first to catch sight of it. "Over there!" she calls excitedly.

Our eyes all follow where she's pointing. Towards the horizon of the seemingly endless expanse of turquoise sea below us, we see a strip of land. The shuttle which has transported us from Torbreg, the Venorian capital where we first landed a day ago, begins its descent, swooping gently towards that sandy shore.

As we reach the shore, the shuttle veers inland a little, circling a large, rambling house with pretty peach walls and multi-colored roof tiles. Two people are standing by the front of the house, looking up at us.

"There's Wyatt!" shouts Kiritela excitedly. It's been nearly three months since we last saw him on his final visit to Krovatia as head of the Interstellar Arts Company. He has since stepped down and passed on the baton to a successor, though he maintains a shareholding in the business. After ten years of continuous travelling, endless cargo runs and putting on show after sell-out show all over this quadrant of the galaxy, he and Rivlor are enjoying their retirement on their newly purchased home on Lirisor. And we're about to enjoy a well-earned vacation on this island paradise.

Kirilaura lifts her head from Kirimor's comfortable lap, blinking sleepily. "Are we there yet, pa?" she yawns.

Kirimor rumbles a quiet laugh. "Yes, little love, we have arrived. Can you not see Wyatt over there with Rivlor?"

Kirilaura looks to where Kirimor is pointing. Her face transforms into a happy smile as she catches sight of them. "Pa, will Rivlor let me ride her griv with her? She promised."

"If she promised, then rest assured she will."

My daughter adores Rivlor, Wyatt's life partner this last decade. She's also been fascinated by grivs, a magnificent horse-like flying creature that's native to the planet Ven, ever since she learned about them at school. On her last visit to Krovatia, Rivlor told Kirilaura that she would be purchasing a griv to help her get about on Lirisor, and that the children would get to ride on it if they behaved well and studied hard at school. My daughter has been as good as gold ever since, which is no hard feat.

The shuttle comes to land a few yards away from the house. Kiritela jumps up to open the door. At fourteen, Kirimor's little star is no longer so little, but a tall and graceful young lady — and a dancer. Kiritela caught the dancing bug, all those years ago watching the first ever ballet performance on Krovatia. It was her eagerness to learn how to dance that instigated the launch of the Krovatian School of Ballet a year later. Using Wyatt's contacts with various ballet companies on Earth, I worked strenuously to make her dream a reality, inviting top ballet teachers to come over and help set it up. It's been a resounding success, oversubscribed year on year, and one of the achievements I'm proudest of in my role as Earth Federation's ambassador to Krovatia, a role I continue to hold.

We all step out of the shuttle and rush towards Wyatt and Rivlor, surrounding the two of them, demanding our hugs and kisses. Finally, I get a turn. Wyatt shines his sweet, sexy smile as he enfolds me in his arms. "Hey, honey," he whispers. I breathe in his familiar woodsy scent and hold him tight. I've loved this man for over three decades. We've had our fair share of pits and falls, but we've come through stronger than ever, the best of friends.

"I've missed you," I murmur back.

He brushes the hair from my temple gently, his bright blue eyes warm with love. "I've missed you too," he says softly.

A strong tail wraps itself around the two of us. "Wyatt," Kirimor growls.

Wyatt grins at him. "Good to see you, old man."

Kirimor smirks, "And it is good to see you too, cute boy."

Wyatt and he are not quite best of friends, but they have grown closer over the years, enjoying a little teasing banter. I feel a gentle hand on my shoulder. Looking to my left, I see Rivlor smiling benignly at me.

"Melinda, you are looking beautiful as ever."

"And you, Rivlor. Retirement on Lirisor suits you."

She grins. "It is good," she says simply.

Then the children clamor for attention again. We follow Wyatt and Rivlor into their new home, taking a tour around the large, spread-out house. We walk from room to room, most of which boast panoramic views of the cerulean sea. A fresh, salty breeze blows in through the slatted windows. The décor everywhere is minimal, with cool, calming colors. Wyatt told me Rivlor wanted their retirement home to be a place of serenity after the hectic nature of their lives the past few years. Perhaps she was also inspired by our home in the Krovatian mountains, which Kirimor extended as our family grew. Throughout our home, Kirimor's aesthetic shines through, favoring simplicity over clutter, with graceful lines that please the eye.

"And here's your room," says Wyatt as we enter a pretty bedroom painted a pale peach color.

I look around. "Nice," I say.

There's the sound of feet clattering, then Kirilaura bursts into the room. "Rivlor, when can we see your griv?" she asks excitedly.

"Why not now? But first I need to ask your ma and pa if you've been good."

"I have! I have!"

Kirimor chuckles, ruffling our girl's hair. "I can attest to that."

"Well then, let us go and meet Ruala."

"Is that her name?"

"It is."

She steers her out of the room and down the stairs. Kirimor comes closer to wrap his tail around me. "I will go settle the children into their rooms and bring out our belongings from the shuttle," he says. "I know you will appreciate a little quiet time with Wyatt to catch up." As he turns to go, he calls out, "Behave!"

I chuckle at this and lean my chin on Wyatt's shoulder. "How are you doing, sweetie?" I ask him. "Is this lovely piece of paradise working out for you?"

"Hmm," he grunts, kissing the top of my head. "No complaints so far. We've already got into our little routine. We wake, go for our morning swim in the sea, bathe and eat, then we spend the rest of the morning working on our novel."

"Ah yes, how's your space opera coming along?"

"Not too bad," he says, releasing me and going to sit on the edge of the bed. "It's still early days. We're about a quarter of the way into the writing, though we've already worked out our plot."

I kick off my sandals and slip my dress over my head. I've been wearing it ever since we arrived on Ven. Under it, I'm in my Krovatian loin cloth. Wyatt surveys me from head to toe, taking in my latest body art. "Very nice," he drawls.

"Thanks." I go to sit beside him.

"How's Kirimor's arm? I noticed he was still favoring his left earlier."

Kirimor's arm is still healing from an accident while playing bong at the water city a few weeks ago. He fractured the bone which had to be set, and the cast has only recently been removed.

"He's a lot better. He's being extra careful with it, that's all. I'm sure he'll grow in confidence using that right arm again in no time. Let's hope he's learned his lesson about playing bong at his advanced age."

Wyatt snorts. "Unlikely! I'll take a look at it later. Perhaps I can massage it to help the healing along." It's been a long time since Wyatt has practised as a chiropractor, but the skills and knowledge are still there.

"While you're at it, can you take a look at my left shoulder? I don't know what's the matter with it. Maybe I slept on it wrong, or I've just strained it reading on my communicator. I don't feel it during the day, but when I lie down at night, I get the occasional pain shooting down that arm."

"Lie on your stomach, let me have a feel."

I do as instructed. He presses a few points along my shoulder blade and I moan. "Yes, right there."

He chuckles, kneading the sore spots until I'm close to purring with pleasure.

"Ah, that's what I've missed these last few months. Your healing touch," I grunt as he presses down on a particularly painful joint.

"Not my irresistible charm?"

"That too."

There's a knock on the door, and Kirimela enters the room. "Melinda, are you alright?" she asks in concern.

I hold out my arm in invitation and she climbs on the bed with us. Kirimela, at nine years of age, is the product of that fateful union between Pirofena and Kirimor. She has Kirimor's dark hooded eyes, his hair, his cheek bones, his smile. She also has his deep loving nature. The child whose conception caused me so much pain has ended up becoming one of the greatest blessings of my life. I love her as my own.

"I'm fine," I reassure her. "Just letting Wyatt ease some aches in my old body."

She sits beside us, observing his actions. "Wyatt, will you teach me how to do this, so I can help Melinda when we're back home?"

Wyatt smiles warmly at her, "Of course, honey. I'd be happy to demonstrate a few moves. That way you can take good care of both Melinda and your pa when I'm not around."

He goes on to do just that while I close my eyes and enjoy my massage.

Kirimor

The children have gone to sleep, and Melinda and I are finally alone in our bed chamber. She gets under the covers beside me and out of habit, I wrap my tail around her as I tuck her to my side. "How was your catch-up with Wyatt?" I ask, kissing the soft fragrant flesh of her neck.

"He and Rivlor seem well settled here. This life suits them."

"You do not think he will miss gallivanting about in space?"

"Perhaps occasionally, but I believe there will be adventure enough in the stories they're both writing together. By the way, he said he'd take a look at your arm."

I grunt.

"Did you speak to Kiristen?" she asks.

"I did. He is enjoying this California road trip greatly. He and Troy visited a museum of past Human entertainment called Disneyland. He said some parts reminded him a little of the water city."

"I remember going there as a kid before it shut down. Mom and dad had to save for months to take me there."

I tighten my arms around her. She has told me about her childhood. There was no shortage of love, but little money to go around. Now I make sure my Melinda gets every material need, including this well-earned vacation, even if it is at her ex-mate's house.

I remember something else Kiristen said. "Guess who they saw working as a host at this Disneyland?"

"Who?"

"Avery."

"Ha! How the mighty have fallen."

"If it were up to me, her fall would be even greater." In my meeting with Denishar after that fateful attack on the command center, I shared with him the information I had gathered as I sucked in Desimar's evil energy. One such piece was that Avery had been involved with Desimar and had some inkling of what was to happen—her illness on that day was feigned. As a result, Avery was ejected from Krovatia in disgrace and sent back to Earth. We have not heard any further news of her until now.

Melinda shifts and turns to face me. "She got her just deserts. No government department will ever employ her again." She kisses me lightly. "Now there's something I'd much rather do than talk about her."

I gaze at her in amusement. "And what would that be, my lovely?"

"Why don't I show you?"

She shimmies under the sheet, dropping kisses down my newly inked chest until she reaches the prize she's looking for. My cock is already hard and aching for her. She does not keep me waiting. Her tongue flicks over the tip, licking off the oozing droplets of my cum. I groan. Gripping my thick shaft with both hands, she brings it to her lips, opening her mouth wide to take as much of me in as possible. "Ah Melinda, you feel good." She sucks me down for a good half beat, until I can take it no longer. Grasping a handful of her long brown tresses, I pull her off me.

"Get on your back, my lovely," I rasp.

I flip her over and throw off the clinging sheet. "Open wide for me."

She obeys me without question, revealing her beautiful wet cunt, pierced through with my gleaming jewelry. A cunt I want to devour. I kneel at the junction of her legs, admiring the view for an instant before I lift them up over my shoulders and bury my face in her mound. Grasping the perfect globes of her ass in both hands, I hold her firmly to me as I lap at her damp, fragrant folds. Her moans of pleasure are music to my ears, driving my hunger for her. I spear her with my tongue, licking the grooves of her inner passage. "Ah," she moans. "Kirimor!"

I know what she needs. With rapid precision, I whip my tail over her breasts, lashing her sensitive teats. She cries out in momentary pain which turns into pleasure. I do it again, and again, as my tongue feasts on the banquet of her cunt. I feel her pleasure nub swell under my tongue. She is close. I bring it into my mouth and suck hard. "Ahh," she cries as she reaches her peak. I let my tongue flutter over her nub, not stopping until her climax is over. When she eventually stills, I let her fall gently back to the bed.

"Ah, that felt so good," she purrs.

"I am not done with you yet, my lovely." Still kneeling, at the juncture of her legs, I grasp my throbbing shaft. "I need to plunge this thick cock into your glorious cunt."

"I need you to," she sighs.

"Then come sit on me."

She pulls herself up and comes to straddle me, her back to my chest. "Take my cock, Melinda." Slowly, she eases herself down. Even after all this time, it is a tight fit. We both grunt in relief when I am finally buried all the way inside her. I clasp a perfect breast in each hand and squeeze the soft flesh.

"Mmm," she moans.

"Ready to ride me?" I whisper into her ear.

"Always, my love."

My chest rumbles in pleasure. I let one of my hands slide down her smooth belly until I reach her mound. With two fingers, I begin to stroke her wet, sticky folds.

"Ah, that feels good."

"I am going to fuck you hard, Melinda, and choke you with my tail. If it gets to be too much, slap one of my hands."

"I know the drill. I can take it. Fuck me, Kirimor."

I growl and begin to fuck my female. With each powerful thrust, she cries out. "More, I want more."

"I'll give you more," I grunt, and piston into her, holding her firmly to me, one hand on her breast, the other on her mound.

My tail winds around her neck, squeezing gently. I fuck her hard and rough and possessively, just the way we both need. Her cunt grips me tight, claiming her possession. I am hers just as she is mine. I pound into her harder and harder, lost in agonizing ecstasy, the noose of my tail tightening around her. I ache for her pleasure. "Come for me," I roar.

With a quiet gasp, she comes on my cock, choking it until I too reach that pulsating peak, drenching her with my cum. My tail comes down, releasing her from its hold. She pants, filling her lungs with air, riding the crest of that powerful wave. I clutch her tight to me, riding that wave with her, feeling every pulse of her cunt on my cock. At last, I bring us down to lie on our sides, keeping myself embedded deep inside her. I like us to remain joined for as long as possible. "I love you, Melinda," I whisper roughly.

"I love you, Kirimor."

We stay like this for a long, long time. Eventually, I reluctantly pull out, going to the ablution room to fetch a washcloth. With reverence, I clean my female, making her comfortable for the night. Then I rescue the covers and tuck them around us. "Sleep, my lovely."

"Goodnight, my love."

"Goodnight."

THE END

Are you wondering what happened to Wyatt at the end of the story? Wonder no more. Read **Wyatt's Redemption** *in the following pages, a 3-chapter story about how Wyatt and Rivlor get together.*

WYATT'S REDEMPTION

A short story

Chapter 1

Wyatt

My first glimpse of the cargo ship fills me with a strange mixture of relief and dread. I'm not looking forward to experiencing another take-off—the roar of the ship's thrusters under me and the rapid, dizzying acceleration as we break the planet's atmosphere to enter space. Despite all this, the presence of the ship brings a feeling of reassurance. It's all because of one person. Rivlor. I've missed my friend and the calm assurance she exudes.

We've been in constant touch since she deposited me here almost three weeks ago. After the attack on the command center, she refused to leave until she made sure I was truly ok, and then, she made sure to call every day to check up on how things were going down here. I can't wait to see her again.

It's time to leave Krovatia and continue on our next leg of the journey to the planet Ven. Around me are the assorted members of the Interstellar Arts Company, and crates of our equipment. I hope loading it on the ship will be an easier task than the last time.

Earlier, I said my goodbyes to Mel, who seemed ecstatically happy in the arms of her gray alien. The grief of losing her is still a deep, gnawing ache. I've loved this woman for over two decades, and it's going to take time to come to terms with the new reality. She's with Kirimor now, not me.

The cargo ship's door slides open, and out steps Rivlor, followed by her second-in-command, Shular. She stops a moment to run her eyes around the group of assembled people, until they land on me. Then a slow smile spreads on her face. "Cute boy, it is good to see you."

I step towards her. "It's good to see you too." Once I'm within reach, I look up into her magnificently tall frame and put a hand to her cheek in greeting. She does the same to me and we bring our foreheads together. *I've missed you.*

She steps back with a smile. "I have missed you too, cute boy." Then she turns brisk. "Let us load all your belongings on the ship." And she begins marshalling us, directing the proceedings with calm efficiency. In less than an hour, we're fully loaded up and ready to go. We begin strapping ourselves in for take-off. My heart starts beating wildly. Will Rivlor hold me, or am I expected to do this on my own now? I stand, undecided, casting my eyes for her.

With relief, I see her walk into the cabin holding the seat extension in her hands. She attaches it to her seat and settles herself on it. "Come, Wyatt," she commands. With no hesitation, I scrabble into her lap, not caring about what others might think. Right now, I need to be in the comforting shelter of her arms. She buckles the seat belt around me and pins me with her arms and legs. My head is pillowed on her soft breasts. I close my eyes and inhale her fresh, lemon and herb fragrance. I'm filled with a sense of wellbeing.

The ship's engine roars and we are tilted backwards, readying for take-off. *Oh God! I can't fucking do this again.*

"Yes you can. You are safe with me."

Hold me. Don't let go.

"I will not ever let you go." Her arms tighten around me. I'm surrounded by noise and vibration as the ship is propelled into the air at breakneck speed. My eyes are tightly shut. It seems an eternity before we are finally upright again and cruising in space. My face is clammy, my breath shallow pants. She ruffles my hair. "You are fine, Wyatt. Come, let me unstrap you."

With this, she undoes the seat belt and releases me from her hold. Shakily, I slide down the seat and get to my feet. She stands and puts a hand on my arm. "I have much to do, Wyatt.

Go settle yourself on the ship and I will see you at the evening repast."

"Ok." I pause. "Rivlor."

"Yes?"

"Thank you."

"It is my pleasure, cute boy." With this, she turns and goes.

I join the rest of my fellow humans in the cargo bay where our pods have been set up and start the process of getting settled in for this journey, which I'm told will take five days. It feels different than the last time I did this. Then, I was filled with hope and anticipation. I was on my way to see Mel and win her back.

Now… I suppose I should look forward to my next run of shows, but I can't work up the enthusiasm. Alone in my pod, I lie on my narrow single bed and ponder my future. What next for me? Do I continue with this venture or do I just fulfil this run of shows on Ven and Driskia then go home for good?

Surely I can't just give up after all the blood, sweat and tears I've put into getting this venture off the ground? I blow out a frustrated breath. If I'm honest, I know that I took on this great big project in an effort to impress Mel and convince her to take me back. Well, she was impressed and proud, especially after that Ricky Charles concert. But it didn't translate into success in winning her back.

Then I recall what I said to Dwight during one of our therapy sessions. *I'm doing this for me just as much as for her*. I've always been fascinated by alien worlds and distant planets. Well, here's my chance to experience all of that. It would be mad to throw it away because I didn't get my girl back.

I sit up and try to shake off this feeling of depressed lethargy. I need to keep going and grow my new company into a profitable business. When I get back to Earth, I'll start planning our next arts program to take with us into space. Perhaps some opera this time. La Traviata? The story of a fallen woman forced to choose between love and honor might go down well with our alien audiences.

Time to get to work.

◆◆◆

I make my way to the ship's dining hall. Lacey Holmes, the principal dancer leading our ballet troupe, falls into step beside me. I nod my head in welcome. "How's it going?"

"Good. Now that we know what space flight feels like on our bodies, we're getting better at adjusting our practice routines. We just did a quick workout on the barre and are taking it easy for today."

"That sounds sensible. We're only five days away from Ven, so maybe use this time to recuperate rather than do any heavy duty training. The ballet performances are last on the program, so you'll have time to rehearse and get into tip top shape once we land."

"Do you know where we'll be rehearsing and performing our shows?"

"Not yet, but Rivlor has found a space she thinks will work for us. She's taking me to see it as soon as we arrive."

"That's good. I hope the stage is a little bigger this time. That lecture theater in Krovatia was a little cramped for our needs."

"We'll see, but I have a good feeling it will be."

We reach the dining hall and slide into the first available seats. I find myself wedged between Lacey and a violinist called Winston. "What's on the menu tonight?" I ask.

"I hope we get more of that *kroot*," says Winston. "I liked it — reminded me of a folded pizza without the tomato sauce."

"As long as it's not *pilat*, then I'm happy." I've mostly enjoyed Venorian cuisine, but that chewy meat with a sour tang, not so much.

Shandral, the ship's resident cook, bustles in carrying a steaming platter of something that looks like noodles with some kind of creamy vegetable sauce.

"Mmm, that smells good," says Lacey.

Shandral beams at her. "I think you will like it. It is called *krepso*."

"I'm sure we will."

From the corner of my eye, I spot Rivlor entering the dining hall with Shular in tow. Our table is full, so she moves to the one beyond and settles herself there with her crew. Damn. I wanted to sit near her at dinner. God knows when we'll be able to have a catch up. Just then, she looks my way. I stare at her wordlessly and give a slight smile. She nods and continues with her meal, conversing calmly with her neighbors. I try to do the same, and focus on my fellow humans, many of whom I've become friendly with over the past few weeks. We enjoy the *krepso* and the sweet, moist cake that follows.

Our meal over, we start filing back toward the large cargo hold that is our home on this ship. I'm halfway out of the dining hall when I hear myself being hailed. "Wyatt!" I turn to see Rivlor behind me.

"Hey."

She steps closer and puts a hand to my arm. I can tell by the focus in her eyes that she's reading me. I let her delve into the different emotions I've been feeling the last few hours. She examines me a moment more, then comes to a decision. "Come."

She strides off in the opposite direction, and I follow at her heels. We come to a door—her chamber—and she opens it with a touch of her hand to the wall scanner. I step inside behind her, not exactly sure what we are doing here.

She goes to her bed and sits, pulling off her shoes. Then she stands and unties her pants, dropping them down to the floor. Underneath, she is bare. I stare at her pussy, covered in a silky bush of honey brown hair. My eyes race back up to her face in confusion.

"Be a good boy, Wyatt. Take off your clothes," she raps out.

"Huh?"

"You better do as I say. I punish naughty boys."

With that last statement, she pulls her tunic over her head, letting my gaze fall on her magnificent breasts. They're large—more than a handful—but rounded and pert, with firm, dark nipples, just begging to be suckled. I can't take my eyes off her. My cock pushes painfully against my zipper.

She reaches over to a side compartment by her bed and takes out a long object with a paddle at one end. She taps it gently against her palm. "Make me wait any longer, Wyatt and I will need to punish you."

I'm still not computing. "You want me to get undressed?"

She raises her brows and starts tapping the paddle on her hand.

"Err, what are you going to do to me if I get naked?" Stupid question. She doesn't honor that with a response.

As I continue to hesitate, she begins to walk towards me, a dangerous gleam in her eye. "Are you looking to get punished, Wyatt?" she asks softly.

"N—no," I stutter.

"Then do as I say."

I don't know what strange reality I have walked into. One minute ago, I was chatting with my friends at the dinner table. Now I'm standing in front of an imposing naked woman holding a paddle and asking me to get naked. My brain is fizzing with a million and one reactions, chief of which is the urge to obey. I begin to undress.

With clumsy fingers, I unbutton my shirt and let it fall to the floor. She hums under her breath and observes me intently. My hands go to the waistband of my jeans. I undo the clasp and push down the zipper, then slowly let my pants drop to my feet. With a tug of my heels, I nudge my sneakers off, then release my feet from my pants. Straightening up, I put my hands to my one remaining piece of clothing. I'm tenting in my boxers and my cock has left a discernible wet patch. Taking hold of the waistband, I pull them down in one quick move, tugging them off my legs. Then I stand, and let her gaze at me.

"Hmm," she hums again, getting to her knees to inspect me more closely. A grin tugs at her cheeks. "It is just as I thought. Hair the color of a golden sunrise. And what's this?" Her eyes spy my frenum piercing, plainly visible with my cock standing to attention. She looks up at me. "You have been a naughty boy, haven't you, Wyatt? Putting that pretty decoration on your cock."

"It was for our tenth anniversary. Melinda and I each got ourselves pierced."

She gazes interestedly at me. "Really, so your former mate also has this on her private parts?"

"Yes."

She whispers under her breath, "That I would like to see." Her eyes return to my cock. If anything, it swells even more, dewy precum gathering at the tip. She's so close, I can feel the warmth of her breath on my skin, making my hair stand on end. She raises a hand and runs careful fingers along my chest, grazing a nipple along the way. I shudder.

Her hand travels down my happy trail, fingers gently caressing the hair on my abdomen. "Golden sun-kissed skin, soft golden hair, and …" Her fingers reach my patch of pubic hair, which I keep in its natural form. It's a thatch of dark blond hair that Melinda has always loved to play with, so I've never felt the need to trim it, unlike the dictates of modern fashion. Rivlor too, seems fascinated with it. She threads her fingers through it, feeling the slightly wiry texture.

Her fingers reach the base of my cock and ever so slowly, trace a line to my wet tip. My whole body trembles. "… And a cock that is decorated for my pleasure and just the right size to fit in my mouth." Her hand falls to her side. "You are beautiful, Wyatt."

"You too, Rivlor," I say huskily.

She smiles and gets back on her feet. Pushing her palm gently to the middle of my chest, she guides me towards the bed. "Sit, and open your legs for me." I do as she says.

Rivlor walks into the space between my legs and looks down at me from her great height. She brings a hand to my hair, stroking the tousled strands, each touch of her fingers sending delicious waves of pleasure through me. Her other hand drops the paddle on the floor behind her and comes to my face, gently exploring the feel of my skin from the smoothness of my brow to the stubble along my jaw. She runs a finger along the straight line of my nose, bringing it down to my mouth, wandering over the soft skin of my bottom lip. Something about this careful, slow exploration awakens an intense response in me—both physical and emotional. I feel seen, valued, revered. It's a balm to my broken and battered soul.

Both her hands cup my cheeks, and she brings her forehead to mine, reading my jumbled emotions. "Yes, I see you, somewhat cute Wyatt."

"Isn't it time you changed it to very cute Wyatt?"

"Maybe," she teases. She leans forward and brushes her lips to mine. It's a feather light touch, but I want more. I catch her head with my hand, pulling her back toward me. She doesn't resist the pressure of my hand, bringing her mouth to mine again. We both part our lips and this time, the kiss is long and deep. We plunge our tongues into the wet warmth of each other's mouth. I caress the soft underside of hers, sucking in Rivlor's sweet, tangy essence. She explores the rougher texture along the top of my tongue, and we tangle together in long, hungry licks. It's not enough. Soon, the licks become protracted sucks, each of us needing to devour the other. I can't get enough of her—the texture of her soft lips on mine, her taste, the feel of silky, moist skin. I could die of pleasure just from this kiss.

All too soon, she releases my mouth and pushes me back on to the bed. My head falls on to the springy mattress and I close my eyes for a brief instant, catching my breath. When I open them again, she's kneeling on the floor between my spread legs. Her face burrows in my groin, inhaling my musky scent. I hear her make that humming sound of satisfaction again. Then her tongue comes out lapping at my balls, lavishing hot wet strokes on the twin swollen sacs. I tremble at her touch. She takes one sac fully into her mouth and gently sucks on it.

"Ah," I moan. "Please, baby, please."

She looks up. "Please what?"

"Suck my cock!"

She gives a wicked smile. "With pleasure." And with no further preliminaries, no gentle licks to the tip of my shaft, she takes me into her mouth, sheathing my entire length in her moist heat.

"Jesus!" I cry. Her mouth clamps around me and sucks, the suction strong and continuous. "Oh fuck!" She doesn't let up, maintaining a constant rhythm of sucking, letting her tongue run along the underside of my cock, tugging at the barbells on my frenum piercing. I'm not going to last much longer. Already, I feel my balls tightening, my cock swelling. "Rivlor, I'm coming!"

The warning only seems to fire her up more. The sucking speeds up, and I come undone. With a cry, I spurt my release into her welcoming mouth. I tremble with the force of my orgasm. More cum erupts from my tip, which she swallows, licking me clean. When finally, I'm done, she releases my cock and crawls up on the bed, pulling my body up with hers and twisting it so my head lies on her pillowy breasts. I place a hand on the mound closest to me and squeeze gently. I'm too drained to speak, so I just do so in my head. *"Thanks, Rivlor. I think I've just died and gone to heaven."* I feel the rumble of her laughter as she reads my mind. Her hands gently stroke my hair. My eyelids shut and I drift off.

◆ ◆ ◆

I come to sometime later. My head is still on her chest, my right hand cupping a breast, laying a claim on it. Her arm is around me, a hand occasionally stroking my hair. Her other hand holds her communicator, scrolling down with her thumb. She's reading her sci-fi novel.

How's the book?

"It is good. I only have one last section to go."

Will you share it with me after? I'd like to read it.

"Of course. Perhaps you should start with the first one in the series."

I'd love to.

"I will send them to your communicator."

Thanks. Hey Rivlor.

"Hmm?"

Thanks for everything. You make me feel so good.

"I am glad." Idly, I stroke the breast under my hand, squeezing the nipple between my thumb and forefinger. "Mmm," she purrs. "Keep doing what you are doing. I like it."

How about if I do this? I shift my head so I can take her nipple into my mouth. I savor the pebbled texture, licking it gently.

"Keep going, somewhat cute boy."

We said you'd stop calling me that. It's very cute Wyatt.

"Hmm."

I stop and lift my head, looking up at her with steely eyes. She barks out an order, "Go back to what you were doing, boy."

I don't move, just narrow my eyes.

"Oh my lord Lir, alright. You are very cute. Now suck me!"

I can't hide my grin as I dip down to take her breast in my mouth again. I tug at the nipple with my teeth then start to suck. I feel her buck under me. I suck harder. She emits a long, drawn out moan. After a while, I transfer my attention to the other breast. My wandering hand travels over the smooth, taut skin of her abdomen, looking for the prize. I reach her bush of hair and tangle my fingers in it. Then I bring my index finger down further and find her nub. Still sucking on her nipple, I start rubbing her clit in a circular motion. Her moans tell me I'm on the right track.

"Yes, Wyatt, do not stop!"

I have no intention to. I keep up my rhythm on her clit and her nipple. Sticky wetness oozes out of her. I dip my finger into her slit, coating myself in her juices, then come back to her clit, using the wetness to rub my finger around it faster and harder. She writhes under me.

Want me to eat you with my tongue?

She lifts her groin to me in supplication. "Yes! Yes!"

I release her nipple with a wet, slurpy pop, and quickly swivel around to bury my face in her mound. I take a moment to run my nose through the honey hair, inhaling the deeply musky, intensely arousing fragrance.

Fuck you smell good.

"Wyatt!"

Ok, ok, I'm getting there.

I lean forward a bit more and drag my tongue over her pussy, starting from the top and going all the way down to her slit. She parts her legs wide in invitation, and I shift my body to settle into a more comfortable position, my own legs astride her, my cock resting in the crook of her neck. She runs her hands over my ass cheeks while I continue to explore her. For a woman of her size, her pussy lips are curiously small and delicate, cute folds of slick pink skin. I lick her, memorizing the shape, feel and taste of her. With every lick, she drips more sticky wetness onto my tongue. I lap at it eagerly, savoring the sweetness of her. I'd heard stories that Venorian men have sweet tasting cum. I hadn't realized their females also produced a sweet nectar. I'm a kid in a candy store, lapping her like a lollipop, sucking in her flavor.

I hear a sort of rumbling noise from above. "Wyatt!"

That's my cue that she's close. That and the throbbing, swollen nub of her clit. I flutter my tongue over it, again and again, faster and faster. "Ah! Wyatt boy! Ah—"

With a loud cry, she comes, showering my face with her sweet, sticky juice. Oh my good heaven how divine she tastes. I drink her up, licking every single drop. She continues bucking under me, and I keep going, not stopping until I feel her come apart under me again. On and on I lick, I suck, I savor. I thought I was in heaven earlier, but this, this is perfection. The combination of her musky scent and syrupy cum is overpowering. I'm already addicted to the most perfect pussy in the universe. I'll never get enough of this. I want more, more of this glorious taste, this drugging scent.

Rivlor moans again, digging her nails into my ass cheeks. Then she's parting them, exposing the brown rosebud of my back hole. I feel a breeze of cold, ventilated air on my most private of places, somewhere even Melinda has never explored. Then a warm tongue brushes over it, and I nearly combust. My face is buried in her sweetness, devouring her nectar, while hers is devouring my ass. An ass that is full of sensitive, erogenous zones, as I discover. Her clever tongue does things to me I've never experienced before, tracing over my rim, fluttering over the puckered surface, then lavishing it with long, slow strokes. My cock is rock hard. I'm about to come again.

She pulls her mouth away and slaps me hard on one ass cheek, then the other. "You do not come until I say so!"

My skin tingles where I've been slapped. *Oh fuck that feels good.* She slaps me again for good measure. "Get back up here, cute boy, and put your cock in me."

I lift my head from the paradise of her pussy, my face coated in her sticky juices. Slowly, I shift around until I'm upright again, my cock brushing against the stickiness of her mound. Her eyes take in the messy, wet state of my face and glimmer with approval.

"I should get a condom," I mutter.

"Do you have a communicable disease?" she barks.

"No, but pregnancy?"

"Not a problem. Venorian females can only become fertile if they consciously decide to. Now fuck me."

Relieved, I guide my cock with one hand to her entrance, then start to push inside gently, looking into her eyes. She's so wet that I slide all the way in with just one push. I take a moment to savor the feeling of being buried inside her. The walls of her pussy grip my cock, powerful muscles holding me captive. God she feels good!

My eyes don't leave hers as I start to thrust, slow, deep strokes, filling her with my engorged cock. I hold myself up on my elbows at each side of her, plunging in and out while I stare into her face. She's so beautiful when she's aroused. Her pupils glow a dark shade of honey. Her wide, full lips are red and inviting. They're slightly parted, emitting soft little pants of pleasure. I circle my shaft inside her, finding the friction I want, the piercing on my cock dragging along her inner walls. I thrust again, and she gasps in pleasure. I smile in satisfaction. I may not have the biggest cock in the world, but by God I know how to use it.

She reads my mind and gurgles with laughter. "Yes, cute boy, you do know how to use that cock. Now fuck me."

I grin. "My pleasure, madam."

She makes a humming sound of satisfaction. Then I clear my mind of everything except the need to fuck the shit out of this incredible woman. I angle my cock for maximum friction and thrust, and thrust again. After a while, I bring her knees up and deepen my penetration.

"Oh yes, clever boy!" she cries.

Oh Rivlor, you ain't seen nothing yet. I angle my body so my groin rubs into her clit with every thrust. I plunge in deep, then keep myself there, making small pushes in and out. From the way she gasped just now, I know I've hit her G spot. I focus on rubbing my shaft against it in small, circular thrusts, letting my frenum piercing do its magic along her sensitive walls. Her grip on me increases, and her pants get louder and quicker. *Oh pretty lady, I'm about to make you come big time.* Her eyes flicker in response, almost like a challenge. I smile, with a hint of smugness. Challenge accepted.

I try for some dirty talk, realizing I can say it in my head, and she'll hear me loud and clear.

I'm gonna fuck your sweet pussy until it begs for me. Feel me, baby!"

She tightens around me in response.

I groan. *God you feel so good on my cock. Take me baby, take all of me.*

And I start to fuck her in sharp, hard thrusts. The rougher I get, the more she gasps and tightens her grip on me.

That's it, baby. Come on my cock. I wanna hear you scream.

She moans and thrusts her pelvis up at me, meeting me thrust for thrust. I pick up the pace, slamming into her.

You want my cum, baby? Scream. I wanna hear you!

She grunts. I slam into her with all my might. *Take my cock and choke it. I wanna feel you cum on me.*

Her walls tighten around me like a noose. I'm wild with desire, driving into her with a roughness like never before. I want to hammer her with my cock. I want to nail her. Claim her.

You're mine, baby. Now come, and scream for me.

With my next thrust, I feel it—her walls clamp tight around me and begin to pulse. Then I hear her. She gasps out loud and lets out a piercing scream.

All my control deserts me. I drive into her wildly, desperate for release. I come with a loud groan, a deep guttural echo to her scream. My cock pulses jets of cum deep inside her for what feels like endless moments. Then, utterly drained, I collapse on top of her, still intimately buried in her tight pussy.

I pant shallow breaths, slowly coming down from my high. My face is buried in the silky warmth of her neck. As my wits return to me, I'm struck down by a thought. This wasn't just a simple rebound fuck. This was seismic. I can't go back to the Wyatt I was before this. I'm changed. Owned. *Shit.*

With slow, deliberate movements, I slip my cock out of her and turn to lie on my back beside her, staring at the ceiling. *Oh shit.*

I finally lift my eyes to hers. She's regarding me, a thoughtful expression on her face. "That was interesting," she says in her deep, melodious voice.

"That's one way to put it."

"I did not expect this."

"No shit."

"You are very good at fucking."

"Thanks."

"I have had good fucks before, but this was something more."

I stare into her honey brown eyes. "I know."

"Like I said, I did not expect this."

"Neither did I."

"You will share my bed from now on."

"Yes."

"While we are on this ship, you are mine."

"Yes." Then I add, a touch defiantly. "And you're mine."

"Of course, cute boy."

I bury my face in her neck and hold her tight. "How did this happen?" I ask gruffly.

"I do not know. The mysteries of the universe are not mine to decode. But there it is. We have found each other."

Mysterious universe indeed. I had no thought, no intention to ever love another woman again. Especially not so soon after my break-up with Mel. But there it is.

I kiss the soft fragrant skin of her neck, feeling a wave of happiness wash over me. We stay, wrapped in each other's arms a long time. Eventually, she stirs. "We need to wash. Come with me."

She gets out of the bed and pulls me with her. I follow to the bathroom and watch as she sits on the toilet and relieves herself in front of me, as if it is the most natural thing in the world. She stands, and goes to the shower, starting the water while I take a quick pee and flush. She waits for me, and I join her under the hot stream of water. With careful, gentle hands, we wash each other, every touch a loving caress. Once clean, she stops the water with a touch to the console button, and steps out throwing me a towel. We dry ourselves and return to the bed, lying next to each other under the covers. She pulls me to her, caressing my hair softly. "Sleep." I close my eyes, contentment seeping through every pore of my body, and do just that.

Chapter 2

Wyatt

The planet Ven blows my mind with its glorious sunshine and vibrant colors. I have never before seen trees with such bright purple and pink blossoms, dotting the blue sky like sprinkles on a cupcake. As we make our way downtown, I gaze admiringly at the grand villas that line the wide, majestic avenues of Torbreg—the capital city. The houses are built with generous proportions, as befits a tall race of humanoids such as the Venorians. They are large rectangular edifices painted in pretty pastel colors, and decorated with windows in a variety of geometrical shapes. One house has huge panes in a combination of circles and semi-circles. Its neighbor has pentagon-shaped windows and the one after that is populated with a repeating pattern of triangles, squares and circles, as if the architects couldn't decide which shape they preferred best. To complement the quirky character of the buildings, their roofs are tiled in bright colorful patterns.

Looking around, I feel like I've landed in some strange, magical kingdom. I've always fantasized about alien worlds, growing up reading science-fiction novels, but this exceeds my wildest imaginings. Rivlor sits close beside me in the drone, her hand on my thigh, a reassuring presence as we fly low in the hustle and bustle of the city. I don't know what it is, but I'm not feeling any of my usual nausea. Perhaps my days spent on a spaceship and the experience of careening in and out of a planet's atmosphere has cured me of my fright. Perhaps it's the presence of this amazing female beside me. Or perhaps, it's a combination of all the above, including my wonderment at the sights I'm seeing outside our window.

"You are liking what you see of my world," Rivlor muses.

"I love it. Rivlor, if this were my home, I would never dream of leaving it."

She laughs. "It is nice to come home to, but as you know, I like variety in my life."

Earlier today, after docking the ship on Ven, we were taken to the Interior Ministry, where all new visitors to the planet are processed. We were given a medical test, inoculations, and asked to sign a document to say we would abide by Venorian rules during our stay. Once that was out of the way, we then went to get settled in our new quarters. I had arranged through Flidar, Treylor's mom, to rent a large house for my troupe of performers to stay in. Our new temporary home is a pastel blue building with massive octagonal windows, featuring a roof tiled in an alternating pattern of navy blue and pink. Rivlor had wanted me to reside at her family home while here on Ven, but I felt it was important, as the leader of this artistic troupe, to remain close to my group of fellow humans.

Rivlor had stared at me appraisingly for a few moments then stated, "Very well, I shall bring my belongings here." And that was that. It seems our relationship is set to continue even now we are off the ship. We haven't really talked future plans. We only agreed to being exclusive while on board the ship. I moved into her cabin for the remaining days of our journey, but I didn't for one minute take for granted that we would continue sleeping together once we got here. I had hoped though. I've grown addicted to being in her bed. Sex with Rivlor is out of this world, but it's not the only thing that draws me to her. There's something about her calm, logical presence that soothes my soul. When I'm with her, no problem seems intractable. I can speak to her in my mind and she understands me. Being with someone who truly sees me has blown all my previous relationships out of the water—even my long marriage to Melinda.

Barely had a drone arrived with Rivlor's belongings than she was dragging me out again, this time to go inspect a venue she thinks might work for our shows. That's where we're heading now, sitting side by side in the drone.

"So, tell me about this place we are going to," I say as I nip her ear gently, then continue my journey down her neck, dropping light kisses along the smooth, fragrant skin.

She taps my thigh in warning. "Are you looking for punishment, cute boy? Do not turn me on when my mind needs to be on business."

"Sorry," I reply penitently. *Not really sorry.* What is it about being called "cute boy" that turns this forty-one year old grown man to mush?

Rivlor's expression softens. "You like being mothered, Wyatt. It takes you back to that time when you felt secure and cherished as a child."

I love it when she reads my mind. There's never any need to explain myself. "Yes, I guess you're right. I never thought I had that kind of fetish."

"It is more common than you think."

"Maybe that's where things went wrong with Mel. She doesn't have that mothering instinct. We talked about having children, but she never really wanted to disrupt her life to have them."

"Did you ever want to have children?"

"I wouldn't have minded either way, but on balance probably not, otherwise I would have pushed for them a little more."

"Maybe unconsciously she sensed that from you and told you what you wanted to hear."

I frown at her. That thought had never occurred to me. I consider the idea then dismiss it. "No, she's not the type to repress her needs. When she wants something, she goes for it."

Rivlor shrugs. I steal a kiss from her cheek, then ask, "What about you? Do you ever want to have children."

"No, that is never going to happen," she says flatly.

"That sounds awfully final. Why are you so sure?"

"I decided it a long time ago, and I never go back on my decisions."

Hmm, I'm not convinced. She sees my doubting look and reluctantly explains. "I told you already that I have no plans to ever mate, Wyatt. That includes no plans to ever have children either."

"There must be a reason."

"Why? Can it not simply be a preference?"

"It could, but I sense a reason behind all this."

She sighs. "You may be right, but now is not the time to discuss. We have arrived." In thrall to our conversation, I had not noticed the light bump indicating we had landed.

"Oh right. But we will discuss this another time."

"Hmm."

That is all the reply I get from her. With nimble movements, she unstraps the safety belt and gets to her feet. "Come, Wyatt. There is much work to be done."

I follow her out of the drone. We're in front of a large, wide building, this one, unusually, not painted a pastel color but stark white.

"What is this place?"

"This is the vibor academy."

"What's that?"

"Vibor is a popular sport here on Ven. It consists of two persons fighting each other until one person is able to bring the other to the ground and hold their neck down in victory."

"Oh, some type of martial arts. We have similar sports on Earth."

"It is a type of art. The contestants have no weapons and fight in bare feet wearing only a loincloth. They are not allowed to hit or punch each other. In order to win, they must gain supremacy through strength and agility. It is very beautiful to watch—" she grins mischievously, "particularly when two females are competing."

I grin back. "I bet! So, why are we here?"

"Vibor tournaments are held at the academy, and many people come to watch. There is a large rectangular space where the contestants fight, and around it are seats for the audience. I believe this could work for your shows."

"Let's take a look."

She leads the way, going through a large set of double doors at the front of the building. Inside, we follow a path down a long corridor with windows opening onto various practice rooms, in which I spot both male and female Venorians partaking in the sport. I pause at one window, my eyes unable to look away from two tall, well-built Venorian females in nothing but skimpy thongs, wrestling each other. My gaze is drawn to the jiggle of their tits and ass while they perform their energetic, yet graceful acrobatics. Rivlor notices where my attention is and comes to my side, watching the show with me.

"They are good looking, no?"

"Yes," I breathe, unable to glance away from their bronzed, athletic bodies.

"The one on the right is called Larbren. I fucked her on my last visit home. Her cunt was delicious."

My cock, which was already at half-mast, now rises to full attention. Rivlor takes it in her hand, through my pants, feeling how hard I am. "You are turned on when I tell you about the women I fuck," she states matter-of-factly.

There is no denying it. The evidence is twitching in her hands. "Yeah."

"Perhaps one day, Wyatt, you would consider joining me as I fuck another woman."

"I've never had a threesome."

"Then you have missed out on much in your life, cute boy."

"I got together with Melinda when I was twenty-one. I haven't had much opportunity to do that kind of thing."

"Would you like to?"

"I—I don't know what that would mean for our relationship. We haven't talked about it, Rivlor. All I know is that on the ship, we were exclusive."

"Then we shall talk about it—when we are alone in our bed tonight."

"I love you, Rivlor." I don't know what has prompted me to blurt that out here, as we watch two nearly naked women wrestle through a window.

Rivlor pulls me into her arms and rests her chin on my shoulder. "I know."

I chuckle nervously. "I guess there's not much I can hide from you."

"There is no need to hide how you feel, Wyatt boy. I also love you."

I hold her tight to me. "I'm so glad," I say huskily.

She kisses me softly on the lips then steps back. "Come now, Wyatt. We have business to attend to."

With my hand in hers, she leads me down the rest of the corridor. We come to a large set of stairs, which we take two at a time. Upstairs, the layout is rather different. Instead of a corridor with practice rooms on either side, there is a large open space taking the length and width of the entire building. In the center of the space, on a raised dais is a large, rectangular stage. Surrounding the stage are bench seats that go all the way around.

I walk forward, assessing my surroundings. "We would have to block off part of the seating so it doesn't go all the way around the stage. Dancers need to have their audience on one side only, not behind them too."

She follows my gaze. "That can be done, though it reduces the number of tickets we can sell for each show.

I look up at the ceiling, which is at least fifty feet high. "Perhaps we could build a raised platform, so the audience can sit on several levels, maximizing the number of people we can accommodate. What do you think?"

She ponders the question. "It can be done. I know a good carpenter who could make the seating for us quickly and cheaply. He kitted out part of my ship. I will contact him shortly so he can get started on adapting the stage for your needs."

"How much will this space cost us?"

"I will find out now. How many rotations will you require it for?"

"I was hoping to do a two-weeks run of shows, starting with two concerts by Ricky Charles, then five nights of theater performances, with the final week devoted to the staging of various ballets. Something else to bear in mind is that we plan to return at different points of the year with other performances, so we would want to negotiate a long-term contract."

"How often do you see yourself returning here, Wyatt?"

"My plan is to return every three months for a two-weeks run of shows, but of course a lot depends on the demand we get for tickets."

"Understood."

She taps away at her communicator. The response she receives makes her grunt in displeasure. She fires off another message. This back and forth continues for a few minutes until finally, she faces me with a satisfied smile.

"It has been arranged. The owner of the building will let us have this space for half a moon rotation at a price of eighteen thousand five hundred Litors, our Venorian currency, which is equivalent to five thousand international credits."

I do the math quickly on my communicator. The space can fit approximately four hundred seats, possibly more. At full capacity, with a ticket price of twenty credits per person, that would give us revenue of eight thousand credits per performance, amounting to one hundred and twelve thousand credits overall. With the wage, accommodation and transport bill, in addition to the costs of staging our performances, there should still be a decent profit of over thirty thousand credits for me and Rivlor to share.

"Do you think twenty credits per person is a reasonable price to charge for tickets?"

"It is entirely reasonable. I would perhaps charge more for the better located seats at the front."

"How soon can we start marketing? I already have the promotional materials designed."

"With a little work, I believe we could pull this together to release the information to the public in the morning news cast next rotation. Would you be willing to be interviewed on the news cast? It will be beamed across the planet and will bring you much attention."

I run a nervous hand through my hair. I'm not a great one for public speaking, but an interview I think I could manage. "Yes, I can do that. I'll ask Lacey and Rinaldo to join me, maybe also Ricky Charles. When would this space be available to us?"

"There are two more rounds in the current vibor tournament, but after this there is a recess, so our rental of this space could begin in four rotations' time."

I nod. "That works within our time frame. We can use those four days to do our preparations, rehearsals and begin selling tickets."

"So, shall I accept the rental offer?"

"Yes, please do."

She taps her communicator a few times more, then puts it away in her pocket. "It is done. I have also taken the liberty of booking tickets for the final round of the vibor tournament three rotations from now. I think you will enjoy it."

"Thanks, Rivlor."

She runs her hands through my tousled blond hair and kisses me. "Now, cute boy, let us get started with the preparations. There is much work to be done."

That turns out not to be an exaggeration. Over the next few days, I run on adrenaline as I do interviews, run promotional slots and begin ticket sales. At first, sales are slow and my confidence in the project hits another low. Lucky for me, Rivlor is there to lift my spirits with her down-to-earth attitude and awesome blow jobs. Each night, I collapse on the bed, shattered. Each night, Rivlor pulls my head to her breast and holds me as I sleep. There is no further opportunity for that relationship talk we promised each other.

On the third day, I wake to the ping of notifications on my communicator. I blink open sleepy eyes. I'm on my side, my face tucked into Rivlor's shoulder as she lies sleeping on her back, my right hand possessively cupping her breast. With a grunt, I release said breast and reach over to the side table for my communicator. Returning into position, I check my messages and give a whoop of delight, which awakens my slumbering partner.

"What is it?" she growls.

"We've sold out tickets for both Ricky Charles performances and our other shows are booking up fast. Yes!" I give a fist bump.

Rivlor observes me the way someone would study a curious phenomenon in a scientific experiment. "There was never any doubt, Wyatt, that the shows would sell out. There has never been anything like this before on this planet. Naturally, many people want to come see what it is all about. Your challenge will be in ensuring they have a positive experience and want to come again next time you return."

"You could have told me! I've been stressing about it like crazy these last few days."

"I thought I had, but obviously I must learn to communicate more clearly."

I look at her in mock frustration, then can't resist leaning over to give her a long, satisfying kiss. "Good morning, baby."

"Good morning, very cute Wyatt."

"Oh, I merit a very cute this morning do I?"

Her laughter vibrates. "You are too cute in your joy, sweet boy."

I kiss her again, bringing a hand down to finger her luscious cunt as I do. *I need to fuck you.* In response to my thought, she brings a hand to my hard cock, not breaking our kiss, and guides it to her entrance. I push inside and sigh in pleasure at the feel of her moist heat wrapping itself tightly around me. *You feel so good, baby.*

She grasps my ass cheeks and pulls me deeper. I pulse into her, kissing her hungrily. *I'm not going to last, baby. I need you to come.* Knowing how sensitive her neck is, I move my mouth down her jaw to that sweet spot at the junction with her shoulder, showering her with urgent, sloppy kisses. She quivers at my touch. I love that she's so responsive. And then I start to pound into her, angling my hip to grind against her clit. I hear sharp little pants as my frenum piercing creates delicious friction inside her, and I know she's close. *Come for me, baby. Come now.*

With a sweet cry of pleasure, she reaches her orgasm just as I drop my load into the depths of her pussy. When I regain my breath, I lift my head to kiss her lips, my cock still buried inside her. Cupping her lovely face with one hand, I murmur, "I love you."

Ever since a few days ago when I blurted it out, I've been telling her I love her at least a half dozen times a day, like a dam has been broken and my feelings have flooded out. It might make me sound like a lovesick fool, but I can't help it. The words just come tumbling out. She smiles, "You can say it as often as you like, Wyatt. I am happy to hear your words of love and to say them back to you. I love you too."

I swoon. Then I decide to kiss her and whisper "I love you" one more time for good measure.

As we're emerging from the shower, I hear a ping on my communicator again. I rush to pick it up, hoping to read more sales figures. Instead, I see it's a message from Mel. I haven't heard from her since saying our goodbyes a week ago. Rivlor notices the changed expression on my face. "What is it?" she asks.

"It's from Mel."

"Ah. Do you want me to leave so you can listen to it in private?" She picks up some clothes and begins to dress as she says this.

"No, baby. Stay."

I turn to her and drop a kiss on her cheek. "I love you, Rivlor," I say, sounding like a broken old vinyl record.

She ruffles my hair and chuckles. "I know, but you still love her too."

"Are you not jealous? I would be in your place."

"There is no point in being jealous. But I am hoping, Wyatt, that now she is to be mated to another, you will choose me as your life partner. I would like that very much."

"You want us to mate?"

"No, not that. I already told you. I have no plans to ever mate."

"Isn't that what a life partner is?"

"In my world, mates are faithful to each other. The mating bond does not allow for either person to stray. I cannot make such a commitment to anyone. I know that I will always be attracted to other women and there will be times I will want to fuck them—and maybe also some other males."

513

I gulp, suddenly feeling unsure. "So what would I be as your life partner?"

"You would be the person I love and the person I share my life with. But you will need to accept that I will want to fuck others too. Perhaps, we could do this together."

"Have threesomes together?"

"Yes, or maybe foursomes where we play with another couple."

"Will you ever fuck others without me being there?"

She considers for a moment. "If that is a condition of your becoming my life partner, then I will only do it when I am with you."

"So, we would be exclusive, except when we play together with others."

"Yes, cute boy."

"Forever?"

"For as long as we live, yes."

My pulse beats rapidly as I take stock of this scenario. It's not like anything I've ever done before. There again, I tried the traditional marriage construct and look where it got me. Maybe I should loosen up, live a little. Who better with than this magnificent female I'm crazy about? I take a deep breath. "Then yes, I want us to be life partners."

She kisses me hungrily then, holding me tightly to her. I don't need to be a mind reader to feel the depth of her emotion. This means just as much to her as it does to me. We're pledged to each other.

Chapter 3

Wyatt

It's been another manic day as we prepare for our first night of shows tomorrow evening. The carpenter Rivlor introduced me to, a Venorian named Shanlor, who turns out to be a distant cousin of hers, has been hard at work building a platform with extra bench seats for us, which he'll fit as soon as our rental of the space begins. Ricky Charles is all set to have a sound check there tomorrow afternoon, in time for his first show on Ven. Our dancers and actors will be using a few of the practice rooms downstairs to do their rehearsing, which we have hired for a minimal extra cost. And best of all, our tickets are selling like hot cakes.

Tonight is all about kicking back and relaxing after all the hard work of the last few days. Rivlor is taking me to my first ever vibor tournament. Yesterday was the final of the men's, and today is all about the women, with a champion being crowned at the end. I'm looking forward to watching the wrestlers in action, and not just from a horny old man's perspective. I mean yes, I can't deny the sight of nearly naked women wrestling is a massive turn on, but also, from what I've seen of the sport so far, there is great skill and artistry involved.

For the occasion, Rivlor has dressed in fancy midnight blue pants and a shimmery silver top that plunges sexily down the middle to show off her amazing cleavage. She looks hot, and I'm so proud to have this goddess of a woman on my arms for this, our first ever date. Well, it feels like a date to me. I've dressed up too, wearing my smartest pants and a crisp pale blue shirt. Before leaving the house, Rivlor eyed me up and down, then nodded in satisfaction. "Yes, very cute," was all she said. I'll take that.

And now we're sitting on a bench in prime position to see the action on the stage. The place is heaving, with not a single spare seat available. It truly is a popular sport on this planet. First order of business is the semi-finals, after which the winners of this round will face each other. The spotlight over the stage comes on, while above us the lights dim. A hush comes over the crowd, only for them to begin stamping with their feet and to chant, "Hayya," which my ear piece is struggling to translate. I gaze around me in bemusement at the transformation of these sedate Venorians into an excited, rowdy bunch. Even my partner—that's what I now like to think of her as—is stomping like mad and shouting out, "Hayya."

She sees me stare and mock punches me in the arm. "Come on, Wyatt, we need to make our wrestlers feel welcome." And so I join in, stamping my feet and calling out "Hayya", whatever that means. In the melee, I see two female wrestlers emerge on to the stage. One of them, I recognize as Larbren, the female we saw fight in the practice room, the one whom Rivlor has intimate knowledge of.

Both the females are tall and athletic, although not overly muscled. They stand in nothing but flesh colored thongs, giving the illusion that they are totally naked. On seeing them, the crowd erupts into even more stamping and crying of "Hayya". The two contestants greet each other the traditional Venorian way, with a hand to the cheek and foreheads touching. Then they step back from each other and bow.

In this instant, the crowd hushes, waiting for the contest to begin. A loud series of gongs are heard in the auditorium, signalling the start of the fight. And then they're at each other. It's like they get into an intimate embrace. As they're not allowed to punch or kick each other, their movements are contained into pushes with their whole bodies and a tangling of their limbs to get better grip and control over the other. At one point, Larbren lifts her opponent in the air, gripping her by the hips, only for said opponent to wrap her legs tight around Larbren and dive backwards with her arms to the floor, performing a magnificent somersault.

I watch enthralled, marvelling at the strength and agility of these female wrestlers. Beside me, Rivlor holds my hand, using the contact both to show affection and to read my reaction to the fight. Now it's Larbren's opponent's turn to hold her up in the air, bending her body in a type of fireman's lift, grasping her by the globes of her firm, rounded ass. It's an erotic pose. I wonder fleetingly what it would be like to sink my teeth into that ass.

Rivlor bends towards me and nips the side of my neck. She whispers into my ear, "Say the word, Wyatt, and I can arrange for you to bite that delicious ass."

My breathing quickens; my skin breaks out into goosebumps. The thought of watching Rivlor devour Larbren, and then inviting me to devour her too, is tantalizing. Dirty thoughts of me sinking my cock into both women have me swell uncomfortably in my pants. I've lived quite a staid life, I now realize. What would it be like to let loose and do something so incredibly sexy? Even better, it wouldn't be a guilty little secret I'd have to hide, because right there with me would be my life partner, sharing in the pleasure and decadence. Could there be any negative consequences to this?

I turn to Rivlor and whisper back, "Are you ok with me fucking her? Please tell me the truth."

Her hand slides down to my straining erection. "Wyatt, this cock belongs to me. You are mine. And I can do what I like with what is mine. It will be my great pleasure to watch you sink *my* cock into her cunt while I kiss her and feel each sensation through our minds."

I place my hand over hers on my cock. "It is yours," I whisper. "And I am yours. Do with me what you want, baby."

I hear her pleased hum as she pats my straining cock one last time before withdrawing her hand. We watch the rest of the tournament in charged silence. Larbren wins the semi-final, then come the second round of semi-final contestants. After a short intermission, the final begins. Larbren walks onto the stage once again, this time to meet her next opponent, a shorter and slighter female, about five feet ten, but with amazing prowess as we saw in the semi-final. This will be no easy contest.

It isn't. We are treated to an epic fight, leaving me on the edge of my seat throughout. Without consciously meaning to, I join in the shouting, calling out "Hayya" time and time again, although I still don't fully know what it means. When Larbren scores a killer move, I stamp my feet in approval. I'm fully invested in this match. And when it finally ends in victory for Larbren, I get to my feet whooping wildly along with the rest of the crowd. In celebration, Larbren is pelted in pink and purple petals, the same as the ones on the trees that line the graceful avenues of Torbreg.

She beams at the crowd, accepting their congratulations, then grabs her losing opponent and kisses her long and hard on the lips, to the cheering of everyone. My body is on fire with excitement and anticipation.

Eventually, the contestants clear the stage and the crowd begins to file out. Rivlor takes my hand, leading me to a door in the far corner, through which the wrestlers had emerged and disappeared. It's guarded by a large, burly Venorian who growls at anyone daring to go past. On seeing us though, his face becomes wreathed in smiles. He wraps his arms around Rivlor and brings her lips to his for a smacking kiss. Now this, I am less than happy about. I'm about to intervene when she puts both hands on his chest to push him away.

"Do not put your hands on me again, Dovsan. My partner will not like it."

I scowl and fist my hands to show my displeasure. He raises his disarmingly.

"Apologies, Rivlor, I was only wanting to show my joy at seeing your lovely self again."

"You can show it by letting us through."

"Ah, of course."

He opens the door behind him and ushers us through. Rivlor takes my hand and marches me forward. She casts an amused glance at me. "You are extra cute when you get possessive and territorial."

I grunt, "You're mine, Rivlor. Don't ever forget it."

She grins and responds in kind. "And you are mine, Wyatt, no matter how many females I let you fuck."

I stop her with my hand, my expression going serious. "I don't have to fuck anyone else but you, Rivlor."

She looks down at my still half-hard cock. "Your body says otherwise, cute boy."

I push my hair back in frustration. "Rivlor, I can get turned on by others, sure, but that doesn't mean I have to do something about it. I was faithful to Melinda for over twenty years. I can be faithful to you."

Her honey eyes burn like fire as she grabs hold of the back of my neck and fixes me with her stare. In a deep, velvety voice, she enunciates, "Wyatt, you *will* be faithful to me and only fuck the females of *my* choice when *I* desire you to. You are mine, boy, all mine, and your pleasure is also mine. I want you to have sensual experiences like you have never had before. You are going to come so hard tonight, cute boy. And Larbren will be in no doubt who you belong to."

Oh God what this woman does to me. I'm buzzing with energy, my heart hammering in my chest. "Yes, baby," I breathe.

She lets go of me and takes my hand again, resuming our walk towards another door that opens into a large communal bathing room. Lounging in the water are the two female wrestling finalists, and around them bustle a small group of friends or assistants, I'm not sure which. Larbren's eyes widen as she catches sight of Rivlor.

"Well, well, this is a pleasing surprise," she smiles.

"Congratulations on a win over a very worthy opponent," says Rivlor, nodding to the other wrestler.

"Thank you. It was a great challenge, and I am very glad to have come out victorious."

She rises from the bath, uncaring of her nudity, and begins to dry herself on a towel. She casts a glance towards me. "And who is this?"

"This is my partner, Wyatt Garcia," Rivlor says proudly. "We would like to invite you for a celebratory meal with us."

Larbren's gaze sweeps over me. "I have not had the pleasure of meeting a Human before, though I have heard much of your kind. Greetings, Wyatt." Totally naked still, she walks to me and places a hand to my cheek, looking me in the eyes. Then she brings her forehead to mine, staying there long enough to get a read of the million and one emotions in my head. She steps back, a twinkle in her eyes. "Oh yes, I would very much like to spend the evening with both of you."

I'm blushing, I just know it. This Venorian mind reading thing can be quite unnerving.

"Good," says Rivlor briskly. "Meet us at Venji's as soon as you are ready. I will make the reservations in my name."

"Understood," nods Larbren.

Our business concluded, Rivlor takes my hand again and guides me out, this time through a back entrance to the building. We walk over to a set of empty taxi drones and program one of them to take us to our destination. Over the course of the short journey, Rivlor taps on her communicator, making our dinner reservations.

"So, Venji's…" I wonder.

"It is a very nice place, and the food is good. I think you will like it."

"I'm sure I will."

"Have you noticed something, Wyatt?"

"No. What is it?"

"We are in a drone and you are not at all concerned about it."

I grin. "I'm cured!"

"I am glad, for to live with that kind of fear is very limiting."

"Don't I know it. I feel like I've been given a new lease of life."

She runs a hand down my chest, making me shiver. "That is also because you are having the best sex of your life with me," she states unequivocally.

I can't argue with that, so I kiss her and bleat, "I love you."

"And I love you, cute boy."

The drone lands outside an eccentric looking small building sandwiched in between two larger ones. The windows are star shaped, the pale gray rendering on the walls glowing silver in the light cast by the moon and a distant street lamp. Rivlor leads me through the front door and I catch my breath. Inside, I'm surrounded by a night sky glimmering with thousands of tiny stars. Soft music plays in the background, a haunting melody on some harp-like instrument.

A host glides towards us. "Welcome," she says in a gentle voice.

"Greetings. I am Rivlor and I have a reservation for three in the top nook."

"Indeed. Please follow me."

We follow her past discreetly spaced tables with diners enjoying their food, and up a winding staircase to a circular platform with a round table and plush velvet bench seats. As we take our seats, the host says in a smooth voice, "The special tonight is roast *prot* with a *dria* sauce, which I do recommend.

Other options are on the menu. I will leave you to make your order, but before I do, may I get you some refreshments?"

"Mmm, seeing as there is roast *prot,* then I think a bottle of *sloh* would go nicely."

"Of course, I will bring it up shortly."

She glides away, and we're left alone. From our vantage point, we look down at the rest of the dining room, which now that my eyes have gotten accustomed to the light, is bustling with diners. The glow of countless stars illuminates a set of dark circular tables surrounded by burgundy colored velvet seats, just like the ones we're sitting on. The distant hum of voices mixes with the unearthly, melodic sounds of the music.

Rivsor strokes my arm gently back and forth. I found out not long ago that she likes the hair on my forearms, a contrast to the hairless smooth bronze skin on hers. It's become a habit of hers to tangle her fingers through that soft hair. I pick up her hand and kiss it. "This is very romantic. I almost wish we didn't have company."

"It will take time for Larbren to join us as many of her fans will want to congratulate her. We can enjoy this meal just the two of us until she comes."

"What are we going to eat? The roast *prot*?"

She glances at the menu on the table's console. "I think so, yes. When cooked well, the meat is meltingly tender. We can also order some *kroot* and crisped vegetables to go with it. Would you like that?"

"I trust you to feed me well."

She casts me a humorous look as she places our order. "Do not worry, cute boy. I will take good care of you." She pauses a moment, then adds, "Not just with the food."

Right. I use this opening to ask. "So, this threesome. What's going to happen?"

She strokes my arm again. "Once our meal is over, I will ask Larbren if she wishes to accompany us to a *mero.*"

"A *mero*? What's that?"

"It is a place where Venorians go when they wish to fuck. It is rented by half or quarter rotations."

I gaze at her startled. I'd like to think I'm not easily shocked, but I am. What she's describing sounds like a sleazy motel Venorians can rent by the night, or half the night, to have sex in. Our sexy encounter just got a little less sexy.

Still holding my hand, she feels my reaction. "Wyatt, I do not know what a sleazy motel is in your world, but I can assure you that a *mero* is a clean, respectable place. The rooms are comfortably furnished and supplied with fully sanitized sexual objects to use for our pleasure."

"So it's some kind of sex club where you can rent rooms with sex toys?"

"If by sex club you mean a place people go to primarily for sexual pleasure, then yes. You have such places on Earth?"

"Yes, but I've never been to one."

Her look is almost pitying. "Wyatt, it seems that there are many things you have not done in more than four decades of your life."

I blink, trying to hide my discomfort, but of course, there is nothing I can hide from my partner. Her gaze softens. "I am sorry. I did not mean to make you feel bad." She kisses me softly. "It seems tonight will be more than one new experience for you. Trust me to take care of your pleasure, my heart. I will make sure you enjoy it."

We're interrupted by the server bringing a bottle of *sloh*. She pours the sparkling drink into two glasses, then leaves us again. I bring the *sloh* to my lips and take a sip. It's fruity and dry, not too sweet, with a bit of a kick.

"Mmm, it's good. How strong is this stuff?"

"A glass or two will make you feel happy and relaxed. Any more and it might put you to sleep. It goes well with our meal, but I also thought it would help you get over any nerves with Larbren."

I smile. "You thought right." I take another sip then place the glass back on the table. "So, back to Larbren. You'll suggest we go to a *mero* and if she says yes—"

She grins mischievously. "If she says yes, which she will, then we go to a *mero*. Fortunately, there is one in the building next door."

"And once we're there, what happens?"

She looks at me puzzled. "All three of us will fuck."

"I need details, Rivlor."

Her look turns severe. "No, Wyatt boy, you do not. I will instruct you on everything you do. Just remember to follow my instructions. If not, I might be tempted to punish you."

I remember that paddle she held last week when she first asked me to get naked. I've not seen it since, though I've wondered about it—specifically if and when she might want to use it on me. I've spanked Melinda on occasion during sex, but she's never returned the favor, and it was always with my hands, not with any kind of instrument. Perhaps one day, I should be naughty and not follow her instructions. But not tonight.

Our food arrives. As promised, the *prot* is tender and the *dria* sauce is both sweet and sour, a little bit like cranberry sauce if I were to compare it. The *kroot* is a freshly baked bread, crisp on the outside and doughy on the inside, with some cheesy type filling. We're about half-way through our meal when Larbren finally arrives. I stand politely to greet her. She towers above me at close on six feet two. Ruffling my hair, she grins, "Hello again, Human." Her grin widens as she takes in the generous amount of food spread on the table. "*Prot* and *kroot*, my favorite!" Without any further ado, she settles herself next to me and begins filling a plate with the food. "Thank you for this. I get so hungry after a fight."

Rivlor laughs. "That is why we ordered twice as much food as we would normally eat."

Larbren bites into her *kroot* and chews, then replies, "That was thoughtful; I thank you." Turning to me, she asks, "Did you enjoy watching the vibor tonight? I am guessing this was your first time at a tournament."

"I loved it, and you were amazing."

"Thank you, Wyatt."

"So, now you have won the championship, what next?"

"When the vibor season is over, I go back to my main job. I have a shop that sells and fixes drones. I run it with my brother."

"And when does the next vibor season begin?"

"In another three moon rotations, so I have time to enjoy myself before I begin training again." She looks at me with a meaningful smile.

Up close, Larbren is strikingly attractive. Now that I've had the chance to relax, with the help of a glass of *sloh*, I've been checking her out. Like all Venorians, her skin is a tanned shade of bronze, but unlike Rivlor's honey hair and eyes, Larbren's eyes are a deep blue and her hair a tumble of black silky locks, loosely braided with a few wisps escaping here and there. When she smiles, which she does a lot, a sexy dimple appears on both cheeks.

I grin back, flirting a little. "Well, we're happy to help you enjoy your victory tonight. Would you like some *sloh*?"

"Oh yes, thank you."

I pour her a glass and as she takes it from me, her fingers briefly touch mine. I feel a zing of electricity shoot up my spine. Rivlor, who is sitting at my other side with her hand on my thigh, now moves that hand to cup my crotch, her meaning clear. I remember her words from earlier. *This cock belongs to me.* I place my hand over hers. *Yes, this cock belongs to you.*

The meal continues, with me bantering back and forth with Larbren, getting more and more flirtatious as the evening progresses and as I make inroads into my second glass of *sloh*. Rivlor is mostly silent, observing us avidly, a gleam in her eyes. Her hands caress me, claiming me as hers. Yes, Larbren is in no doubt who I belong to. It's strange but seductive to be claimed—*owned*—and yet also engage in a flirtation with someone else. I feel wickedly decadent and safe all at once.

The meal draws to an end, and now Rivlor rouses herself to speak. "Larbren, we were hoping you would come to the *mero* next door with us for further enjoyment of our evening."

Larbren leans across me and kisses Rivlor on the lips. Pulling back, she purrs, "I would very much like to continue our enjoyment together at the *mero*."

"Good, then let us go there now."

We stand, walk down the winding stairs and to the entrance of the restaurant. We bid the host goodbye and make our way out of the building, only to climb the short set of steps to the front door of the next building. Inside, we are greeted by yet another host, this one a male Venorian. He smiles at us politely. "Greetings. How may I be of assistance to you?"

"We would like a room large enough for three."

"Yes of course. How long will you need it for?"

Rivlor glances at me then back at the host. "A quarter rotation I think will be sufficient." She hands over her communicator. "Please charge it to me."

He completes the transaction, requesting her handprint on the scanner. "Please make your way to the top floor, your room is number 47."

"Thank you. Is there an attachable male appendage there?"

"Of course. There are several in different sizes to choose from."

"Perfect."

Rivlor takes my hand again and leads me towards the set of stairs, Larbren at our heels. We make our way up to the second and top floor, then find room 47. Rivlor places her hand on the scanner to unlock it and we walk inside. I don't know what I was expecting, but this room is charming and not remotely sleazy looking. The dark wood floors are in sharp contrast with the tasteful pastel yellow walls. It is, of course, dominated by a large bed, with white satin bedding and colorful pillows. Next to it is a large chest of drawers, which Rivlor goes to and opens, rifling through the contents. Behind me, Larbren is already removing her shoes and undoing the laces on her pants.

I walk to stand by Rivlor, looking over her shoulder as she removes what looks like a tub of lube, and what I recognize as the attachable male appendage. It's a realistic looking erect penis attached to leather pants which can be secured around a woman's crotch with the available straps. Rivlor sees me glance down at it and smirks, "When I say I fuck females, Wyatt, I mean I really fuck them—with this. And sometimes, I also fuck men with it."

I gulp. "Any plans to fuck me?"

"What have I said, boy?" Her tone is sharp. "It is not for you to ask. You will do as I say, unless it is something you have a grave problem with. If so, you must let me know. Now, remove your clothes."

I stand frozen for a fraction of a second, but the look in her eyes spurs me into action. I unbutton my shirt, keeping my gaze fixed on hers. I discard it on a nearby chair and take off my pants, then my boxer briefs. My cock is already hard and straining up towards my navel, a drop of precum glistening on the tip.

Rivlor's nostrils flare. I know her superior sense of smell is catching the musky aroma of my sex. Looking behind me, she address Larbren. "Come see my beautiful male, Larbren, and have a taste of his cock."

Larbren, fully naked now, walks over to stand before me, taking my body in from head to foot. She runs her fingers down my chest, delighting in the golden blond hair that grows thicker as it reaches my happy trail. Then, her attention is caught by the piercing on my frenum. She gets to her knees and slides a delicate finger along the silky, throbbing flesh, and over the piercing, all the way to the tip. I shudder.

Looking up at my partner, Larbren murmurs, "He is indeed beautiful."

"Taste him."

Larbren turns back to me with that dimpled smile and licks my tip with her tongue. "Hmm, different. Not sweet, but good." She opens her mouth wide and takes my length in, all the way to the root, applying powerful suction. I grunt. What is it about these Venorian females and their incredible blow jobs? If she carries on like that, I'll be a goner.

As if reading my mind, Rivlor slaps Larbren hard on her right breast. "I said taste. Do not make him come."

Larbren lets me go, exclaiming, "Ow!"

Rivlor issues another set of commands in her clipped voice. "Both of you. Undress me now."

I go to Rivlor and lift the tunic over her head. Meanwhile, Larbren rises to her feet and begins unlacing Rivlor's pants. A few seconds later, we're all naked. My eyes devour Rivlor's generous, rounded breasts, which never fail to turn me on. My voice husky, I say, "You're the beautiful one, Rivlor."

She smiles and rewards me with a light kiss on the lips. Then she commands Larbren, "Go sit on the bed, your back to the board." It's an unspoken agreement between the three of us that Rivlor is in charge of the proceedings. Larbren obeys without a word.

"Wyatt, go sit beside her on the bed."

I follow the instructions. Rivlor settles herself on the other side of Larbren and takes her face in both her hands, kissing her long and deeply. I watch the two of them kiss, incredibly turned on. Finally, they break apart, their lips plump and glistening. Rivlor turns to me. "She tastes good. Now you kiss her."

Obediently, I lean towards Larbren and capture her lips with mine. She does taste good, and her full lips are soft, cushiony and inviting beneath mine. She parts them, allowing my tongue to plunge in and duel with hers. I ravish her mouth, kissing her for long, endlessly pleasurable minutes, before I pull away, breathless. My eyes go to Rivlor, waiting for my next instruction. She cups Larbren's right breast in her hand, still a little pink from the slap earlier, her fingers gently rubbing the dark brown, pebbled nipple. She nods towards the other breast. "Touch her boy, feel her gorgeous booby."

I plant my palm on Larbren's left breast and begin fondling her, enjoying the feel of it in my hand. Her breasts are a lot smaller than Rivlor's and fit easily into my hand, reminding me a little of Mel's breasts. I used to love cupping them like this. My chest tightens at the memory, but I push it away. I'm determined to stay in the moment.

"Put your mouth to it and suck."

Rivlor follows this instruction with a modelling of what she wants me to do, capturing Larbren's nipple in her mouth and applying suction. I watch, mesmerized, before remembering to do what I'm told. I bring the other breast to my own mouth, putting my lips around the dark puckered nipple and sucking. Above me, I hear Larbren's moans as both Rivlor and I suckle her breasts. My hand strays to my cock, giving it a satisfying tug. Immediately, it's slapped away. Rivlor interrupts her sucking of Larbren's breast to chide me.

"I did not give you permission to touch your cock, Wyatt. If you need to use your hand, use it on Larbren. Stroke her cunt and make her wet, so I can fuck her."

Yes Ma'am. I resume my ministrations to Larbren's breast and slide my free hand down to her pussy, which is already nicely moist. My seeking fingers search for her clit, and it's not long before I find the engorged nub. Larbren's moans escalate. Her pussy becomes slicker and slicker with every touch. I'm seized with a sudden desire to bury my face right where my fingers are probing.

Larbren gives a strangled cry, "Do it!"

Is she talking to me? Not sure, I continue as before. Now it's Rivlor's turn to issue the order. She ejects the fat nipple from her mouth with a wet pop, and barks, "Do it boy! Eat her cunt."

Seeing as Rivlor isn't touching me right now, she must be reading my thoughts second hand through Larbren. My mind boggles at the idea.

Releasing the breast I'm sucking from my mouth, I trail kisses down Larbren's abdomen as my hands skim over her body, appreciating the taut musculature and wonderfully satin skin. Down I go to her mound covered with well-groomed silky black curls. I run my nose through them, inhaling her sweet and musky fragrance.

Gently, I part her legs and set my gaze on the pink, wet folds of her pussy. *Oh so pretty.* I take a moment to admire the sight before me. I don't think I'll ever tire of a woman's pussy. Each one is individual, unique, special. Where Rivlor's pussy lips are small and delicate—a delicacy to savor—Larbren's are puffy and swollen, crying out to be devoured. Without further ado, I set to doing just that. I give her pussy an open mouthed kiss for several sweet moments, then begin to run my tongue over her slit and all the way up to her plump clit.

"Ahh," moans Larbren.

Encouraged, I continue my explorations, lapping her with long licks from slit to clit, building a slow, constant rhythm. Each lick produces more flow of her pussy juice, drenching the bottom half of my face. Like all Venorians, Larbren's pussy tastes sweet, like a soft pancake drenched in maple syrup, but with a sexy musk infusing the sweet. I feast on the banquet before me; I always knew I had a sweet tooth.

Time passes. I forget myself, buried in the heaven of Larbren's cunt. I lick and lick, becoming conscious of the ratcheting up of her moans above me. Under my tongue, her clit is swelling. She's close. I speed up my rhythm, fluttering my tongue on her nub, then alternating with long licks the length of her pussy. *Oh yeah, sweet goddess. Come for me.* As if on cue, I feel her beginning to pulse beneath me. I keep licking her through each sweet spasm of her orgasm, relishing the sound of her wild moans.

Finally, I lift my head away and look up to Rivlor. She takes in my face, smothered in pussy juice, and her honey eyes flame with desire. "Come here," she orders.

I crawl back up to the top of the bed. She grabs the scruff of my neck and pulls me to her, across Larbren's body sandwiched between us. "Let me taste her on you."

Then her mouth is on mine, licking the seams of my lips and all around to where the pussy juice has leaked on my chin. Her tongue demands entry past my lips, and I gladly let her in, deepening the kiss. *I love you.* I telegraph the thought to her in my head. *I couldn't do any of this without you.*

She pulls back and smiles. "I know, sweet boy."

Then it's Larbren who takes hold of my head, demanding a kiss. She tastes herself on me as our tongues meet. When finally we break the kiss, she says in a husky voice, "Thank you, Wyatt. That was good."

"My pleasure."

We turn to observe Rivlor who has gotten off the bed to lace up the attachable male appendage. When she faces us with the large erect cock on her groin, a shiver of excitement goes through me. I never thought I'd find the sight of a woman with a cock strap sexy, but my God she takes my breath away.

Rivlor climbs back on to the bed and lies down on her back, her cock springing up in the air like a rocket about to launch. She issues her next instructions. "Larbren, you will sit on this cock and lie down on me. I want to devour your mouth while I fuck you. And you, Wyatt, play with that ass you've been wanting to sink your teeth into. Slap it, bite it, worship every curve of it while we fuck. And then, using this lubricating gel, get your fingers as deep in her ass as you can go, and fuck her with them."

"Understood." I'm beginning to speak like a Venorian.

She smiles approvingly, then nods to Larbren who mounts her, sinking on to that artificial cock with a hiss of pleasure. Once the cock is fully sheathed in her, she bends forward, lying on top of Rivlor. The two embrace, kissing passionately while Rivlor thrusts her groin up into Larbren, who moans in pleasure. I watch them with the illicit delight of a voyeur. They've almost forgotten my presence, humping and devouring each other—two sexy goddesses worshipping each other.

After a while, the sight of Larbren's ass jiggling with each thrust of Rivlor's cock reminds me of what I've been tasked to do. Bringing the tub of lube with me, I shimmy down the bed once again and sit astride them low enough so I can reach that luscious ass. First, I fondle each cheek with my hands, squeezing the firm, rounded flesh as it grinds on that cock. I love pussy, but I'm an ass man too. At least when it comes to this magnificent ass.

Soon, I'm aching for more. I bend down and nuzzle it with my lips, enjoying the soft texture of her skin. Like a tasty apple, I take my first bite. Moving across to the other ass cheek, I sink my teeth into that soft, inviting flesh. Then with both hands, I give each ass cheek a light slap. Larbren moans. I spank her ass again, this time a little harder. She moans louder. *Oh yes, sexy goddess. You like your ass spanked.*

I give each cheek a set of slaps, alternating back and forth, until the rounded globes are stained a dark red. I stop then and stroke my hands soothingly over the stinging flesh. All the while, Larbren continues grinding her pussy on Rivlor's attached cock. I decide it's time to get the lube. Reaching out a hand to it, I dip a finger into the cold wet gel. With my other hand, I part Larbren's ass cheeks to bare her brown rosebud. *Such a pretty little thing.* I touch my finger to it, pressing lightly. Larbren emits a sound of pleasure. Gently, I bring more pressure until my finger pushes through into the tight heat of her back passage. Larbren moans her approval. I push deeper into the recesses of her ass, until I'm as far in as my finger will go. I rotate it about, then start plunging in and out, trying to match the rhythm of Rivlor's thrusts into Larbren's pussy.

My partner rips her mouth away from Larbren to command breathily, "Now two. She's close." Then she resumes their passionate kiss.

I withdraw my finger to gather more lube, then return to the rosebud of Larbren's ass, which is gaping slightly from my earlier efforts. Gently, I now push in two fingers.

"Ah," grunts Larbren.

I take that as a good sign, and start fucking her ass with both fingers, trying to find a corresponding rhythm. Rivlor speeds up, thrusting wildly into Larbren, and I start fucking her ass more rapidly too. I can feel Larbren's climax building with the clench of her flesh on my fingers and the moans she's making. I know the moment she reaches the precipice. She emits a harsh groan and her tight passage pulses on my fingers, nearly cutting off the blood flow in the strength of each spasm.

Slowly, I remove my fingers. Larbren lifts herself off Rivlor and collapses on the bed beside her. I exchange a look with my partner. She pants, a little out of breath, "You did good, Wyatt. Go wash your hands and come straight back."

I do as she says, finding the bathroom—which the Venorians cutely call the ablution room—and wash my hands thoroughly. On my return, I find Rivlor sitting up on the edge of the bed, still wearing her cock strap. She glances at Larbren, who is reclining on the bed in spent exhaustion. "I do believe, Larbren, that it is time we reward Wyatt. I am thinking, it is his ass's turn to get a fucking, do you not agree?"

Larbren sits up and smirks, "Oh yes, I think it is time for Wyatt to get a fucking in his beautiful ass."

I pale. "Err, are you sure that's what you want to do? I mean, I'd be happy to simply fuck your wonderful pussies, if you would let me."

"We will get to that too, but first, your ass."

"Umm, I should let you know that this is a virgin ass that has never been fucked before."

Rivlor smiles wickedly. "All the more reason to get it fucked then. Get on your hands and knees, boy."

"Rivlor—"

Her tone becomes sharp. "Do as I say!" Then she softens, "Trust me, Wyatt, this will be good."

I hesitate for a moment, then acquiesce. Slowly, I crawl on the bed and get into position. Rivlor kneels beside me, ruffling my hair affectionately. I turn my head towards her, begging for a kiss, and she rewards me. Over the years, I have on occasion wondered what anal sex would be like, but was never curious enough to explore this side of things or suggest it to Mel. Tonight, I'm putting my trust in Rivlor.

She pulls her soft, full lips from mine to say, very gently, "I know, my boy. I promise to make it good for you." Then she directs her gaze at Larbren and issues her next command. "Prepare him for me."

I feel Larbren part my ass cheeks and bring a lubed finger to my pucker. She doesn't push in, but rubs it in a circular motion. *Ah, that feels good.*

Rivlor smiles. "I know, my love. And it will feel even better soon."

Gently, Larbren begins inserting her finger into me, breaching my back passage for the very first time. The sensation is odd, but not unpleasant. Her finger goes in deeper and deeper until—

"Ah!"

"You have found his sensual spot," states Rivlor. I guess she must be referring to my prostate.

Larbren begins to massage her finger back and forth, finding that sensual spot and making me gasp.

"Two fingers," instructs Rivlor.

The finger withdraws and shortly later returns with more lube and a second digit. Slowly, she enters me again and burrows deep until she finds my prostrate. I can't help the moan that comes out of my lips at the contact.

"Good," purrs Rivlor. "Now fuck him with them."

Larbren does as instructed while Rivlor strokes my back soothingly and showers me with light kisses along my jaw and neck. My cock is ramrod stiff and leaking at the tip.

"Three fingers."

Larbren repeats the process, this time stretching me with three fingers. The initial discomfort is soon replaced with a blissful feeling as she massages me in my darkest, most intimate place.

After a few minutes of this, Larbren says, "He is ready, I think."

"I agree."

Larbren slowly takes her fingers out of me and I start to feel both dread and anticipation. Rivlor reaches for the lube and wets her attached cock with it. Then she looks intently at me. "Wyatt, I am going to put this giant cock up your ass and fuck you with it. Then Larbren is going to position herself under you so you can fuck her cunt at the same time."

The image she conjures has me inhale sharply.

Rivlor shifts to kneel behind me. She grabs both my ass cheeks and squeezes, then gives each of them a couple of loud spanks.

"Mmm," I moan.

"Let me get my cock inside you," she whispers.

I feel her spread my ass cheeks. The cold tip of her lubed cock taps against my pucker, then starts to push slowly in.

"Take my cock, Wyatt. You can do it."

I listen to Rivlor's encouraging croons as she grips me by the hips and very slowly, pushes that great cock into me. After a few light thrusts, she eventually manages to get past the tight ring of muscles and sheath it fully in my ass. The sensation is unlike anything I've ever felt before. Not quite pain, but on the edge of it.

"Good boy, Wyatt. Stay still for a while and let your body adjust."

I stay still on my hands and knees, feeling this new intrusion inside my body. "I can read your mind, Wyatt, and feel what you are feeling." Rivlor's voice is gruff. "I will experience everything with you as you get fucked in the ass for the first time." Rivlor pulls out about an inch then slides back in, filling me even deeper than before. "I can feel my cock filling you up, Wyatt," she groans. She pulls back again, this time nearly all the way, then thrusts powerfully into me.

"Fuuuck!" I cry.

"Oh fuck yes!" she cries in unison with me.

Then she thrusts again, and again. The pain is gone now, replaced by intense sensation as Rivlor nails my prostate with powerful plunges into my ass. Each nudge of my prostate elicits a groan not only from me, but also from Rivlor as she senses what I'm experiencing through our mind connection. My mind cries out to hers. *Oh God that feels good.*

"So good!" she pants.

She gives one more thrust then pauses, buried deep in my back passage.

"Larbren!" she calls out sharply.

Larbren needs no second invitation. With a dimpled smile, she shimmies herself into position under me, putting a hand around my cock to give it a few tugs. Then, carefully, I lower myself onto her as she guides my cock to her entrance. I push in gently, her slick pussy making it easy for me to glide all the way in. Her walls are snug around my cock, gripping me tightly as Rivlor begins thrusting into me once more.

With each thrust of her cock, Rivlor pushes me deeper into Larbren's pussy. She dictates the pace, almost as if she's fucking the two of us at once. Once we have established a rhythm, Rivlor increases the power of her thrusts, hammering me with that great cock over and over again. I nuzzle my face in Larbren's neck and surrender to the pounding I'm being given. On and on, Rivlor nails my ass, hitting my prostate every time and making me gasp as my dick plunges in and out of Larbren's moist, tight cunt. I'm sandwiched between these two goddesses and I'm in heaven.

"Oh Holy Lir," cries Rivlor. "I can feel your tight cunt on my boy's cock! You feel so fucking good."

Through her mind connection to me, Rivlor's reading what I'm feeling as my cock pounds into Larbren's cunt. We ride this rollercoaster together, sharing each sensation as if we were one. Rivlor fucks me on and on, as I fuck Larbren's sweet, tight pussy. We thrust and grind and moan, all three of us locked in a mind blowing rhythm of carnal pleasure which builds and builds. I know I'm close—I don't think I can hold off much longer—and my two Venorian mind readers feel it too, reaching for the precipice with me. In synch, all three of us find our climax, one glorious pulse after another. I groan loudly as I come, and hear echoing groans from Rivlor and Larbren. I don't think I've ever come so hard. I'm gripped by wave after wave of powerful pulses as I empty my cum into Larbren's welcoming pussy and clench my ass around Rivlor's great cock.

Spent, I collapse on top of Larbren while Rivlor gently withdraws from my ass. Once free, I pull out of Larbren, my cum dripping down her cunt. I roll over to my side and lie on the bed, still coming down from my high. Rivlor undoes her cock strap and joins us, spooning me from behind. She kisses the back of my neck and strokes her hand down my arm. "That was good?"

"So good," I reply. "Thank you, both of you."

Larbren turns to face me and brings her lips to mine, kissing me long and deeply. "No, thank you. This was an excellent way to celebrate my tournament victory," she finally says.

We repose like this for some time, getting our strength back. Finally, Rivlor sits up, saying briskly, "Let us bathe now, for we must get going. Wyatt has a big day tomorrow and needs his sleep."

Leaving us still resting lazily on the bed, she goes to the ablution room, and I can hear her start the large communal bath that Venorians favor. With an effort, I rouse myself and make my way to the bathroom, followed by Larbren.

"Good," says Rivlor. "I was about to come fetch you. Get yourselves into the water. I have added some special salts to soothe your aches."

With this, she steps into the sunken bath and submerges her body in its steaming, fragrant depth. Larbren and I join her, each of us sighing in satisfaction as the warmth of the water surrounds our bodies. The three of us gather close, our arms around each other in a group embrace. I kiss Rivlor, telegraphing my thoughts. *Thanks, baby. I love you so much.* Being able to kiss and communicate at the same time is such a cool thing. Then I'm kissing Larbren, transmitting my thanks to her too. *You are hot, and I'm the luckiest man alive to get to fuck you.*

She laughs, "Thank you, Wyatt, the pleasure was mine."

Then her lips are on Rivlor's in a deep, intimate kiss. I watch them, the sight beautiful to my eyes. Before long, Rivlor transfers her lips to mine, kissing me again, then murmuring, "I love you too, my sweet, cute boy."

We take our time, holding and stroking each other as the three of us take turns to kiss. In the afterglow of our lovemaking, it feels right to spend this time showing mutual love and care for each other, elevating our encounter to more than just a sexy hook up. I don't know whether we'll ever do this again with Larbren—I hope we do—but this brief time we had together will be etched in my memory.

Eventually, we come out of the bath, dry ourselves and get dressed. Emerging from the *mero*, we give Larbren one more kiss goodbye, then get into our separate drones to make our way back home. In our room, Rivlor and I quietly undress, wash and get into bed. I wrap my arms around her and kiss the back of her neck as I spoon her to me.

Rivlor?

She grunts sleepily.

Tonight was incredible. Thank you, baby.

"It is just the beginning of what our life together will be," she murmurs.

Will we do this often, do you think?

She snorts. "Not too often, cute boy. I like having you to myself. But when we feel the need or meet someone who attracts us, then we can explore this further."

I like the sound of that.

"Good, now go to sleep."

Goodnight, baby. I love you.

"I love you too."

Main Krovatian Characters

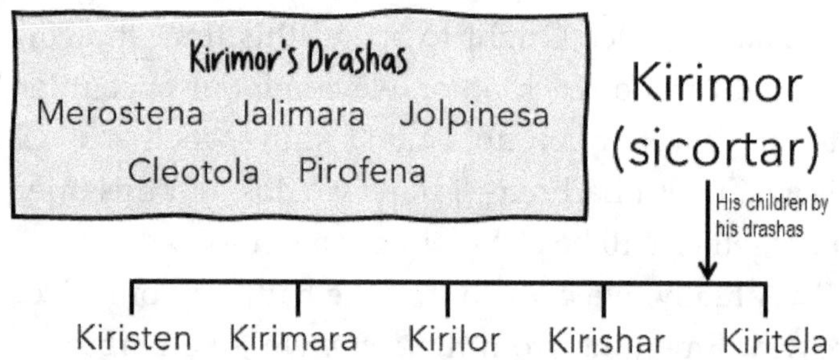

People who work for Kirimor

Sholinar – aide
Dresolor – cook
Jenisor – groundskeeper
Dorinor – body artist

Sector Leaders

Denishar – northern sector
Nevestor – eastern sector
Dorishena – southern sector
Lorifena – western sector

Other Characters

Desimar – liaison officer to the humans

Turi – a dolphin-like creature that Kirimor has befriended

Melistor – a sicor who will succeed Kirimor as sicortar

Main Venorian Characters

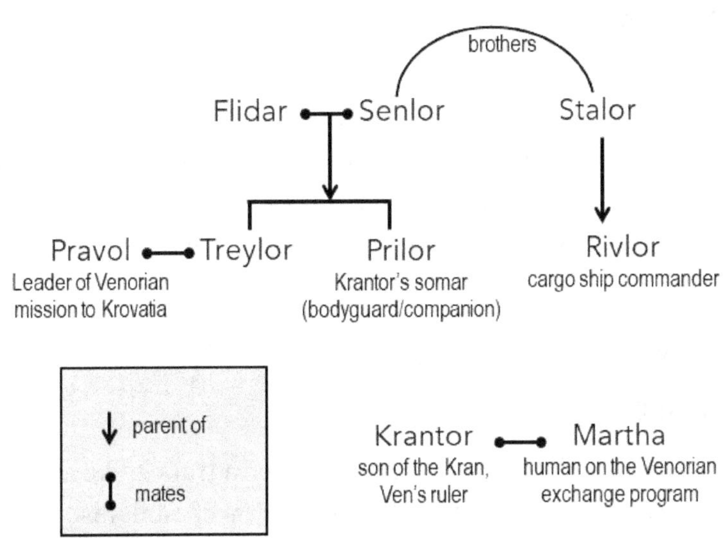

Glossary of Krovatian and Venorian terms

Ablutenizer

An automated system for brushing teeth located in the ablution room of Krovatian and Venorian households. A person places their lips around the spout and presses a button to start the process. Warm liquid enters the mouth followed by a set of automated brushes that cleanse teeth guided by a sensor.

Bilos

A Krovatian farm animal similar to a cow.

Boral Crystals

Crystals used by Krovatians to induce a trance-like state where they can read other people's auras. Boral crystals also inhibit the neural transmitters of the Venorian people and can induce a mild soporific effect on them when used alone. Combined with dorenium, boral crystals can cause unconsciousness in Venorians.

Chilos

A Krovatian food, similar to a pizza.

Drasha

A concubine to a sicor or sicortar, whose duty is to provide sexual relief during a holy trance.

Dorenium

A mineral used as an energy source to power Krovatian and Venorian ships.

Drelan

A mud spa that Krovatians go to for mind and body relaxation.

Dren

A Krovatian woolly animal that is farmed for its tender meat and wool.

Driskians

A friendly reptile-like race of people from the planet Driskia, allies of both the Krovatians and Venorians.

Frekium

A chemical that stimulates the neural transmitters in Venorians, used to treat telepathic blockages. It can also be used as an antidote to boral crystals. A side effect of using frekium is that it stimulates fertility in Venorian males and females.

Griv

A large four-legged animal, native to the planet Ven, that is a cross between a horse and a dragon.

Joh

A hot and spicy beverage drunk by Venorians, similar to a Chai Latte.

Jujo

A Krovatian feathered farm animal, similar to a chicken.

Kran – also known as the Holy Father of Ven

Both a spiritual and military leader in charge of defending the planet Ven. The Kran is gifted with special telepathic skills upon bonding with his fated mate. Once mated, he is able to mind meld with his mate as well as read the minds of people around him. His blood and saliva have special healing powers.

Krovatians

A secretive race of people, allies of the Venorians and Driskians.

Klixians

A slimy race of people known for their deception and treachery. Venorians and their allies do not engage in trade with them.

Lanjo

A Krovatian musical instrument that sounds like a cross between a guitar and a harp.

Lir

The god worshipped by Venorians.

Lam

Krovatian savory bread, eaten at breakfast.

Lom

A Krovatian fizzy, sherbert-like drink that induces a mellow feeling.

Loshi

Krovatian type of food, consisting of seared meat in a green sauce rolled in a lettuce-like leaf.

Mishu

Krovatian type of food, consisting of a crispy green ball with a soft meat and herb filling.

Moon rotation

The Krovatian/Venorian equivalent of an Earth month.

Nari

A refreshing drink, similar to iced tea, drunk by Krovatians.

Olar

Venorian cargo ship that takes Melinda Garcia to Krovatia.

Rotation

Krovatian and Venorian word for a day.

Saraxians

A race of people who are kin to the Krovatians, and live on the planet Sarax. The Saraxians have a history of conflict with the Venorians. Krovatians are banned from any contact with the Saraxians.

Sicor

A member of the Krovatian priesthood.

Sicortar

The head of the Krovatian priesthood, responsible for the spiritual wellbeing of Krovatia.

Somar

A male Venorian who has pledged his life to a kran. Each kran has four somars. They act as both his protectors and sexual companions. A somar is not allowed to have his own mate but must mate with the kran's fated mate. He is allowed to procreate with her once she has begotten an heir for the kran.

Sun rotation

The Krovatian and Venorian equivalent of an Earth year.

Taya

The goddess worshipped by Krovatians.

Torbreg

The capital city of Ven, named after the Tor family (the Kran's clan).

Utar belt

A neutral zone separating the planet Ven from Sarax, a planet whose people have been in conflict with the Venorians. A peace treaty was signed with the Saraxians seven years ago which states that Saraxians should not enter this neutral zone. The Saraxians broke this peace treaty when they attacked Ven last year.

Venorians

A friendly race of people from the planet Ven. The first alien race to make contact with humans.

Vlor

A precious stone mined on the planet Ven that comes in shades of pink and purple. The purple vlor stone is known for its healing properties. It has a powerful regenerative effect on the body and can cut healing time for wounds by being placed on the affected area. It is also used to combat the effects of aging.

AFTERWORD

Dear reader,

I hope you enjoyed reading **Melinda's Choice** and its sequel short story, **Wyatt's Redemption**.

May I ask you for a small favor?

Reviews are the life blood of independent authors. Please could you help spread the word about this book by submitting a review on Amazon, Goodreads or any other book reader platform. Thank you! For latest news and freebies, please subscribe to my newsletter on my website, **mw-author.com**.

M.M. Wakeford

ABOUT THE AUTHOR

M.M. Wakeford lives with her husband and son in a London terraced house that gathers dust while she loses herself in her writing. A lifelong reader of romantic novels, she writes in many genres including contemporary, sci-fi and historical romance. All her stories strive to capture that heady feeling of falling in love, with authentic characters whose journey to a happily ever after is lined with dilemmas to overcome. If you're looking for a page turning romance with high emotion and a good dose of spice, you've come to the right place.

ALSO BY THIS AUTHOR

One day, on a planet far from Earth, I meet my fated mate.
The only problem is, he's in love with someone else.

Martha has enrolled on a six-month exchange program to the planet Ven, whose people have recently made first contact with Earth. Newly single and broke, Martha looks forward to this once-in-a-lifetime opportunity to find out more about the Venorians, an intriguing humanoid race of massive bronze-skinned people.

As the son and heir of the Kran, planet Ven's ruler, Krantor has four somars—men who are his lifelong bodyguards and companions. He loves them all dearly, but one of them, Prilor, he loves best of all. Krantor knows he's destined to meet his fated mate one day, but it's Prilor he wants to spend his days and nights with. And he certainly hadn't banked on his fated mate being a human!

Will Martha give up her life on Earth for a fated mate who already loves another? And what of the feelings she has developed for Shanbri, another of Krantor's somars?

Author's note: this is a standalone sci-fi romance with steam and spice aplenty, featuring FM, MM, and MFM relationships, and a guaranteed HEA for all.

What people say about Krantor's Mate:

"What a phenomenal read. The worlds, culture, and species created were diverse and detailed… I went on such an emotional ride with this book." 5* Amazon review

"I found this an interesting and original approach to the reverse harem and fated mate tropes… Thought-provoking and provocative, with high heat throughout." 5* Amazon review

"M.M. Wakeford offers a completely new take on fated mates. With all the expectations that are set with a trope, the author blows it out of the water with her fabulous storytelling." 5* Amazon review

"This is a fantastic sci-fi romance… I loved the characters and I highly recommend this book." 5* Amazon review